BLACK
WATER
GREEN
HILLS

J R HARRISON

ISBN 978-1-68526-005-7 (Hardcover)
ISBN 978-1-68526-004-0 (Digital)

Covenant Books
11661 Hwy 707
Murrells Inlet, SC 29576
www.covenantbooks.com

To my mom, Journala Marie Harrison.
Thank you for all your love and support.

PROLOGUE

India 1936

"Where are you getting off, my friend?"

The stranger's voice startled Chandu away from his thoughts and the bucolic images reeling by his window. He turned, but the man's face was hidden by the newspaper he was reading. Exposed were his black, sinewy legs. They were crossed, and thick calluses padded the bottom of his feet. The train swayed gently side to side, the stranger and his paper along with it.

"Rajahmundry," Chandu replied, awkwardly. He paused for the stranger's next question, but he was silent. *Just as well*, Chandu thought to himself. He turned his attention across the aisle through the barred window. Flowing steadily in the opposite direction was the mighty Godavari River. In his youth, he had seen her in many different moods. Today she looked lazy and unhurried, meandering slowly to her destination.

It occurred to him that the once-full passenger car was nearly empty. Aside from the stranger hiding behind the newspaper, only a few lonely passengers remained. Absorbed in his thoughts, he hadn't noticed the mass exodus at the last several stops or the fact that the train was lighter, skipping along at a swifter clip.

He returned his gaze to the window on his right, where small, rural villages untouched by time clacked by. The stranger noisily rustled through the pages of his newspaper, and Chandu tried to ignore him.

"Wish I could watch," said the stranger, barely audible.

He glanced over in his direction, unsure how to respond.

"I can't look out the window of a moving train," he continued, this time more audible. "Makes me ill, you see."

"Oh—I'm sorry," he responded but still not sure to whom he was responding.

"You visiting?" he inquired.

"Yes, I am. But—how did you know?"

"Your accent."

Accent? I couldn't possibly have an accent, he thought to himself. While he hadn't spoken Telugu for quite some time, he was sure he hadn't lost his ability to speak it.

"Where are you staying?"

"Staying?" he asked, wondering if the man could hear the hint of exasperation in his voice.

The man closed his newspaper and folded it over his knee, and Chandu's eyes instinctively shifted toward him. He wanted to look away, but he couldn't.

"Yes," the man said politely, "where are you staying?"

He tried to reply, but the words got stuck on the back of his tongue.

"Are you staying in Rajahmundry?" the stranger asked patiently.

"Uh—yes, er, no," Chandu replied awkwardly.

The stranger reached his hand up to adjust the yellowed cloth that wrapped around his forehead, making sure it was covering his left eye. The top of his head was burned, leaving scars and random tufts of black-and-gray hair. His right ear and neck were also scarred. It was hard looking at him, yet he didn't want to look away.

"Not sure?" asked the stranger.

"Actually, I'm going on a little further—to a small village called Korlakota, about fifteen miles away on the Godavari River."

"Korlakota!" A broad smile swept across his face, exposing the few teeth he had left. He uncrossed his legs and leaned forward. "You have someone to stay with?"

"No—I, uh, I'll stay at an inn, I suppose."

"There's only one in Korlakota." He leaned closer and whispered, "And it's not fit for a beggar." He gently tapped Chandu on

6

his knee and, with a glint in his eye, said, "You'll stay with me and my family."

"You live in Korlakota?" Chandu asked.

"That's right."

Chandu chuckled under his breath. He had given little thought to where he might stay upon his arrival. He assumed that the little village in which he was born and left as a boy had grown up into a—well, a big village complete with hotels, temples, and a bustling marketplace. After all, Korlakota now had its own train depot.

From the time he disembarked the steamer ship in Madras and boarded the northbound train that would terminate in Hyderabad, he had been considering the true purpose of his journey. A pilgrimage…okay. But he sensed that there was something more meaningful awaiting him.

He pondered whom he would find in Korlakota. Old friends, distant relatives…perhaps. But after nearly half a century of living in a foreign land, he would be a stranger—a foreigner in his own country.

He wondered if he would still be welcomed once they knew he was an Indian who dared to cross the *Kala Pani*, that vast expanse of black water. To those who held fast to the Hindu traditions, crossing the Kala Pani meant certain death. To survive was considered an act of divine favor. To others, it meant defilement—that he was no longer considered a Hindu.

Perhaps his return was an act of the divine, and perhaps he had been defiled.

Indians living abroad were always aware that they were never completely accepted as citizens of their adopted homeland. Now returning, he felt like an orphan hopelessly disconnected from his heritage.

The man picked up his paper and started singing, but Chandu didn't mind. He now knew it was no mistake that He had run into this kind man who appeared to own nothing more than the bag by his side. He glanced down at his blackened, callused feet and found them strangely beautiful.

His eyes returned to the window when he suddenly recognized the song. It was the same one his father often whistled—usually when he was in a good mood. Sometimes he hummed it but never sang it because he only knew a few of the words. He started humming along, and the man sang louder still. Then he abruptly stopped and lowered his paper. "How do you know this song? Not many people know it."

"My father," Chandu replied.

He smiled, but his face was serious. "He must be a good man."

"He was. He was a very good man."

The man resumed singing, and Chandu slipped away—into a sea of memories.

CHAPTER 1

Korlakota, India 1888

The rains still hadn't arrived. Chandu's father, Nayadu, shielded his eyes from the hot, late morning sun, hoping to glimpse the slightest formation of a dark cloud on the horizon—but nothing. He drew a heavy sigh and mumbled under his breath. The temple priest had promised that *Lord Shiva* had been appeased. That no longer would the temperamental god withhold the rain the farms in their village so desperately needed.

Nayadu pulled his straw mat underneath the sparse shade of a tamarind tree. It was there, just steps from their small, thatched-roof house where he found daily solace, sipping his *masala* tea. And it was while sipping his tea on that hot, dry morning that he noticed a stranger sitting on a horse perched high on the top of the steep, narrow trail that connected the small home and the road that ran alongside of the Godavari River. The trail was steep, and most animals, bovines and equines alike, navigated its sheerness hesitantly.

The horse snorted loudly, and Chandu rushed to the window to see who was paying a visit. He had never seen such a horse. She was silvery-gray with a dappling of sabino markings on her belly. Her neck was long and slender, and her eyes were large and dark. Her high-stepping, springy gait was one of confidence and elegance making her rider appear as if he were descending on air.

As they neared, it became apparent that the short, stout rider was not from Korlakota. His rubicund complexion and expensive, wire-rimmed spectacles were evidence that he was high-caste, likely from the big city.

Nayadu stood slowly from where he had been enjoying his tea and with a curious gaze, pressed his hands together high in deference to the man's higher caste.

The stranger dismounted with a skill and alacrity that belied his stature. He pulled a handkerchief from his rear pocket and wiped his face. Then he smiled and said, "Greetings, my name is Sreenivasu Rao. But please, call me Rao."

Again, he pressed his hands together with a nervous smile and replied, "I'm Nayadu." His dark, thin frame contrasted dramatically with the fleshy, fair-complexioned stranger.

"Well, Nayadu, it's a pleasure to meet with you. I've come all the way from Hyderabad to see you."

From the corner of the front-facing window, Chandu watched his father hastily pull the string cot over next to his mat under the tamarind tree. "Please sit, Rao *garu*."

Embarrassed that he was unable to offer tea to his guest, Nayadu hastily ran behind the small house, where he was able to glimpse his wife washing clothes in the riverbed. He flapped his arms frantically and yelled, "Amma! Come!"

Returning to his guest, he sat down anxiously on his straw mat, hoping that she wouldn't delay.

"You came to see *me*?" Nana asked.

He smiled unctuously and said, "That's right." Then his face turned serious. "Excuse me while I get straight to the point, Nayadu, because time is short. We are in dire need of agricultural specialists, and we believe that you're right for the job."

Nayadu's eyes widened, listening intently to what the man had to say.

He leaned forward, resting his elbows on his knees. "Well, what do you think?"

Nayadu's brows furrowed, and his head tilted slightly. "About what?"

"About working for us as an agricultural specialist."

His head cocked back several inches. "What's an agricultural specialist?"

Rao grinned. "It's you, Nayadu! You're an agricultural specialist. Someone who knows farming, who knows what it is to earn an honest living."

He nodded and started etching nervously with his fingers in the hard clay. Nayadu knew how to farm, and he knew what it was to earn an honest living, but how did this man whom he never met know this? He looked up at Rao with one eye squinting from the sun. "The wage?" he asked, sheepishly.

Rao reached down and patted a worn leather case by his side. "Nayadu, I represent wealthy plantation owners overseas. You can be sure that it will be more than what you're earning now."

Rao must have known his timing was ideal. Korlakota had fallen on hard times. Ashen-gray dust had swallowed any evidence of the former lushness which made these farming villages the bread-basket of Rajahmundry. For the second year, the monsoon rains had forsaken Korlakota along with every other village concentrated in the southern parts of India.

The former greatness of the Godavari River, normally an undulating mass of milky-brown water, was only a memory. The numerous rivulets flowing from the Eastern Ghats into the verdant plains below had long been dry. Villagers whose very existence depended on the mighty Godavari were left with a mosaic of dry, cracked mud, and a few precious streams that were still trickling east toward the Bay of Bengal.

Nayadu sat intrigued by the proposition. "Agricultural specialist," he said softly to himself.

"*And* we pay your passage."

"Passage?" he repeated, scratching his head.

Rao smiled. "Nayadu, we're going to have to move you overseas."

"Oh." Nayadu lowered his eyes. "I don't know, Rao garu, this is where I was born, and this is where I—"

Rao interrupted, "I know, this is where you should die." He cleared his throat. "Don't you worry, my friend. You go, you make your money, and you come back. Sound good? In fact," he said before

11

Nayadu could answer, "You should come back with enough money to buy your neighbor's farm."

At this Nayadu smiled, but the conversation was interrupted when his wife finally arrived. "Amma, Rao garu is our guest. Bring him some tea."

Chandu abandoned his vantage point and quickly scampered back to the mat on which he had been lying. Without saying a word, Amma disappeared into the small kitchen attached to the back of the family's small house.

"Surely, Rao garu, you will be able to join us for some lunch," said Nayadu.

"Well, I—"

"Please, your staying here for lunch will honor us."

"When you use these kinds of words, you leave me little choice. Besides, I'm sure that your wife cooks the finest food this side of the Godavari." Rao could feel the words sticking to his tongue. He wasn't accustomed to eating with the villagers, but he knew that this villager was on the hook, and he wasn't going to let go. He was sure, with a little more persuasion, he would land him before lunch was over.

Meals in the Nayadu home hardly ever deviated from the staple of rice and lentils, and today would be no different. Archana, or Amma as she was affectionately called, didn't cook especially well, but the family never let their feelings about her cooking be known. Instead, on the rare occasion when all the ingredients and spices came together into a serendipitous harmony, they rejoiced with second helpings.

But ingredients were increasingly hard to come by during these days, and spices were a luxury. They were just happy to have something fill their stomachs.

When Archana heard her husband invite Rao to stay for lunch, she looked into the small pot hanging over the fire to confirm what she already knew. There was barely enough rice for her own family. She peered into the limp, burlap rice sack and found two rats competing for the remains. She turned the bag on its side. "Shoo, shoo!" she exclaimed, hoping to salvage what little rice was left. She pushed the wooden spoon through the boiling water and felt her stomach moan with emptiness.

"Amma!" Nayadu yelled as he entered through the door. "Rao garu is ready for his tea." Rao followed and noticed Chandu and his brother Pradip lying on their mats in the corner.

"Just two boys?" asked Rao as Archana brought out the tea.

"Yes, Pradip is six, and Chandu is nine. Both are sick today."

Rao nodded. "Must be something going around. I visited two other families here in your village this morning. Their children were also sick."

Nayadu turned abruptly in Archana's direction. "You hear?" he said sternly. "Other children are sick too."

She said nothing as she returned to the kitchen. Chandu nudged his little brother, but he was sound asleep. News that other children in the village were ill caused Chandu to wonder if they too were malingering like he and his brother or whether there really was a contagion slithering through the village, preying on children.

Nayadu turned back to Rao. "It was the ceremony at the temple yesterday."

"Ceremony?"

"Do you have children, Rao garu?"

"Four."

"Would you put their lives in danger if a temple priest asked you to?"

"No, why do you ask?"

Nayadu was not one usually given over to emotion, but his eyes welled up with tears. "Neither would I, Rao garu. Neither would I. I didn't want to bury our children in that pit yesterday, but we were forced."

Chandu peeked through his closed eyes just as Rao glanced over at the two boys. He could see the confusion on his face. The man squinted in the direction of the two boys, looking to see if they were breathing.

"It was the most painful thing I ever had to do," said Nayadu, cuffing his hands over his mouth.

"But why—why were you forced to bury them?" asked Rao.

"The priest told us that if we didn't bury our children as a sacrifice to Lord Shiva while he did his *puja* offering, then the rains would never come back to our village. I said I will never let my boys be buried for one minute—one second even."

"Then," said Rao.

"He scolded me. Told me that my family would be cursed." Nayadu glanced over at the boys, and Chandu could see the anguish on his face. A sensation of guilt swept over him. All they saw in him the previous day was anger and little sympathy for what he and Pradip had to endure. And though they knew in their hearts that it wasn't them with whom he was angry, they both conspired the previous night that they would feign sick in the morning out of retribution. It was their way of avenging themselves.

He turned back to his guest. "What would you've done, Rao garu?"

Rao cleared his throat. "So all the children in the village were buried in a pit during this ceremony and had to hold their breath while the priest did his puja?"

"Yes," said Nayadu. "The children were terrified. And we had to shovel the dirt back into the pit. The priest said that if any of the children moved during the puja, they would have to pay 200 rupees."

As Rao listened, he knew that he would need to use wisdom in responding to Nayadu. Rao wasn't unfamiliar with the homespun superstitions perpetuated by *Brahmins.* In fact, he was keenly aware that the acts of worship were a means by which they kept themselves elevated as superior human beings in Hindu society. As long as temple priests were able to keep the peasants cloaked in ignorance, they would be able to keep themselves free from the toil of physical labor.

"I admire your desperate courage, Nayadu. It would have been hard for me to sacrifice what you did."

Archana brought out a small pot of rice and smaller pot of dhal along with two plates and put them between her husband and Rao.

She sat next to the boys and whispered, "Don't worry, I'll see that you eat before the sun sets."

The man mashed some rice and dhal together with his hand for several minutes before he finally pushed it into his mouth. "Very good," he said to Archana, who sat quietly next to the two boys.

She blushed at Rao's unexpected remark. But Chandu knew better and immediately became suspicious of the man.

He continued, "Life's hard around here, huh?"

Archana lowered her head and then warily lifted her eyes.

Rao pressed further, "How would *you* feel about leaving this life behind for something better?"

She glanced over at her husband for a nod of approval before responding. He simply shrugged in indifference.

"I don't know," she said shyly.

"Sure you do," he responded. "Tell me."

Again, she looked to Nayadu. It was rare that a man other than her husband would solicit her for her personal thoughts. Nayadu smiled awkwardly and nodded. She straightened her back and lifted her head. "Garu, I don't know what we did in our previous life, but it must have been bad. But I know…," her voice trailed off.

"Know what?"

"This is our karma."

Rao pushed his food aside and removed his glasses. "Do you good people believe that my coming here to offer you a chance to make a better life for yourselves is something that you should ignore?" His tone was indignant, and he sensed his edginess getting the better of him. He softened his tone and continued, "Listen to me—good fortune has found you. All the stars have aligned themselves for this most auspicious of days. If I leave here today without your signature, then you will never get another chance like this." Rao lowered his voice. "Good people—look around," he said, glancing around the room. "You have nothing to lose except hardship and heartache. Why are we waiting?"

The couple glanced at each other before Nayadu spoke, "Rao garu, can we think about this?"

"Yes, but you have to decide before I leave here."

"If we go, how much time do we have before we leave?"

"The steamer ship leaves late next week from Madras, but the train only goes down to Madras two times a week. We should get you and your family onto a train in Rajahmundry by this Saturday so that you get there by Sunday. You can get someone to see to your farm?"

Nayadu scoffed, "Rao garu, you've not heard who owns our farms here in Korlakota?"

"Uh, no," said Rao, pulling out a contract from his leather bag.

"Ever hear of R. K. Chouderey?" he asked.

"No."

"He works for the British—Indian—uh—"

"British East Indian Company?"

"That's it. He controls the whole village."

"Ahh," Rao said, nodding. "He's the *Zamindar*."

"So you do know him,"

"No, I don't know this Chouderey fellow you speak of, but these Zamindars are quite common throughout these parts. But carry on," he said with a motion of his hand. "I'm listening."

"Well, he arrived here in our village some years back and spoke to Sangam Bukkaya. He's our village elder." Nayadu's eyes suddenly grew. "Next thing we know, a village meeting was called. R. K. Chouderey said that he and his men were here to protect us from foreign invaders and that we were to pay him."

Rao shook his head side to side and scoffed. "Foreign invaders? That's a good one. These men are nothing more than tax-collecting landlords for the British."

Nayadu shrugged his shoulders. "What do we know about foreign invaders or Zamindars? All we knew was that this was a high-caste fellow. Nobody questioned him. I always paid but some didn't, and I don't blame them—we never saw anything in return. Is that fair to us, Rao garu?"

"I don't think it is," said Rao.

"I don't either. One month, a couple of years back when times were better, I told him I didn't sell any of my crop and had no money to pay him. But he knew better and threatened me—said he would have his thugs come and beat me."

"How does this man know better?" asked Rao.

"Sangam Bukkaya," he replied. "When the Zamindar took over, Bukkaya added a new verandah and a built a new roof. His old broken-down buffalo turned into four fat buffaloes. Even now, you can spot his family stocking up with grains, rice, and other things while the rest of the village barely survives. Everybody knows that Bukkaya works for the Zamindar."

"And you people have never turned on this Bukkaya fellow?"

"Rao garu, you know that we respect our elders."

"Yes, but how can you respect someone who has turned on his own people?"

"This is our culture. Bukkaya is the oldest man living in the village—that gets him our respect. What's more, Bukkaya has wealth, which gets him more respect. We don't look at how he got the wealth because he—"

Rao interrupted, "Because he's the village elder."

"Yes!"

Rao knew the agrarian ways and customs of the low-caste Kapu villagers were more conservative than the ways in which he was raised. Elders, in his opinion, were certainly to be revered but not to be regarded as infallible. But what struck him, as he listened, was the cleverness of this landlord. The man knew that the best choice for an indigenous traitor wasn't necessarily the strongest or even the smartest but, rather, one that the other villagers would hold in the highest esteem—no matter what. The elder could effectively inform on his own children and never lose a degree of respect, thus keeping order in the ranks.

"Every year the Zamindar took more and more money from us till it became impossible to pay both him and feed my family."

"And then?"

"Sudhakar, he's the man who collects the money for the Zamindar, offered to loan us money." Nana raised his trembling right hand and covered his heart. His sad, misty eyes pierced Rao's defenses. "I never borrowed a lot of money, Rao garu—only enough to buy what we needed to live."

Rao squirmed in discomfort.

"Then one day the Zamindar himself told me that we owe hundreds of rupees. He showed me papers, but I don't read. He told me that he had no choice but to take my land from me. This is his land now—I just live here and work for him."

Evidence of an internal struggle etched Rao's face. Sudden feelings of sympathy must have been warring with the mission in front of him. Exploitation of the underprivileged castes was a part of Indian society—it was their lot in this life. Rao's conscious started gnawing at him.

He sat silently, pondering the Zamindar's calculated, heavy-handed takeover of all farms in Korlakota. He considered that both he and Zamindar were representatives of the Crown with conflicting agendas. The Zamindar was there to exact levies from the villagers, albeit with a corrupt heavy-handedness, while he was there to lure them away from their homeland with the promise of prosperity.

But he really wasn't sure what awaited recruits on the other side. He was simply parroting the smooth parlance of the British landowner's agents. Until now he had given little thought as to whether he was using deceit as a means to contract unsuspecting Indians. But it was easy to ignore such knotty thoughts when promised twenty-five rupees for each able-bodied recruit and ten rupees for each woman and child over the age of seven. A good day of prospecting might easily yield a recruiter a few hundred rupees.

But Nayadu's story somehow managed to alter Rao's perspective. He wondered whether he had become a pawn in a cruel game perpetuated by the British Empire's insatiable quest for world dominance.

Rao took the contract and rolled it up. "Nayadu, I've been doing this for six weeks now."

"Doing what?"

"Recruiting hardworking men like you." He cleared his throat. "Nayadu, I honestly don't know what kind of life awaits you on the other side of the *Kala Pani*. I've cared little about such things until I met you."

But Nayadu was oblivious to Rao's awakened conscience and said, "We'll go, garu."

Rao replied with raised eyebrows, "You want to go?"

Nayadu looked over at his wife before he answered. "What do we have to lose?"

"Uh… Very well then," Rao said as he unrolled the contract. Nayadu's eagerness managed to melt away Rao's guilt. "In several days, my man will come to fetch you, people. He'll come with an ox-drawn cart to bring you to the Rajahmundry train station. Please don't keep him waiting. Any questions?"

"Yes, Rao garu, what does this say?"

Rao chuckled. "Oh, of course, Nayadu. This is an agreement of indenture. That means you agree to work for whoever buys this contract for the term specified."

"What is the term?" he asked.

Rao took the contract and looked at it closely as if he wasn't sure and then handed it back to Nayadu. "Five years," he answered.

Again, he looked over at Archana, who showed no emotion. "All right," he said. "Where do I—?"

Rao took Nayadu's right hand and pasted it with ink then impressed it on the bottom of the contract. "Anything else before I leave you, good people?"

Nayadu wiped his hand on the ground trying to remove the ink. "Uh, yes, Rao garu, where will you be taking me and my family?"

Rao looked at him and hesitated for a moment. "I'll let you know once you arrive in Rajahmundry."

CHAPTER 2

The next morning Nayadu went to notify Chandra Sudhakar, the Zamindar's agent, of his overseas work contract. The trek took him to the other side of the village next to the tracks where the agent had a small office. It was there that the villagers would bring money each month, and Nayadu loathed the journey. But not today. Nayadu's steps were lighter, and the air—even it felt cooler. He found himself whistling a tune—a tune that he only whistled when he was feeling a bit sanguine. *I might even miss this place*, he thought to himself.

He came around the final bend so that the agent's office was in sight. The office sat at the end of a strip of ramshackle buildings lined up on the north side of the railroad tracks. There was no door to the office but only a piece of cloth hanging from some hooks above the entrance. Today the cloth was pulled to the side and Sudhakar was in plain view from the road, sitting behind his desk. Nayadu always felt a lump rise in his throat when he would come around the bend and neared the agent's office. This time was no different.

He warily poked his head in. "Greetings, Sudhakar garu."

Chandra Sudhakar was an irascible bully responsible for doing the Zamindar's dirty work. He had a wide waddling gait and a thick, overgrown moustache which always dangled a remnant or two of his last meal. Behind his back, the Kapu villagers joked that there was no worse karmic fate than that of being the agent's horse. But face-to-face villagers trembled. One rumor circulating around the village purported that the Zamindar's right-hand man once killed a man for lying to him. Whether true or not, it was enough to keep most Korlakotans honest.

The agent shifted his dark beady eyes away from the paper laid out on his desk. "Nayadu, you're early this month. You have money for me?"

"Uh, no, garu," he said, stepping warily into the office. His legs suddenly felt weak.

"Then why are you here?" he asked, glancing back down at his paper.

"I've been given a job—overseas—as an agricultural specialist."

He lifted his head again and, with a harsh tone, asked, "A what?"

Nayadu moved back several steps. "An agricultural specialist."

Sudhakar leaned his thick frame back in his chair, and with a mocking tone, he scoffed, "An agricultural specialist!"

The little bit of confidence that Nayadu had gathered while walking across the village was gone, and beads of perspiration started to dot his forehead.

He laughed contemptuously and said, "Forget it, Nayadu!" His words spittled across the desk. "You work for the Zamindar, and you owe him hundreds of rupees."

Nayadu tried to reason with him, "Yes, garu, I know, but now I can make enough money to pay back what I owe the Zamindar."

"Nonsense!" he barked. "It will take you a lifetime to repay what you owe, and besides, who is going to work that farm if you're gone?"

Nayadu recoiled at the agent's merciless response and lowered his head in shame.

"Who was this person who hired you?"

"Sreenivasu Rao."

"Rao?" His eyes squinted. "Short, fair-skinned with glasses, from Hyderabad?"

Nayadu nodded.

The agent shook his head side to side, and he wagged his finger at Nayadu. "Don't think about it, Nayadu. The Zamindar won't hear of it." He shooed him out of his small office. "And if you see that Rao fellow again, tell him to come see me."

With his head hung low, Nayadu backed out of the agent's office. He slowly started to make his way back home wondering now whether he would be able to get out of the contract he signed with Rao. He looked down at his hand and started rubbing at what remained of the dried ink stained into the cracks and calluses of his right hand.

Nayadu believed the contract would be welcomed news to Sudhakar and the Zamindar. *Why couldn't laborers be hired to work the land once the rains returned,* he thought to himself.

*****

Along the way back, he passed Sangam Bukkaya's house. Up high in one of the Palmyra palms was Bukkaya's nephew cutting the greenest fronds and dropping them to the ground. Bukkaya's son was busy on the ground gathering the fresh cuttings. The fronds were a last resort to extract any remaining sap still left in the tree. All the veins within the trunk itself had been tapped dry months ago. A fellow that Nayadu didn't recognize was busy pressing sap out of the freshly cut stalks into earthenware jugs to make ready the sticky white liquid for a fermentation process. The result was a fizzy alcoholic drink known in the village as *kalloo*.

"Nayadu," Bukkaya called out from his palatial verandah. "Come, my friend, and have a toddy with me." Rarely did Nayadu imbibe, but he would never disrespect Bukkaya by refusing his offer. He knew the routine. Plucking a choice leaf from a nearby almond tree, he skillfully rolled it up into a cone shaped cup.

The verandah still smelled of freshly cut wood, but Nayadu avoided commenting on it. Deep down, he wondered what Bukkaya would say if asked about his newfound wealth. The old man hadn't worked in years and up until recently, relied mostly on his two sons just to survive.

Bukkaya sat on the steps wearing nothing more than a *pancha*. His dark, leathered skin hung loosely on his gaunt frame while his stomach paunched outward. With his head tipped back, he quickly poured a shot of the white effervescent concoction down his throat. One could only assume that the vigorous nod and guttural heave that followed was a sign of satisfaction.

"So, my friend, I hear that you're leaving us."

Nayadu dipped his makeshift cup into the pot which held the tropical potation. "You know this already?" he asked before belting down the libation. He winced at the bitterness. "How do you know this?"

"Heard if from the priest, Sai Komdaari"

Nayadu's lip curled upward. "How does he know such things?"

Bukkaya shrugged. "Never mind, Nayadu, tell me where you're going."

"I've taken a job as an agricultural specialist over—"

"A what?"

"An agricultural specialist."

"That's what I thought you said. Okay, Nayadu, I'm listening."

"This high-caste city fellow came to my home yesterday and told me that there aren't enough people who know how to farm. So," he said, shrugging his shoulders, "they're hiring people like me—who know how to farm."

"This high-caste man you speak of is fat, light skin, glasses—from the city?"

"You know him?"

"No, no. Saw him though. He came riding by yesterday and stopped right there," he said, pointing out toward the road. "I waved to him, and he waved back, then he rode off."

"Yes, his name is Rao. He works for rich foreigners."

"Okay, so tell me where you're going."

"Across the Kala Pani."

Bukkaya's bloodshot eyes opened wide, crinkling his forehead. "I always wanted to travel across the Kala Pani."

Nayadu continued, "At first, we weren't sure if it was wise to leave our homeland, but Rao convinced us."

"Nayadu, you've known me your whole life, and you know I'm not much into tradition. I believe that a man must do whatever he must do to get ahead in this life." Nayadu tried to keep a straight face. "If you're being given a chance to make a better life for yourself, take it!"

"But what about Sudhakar? He says we owe the Zamindar money—a lot of money."

Bukkaya pulled himself up out of his reclined position to refresh himself with another dip into the kalloo pot. "Please, my friend, help yourself to another drink," Bukkaya motioned with his bony finger. He continued, "Nayadu, maybe you don't understand that the Zamindar has you right where he wants you. He owns your farm, *and* he owns you. Leaving here and abandoning your farm will upset his—his little kingdom."

"But I can go earn enough money to pay the Zamindar what I owe him and buy my farm back."

Bukkaya shook his head sharply. "By the time you return, my friend, you will owe more interest than can be paid in this lifetime—and the next."

Bukkaya's frankness was sobering. Nayadu dipped his cup back in and made sure that it was full this time. He tipped his head back and poured it down his throat. "Aaacchh!" Nayadu's face winced at the bitterness of the kalloo.

"Sorry, my friend, I'm afraid that the sap from the fronds doesn't make as sweet a batch as the sap from the shaft." Bukkaya looked up toward the cloudless sky. "Oh, how I wish the rains would return."

"Excuse me, Bukkaya garu, but I should go now."

"Yes, go if you must. But don't let the Zamindar or that agent of his stop you. You're being offered a new life. Sometimes we have to take chances and step into the unknown. Anything worth having is worth taking a risk for. Just go, I say."

"Thanks, Bukkaya garu, I will consider all of what you've told me. Please, you must excuse me now."

It didn't matter to Nayadu that Bukkaya had become a traitor by working for the Zamindar. He still reserved considerable respect for the village's most senior, albeit venal, resident.

*****

As Nayadu made his way home, his stomach began to rumble, and it occurred to him that he had not eaten the entire day. With each step, the uneasiness in his belly intensified. He realized that he should have forsaken that second helping of kalloo. Never had it made him feel so bad. But then he had never consumed a batch made from the fronds, and he certainly wasn't an experienced imbiber. Suddenly his stomach lurched violently, expelling every last drop of the caustic substance along the roadside.

Feeling better, Nayadu used his shirt to wipe the perspiration from his forehead. He hadn't walked twenty feet when he began to ponder the different encounters throughout the day. Images of Sudhakar's angry face flashed before him, along with his piercing words, *Forget it, Nayadu. You work for the Zamindar.* Nayadu's chest tightened.

Then Nayadu thought about Bukkaya's emboldening words, *Don't worry about the Zamindar or his agent.* His tensions slowly waned. *Just go, Nayadu*, he heard in the back of his head.

But Nayadu knew little about taking risks. The extent of his bravado was wading out into the Godavari up to his waist to bathe during peak monsoon season. With no swimming skills whatsoever, he was always aware that a sudden slip might mean being swept to his death by the swift moving river.

He felt himself breathing heavily and slipped some *betel nut* into his mouth to calm his nerves. The sun was starting to set, and the shadows from the trees lengthened but that did little to abate the warm temperatures. Nayadu, however, was thinking little about the heat.

Ahead on the right was the *Shiva* temple. Nobody knew how old the temple was or who built it, but it was impressive in workmanship. Hundreds of intricately chiseled deities, juxtaposed with mythological scenes carved into the white marble facades, overlooked all four sides of the temple. They provided an ominous vigilance over the surrounding area. The black moss and dark green lichen that pervaded over much of outside walls somehow managed to add beauty to the structure. The marble still exposed luminesced in the remaining rays of sunlight.

Outside the front of the temple sat a young girl delicately threading garlands of marigolds so as not to damage the decorative orange, copper, and buttery yellow flowers. They hung in uniformity, waiting to be purchased by temple patrons.

Nayadu shuffled quickly by the girl without looking at her. At the entrance of the temple was a bell that pilgrims were expected to chime before entering to ensure that the gods were awake, but he ignored that also.

In the center of the temple was a large shrine which housed the image of Shiva.

His likeness dominated the handful of other deities that occupied the different corners of the temple. The sweet, pungent smell of incense permeated the air.

Nayadu expected to find Sai Komdaari, the temple priest, sitting in his usual place next to the *Hanuman* shrine. The holy man had an ability to sit for hours, even days, cross-legged without moving—not unlike the other statues. Korlakotans believed he was the closest thing to a god they had ever seen.

But the priest was nowhere in sight, and Nayadu was glad. He was still bitter about the ceremony in which his two sons were buried alive. He just wanted to offer a quick puja and be on his way.

"Greetings, Nayadu," came the voice from behind, startling Nayadu. He turned quickly to find Sai Komdaari holding a lamp, its flame a mere flicker.

Pressing his hands together above his head, he smiled awkwardly. "Greetings, Komdaari garu."

"Exceptionally warm this evening, Nayadu."

"Er—yes, very warm, Komdaari garu.

"I haven't seen you here for some time," the priest said, rolling the length of his unshorn beard around his index finger.

Nayadu lowered his head. "I know—I'm sorry."

"Are you troubled, Nayadu?"

"You can tell?"

The priest continued, "Is it because you're going overseas?"

Nayadu gaped. "H—how did you know?"

"Nayadu," said Komdaari, shaking his head, "does it surprise you that I am able to know such things? And I suppose you want favor from the gods."

Nayadu lowered his head but kept his eyes fixed on the priest. He nodded shamefacedly.

The priest lowered his head, staring back into Nayadu's eyes. His voice was calm. "Your ambition to make a better life for yourself is admirable. Who in their right mind would not want to escape the toil and trouble of this existence? But this is the life that you have been born into, and you cannot change that. Do you not know that the *Bhagavad Gita* says that it is your duty to perform the job that your birth ordained, regardless of how you like it?"

Nayadu didn't answer.

"In fact," he continued, "it is better for you to perform poorly at what you were intended to do than to do well at someone else's duty. Everyone must perform what he was predestined to do. This is one's *dharma* according to their karma and what helps maintain order in the cosmos. But something else you should know, Nayadu."

Nayadu's eyes widened. "Tell me, garu."

"Our scriptures forbid our people from crossing the Kala Pani."

Both men stood silently for a minute, and then Nayadu asked sheepishly, "So do you think we can still offer puja?"

The priest smiled and turned the question around, "Nayadu, would you plant seeds on your farm if you knew there was no way to water the seeds?"

Nayadu's heart sank.

"And besides, you've brought no offering."

Now he felt sure that his leaving was a bad omen. He bid the priest an awkward farewell. Outside the temple sat the little girl, her hand extended outward. Nayadu dared not risk the wrath of an angry god and hastily reached into his pocket for change.

"Here!" he said, pressing fifteen paise into her small hand. "Now you have all my money."

He headed home, his head swirling with all the different advice he had been given. One thing he knew was that he didn't want to go against the edicts of ancient scripture.

*****

Archana had already started dishing out rice and dhal for the boys by the time Nayadu arrived. She instinctively knew something was wrong.

"You were away for a long time," she said calmly.

"We're not going," he blurted out.

"But why, Nana?" Chandu cried out.

"Come, sit," said Archana.

Nayadu sat for a moment then started eating. He stopped and looked at each one of them. "We're Kapus," he said, "and Kapus are farmers. This is what we were born to do!" He jumped up and walked outside.

"*Ammandi!*" Archana cried out, following Nayadu out the door. She found him sitting in his usual spot etching with his fingers in the hard, dry clay.

"Tell me," she said, pulling his hand into her lap.

"We can't go," he said softly.

"But why?"

"The Zamindar will be angry—and the gods will be angry. There are too many bad omens."

Gently stroking her husband's weathered hands, she asked, "Why will the gods be angry?"

"Our dharma—we have to be farmers. That's what we were born to do," he said, pulling his hands away from Archana.

"But, Ammandi, won't we be farming overseas?"

Nayadu hesitated. "Yeah, but…we're not supposed to cross the Kala Pani."

"Why not?"

"Hindu scripture forbids us."

Archana persisted, "But why, Ammandi?"

"I don't know, but this is what Komdaari told me," he said, sweeping the dust off the ground in front of him.

Pradip and Chandu inched closer to the door listening closely as their fate unraveled.

"Have you so quickly forgotten what Rao told us?" asked Archana. Nayadu didn't respond. She reached over gently pulling his gaze toward her. "The stars—they're lined up in our favor, Ammandi."

Nayadu looked up into the cloudless night sky for some sort of confirmation and the two sat without a sound for some time. The silence was painful for the two boys as their fate weaved back and forth.

"What about her?" she asked motioning toward the River.

"What *about* her?" Nayadu asked.

"You say that she sometimes speaks to you. Is she saying anything to you now?"

Nayadu chuckled. "Haven't heard anything from her in some time. It was months ago that I felt her say she was tiring, and she's been weakening ever since." Nayadu had a unique relationship with the river and talked with her frequently. Sometimes he prayed and worshipped her along her muddy bank, and sometimes he talked to her as if she were his mother.

"Maybe she's gone," said Archana.

Nayadu clapped the dust off his hands and turned to Archana. "You really want to go, huh?"

Archana smiled and nodded. "What do we have to lose, Ammandi?"

He sat silently weighing all the advice that he had been given since Rao's visit. Nayadu was not a deep thinker, but he considered that Bukkaya was the only one who didn't have a selfish motive behind his counsel.

The words suddenly echoed again, *Just go, Nayadu!* He jumped up, "You're right, what do we have to lose?"

Chandu knew that moment of revelation for his father had forever altered their lives, that he had found an inner peace that managed to walk a fine line between tradition and self-determination.

Pradip looked at his older brother, and Chandu knew he was troubled. "What's wrong?" he asked him.

"*Ammamma* and *Thathiyya.*" His voice quivered and a tear rolled down his eye. "Don't worry, Pradip. We'll see them again—someday."

Chandu's words did little to comfort him. He lowered his head onto his knees and started sobbing. "I don't want to go," he whimpered.

"Stop crying," he scolded. "We have to go. There's nothing here for us."

"Ammamma and Thathiyya are here. Why can't they come with us?"

"You know Nana would never allow that. Now be quiet."

29

CHAPTER 3

The coolness of morning had dissipated into late summer heat long before the bullock cart arrived to fetch the Nayadu family. The precipitous path leading down to their home was too narrow for a cart to descend, leaving the driver no choice but to wait for them on the road. Already in tow was another young family whom Rao had contracted.

Pradip and Chandu had been ready for hours. The anticipation of journeying to another land broke their sleep long before the half a dozen or so roosters that normally interrupted the morning calm. With their allowed essentials tied up securely in their bedding, they found time to amuse themselves with a game of *tokuddu billa*. This was a game they played by etching squares into the dirt and hopped from square to square to square on one foot. But Pradip quickly lost interest in the game and wandered over to his father who was securing the front door of their home.

"Nana, is five years a long time?"

Nayadu chuckled, and his mother answered, "To you, yes.

Disappointed, he returned to where they had their belongings piled. "Chandu, are you scared?"

"No," he answered hesitantly. "Why, are you?"

"Uh, no. Well, maybe a little."

"Of what?" he asked.

"I don't know, but I'm afraid something bad is going to happen."

"Don't worry," Chandu said, putting his arm around him. "The gods will protect us." He reached over to the satchel and pulled out a statue of *Ganesha* and handed it to Pradip. "He's the destroyer of all evils."

Pradip ran his hand over Ganesha's protruding belly. "I've always wondered, Chandu, why does Ganesha have an elephant head?"

"Because."

"Because why?"

"Because Shiva got mad at him, cut his head off and then gave him the head of an elephant."

"How do you know that?"

"I just know."

Pradip studied the statue some more. "And he's gonna protect us?"

"Of course," he said.

Pradip smashed the deity on the ground, breaking off one of its arms.

"What are you doing?" he scolded.

Using the broken appendage to break through the hard packed earth, he started digging fervently into the ground. "I want him to protect our home while we're gone," he said, carefully placing the deity's arm in the hole he created. "Promise me something, Chandu," he said as his older brother helped him push the dirt back into the hole.

"What is it?" he asked.

"Promise me that nothing will keep us from coming back here."

"We will," he replied.

"Promise, Chandu."

"I promise."

"Wait," he said before running over to the tamarind tree. He picked up a pod off the ground, broke open the brittle shell and brought the seeds back, placing all five of them into the soft dirt. He then took the broken Ganesha statue and carefully wrapped it up in his blanket. "He can still protect us with one arm, can't he?"

"He can protect us with no arms."

Pradip smiled. "Good."

*****

As Nayadu tied off the last knot tightly securing the door, he glanced over at Archana as if to seek her approval. A tear rolled down her face. The emotions that had been building up inside her from the time they made a decision to leave now culminated into a combination of melancholy, fear, and joyful anticipation. How their simple, uneventful lives had drastically changed since Rao's visit earlier that week.

"Are we making the right decision?" he asked somberly.

"Don't you remember what you said, Ammandi?"

He paused, looking toward the sky. "You mean, 'What do we have to lose'?"

She smiled and used the sleeve of her *sari* to wipe his face.

"Come on, boys, let's go," he said as he hoisted a satchel of their meager belongings over his shoulder.

Chandu didn't wait for his little brother. He ran to the bullock cart dragging a small bundle of their belongings. Little consideration was given to items they knew they couldn't bring. Cooking essentials, some clothing, and of course, their gods and lamps were the only things deemed necessary.

Nayadu stopped halfway up the steep trail and turned around to look at their home—the home that he had helped build with his own hands.

"Come, Nana!" Chandu yelled from the top of the trail.

Nayadu reached down and picked up a smoothed rock and slipped it into his pocket. "Coming," he said.

*****

Ram Velu, his wife, and four-year-old daughter, Manisha, rearranged themselves and their belongings to make room for Nayadu and his family. They lived on the other side of the village, but Nayadu would occasionally meet Velu at the market or temple.

Velu was thin and wiry like Nayadu but shorter. He was known for a certain level of toughness that made other men in the village respect him or at least avoid confrontations with him. It was understood that the scar that ran from the outer edge of Velu's right eye-

brow to his lower cheekbone was the work of the Zamindar's henchmen, though nobody was sure what caused the scar, and Velu was
never known to speak of the incident.

"Greetings, Velu," said Nayadu.

Velu jumped down from the cart to help and replied with a
reluctant smile. He took Nayadu's satchel and tossed it onto the cart.

"Agricultural specialist?" Nayadu asked, assuming that Velu had
been recruited for the same job.

Velu snickered. "If that's what they want to call it." Velu had a
high, scratchy voice that would make your eyes water until you got
used to it.

Nayadu turned to greet Velu's wife. Her eyes were swollen and
moist from tears. Feeling awkward, he quickly turned to his boys.
"Say hello to Uncle and Aunty."

"That's Prema," said Velu, motioning toward his wife. "She's
very sad this morning—leaving her family. The little one is already
missing her grandparents."

Pradip inched next to Manisha to show her the stone he'd been
using to play tokkudu billa. Manisha turned away, latching onto her
mother, but Pradip was unfazed by her rebuff.

"No family here to see you off?" asked Velu.

"What family?" Nayadu retorted.

The driver interrupted with an unsympathetic warning, "Finish
loading and get on!"

"Pass me your other satchel so we can get moving," Velu said to
Nayadu.

*****

"Hyaahhh!" barked the driver, putting into motion the beast of
burden. Nayadu took one last look down at the family home before
turning away. The terraced fields that once boasted some of the finest
harvests of rice in South India were quiescent. Brown, lifeless stalks
covered with dirt and dust were all that was left from Nayadu's futile
attempt to bring forth a crop this year. His hopes were high that the
rains would return this year and in the interim he put the whole

family to work along with the buffalo toting buckets of water from the Godavari to the terraced paddy fields. It seemed that there was no other way, so they toiled from sun up to sun down, back and forth from the river to the paddies with buckets of muddy water. After several months, their hands developed thick calluses and their skin blackened from the cloudless days. Nevertheless, the hard work paid off. The seedlings took root and started to grow. They were sure that they had managed to foil the capricious Shiva and his alleged plan to spoil their crops yet again. But alas, Shiva had the last word. He reduced the river to a mere trickle, bringing all their hard labor to naught.

He reached into his pocket and took out the fifty rupees he made from the sale of his buffalo and wondered how he might need it. He wondered if rupees were of any worth where they were going. Then he glanced over at Archana, who had already taken to Prema.

The two women were chatting as if they were sisters though they hardly resembled each other. Velu's wife was plump which was rare in the village, and her features were fair and pleasant. Her eyes sparkled with intelligence, and her cheeks dimpled when she smiled. There was an attractiveness to her that was not seen in most Kapu women. Nayadu's wife, on the other hand, was thin with angular yet ordinary features. Her hair with thick and wild, and she was forced to keep it tied back. He was glad that the two women were getting on well.

Nayadu smiled upon Pradip, who had withdrawn into his own little world. Chandu, however, saw concern on his father's face. He pulled his elder son close to his side but said nothing. The events of the past week weighed heavy on him. He wondered whether he made the right decision uprooting his family from everything that felt safe and familiar.

"You were saying, Nayadu?" asked Velu.

"Saying?"

"About your family."

"I thought the whole village knew," said Nayadu.

Velu abruptly sat up from his reclining position, his eyes firmly fixed on something in the distance behind them.

Nayadu looked back to see what had alarmed Velu. Barely visible were two men on horseback riding swiftly toward them. Still, there was no mistaking the pair. The Zamindar with his slight stature led the way, flanked by the more imposing presence of his lackey, Chandra Sudhakar. Together these men had managed to bring the village of Korlakota to its knees.

When Nayadu turned to see the men riding in their direction in a furious cloud of dust, he instinctively latched onto Chandu's arm. But before he could say anything, the two of them took a sudden turn down the narrow road leading to their empty house.

"You think they saw us?" Nayadu asked while trying to remain calm.

"Faster!" Velu yelled to the driver.

"What's wrong?" the driver asked.

"We might have trouble."

The driver took his long stick and swatted the bullock, prompting the animal to scuttle.

"Won't take them long to realize you've abandoned the farm. My guess is that they'll come looking for you," Velu said.

Archana pulled Chandu out of his father's clutches over to her side. Nobody spoke as if chatter might give them away. The only sound heard was that of the bullock's hooves clapping frantically against the ground.

After several minutes had passed, the driver allowed the bullock to slow down. "Good thing we left when we did," he said.

"Why are we slowing down?" asked Nayadu.

"This girl is old," the driver replied. "Don't want to kill her."

"Maybe they went back," said Velu.

Nayadu nodded defiantly and continued to watch the road behind them.

"Hey, Nayadu, if they were after us, they would've caught up with this vegetable cart a long time ago."

Nayadu wasn't amused. Velu leaned over to the driver and whispered into his ear. The driver urged the bullock on with a sharp swat and the cart started making ground again.

The driver turned around and said, "I'm not gonna race her, or we'll never make it to Rajahmundry."

All of a sudden, the cart jolted and then again when the left wheels rolled over a large tree branch that had fallen onto the road. Nayadu and Velu, who were sitting on the left side of the cart, were joggled several inches from where they were sitting. Suddenly, the left rear wheel broke loose from the axle and rolled off the side of the road. Nayadu quickly tried to move toward the front of the cart to keep it from tipping, but it was too late. The left rear of the cart dipped before he could move to the other side of the cart. The bared axle gouged the road as the passengers desperately clung to the edge of the cart. Everyone—that is, except Nayadu, who rolled off the back along with several satchels.

Luckily, he was unhurt save for a few scrapes. The wheel was also in one piece. The violent jolt snapped the pin that held the wheel in place on the axle. The driver surveyed the situation, walked over to a nearby tree, and broke off a small branch. With the help of the two men, he had the wheel back in place and modeled the small branch into a temporary pin.

"Clever, this guy," said Velu patting the driver on the back.

"Don't know that it will hold but we'll see. Let's go," said the driver, showing no emotion.

"Shh!" said Nayadu. "Hear that?"

"Horses," said the driver.

"And they're heading this way," said Velu.

The road behind them was curved and lined with brush and trees. They couldn't see beyond the bend in the road and could only hope that the horses heading in their direction were anyone but the Zamindar and his henchman, but Nayadu's instinct told him different. Rarely was anyone in a hurry to get somewhere.

There were no trees where they had broken down, however. There was nowhere to hide. There was just the shallow Godavari that had been following alongside them ever since they left their home.

"This is it," said Nayadu. "I knew this was a bad omen." He reached into his pocket and pulled out the small stone that he had taken from the farm. Then he threw it as far as could in the direction of the river. "There! Take it!" he yelled, convinced that its removal had brought bad luck upon them.

"I have an idea," said the driver. "All of you, go down to the river and make like you're washing your clothes. I will start moving slowly down the road. Move quickly before they get here!"

They wasted no time. Nayadu grabbed Pradip off the back of the cart while Velu snatched Manisha. Within seconds, they were spread out down by the meandering streams of the parched river. Archana took her husband's shirt, dipped it into the water, and then proceeded to swing it violently onto a large flat rock protruding out of the water. It was a task she knew well. Prema followed suit while Nayadu and Velu each kept one eye on the road above.

As expected, the Zamindar with Sudhakar close behind stopped to interrogate the driver who was rolling slowly down the road. Archana kept the boys close and instructed them not to look up. But Chandu snuck peeks of the men out of the corner of his eye. The driver kept lifting his hands as if to convey his ignorance. Archana kept beating Nayadu's shirt against the rock while Nayadu and Velu walked further upstream to distance themselves from the families. Nayadu, however, snuck nervous glances up toward the men.

"Act natural, Nayadu, or you'll give us away."

"Komdaari warned me," said Nayadu. "Said we Hindus are forbidden to cross the Kala Pani."

Velu laughed. "He wished me a safe journey. I was surprised because he never says anything nice to me. Didn't think he liked me."

Nayadu couldn't laugh. Despite Velu's warning, he kept peering up toward the road. After what seemed like an eternity, the men turned their horses and started back. The driver waited several minutes until they were well on their way and then waved the two families back. Archana, in turn, yelled for the two men to return, and soon, they were back on the cart rolling toward Rajahmundry.

Velu leaned over to the driver. "What did you say to those thugs?"

"Told them I'm just a hardworking man moving some of my family's belongings to a new village." The driver paced the bullock so that she would make Rajahmundry in plenty of time without running her into the ground. Nayadu was relaxed now and managed to find room to recline on one of his satchels.

"Sudhakar warned me not to leave," said Nayadu.

"Then why did you?"

Nayadu thought for a minute. "We decided we had nothing to lose." They rode along quietly for several minutes before Nayadu asked, "What about you? What did you tell the Zamindar?"

Velu laughed. "Nothing. I didn't tell him we were leaving. I haven't moved a handful of dirt on that farm for months."

"So you haven't paid the Zamindar?"

Velu scoffed, "Never!"

"And?"

"Those thugs show up every month to collect, and I tell them to jump into the river."

"And?"

"They beat me like a stray dog. But not without a good fight?" Velu smiled widely to reveal a missing front tooth and then proceeded to show Nayadu the different scars that he had accumulated over the months. "Told them they might be able to hurt me, but they would have to kill me because I won't pay money for my own farm. I would fight them till my last dying breath." He laughed. "They got my farm, but it's not doing them any good."

Nayadu sat amazed at Velu's story. He didn't know whether to chalk it up to brazen courage or plain stupidity.

"But enough about me, Nayadu. Tell me about your family."

"Oh, Archana's family—we haven't seen them—must be a year now," said Nayadu. "Don't know how you can live in Korlakota and not know about them."

Velu shrugged his shoulders. "Know what?"

"Archana's father and mother—they turned their back on our gods and our religion and started following a foreign religion." Nayadu's face grew stern. He didn't enjoy talking about what had happened to Archana's parents. Before this new religion had taken them captive, Nayadu had loved them as much as he had loved his own family.

"And they turned their backs on your family?" asked Velu.

"Well, no, but I didn't want anything to do with this religion."

"So what *is* this new religion?"

"I don't know what it's called," said Nayadu. "It's the White man's religion. They told us that this god had become a man and was sacrificed so that all men can be enlightened—or something."

"But how did they hear about this god?" asked Velu.

"A foreigner who was passing through our village stopped at their home for water and to take rest. The stranger told her mother and father about this god and left a book with them. That was it. They stopped going to the temple. Then they told us we must stop praying to all of our other gods. I told them, 'Never!'" he said, slapping his hand on the wooden planks. "'We will never stop praying to all our gods,' I told them. 'We were born Hindus, and we will die Hindus!'"

"But why do they say that you must stop praying to all the other gods?"

"This is what I asked. They believe that this god is the only true god and that our gods are false."

"False!" exclaimed Velu. "How can our gods be false?" he snickered.

"I don't know, but this is what they believe, and this is what they want us to believe. They threw all their gods and lamps into the Godavari and told us we should do the same."

"And your wife, you keep her from her mother and father."

"It's for her own good. I can't have them poisoning her," he said, glancing over at his wife. She sat innocently holding Pradip by her side. "I just hope these people come to their senses. These boys miss their Thathiyya and Ammamma. They're the only grandparents that they have left.

Chandu looked over at Pradip with a sly smile. Archana looked down and put her finger over her mouth. She had been allowing them to visit their grandparents without their father's knowledge. It was a secret that they had been keeping from him for months.

Archana was indifferent about her parents' decision to change their religion. They were still her parents, and she loved them. But she knew she had to be submissive to her husband. Interestingly, Nayadu wasn't even religious—just traditional. He held Komdaari, the temple priest in the highest regard but grew to dislike him intensely. Archana lived with her husband's inconsistencies doing whatever it took to keep peace in the family.

Archana was especially mindful of the fact that her parents were the only grandparents the boys had. They never knew their father's parents, and it was a story he never talked about. Archana, however, recounted for her boys the amazing tale one afternoon:

It was shortly after the couple discovered that she was pregnant with Chandu that they decided to move out of the small home that they shared with Nayadu's mother and father and build a small cottage for his growing family. He could not have known the fortuitous consequences of his decision to build that cottage just up the bank. Nayadu's mother had insisted that the couple continue to live with her and Tata, as he was called. But Nayadu, was firm in his decision and began the construction of the new home.

Tata, Nayadu, and his younger brother, Nagesh, spent the better part of three weeks erecting the new home. It was an identical version of the family dwelling, complete with an attached kitchen on the back of the house. During those weeks, Nayadu's mother, or Mama, as she was called by the boys, and Archana not only cooked but tended to the farming. Construction of such homes, made mostly of neem wood and thatched palm roofs, was not extremely time consuming, but they had the additional task of creating a flat plot of land.

The Nayadu farm was unusual in that it covered four hectares of riparian land. It was situated between the north bank of the Godavari River and the dirt road, which, for the most part, ran parallel to the river. The uphill grade of the land made irrigation a toilsome task during the dry season. However, the hill offered exemption from the devastating effects of monsoon floods that were common to the low-lying areas. Most of the land was skillfully terraced for the cultivation of rice. A small portion was set aside for the few buffaloes owned by Tata.

It was a mid-June afternoon, and the exceptionally still, balmy air forewarned of a menacing intruder. When the buffaloes pulling the plows started acting erratically, Tata knew something was awry. He knew from past experience that animals were extremely sensitive to abrupt changes in atmospheric pressure.

Tata called Nayadu and Nagesh over to tell them he was sure that nasty weather lay ahead. Within an hour, the jostling of trees disturbed the still air. While the cool breeze brought relief from the intense heat, a foreboding black wall of clouds appeared suddenly and swiftly on the eastern horizon. Dramatic displays of lightning sparked deafening roars of thunder. The rapidly encroaching storm cast an ominous pall over the land.

"It looks like the gods are really angry at each other!" Tata yelled to his two sons. "Tie up the animals. This looks like it is going to be a big one!"

Tata yelled over to Nayadu. "Why don't you and Archana come down and wait out the storm with us!"

"Okay, but I'll see if she's well enough to move. She wasn't able to get out of bed this morning."

By now, the wind had turned anything not fastened down into a dangerous projectile.

"I'll be down if she's well enough to get out of bed, okay?" reassured Nayadu.

"Okay," Tata replied before disappearing into his small home.

No sooner had the men parted ways than the wind and rain began to unleash its fury. Nayadu found his wife awake and feeling much better, but they both agreed that it would be better to stay in their new home until the storm subsided. The storm, however, intensified. Gale force winds started undoing the expertly thatched fronds, which should have lasted for years. Rain started pelting through the walls, and Archana was sure they were going to die that day.

Nayadu felt helpless against the storm's immense power. He wanted desperately to protect his young bride and unborn child. Nevertheless, he could do little more than huddle in the corner and wrap his arms around her. "We should pray and seek favor from the gods!" Nayadu exclaimed out of desperation.

Before she could respond, a gust of wind whipped through the house as if there were no walls at all. The shrine, which housed the images of *Shiva, Ganesha,* and *Hanuman,* crashed to the ground. For a brief moment, there seemed to be no noise. Even the wind had dulled to a whisper. The couple just looked at each other. Nayadu quickly reached over to pick up the fallen deities when the fierce wind resumed with a vengeance.

The small house felt as though it would blow right off its foundation. How thankful he was now that his father had insisted on reinforcing the frame during the construction of the house. He prayed that Tata, along with his mother and brother, Nagesh, were faring at least as well as he and Archana were. He was concerned that the old home was no longer sturdy enough to withstand the brutal punishment of a such a storm.

He got up and moved toward the window to see if he could see his parents' house a stone's throw down the hill, in the direction of the river. Although the sheets of rain made the visibility poor, he was able to make out the faint outline of the beleaguered structure. What he didn't notice was the rapidly rising river just beyond the quaint house sheltering his three loved ones. He settled uneasily back into the corner where the two would wait for the storm's passing.

It was the next morning by the time the storm passed. Somehow, cradled in each other's arms, Nayadu and Archana managed to fall asleep in spite of the storm's fury. The young couple awoke in the same position that they had assumed during the storm. Above them where there was once a roof was clear sky but for a few ambling patches of gray clouds.

The eerie silence was deafening. No roosters cackling, no birds chirping, no buffaloes mooing—nothing but silence. Nayadu jumped up and ran out the front door to see how his family had managed through the night. The waterline left from the swollen river had risen to just a few short yards away from what was left of the young couple's new home.

Below the waterline, there was nothing but debris. Remnants floated on the top of the murky river. Nayadu's boyhood home was gone. There was nothing left where the modest little home had formerly been. Amma told the boys that time seemed to slow down in those dreadful moments as she watched their father from the window.

He searched frantically to find his family. He dug into the banks of the river clawing like an animal trying to find just one piece of his childhood, but nothing remained of his former home. His father, mother, and brother were gone.

Nayadu turned, facing the river, and cursed it, then he wept bitterly.

CHAPTER 4

It was early afternoon by the time the families arrived. Rao was standing under a tree near a large sign that read Rajahmundry Train Depot, and in his hand was a list with all the people he had enlisted. His smile grew wider with each name he was able to check off. He recruited ninety-eight men, women, and children over a seven-week period. If they all showed, he would be paid ₹1,730.

"Velu, Nayadu, so nice to see you again," he said with a courteous nod and checked off their names. After they offloaded their belongings, Rao swept them together with the motion of his hands and said, "Come, come, they have some lunch waiting for you, good people. You must be hungry after such a long ride."

Nayadu smiled and replied, "The boys are very hungry, garu."

"Before you go, take this paper. You're going to give this to an agent in Madras. He should be waiting for you when you get off the train."

"Uh, Rao garu," said Nayadu.

"Question?"

"You told us that you would tell us where we are going."

Rao grinned. "I did, didn't I. You'll be going to a place called Natal in South Africa. Don't know much about the place, but I hear there are green hills as far as the eye can see."

Velu, who was already walking toward the shade of a large neem tree, mumbled under his breath, "Green hills, is that it?"

To Nayadu, it didn't matter. He finally had a name to attach to the wanderlust of his imagination. It didn't matter that he had no

44

idea where this place was. He was just happy to know that this was a real place and not some ruse.

*****

The two villagers would become fast friends. Nayadu admired Velu's boldness and hoped that some of it might rub off on him. From the time they left their little home back in Korlakota, Nayadu had been questioning his decision to leave, and being around Velu managed to quell some of the anxiety he was feeling.

Velu, on the other hand, found Nayadu's honesty rare and refreshing. He instinctually knew that what you saw was what you got with Nayadu. He was sure that there was not a conniving or scheming bone in his body, and he liked that.

Archana, too, found Prema a suitable confidant and when neither family could find a reason to part company and a strong bond of friendship grew between them.

*****

The air was filled with anticipation as they filled their empty stomachs with dhal and parathas that were less than warm but tasty nonetheless. From their little encampment in the shade of a large neem tree, they observed with unbridled curiosity as people from all walks of life arrived. Their faces displayed varied expressions of bewilderment, and Chandu contemplated what circumstances might have brought each of them to this place. Certainly, there were few unaffected by the drought, but for an Indian to leave India was no small decision.

Their inquisitive observation was interrupted when a pair of hauntingly familiar faces appeared. Manisha was the first to notice and exclaimed, "Look, those bad men are here!"

Prema quickly pulled Manisha down to her side and cupped her hand over her mouth. "Look," she said, "there are four of them now."

The Zamindar had recruited two more thugs, but before the men could proceed onto the horseshoe-shaped drive fronting the station, Rao intercepted them to find out their business.

"How did they find us here?" asked Archana.

"Bukkaya," said Velu.

"Couldn't be Bukkaya," said Nayadu. "He was the only one who said we *should* go. He wouldn't tell the Zamindar where we are."

Velu scoffed, "Nayadu, have you forgotten who that old man works for?"

"No," he replied hesitantly. "But he wouldn't put the Zamindar onto us. That uncle likes me and my family."

"Maybe, but his real loyalty is to the Zamindar."

The exchange between Chouderey and Rao intensified. The Zamindar was the same height as Rao but much thinner. And some would argue that he was as ugly as he was mean with his pock-marked face and low-protruding forehead that cast a shadow over his beady eyes.

It was impossible to hear what Chouderey was saying to Rao, but Nayadu knew they were there to take him and his family back to Korlakota.

Rao looked over his list again and shook his head side to side with a shrug of his shoulders that seemed to say, *I don't know these people that you're looking for.*

But Chouderey didn't appear convinced and continued to berate Rao.

Prema gasped as the verbal altercation grew louder, "What should we do?"

"Turn around!" Velu scolded. "That's what you should do."

Archana and Prema turned their backs to the men while Nayadu and Velu positioned themselves behind the two women. Pradip and Chandu shrunk behind the base of the neem tree but found it impossible not to peer out with one eye. Frozen with fear, they watched as Chouderey tried to intimidate Rao with his strident voice and the menacing trio overshadowing him. Rao, however, was unflappable. He stood stoically, knowing that it was unlikely that they would try to harm him with so many villagers present. Sudhakar's eyes scanned back and forth like a hunter looking for prey, and the two boys quickly pulled their heads back behind the tree.

Pradip put his hand on his chest and said, "My heart is beating real fast."

"Mine too," Chandu replied.

Then fear covered his face. "What will they do to us if they find us, Chandu?"

He nodded. "I don't know."

"Do you think they'll kill us?"

"No," he replied. But he wasn't sure.

"How do you know?" Pradip asked.

"I don't now be quiet."

"Maybe they'll drag us back to the farm and flog us."

"And you'll be the first," Chandu replied sardonically.

The confrontation went on for several more minutes. Finally, Chouderey mounted his horse and exclaimed, "You haven't heard the last of us, Rao!"

Rao didn't reply.

"Come, let's go!" the Zamindar barked at his accomplices who were still shifting their glances to and fro. As suddenly as they appeared, they were gone.

Nayadu let out an exhaustive sigh and said, "I don't know if I can take any more of this."

Rao made his way over to the two, pulled his glasses off, and wiped the beads of sweat that dotted his forehead. "You're a wanted man, Nayadu," he said with a half smile.

At that point, Archana burst into tears. Nayadu, too, felt as if he might break down but knew he had to be strong for his wife. He pulled her to his side to comfort her.

"It's okay. Everything will be fine. These men shouldn't trouble you anymore," said Rao.

"Are you sure, Rao garu?" asked Nayadu. His voice was unsteady.

"You're getting ready to board a train for Madras, Nayadu. I don't believe you'll be seeing him for some time."

Velu said, "These men are evil, Rao garu."

"Yes, well, you, good people, please try to rest easy. The worst is over now."

The sound of horses moving swiftly in their direction, however, told them that the worst was not over. They turned to see the four horsemen returning, and with a vengeance.

Rao yelled, "Quick, follow me!"

They started to pick up their satchels, but Rao told them there was no time. Nevertheless, Nayadu grabbed hold of the bag containing the lamps and idols and threw them over his shoulder.

Archana took hold of Pradip's right hand and said to Chandu, "Take your brother's other hand, and don't let go!" There was panic in her eyes.

Prema pulled Manisha up and wrapped both arms around her then started running. The other emigrants were encamped in various shady places around the outside of the station and stared with startled bewilderment.

The thundering sound of the encroaching intruders grew louder. When Archana realized that Pradip's short strides were only slowing them down, she stopped and put him over her shoulder, but this caused her to lag behind. Velu reached the top of the steps leading into the station first with Nayadu right behind him. They both turned toward the rest and motioned anxiously for them to hurry. They had yet to cross the dirt driveway that fronted the steps while Prema and Manisha were even further behind.

Rao climbed several steps, turned around, and yelled, "Hurry!"

It was too late. The Zamindar and his three henchmen were upon them. The men quickly corralled the women and children. One of the henchmen reached down and snatched Pradip from their grip and pulled him up onto his horse while the other thug reached down and grabbed Manisha by her little arm.

Prema held tightly and screamed, "Noooo!"

The third ruffian reached down and thwacked her hard on the side of her head, knocking her off her feet. Manisha, who was crying hysterically, got up and started running toward the steps, but her effort was futile. The henchman who had tried to snatch her just seconds earlier was successful this time.

Prema let out a deafening scream, "Noooo! My baby!"

The Zamindar said, "You think you can defy me and get away with it?"

Rao pointed his finger at him and said, "You have no right to do this!"

The Zamindar ignored Rao and looked at Nayadu. "We'll see you back in Korlakota, Nayadu." Then they rode off.

Archana and Prema fell to the ground, wailing hysterically.

Velu ran down the steps and toward Rao's horse that was tethered a short distance away.

Rao yelled, "Hey, where are you going?" but Velu didn't reply, and Rao ran after him.

Velu quickly untied the Arabian mare and mounted it. The horse was a striking dark gray with light silvery gray spots on her belly. She was Rao's pride and joy.

Rao caught up with him and said breathlessly, "Wait!"

Velu replied, "I'm getting those kids back!"

"I'm not going to stop you." Rao reached into the leather saddlebag hanging on the horse's rear haunch and said, "I have something you'll find useful." He pulled out a loaded revolver and handed it to him.

Velu took the firearm and examined it curiously.

Rao asked, "Ever used one?"

He replied sheepishly, "Never even seen one."

"Pull this hammer back till it locks in place, and pull this trigger." He demonstrated. "But be careful. You don't want to shoot anybody—just scare them." Rao gently released the hammer till it rested softly on the percussion cap and placed it back in the saddlebag. "Leave it here for now."

Then he said, "Chanchita is quite spirited, but she will do what you tell her."

The loud shrill from the train's whistle pierced the air indicating that it was time to board.

"Now go!" Rao bellowed.

Chanchita broke into a sprint while Velu held fast to the reigns. The swiftness of the Arabian mare astonished him, but his mind quickly reverted to the children, especially his precious little Manisha.

Immediately his mind started imagining what he would do once he caught up with the four miscreants. First, he considered shooting each one between the eyes with the revolver Rao had given him. But that would be painless, he reckoned, and he would be branded a murderer. Maybe he would shoot them in their backsides. That way they wouldn't be able to sit for weeks. The thought put a smile on his face as he spurred Chanchita along.

It didn't take long to get the four men in his sight. When he observed that they were trotting at a casual pace, he halted the mare and reached into the saddlebag to pull out the revolver. As he wrapped his fingers around the grip of the gun, his heart started racing. A mixture of fear and anger coursed through his veins. Though he was unable to see the two little ones, he knew they were with those men and could only imagine how frightened they were.

He spurred Chanchita on so that the four men were able to hear him approaching. They all stopped their horses and turned to see Velu with one arm raised above his head and a crazed look in his eye. He fired the revolver into the air. The explosion of the gunpowder sent the horses into a frenzy. The Zamindar's mount panicked, rising into the air and clawing the air wildly with her front hooves until her rider fell helplessly to the ground.

Manisha and Pradip cried uncontrollably amidst the hysteria. By the time the horses settled, Velu was aiming the revolver at the Zamindar. He slowly started to get up, but Velu said to him, "Stay there and get on your stomach!"

Chouderey scowled and said, "Do you think that—"

"Shut up and do what I say, or I'll shoot you dead!" Velu wanted to pull the trigger. He hated the Zamindar with every fiber in his being and felt he would have been justified to end the landlord's life right there on the spot.

"Now you," he said, pointing the revolver in the direction of Sudhakar and the two others, "off your horses and onto the ground next to your boss." They dismounted and lay next to the Zamindar so that the four of them were lying side by side on their stomachs. Velu inched his horse over and rescued Manisha and Pradip and tried to straddle the two of them in front of him, but Manisha clung to her father like a leech and he hugged her tightly.

Velu felt an enormous sense of relief and satisfaction, and no longer did the revolver feel shaky in his hand. He took aim at the Zamindar, carefully pointing the revolver where he knew he wouldn't kill the man but rather leaving him with a painful journey back to Korlakota.

Pradip said, "Are you going to shoot him, Uncle?"

Velu had already cocked the hammer and held the gun steady with his finger firm against the trigger. He replied, "Don't you think he deserves it?"

Pradip's eyes opened wide as saucers. "You're going to kill him?"

"No—just hurt him—like he's hurt so many others." Then Velu pulled the trigger. The hammer slapped the percussion cap, but there was no explosion of gunpowder. The four men heard the misfire and looked up at Velu. Once more, he cocked the hammer and fired, but again, it misfired.

Suddenly, Velu knew he was no longer in control. The men lifted themselves from their prone positions and Velu barked, "Stay down!" But they ignored him. He cocked the revolver again and aimed it at the Zamindar, but none of them were any longer fearful. Velu pulled the trigger a third time, aiming this time at the Zamindar's leg. *Click.* Yet again, the gun misfired.

Velu threw the revolver to the ground and kicked Chanchita in her ribs, sending her into a dash back toward the train depot. He glanced back to see the Zamindar and his men mounting their horses. He knew, however, that he had the advantage on Chanchita. She was a swift moving Arabian mare while the other horses were larger and thicker, better suited for plowing or hauling. Nevertheless, he pushed Chanchita to her limit.

Pradip held furiously to Chanchita's mane while Manisha never let loose of her father. Velu spurred his heels into the mare's ribs again, though he was sure she was galloping at full speed. He instinctively turned his head, hoping that he had left the hooligans in a trail of dust. Indeed, the dry trail was clouded, making it hard to see where the men were, but he knew that the thick dust would also hinder their momentum. He felt the tingling sensation of adrenaline running through his body, reaching all the way to his toes and fingertips.

He yelled out to Chanchita, "Go, girl! Go!" To his amazement, the Arabian mare sprinted faster, and Velu leaned forward, holding Manisha tightly with one arm and the reins with the other.

His thoughts shifted, and he suddenly remembered that the train whistle had alerted passengers of its imminent departure. He never traveled on a train before. He was unfamiliar with the protocol and how much time passengers would have to board before the train started rolling. All he knew, according to Rao, was that Rajahmundry was the starting point for this particular train that was called the *Madras Express* and not just a stop along the way. He desperately hoped that it would be delayed in leaving.

Within minutes, he had the train depot in sight. He saw plumes of smoke and steam bellowing from behind the depot and knew the train must be preparing to leave. Rao stood expectantly on the steps, waving his arms. Next to him were two British officers whose headquarters were nearby. They appeared more inconvenienced than concerned, but Velu was greatly comforted to see them. He halted Chanchita abruptly at the base of the depot steps, creating a small cloud of dust.

Rao ran down and retrieved the two children and said, "You must hurry. The train is getting ready to leave!"

"They're right behind us!" Velu exclaimed.

"Don't worry," Rao rejoined. "They'll hold them off." He smiled and nodded with amazement. "You did it."

Velu smiled back.

"Hurry now, before you miss your train," said Rao.

Just then the four men galloped into sight.

CHAPTER 5

The train whistle pierced the still air as a blast of steam belched from the bowels of the locomotive. The passenger cars lurched forward with a jerk and started rolling slowly away from the depot. Pradip echoed the sound of the whistle and had seemingly forgotten the harrowing episode that had just occurred. He wedged his face in between the iron bars in the window, but Archana pulled him back into the safety of her arms. Nobody would rest easy until they were well on their way and far from the reaches of the Zamindar.

By the time the train left the limits of Rajahmundry, both Nayadu and Velu had dozed off. But the two boys had already decided that they were going to stay awake for the entire trip. They grabbed hold of the iron bars that offered little protection from the elements and gazed curiously at the world beyond Korlakota and Rajahmundry. Watching villages stream by the window, however, didn't agree with Pradip, and he became nauseous. He spent the remainder of the journey with his head on Archana's lap. Manisha held fast to her mother, but her gaze was fixed toward the window. She still bore the trauma of what had happened but was gradually giving in to curiosity.

Chandu was alone as he observed the vast swaths of pastoral land and rural villages that separated him from their destination, and it dawned on him that there was little difference between the villages. Everything looked the same, and before long, the gentle rocking of the train coerced him into releasing his grip on the window's bars.

He laid his head on his father's lap and was lulled into a deep sleep. It had been a long day.

*****

They arrived into Madras the next morning. Archana pulled Chandu and Pradip close to her side as they disembarked from the train. There were more people at the station than they had ever seen at one time in their entire lives, but no sign of an agent, as Rao had promised.

After waiting for nearly an hour, the two men with their families in tow instinctively gravitated toward the harbor and the huge ships. To them, this seemed like the logical place from where they might embark on their journey across the Kala Pani.

As they neared the harbor, the two boys were awestruck at the sight of two modern steamer ships that were moored one in front of the other. The huge vessels floated like twins with their sharp bows and long gray sides.

"Which one?" said Chandu, elbowing his little brother in the ribs.

"Neither," he said, brushing him away. "I like that one."

Further down toward the peninsula jutting out into the bay was an older three-masted wooden sailing ship—a relic of an era past, its three masts rocked gently side to side with its sails draped on the mast's yardarms. Crewmen aboard the old wooden ship seemed to be readying the vessel for voyage. Rigging, swabbing, and necessary busyness were the orders of the hour.

"How does a big boat like that stay on top of the water?" Pradip asked as they walked toward the old ship.

They both looked over to their father, but he looked awkwardly over to Velu for relief. Velu was no more knowledgeable than Nayadu about such things, but he wasn't going to play ignorant. He hesitated for a moment and then responded, "You've seen trees drifting down the Godavari, haven't you?" His voice was scratchier than usual, but his tone was confident.

"Yes," the boys replied.

He continued, "That boat is made from the same kind of trees."

They waited for the rest of his proposed theory, but that was it. That was his answer.

"Hey, *coolies!*"

Velu turned.

"Yeah, you—all of you," said the foreigner.

They knew instantly that this man was from a distant land. His white skin was burned from the sun and flecked with brown spots. His face was ruddy and unshaven, and his eyes were light in color. Straggling from underneath his bandana was unruly, colorless hair.

Pradip looked at Chandu with a puzzled look. "What's a coolie?"

"Don't know," he answered with a shrug.

The frustrated foreigner motioned for an Indian man to come over and speak to them. He walked over and appeared no friendlier or sympathetic than the foreigner. Although clearly Indian, his skin was fair, and his Telugu was heavily accented. He asked, "Did you people just come on that train?"

"Yes," Velu and Nayadu replied simultaneously.

"You're not supposed to be over here. Do you have your papers?"

After he inspected the papers that Nayadu and Velu provided, the stranger returned them.

"Go there," he said, pointing toward a wooden double-storied building just a hundred or so yards south of where they were standing. "Through those doors and wait in the queue."

*****

The two small doors opened up to large courtyard filled to capacity with no less than three hundred Indians from an array of different backgrounds. Every caste occupation under the Indian sun mingled, if not reluctantly, waiting to board the ship that would take them to whatever was promised to them.

Cultivators and cow herders stood alongside the scribes and schoolteachers while street sweepers rubbed shoulders with shop keepers. Even Hindu priests stood in the shadows of non-Hindu *dalits*. There was no queue but only throngs of would-be emigrants trying to move closer the single door on the opposite end of the courtyard.

"Are all these people going to where we're going, Nana?" Pradip asked, but Nayadu stood mesmerized, even confused.

He turned to Velu. "What do these people know about farming?"

"Can't be much," Velu replied.

Nayadu asked a man standing directly in front of them what they were waiting for, but the man didn't speak Telugu.

A man dressed in fine clothes overheard Nayadu's question and turned to answer, "Everyone is getting a medical examination, but there is only one doctor. This queue has hardly moved in several hours."

Nayadu knew the man was of a higher caste and pressed his hands together.

"Are you an agricultural specialist?" Nayadu asked.

"A what?"

"Why are you here, garu?"

"Me and my son are going to start a new life overseas."

"Doing what?" asked Nayadu.

"Business."

"What business?"

The man started to look annoyed. "We're merchants. We left our store back in Hyderabad with my wife and her parents so that we could look for new business opportunities overseas."

Velu asked the man, "Who told you to come here?"

The man lifted his hand in a threatening gesture and scolded Velu, "That's none of your business."

Nayadu pulled Velu out of the man's reach and whispered into his ear, "Let's not get into trouble here."

"I just wanted to know who recruited him."

"Yeah, didn't Rao say all the men going overseas are agricultural specialists?"

"This fellow is not an agricultural specialist, Nayadu."

Nayadu's brows furrowed. "I know. I don't understand."

*****

Nayadu was still scratching his head when an elderly foreign couple walked into the courtyard. The man who was tall, thin and slightly stooped scanned his gaze over the heads of the gathering. His wife, a short, determined looking woman with pale skin and a pointed nose, held fast to the waist of her husband's trousers. Then they moved purposefully and graciously parting their way through the crowd. When they found the individuals they were looking for, the throngs of emigrants gradually spread out and a mock stage was set.

In the center were two young girls. They appeared scared and most assumed that it was because of the foreigners they were frightened. But when the two young girls finally embraced the couple with a heartfelt hug, it was apparent that it wasn't the couple whom they feared.

Suddenly, several recruiters forced their way through the crowd, and a confrontation ensued. One could have heard the steps of an insect except for the animated exchange between the elderly couple and the recruiters. But for Velu and Nayadu, it was unintelligible and impossible to tell who was in the right.

Velu whispered to the man standing next to them who appeared to be of a higher caste, "What's going on with these people?"

"My English is not that good, but it sounds like these foreigners are Christians and have come to take these two young girls back to their village." The man put his finger over his lips, listening further to the exchange. Then he added, "These foreigners claim that the girls were raped by a recruiter when they refused the recruiter's employment offer. The foreigner is saying that he tied them up and raped them and the only reason they came here was because their reputation in their village has been ruined."

"Who are those foreigners?" asked Nayadu.

"Missionaries who have been living in their village. They came to bring the girls back to the village, but the recruiters don't want to let them."

Just then another recruiter made his way through the crowd, said a few words, and motioned for the couple to leave. The man put his arm around one girl while his wife wrapped her arm around the other then proceeded toward door. Tears streamed down the faces of the young girls, but it was hard to tell whether they were tears of happiness or despair.

"The chief recruiter decided to let those foreigners take the girls away," said the high-caste man. "Seems he was worried that the foreigners might make trouble."

Velu's brows furrowed. "Why would those foreigners care about those two low-caste girls?" he asked.

The man shrugged. "Don't know."

*****

The stale, hot air and cramped conditions of the lower deck aboard the old wooden ship made breathing difficult. Several passengers tried climbing back up to the upper deck for fresh air but were prevented from doing so by crew members.

Velu found his way over to where they had squatted just below the hatch. "Are we in jail down here in this hole?" he said, kicking the side of the ladder leading out of the lower deck.

"We just got here. You want to leave already?" Nayadu asked.

"I can't breathe," he replied. "And there's too many people down here."

"Come sit, Velu."

Just then a smartly dressed Indian man descended the ladder into the lower deck. Stopping on the next to last step, he rang a bell to get their attention. He spoke to the passengers first in Tamil. When the two men heard groans emanate from the crowd, they knew the news was not good. Then he announced in Telugu that their departure would be delayed for some time until further notice.

Velu was standing an arm's length from the man and called out to him, "Garu, why are they waiting to leave this place?" Velu was wet with perspiration, and his scratchy voice was irritable. The man glanced over at Velu expressionless and then quickly climbed up to the fresh air on the upper deck.

Moments later two bedraggled women descended hesitantly down the ladder, each clinging desperately to her small bundle of belongings.

"Keep moving," came the voice from above.

The two women clung close to each other, peering anxiously around the crowded lower deck. Nayadu sat quietly with his knees pulled into his chest, his chin resting on his knees. He cared little about things that didn't matter anymore. He had little concern whether they set sail in one hour or in one week. He no longer worried whether the passengers boarding were qualified as agricultural specialists. That wasn't important. All he cared about was his family arriving safely on the other side of the Kala Pani.

The smartly dressed man followed them down. "Anywhere you can find a place," he said, gently nudging them away from the ladder. He stood with his arms on his hips, watching to see where the women would land.

Velu looked over at Nayadu. "They've kept us all waiting for two low-caste women."

The man overheard Velu and commented, "There are still more to come."

Velu glanced around and then replied to the man, "But there's no more room."

He nodded. "I know, but they are under contract to bring at least one female for every three male passengers." The man turned and started making his way back up the ladder.

Velu yelled after him, "Why do they need more women in the…" But the man was gone.

*****

As the late arrivals boarded, throughout the day it was obvious that they had come from the lowest echelons of Indian society. Temple dancers and artisans made up the bulk of those who were boarding late. Young widows who would have no life to look forward to in their own village also joined rank, taking residence wherever they found empty space.

Passengers grew increasingly restless when finally the last immigrant arrived—a young girl no more than thirteen years of age. A dry stream of tears marked her round dimpled cheeks, and her light-brown eyes peered anxiously across the room. She stood frozen at the bottom of the steps.

The smartly dressed man, who followed her down, spoke to her in Telugu, "You'll have to keep moving until you find a space to put your things."

She turned and looked up to him, and her eyes moistened with tears.

The man walked ahead of her and said, "Follow me." Then he led her to an empty space somewhere in the middle of the crowded deck.

Velu commented, "I've never seen a more beautiful girl."

Nayadu nodded. "She looks so young."

"Why do you think she's leaving here?"

Nayadu shrugged and said, "Who knows?"

They sat in silence for several minutes before Nayadu said, "And who knows what awaits us on the other side of the Kala Pani?"

CHAPTER 6

As the wind filled the sails just outside of the calm waters of the harbor, the old wooden ship tilted hard to the left. The passengers below could hear the captain barking orders while the sails flapped furiously in the wind looking for the perfect tack. The *Chadwick*, as the boat was called, creaked and groaned from stem to stern like an old woman troubled with arthritis.

With each downward pitch of the boat waves crashed over the bow sending a salty mist into the lower region of the deck. Whether it was an auspicious day for sailing or not was better left unknown. The *Chadwick* was sailing irrespective of what the pundits would advise.

The man who had delayed their departure reappeared the next morning and found Nayadu and Velu sitting in the same place under the steps. Though it was dirty and cramped, they laid claim to the spot.

"You didn't sleep here did you?" he asked half-jokingly.

"This is the best place. Fresh air and light stop right here," Nayadu replied.

He was right. The further one moved away from the ladder, the darker and fouler the air became.

Velu, who had been eyeing the man with noticeable apprehension, interrupted, "So are you the boss?"

"Assistant purser," he answered. He noticed the blank look on Velu's face and added, "I'm in charge of supplies and your welfare—and you?"

"We were told that we could make a better life for ourselves in this place where you people are taking us."

"Did anyone tell you what you are going to be doing there?"

"We're agricultural specialists."

The man smiled. "Of course you are."

Nayadu said, "We were farmers in—"

"We had *huge* farms back in India," Velu interrupted. "Many crops and livestock, but the drought killed everything. Life became very hard for our families—many problems were there. Then this man came to us and told us that we could have a better life overseas working for wealthy foreigners—that they needed people like me and Nayadu who know how to farm."

The man nodded slowly. "So what did you do with your huge farms?"

"Uh, sold them," said Velu.

Nayadu looked over at Velu, puzzled.

"You must have made some good money from selling your farm."

Velu hesitated for a second. "Of course."

"And you're here because you believe you'll have a better life overseas."

"That's what the man told us," said Velu.

"That'll depend on your attitude and your expectations. I always tell people to pray for the best but expect the worst. That way you'll never be disappointed."

Velu quickly realized that this was a clever man and likely very educated judging by the way he spoke. He decided to let Nayadu finish the conversation.

"You've been to this place we're going?" asked Nayadu.

"Three times—but only long enough to restock our supplies. Can't tell you much else except—well, this is my last trip."

"Missing your family?" asked Nayadu.

"Oh yes, I have a wife and three children in Bangalore. I don't see them for three or four months at a time."

"What is your good name, garu?" asked Nayadu.

"Sivaaa!" came the cry from above deck.

"Ah, there's my boss, Mr. Pickles."

"Your name is Siva?" Nayadu asked.

"Yes." He glanced down at his pocket watch. "It's after two o'clock—he must be on his third brandy by now."

Just then Mr. Pickles swaggered slowly down the ladder, stopping halfway to look around. "Siva!" he bellowed.

Siva jumped up. "Here, sir."

"I'm calling you, man. Come out of this foul-smelling hole so I can talk to you."

"Coming, sir."

Mr. Pickles was a coarse man, grossly overweight with a red, swollen nose. His pate was bald and sunburned, and the hair that remained hung long and straggled. He wore his beard much like his hair. Barely visible on his left arm was a worn tattoo of a scantily clad woman.

"He doesn't like Indians much," Siva whispered as Mr. Pickles climbed back up the ladder. "Another hour or two and he'll be unconscious. It's my job to make excuses for him."

As Siva quickly ascended up the ladder, Nayadu turned to Velu, "Why did you lie to that man about our farms?"

"What?"

"You know what."

"Why not?" Velu retorted. "We can get more respect from people if they think that we owned huge farms back in India. Who will ever know better?"

"Why don't you just tell people you're a Brahmin?"

Velu rubbed his chin. "That's not a bad idea."

*****

The first week passed slowly, and Nayadu noted that Indians were not good sailors. Riding out tempests and high seas was a job better left for Europeans. Nayadu was of the few that had not succumbed to seasickness. But that was not the only thing afflicting the passengers. On day nine, Pradip awoke with a severe fever. Every movement caused him to whimper in pain, and Archana feared the worst. She held him close, trying to draw the heat from his body, and as she did this, she began to weep.

Distressed, she looked to Nayadu and said to him, "I don't know what else to do."

He nodded in despair and replied, "We can't even light our lamps to appease the gods aboard this rotten boat."

Just then a rather short woman appeared before them. She wasn't yet forty years of age but was thin and hunched over. Archana imagined that she was one of the many widows seeking a new life outside of India. Her voice was solemn when she said, "There are bad eyes on this child."

Archana pulled Pradip close to her bosom. "What do you mean?" she asked.

She looked to the left and then to the right. "Someone is jealous of this child. There are bad eyes on him, and they need to be removed." Her voice was more serious now.

Nayadu scanned his eyes across the lower deck. "Who?" he asked. "Whose eyes are on my child?"

The woman nodded. "This, I don't know. What I do know is that you have to remove the curse put on this small boy."

"How?" asked Archana.

"I'll remove the curse if you like."

"Please."

"Okay, I will need some salt, two chilies, and some hair."

"Where will I get these things from?" asked Archana.

"Your husband knows the purser, doesn't he?"

"Purser?" she replied, unsure of who the woman was referring to.

"Yes, the man who comes and speaks for Europeans."

She nodded eagerly in assent. "Yes, my husband knows him."

Just then Siva came down into the deck landing steps away from where the Nayadus were camped. The concern on Archana's face caught his attention. "Is the boy okay?" he asked.

"No, Siva garu," said Nayadu. "This woman says that our boy is under a curse and that we need some salt and chilies to remove it."

Siva looked over at the woman who was known as Sareena and smiled. "You don't give up, do you, woman?"

She lowered her head and inched back toward her mat and belongings.

"She's just tired of eating bland food," said Siva. "You're the third family she's tried to convince that one of their sick loved ones was under a curse."

"These conditions are absolutely dreadful!" said Mrs. Weatherly, who appeared seemingly out of nowhere. "Everything is so cold and damp."

"And we have a sick child here, madam," said Siva.

Mrs. Weatherly, much like Siva, was sympathetic to the plight of the Indian passengers. Her warm smile had a way of putting everyone at ease. With her blond hair hidden beneath her bonnet and her delicate white skin untouched by the harsh maritime sun, one would never suppose that this prim and proper middle-aged English woman was a veteran seafarer. Her demeanor, however, was one of assurance. Having worked as a nurse for a number of years, she knew how to deal competently with minor ailments and afflictions, especially those common to sea mariners.

"May I take a look at the child," she said calmly. "This boy has a high fever and a rash on his chest and arms." She turned her attention to Siva and said to him, "May I suggest that we bring him to the sick bay? I'm sure that the ship's physician will be able do something."

Without waiting for permission, Mrs. Weatherly wrapped Pradip in a warm blanket and carried him straight to the doctor's quarters. The ship's physician, Dr. Wigglesworth, was in the middle of a tea break when she abruptly barged into his quarters with Pradip on her shoulder.

"Mrs. Weatherly, have you misplaced your manners?" the doctor chided. "Is it not polite to first announce yourself before barging in on one's tea time?"

"Never mind with your teatime, Doctor. I have a precious little child that is desperately ill. He has a high fever with a severe rash over his upper body."

"Very well, put him on the table so that I can take a proper look at him."

Pradip coiled up with fear as the doctor tried to examine him.

"Mrs. Weatherly, I need your matronly charm if I'm ever to get anywhere with this young fellow. He's probably never had an unsightly White bloke like myself poking and prodding him.

She laughed. "You're probably right, Doctor." She placed her soft hand on Pradip's forehead, and the tension immediately left his body.

"You really do have a way with patients," he said.

"Thank you."

"Hmm, look here," he said pointing, under Pradeep's arm. "He has bite marks. It looks like he has been bitten by a rat."

"A rat! Is that what caused this boy's illness, Doctor?"

"Oh, I've seen a few cases like this. This is a classic case of rat-bite fever. The organism Streptobacillusmoniliformis causes it."

"Will the boy be okay?"

"I think so. He's starting to shiver, so let's wrap him up with blankets. I could let some blood from the lad, but he's frightened enough as it is."

The captain's wife put her hands on her hips and said, "So we have a poisonous rat running around on this ship."

With raised eyebrows, the doctor replied, "Afraid so, madam. But I'm more concerned with the atrocious conditions down in that hole and the amount of people they've stuffed down there. It's just a matter of time."

"Just a matter of time before what?"

He took a deep breath and said, "Let's just pray that we make it to South Africa without any casualties."

*****

Pradip recovered from the rat-bite fever after several days, but on the twelfth day of the voyage, Dr. Wigglesworth's worst fears were realized. Scores of passengers were stricken with dysentery. The doctor suspected that one of the casks of water had been drawn from a contaminated water source. There was little anyone, including the doctor, could do to alleviate the dehydrating effects of the malady. Even the gentle caring hands of Mrs. Weatherly were powerless.

By the next day, three small children were dead. A depressing pall fell over the ship. The caterwauling of the mourning parents lasted for days. The bodies of the children were wrapped in blankets and unceremoniously tossed overboard. Over the next three days, twelve more children would succumb to severe dehydration. Mrs. Weatherly worked tirelessly with Siva at her side trying to comfort the mothers who had lost their children while Mr. Pickles was nowhere to be found.

Fear and resentment started to take over since most of the Hindu passengers wanted to light their god lamps but were prevented from doing so for safety reasons. Velu became convinced that there was a conspiracy against all the Hindus after Manisha fell sick.

"There won't be any of us left by the time we reach land," Velu said to Nayadu.

Nayadu sat motionless, nodding. "Should've listened to Komdaari. Our leaving was a bad omen."

"These foreigners are bad omens," said Velu. "How can they stop us from offering puja to our gods?"

Nayadu stared ahead blankly. "We should've stayed."

*****

Manisha's condition continued to worsen, and they all started fearing the worst. That evening Velu waited till the passengers were asleep before he pulled out a lamp and a brass image of Lord Shiva. He looked around for any movement before he poured a little oil into the base of the lamp and lit the wick with some flint and sticks that he had stored with his lamp. Then he stood the idol next to the lamp.

Lord Shiva would destroy the evil that was killing these children, he thought to himself. The glow from the lamp allowed him to see little Manisha lying beside him. He could hardly imagine life without his precious little girl. Her face glistened from perspiration. He reached over and gently wiped her face, then fell asleep.

*****

The next morning Velu was awakened by Siva. Velu quickly sat up and noticed many of the passengers peering in his direction. Standing behind Siva was Mr. Pickles, his face flushed with anger.

Siva looked disappointed. "Is this your lamp, Velu?"

Velu looked down and noticed that only a hint of oil remained in the base of the lamp, yet the flame was still strong. He knew he wasn't going to be able to lie his way out of this one. He turned to see that Manisha's color had returned to normal. She sat up and held onto her father.

"Yes, it's mine," he said proudly.

"Bring 'em!" said Mr. Pickles.

"I'm sorry, Velu. You people have been warned about lighting anything below deck," said Siva. He licked his thumb and forefinger and extinguished the flame.

"Now!" said Mr. Pickles.

"You're going to have to come with us," said Siva.

"No!" cried Manisha, instinctively aware that her father was in trouble.

"What's happening, Ammandi?" Prema asked.

"I lit the lamp last night. Now they're taking me somewhere."

"Where are you taking my husband?" she cried out in Telugu, but Mr. Pickles neither understood nor cared what the woman had to say.

He reached down and grabbed Velu by the arm and yanked him out of his bunk. Prema and Manisha cried as they watched their loved one dragged up the ladder.

Siva followed close behind. "Why did you break the rules, Velu?"

"My little girl—all the children aboard this wretched boat are dying!"

On deck, Mr. Pickles turned to Siva. "Tell the coolie, 'Ten days or ten lashes.'"

Siva translated and then added, "I think he would rather take the whip to you—take the ten days."

"Let him whip me."

"Don't give him the pleasure, Velu."

"It will be *my* pleasure," said Velu.

Velu's shirt was removed. His arms were wrapped around the mast as far as they would reach and then tied by two of the crewmen. Mr. Pickles smiled as he pulled out one of his favorite possessions—a *chicotte*. It was a whip fashioned from hippopotamus hide. He had picked one up during a stop in Portugal a year earlier. He had only used it once and had been waiting for an opportunity to use it again.

Siva turned away as Mr. Pickles reared back and, with all his weight, unleashed the twisted strips of leather into Velu's back. Velu let out a cry that could be heard below deck. Prema held Manisha tightly and wept.

Mr. Pickles reared back again when Mrs. Weatherly appeared on deck. "Stop!" she yelled. "Why are you flogging this man?"

"This coolie broke the rules of this ship, madam," said Mr. Pickles.

"What did this man do?" she asked, her face turning red.

"Almost set the ship on fire by burning one of their lamps. You know—the kind they use for their religion."

"Have some mercy on this man," she said, looking over at the thick welt on Velu's back. "I'm sure he won't do it again."

"But this coolie needs to be taught a lesson, madam."

"Untie him—now!"

"I thought these coolies were in my charge," said Mr. Pickles, moving closer to Mrs. Weatherly.

"Perhaps we should take the matter up with the captain. And while there, we can talk about your drinking habit."

Mr. Pickles' nostrils flared, and his face turned even redder than it already was. He turned to one of the crewmen and grumbled, "Untie the bloody coolie."

"That's what I thought," said Mrs. Weatherly.

*****

On the seventeenth day, the voyage took yet another turn. Archana completely withdrew from her family. Nayadu implored her to tell him what was wrong but to no avail. Her boys pleaded with her to speak to them, but it was as though she had taken leave of her body. She slowly became a shell of her former self. She hardly ate, and she stopped bathing. Her long, thick black hair, which she always kept neatly plaited, became dirty and matted. They considered whether she had come under a curse.

Prema continued to console her, hoping that she would eventually open up. Finally, after a week went by, she started to weep.

"It's okay, Archana. You can tell me."

She looked up, her face cloaked in shame. "It was that man," she sniveled.

"What man?"

"That ugly White man—who drinks a lot."

"Mr. Pickles?"

Archana's forehead crinkled as she fought back tears.

Prema turned indignant. "What did that brute do to you?"

"I was bathing," she said, trailing off into tears. "And he…he—"

"Never mind," she said, wrapping her arms around Archana. "We have to tell somebody."

"No! He said he would kill the boys if I said anything to anyone."

"But we can't let this—"

"No!" Archana cried out. "You can't tell anyone."

Prema nodded. "Okay, Archana, whatever you want."

*****

That evening, Prema couldn't sleep. She feared she would be next on Mr. Pickle's list. Convinced that keeping Archana's secret was a mistake, she confided in Velu what happened. He was enraged.

"Do you think you should tell Nayadu what has happened?" she asked.

"No!" he replied. "He must never know about this. It will ruin him."

"Then what are you going to do?"

"I need time to think."

In the meantime, Archana's condition failed to improve. She was still unwilling to tell anybody else what was wrong. She continued to keep herself unkempt. It was as though she was intentionally making herself unattractive. She pulled on her hair and twisted it into knots. Her constant scratching produced open sores on her arms and legs.

Nayadu was unable to reason with her. When he would ask her why she wasn't bathing herself, she would reply, "You can't make me bathe. No one can make me."

Nayadu didn't know what to do with her.

That evening, Velu pulled Siva aside and, in confidence, told him what had happened to Archana. Siva showed no emotion.

"When I was speaking to Nayadu's wife the other day, translating for Mrs. Weatherly, my instinct told me that she had been assaulted. So she told your wife that Mr. Pickles was the one who assaulted her?" asked Siva.

"Yes, and now I'm telling you. If he's done this to Nayadu's wife, he's done this to other women," Velu argued.

"No, I'm sure you're right," he said, motioning for Velu to lower his voice. "I've suspected that he's assaulted many women. Our Indian women will never speak about such things for fear of being rejected by their families or caste. There was a young, pretty *dalit* girl on the last voyage named Deepa. I remember it like it was yesterday. She came to me and told me that Mr. Pickles hurt her. She wouldn't say what he did, but she was crying and in great distress. I asked her what I could do to help her, but she couldn't answer me. I went and told Mrs. Weatherly what the young girl had told me. We both went back to speak to the girl, but it was too late. She stepped off the side of the ship.

"Mrs. Weatherly was more devastated than I was. She found Mr. Pickles and asked him what he did to Deepa that made her kill herself. He told Mrs. Weatherly that the only thing he did was slap the girl because she had gone into the galley without permission. Without Deepa to defend herself, she had no evidence against him.

"That girl wouldn't have killed herself because Mr. Pickles hit her. After that incident, Mr. Pickles asked me what I said to Mrs. Weatherly. He told me that if I knew what was good for me that I better mind my own business or I 'will end up like that girl.' I have been careful ever since to watch what I say to people."

"So you are afraid of this *sahib*?" asked Velu.

"I have a wife and three children who expect me to come home in a few months. I don't want to test this man to see if he is serious."

"Can't we go to the captain?" Velu asked.

"If the captain does anything short of removing him from this ship, then Pickles will come after me. It's too risky. The only way to get this man is to get Nayadu's wife to speak to Mrs. Weatherly. But I don't think she will. Without Nayadu's wife, there's little we can do."

Velu walked away frustrated. He was fed up with the injustices of life. How people with lighter skin were able to lord over people with darker skin. How they were able to cheat, lie, and exploit other people without any repercussions. He knew that he had enough.

CHAPTER 7

"Only girls play hide-and-seek," the boy chided.

Chandu and Pradip recoiled at his stinging response. Chandu turned and started to walk away when Pradip lashed out, "We're not girls!"

"Let's go, Pradip," Chandu said, grabbing him by the arm.

"Wait," said the boy. He jumped up and motioned for the two brothers to follow him. When they were far enough away from his father, he opened up. "I've got something better," he said in a hushed tone.

"Better?" Chandu asked.

"Yeah, better than your game of hide-and-seek."

"Well, what is it?"

He discreetly glanced to both sides and then whispered, "*The Great Room.*"

"*The Great Room*," Pradip snickered.

"Shh!" He again looked around to see if anyone was listening. "I don't *have* to show it to you," he threatened dismissively.

"No, we want to see it," Chandu said, elbowing Pradip in his side.

"Are you sure? If we get caught, it'll mean death."

Pradip's eyes lit up. "Death?"

The boy's thick eyebrows narrowed down toward his nose. "It's the captain's room. We might be thrown overboard if we're found out."

Pradip looked over to his brother, waiting for his reaction. "Uh, maybe we should wait till another time," Chandu replied sheepishly.

The boy grinned from one side of his mouth. "That's what I thought, a couple of scared rabbits."

"Have you been to *The Great Room*?" Chandu asked.

"Many times."

"How many?"

"Okay, once. But I discovered something."

"What?"

"Candies—a whole jarful."

"Candies!" Pradip bellowed.

"Sshh! You want to get us caught before we even get inside the room?"

Chandu's mouth had already started watering even though he could hardly remember the last time he felt the sweet sensation of a piece of candy rolling around in his mouth.

"Okay, I'll go," he said, convinced that the reward of wallowing in a container of sweets would far exceed the risk of getting caught.

"Meet me here tomorrow morning after breakfast. The crew is on deck between breakfast and lunch. That's when we'll go."

"We'll be here," Chandu said before taking Pradip by the arm.

"Wait, what's your name?" he asked.

"Chandu."

"I'm Imran," the boy replied with a broad smile and extended hand.

But Pradip yanked his arm away from Chandu's grip and said, "I'm not going."

"He's my brother, Pradip."

Imran pursed his lips and nodded. "Maybe it's better if he doesn't go. Meet me here tomorrow morning, Chandu."

"I will."

*****

Two wooden doors with small windows built into them separated the boys from the treasure inside *The Great Room*. The very sight of them made Chandu's knees weak. The windows were up high—too high for them to see inside. Chandu swallowed hard and

74

then followed Imran, inching slowly towards the doors. He hesitated before taking hold of the door handle.

"The door was open last time," Imran whispered.

He pulled on the handle, but the door was locked. Suddenly they heard footsteps from inside *The Great Room*. When the two boys suddenly heard the footsteps moving toward the door, Imran's eyes widened with fear. Chandu noted that he wasn't as brave as he pretended to be. He looked at Chandu but seemed unable to move. Chandu pointed to a room adjacent to *The Great Room* since there was nowhere else to hide. All he could hope for at that point was that the door was unlocked and that nobody was in there.

Chandu moved quickly and Imran followed. The handle moved freely, and the door swung open. Behind them they heard the door of *The Great Room* open with a loud creak and knew that it was too late to close the door. They slipped behind the door and held it in place so that it wouldn't move. Chandu wondered if the loud thumping in his chest might betray him.

From a small hole in the door he saw an officer emerge from *The Great Room* that he would later learn was the first lieutenant. The officer hastily ascended the ladder leading up to the main deck, seemingly unaware that anyone had been lurking about. The two boys breathed a heavy sigh of relief and came out from hiding. It was then they noticed that the man left the door of *The Great Room* ajar.

Imran peered into the room to see if anyone else was inside and then motioned for Chandu to follow. The room was plush and full of things made with mahogany. Toward the rear was a large stained glass window. The two instinctively gravitated toward the center of the room where a map and charts were strewn out on a magnificently large table.

Imran pointed and whispered, "Look." What caught his attention was the dotted line that stretched from near the top of a large map down to the bottom. It originated out of the bottom of a pointed landmass.

Chandu whispered, "Home?"

"I think so," said Imran, though neither of them really knew.

The line extended down to a larger landmass.

"This must be where we're going," he said softly.

"What do you think this is?" Chandu said, pointing to a solid line that zigged and zagged along the same course but only reached about half of the distance.

He shrugged and guessed, "Our actual course?"

"But look," Chandu said, pointing to the line, "that means we're way off course."

"Probably because we haven't had any wind for the last week."

"How do you know this?" Chandu asked.

"Just a guess," he replied.

"Okay, but if this is our actual course, then that means we are only about halfway to where we're going."

"Yeah, I guess so."

"That means we have another—"

"Three weeks."

*****

As far as they were concerned, the thought of spending another day on the wretched boat was bad enough, let alone three weeks. As they lamented their discovery, they suddenly heard voices from above that seemed to be moving in their direction. Quickly, they looked for a place to hide. With nowhere to adequately conceal their selves, they scurried out of the room where they were now completely exposed.

Already descending the ladder was the captain with the first lieutenant close behind. They hastily scampered into the same cabin that they hid in earlier. From the shadows, they were able to get their first close-up view of the captain. Until now, he had seemed somewhat of a phantom. His deep, craggy voice often bellowed from top deck to the quarters below, but never was he seen.

As the two men made their way into *The Great Room*, Chandu stood in the shadows mesmerized by the sight of the man. His spiffy whites lit up the room. Rotund with a slight limp, he still outpaced the much younger first lieutenant. He had a neatly groomed white beard, and deep lines etched his face. Chandu wondered to himself what the captain might do if he were to catch them in his Room.

"Sshh," Chandu whispered to Imran as the two men passed.

Imran turned around and was startled to find Mr. Pickles lying in one of the berths. Chandu wondered why they didn't see him earlier, but now there was a thin stream of light coming through the partly open door.

"Sshh," he whispered again.

"Look, his shirt is soaked with blood," Imran exclaimed in a strained whisper.

The two boys dared to inch closer to the man's lifeless body. Their hearts thumped loudly. As they moved close enough to touch him, they heard a raspy, dark gurgling sound that escaped his mouth with each slow, labored rise and fall of his chest. His eyes were open, but he stared madly at the top of the bunk. He made no recognition that they were in the cabin. Now the two boys were petrified.

"Look," said Imran, pointing to the floor.

Just inches from Chandu's feet was a knife, its blade covered with blood. Imran reached down to pick it up.

"No!" said Chandu, almost giving them away. "Don't touch it."

Imran snatched the knife off the floor and ran his finger across the flat edge of the blade. Then he moved the blade in front of the light coming through the cracked door. "The blood's not even dry yet," he said.

Chandu felt his skin tighten. "Let's get out of here."

"Wait," he said, placing the knife back on the floor. "The captain might see us."

"But what if they come looking for this man and find us here in the room?"

Just then Mr. Pickles closed his eyes, his breathing, though still raspy, had become fainter.

"Okay, quick," Imran whispered. "Let's put a blanket over him, and if they come in here, they'll think he's sleeping."

After they covered the man, they tucked their selves away behind a chest and waited. It seemed like an eternity before the captain could be heard leaving his quarters. Thankful that the men had not come seeking Mr. Pickles, Imran and Chandu agreed that they wouldn't say anything to anybody about what they had found. It would be difficult to explain why they were in the man's quarters.

*****

News of Mr. Pickles's demise didn't remain a secret for long. Imran and Chandu remained painfully quiet as rumors abounded. Unaware that the news had already circulated throughout the ship, Siva stopped by and informed them, "Mr. Pickles was found dead in his cabin this morning. If they don't find the killer, the first lieutenant will be asking you people some questions."

"How do they know somebody killed him? Maybe he killed himself," said Nayadu.

"Not likely. Mr. Pickles was stabbed numerous times in the stomach."

"He could have stabbed himself in the stomach."

"Perhaps, but whoever stabbed him wiped the blade with his finger. Mr. Pickles had blood on his hands but not his fingers."

"But why would they ask us about the murder?" asked Velu.

"Everyone will be questioned, including me."

Nayadu leaned over and whispered to Siva, "You didn't kill him, did you?"

Siva chuckled, "Hey, I didn't like the man, but I didn't kill him."

*****

The next morning Siva interpreted as the first lieutenant asked his questions. For each passenger, it was the same:

> *"Where were you yesterday morning?"*
> *"Right here."*
> *"Did you kill Mr. Pickles?"*
> *"No."*
> *"Do you know who did?"*
> *"No."*

Even though Mr. Pickles had few admirers among the Indian passengers, it seemed unlikely that any of them could have been responsible for his murder. They were tame and docile compared to the rough and raucous crew members.

But one Indian did come under intense scrutiny—Siva. Crew members and passengers alike witnessed the extreme dislike Mr. Pickles had for Siva often humiliating him in public. With one less headache and a promotion to head purser, perhaps nobody had a better reason to see Mr. Pickles become fish food then Siva. But most found it hard to believe that he was capable of anything so heinous. His geniality preceded him. Nonetheless, doubt as to his innocence lingered.

*****

With Mr. Pickles gone, Mrs. Weatherly took a more active role in Indian affairs. She was especially concerned for Archana. The boy's mother had grown noticeably weaker.

"But at least she is bathing herself now," Siva said to Mrs. Weatherly after meeting with Archana and Nayadu.

"I noticed," she said. "She hadn't bathed in weeks."

"It's interesting that she started bathing after Mr. Pickles died."

Mrs. Weatherly raised an eyebrow. "What are you inferring, Siva?"

"It's interesting, that's all."

"Are you trying to say that Mr. Pickles interfered with Mrs. Nayadu?"

"I would rather you come to your own conclusion on the matter, madam."

"Can we not ask her if that brute assaulted her?"

"She will never say."

"But why?"

"Fear."

"Of what?"

"It's our culture. If it's revealed that she was defiled by another man, then she could end up being rejected by her own family."

"Then what can we do, Siva?"

"Nothing madam, It's up to her."

*****

Imran and Chandu became close friends. Together, they contemplated the complexities of life, including the murder of Mr. Pickles. It was disconcerting to consider that a killer was in their midst.

"Maybe the killer was in the room with us when we found the body," said Imran.

"No, I don't think so."

"If he was, then he'll know who we are. He might come after us next."

"No, if the killer was still in the room, he wouldn't have dropped the knife. I think the killer got scared after killing Mr. Pickles and panicked, dropping the knife on the ground before running away."

"Hmm, sounds like a good theory, Chandu. You must consider becoming a constable when you grow up."

"You didn't tell anybody what we found, did you?" Chandu asked.

"No, never."

"As long as the killer is still loose, they can never find out that we found the body or they will think we did it."

"I won't say anything."

*****

It was days later before the *Chadwick* drifted out of the doldrums centered around the equator. Once they were far enough south, the winds started to fill the sails and fresh air once again circulated through the lower regions of the ship.

"It's time," Chandu told Imran.

He looked up at his friend and smiled, resting comfortably next to his younger brother, Jamal. "Now?" he asked.

"The captain and crew are busy on deck."

"I'm going to have to bring him," he said, shifting his eyes toward Jamal.

"Then I'll bring Pradip. He's been wanting to go ever since I told him how great *The Great Room* is."

*****

They were in luck—the door was open. Imran locked the door while Chandu scurried over to the large table to look at the map.

"You see, the wind is taking us back on course. We're more than halfway now."

"There's no turning back now," said Imran.

"Where's the candies?" Pradip cried out.

"Sshh!" said Chandu, looking up from the map.

"On that small table." He pointed.

Pradip ran over to the large jar full of multicolored hard candies and shoved his hand inside. He pulled out as many as he could wrap his small hand around, dropping several to the ground, then pushed some into his mouth.

"Give me those!" Imran said, snatching the jar out of Pradip's hands. "We don't want to get caught by eating all the candies."

Jamal jumped up onto the captain's red velvet chair and bellowed out, "I'm the captain, and you have to do what I say."

"Quiet, you cowbrain," said Imran. He picked up a small paperweight and threw it at Jamal. The object narrowly missed his head and shattered a pane within the stained-glass window just feet behind him. All of them froze.

"We're dead now," said Pradip.

Within a few minutes, footsteps descended rapidly down the ladder.

"What are we gonna do?" said Jamal.

"Quiet," Imran said softly.

The handle of the door jostled violently, but it was locked from the inside.

"Open this door!" the officer yelled.

They stood nervously, not knowing what to expect. They had no plan of escape and nowhere to hide. Chandu could already see the look of disappointment on his father's face as all of them would surely be marched up onto the main deck to walk the plank. But there was silence. Then the footsteps moved away from the door and back up to the main deck.

"Let's go," said Imran, unlocking the door. They scampered out of *The Great Room*, down the hall toward the lower deck, where they hoped to disappear among the passengers.

"Quick, we'll go under the blankets at our camp," said Imran.

"Hey, where's your brother?" Jamal asked.

Chandu turned around, and Pradip was nowhere to be seen.

"Pradip!" he called out.

"He must still be in *The Great Room*," said Imran.

"I have to go back and get him."

Imran scanned around, looking for any sign of the captain or crew. "Okay, I'll go with you."

"I'll go to," said Jamal.

"No, you won't."

As Imran and Chandu moved cautiously back in the direction of *The Great Room*, they could only suppose that Pradip's greed for those hard candies had gotten the best of him. Chandu's heart started pounding violently as they approached the rear ladder just steps from *The Great Room*.

With both doors of *The Great Room* open, they could see the first lieutenant and Siva. In the hand of the lieutenant was Pradip, hanging painfully by his left ear. As the ship tilted slightly fore, several small candies rolled out of the room and into the hall in which they were standing. Imran and Chandu moved out of view.

"Please, sir," Siva pleaded, "have some mercy on the boy."

"Mercy! Like the kind that was shown to Mr. Pickles?"

"Sir, are you implying I had something to do with that man's death?"

"Not at all. I'm implying that justice must be carried out on this ship."

"But look, sir, this is just a small boy whose curiosity led him astray. Please, let me deliver him up to his father. He will discipline him."

The lieutenant relaxed his grip on Pradip and looked around the room. "No, bring the boy's father to me." He pushed Pradip away. "Bring him to me—now!"

With no understanding of English, the boys assumed that Pradip had been let off the hook with a stern warning. They stayed out of sight as Siva led Pradip down to the lower deck. He didn't sound angry but rather sad when he said to Pradip, "You've brought a lot of trouble for your father."

Without a word, they followed as Pradip was led back to their bunk. Still clutching the few candies that he was able to hold onto, his dirty little feet shuffled clumsily along the wooden floor trying to keep up with Siva. Chandu contemplated whether he should confess to Siva that they too were responsible for what happened in *The Great Room* but the words wouldn't come.

*****

Nayadu was escorted along with Pradip back to the first lieutenant.

"Tell the father that his son has been found guilty of trespassing, theft, and vandalism. In light of the fact that the defendant is of such young age, I am willing to commute his sentence to three days in the brig."

After Siva translated the lieutenant's verdict, Nayadu looked over at Pradip.

Pradip looked up to his father, his face saddened. "I'm sorry, Nana." A tear rolled down his dirty cheek. An overwhelming sense of compassion welled up in Nayadu's heart.

"Please, Siva garu, ask the sahib if he will allow me to go to the brig in my son's place."

Siva's eyes widened. "You're willing to bear the punishment for your son?"

"Yes."

When Siva relayed what Nayadu had asked the lieutenant, he said nothing at first. "Very well," he said after a few minutes. "This man will serve three days in the brig starting immediately."

CHAPTER 8

"Land! I can see land!" yelled a male passenger peering out of one of the starboard portholes. Hordes of weary passengers scurried over, each hoping for a glimpse of what had been promised.

The atmosphere changed dramatically from despair to joyous anticipation. Even Archana managed a smile. Nayadu put his arm around her to assure her that everything was going to be all right.

"Come, let's go," said Imran.

"Where?" Chandu asked.

"You'll see."

With Imran leading the way, they darted up the ladder unnoticed and hid themselves under one of the lifeboats on the starboard side. The fog was thick and damp, but the faint outline of a grayish landmass loomed on the southwest horizon.

"I discovered this place the other day," he said.

"Why didn't you tell me about it?"

"I'm telling you now."

"We shouldn't be reaching land for another week."

He nodded. "I know." In their minds, they had assumed an imagined responsibility for the ship's course and progress.

"Maybe the charts were wrong," Chandu said.

"I don't mind that they were wrong," said Imran, shrugging his shoulders.

"Neither do I. I just want to get off this boat."

They lay on their sides, mostly hidden by the lifeboat hanging above them and two coils of thick rope lying on the side. Quietly, they gazed upon the calm waters. The cool salty air felt good in their lungs.

"I wish I discovered this place earlier," he said.

"Yeah—hey, do you think we'll still be friends when we get to Natal?"

"Why not?" Imran replied.

"I don't know. Maybe we'll end up living in different villages."

"Doesn't matter," he said, extending his hand. "We'll always be friends."

As the sun slowly ascended, a light breeze started to texture the dark water and the fog gradually dissipated. The grayish landmass took the shape of splendid black cliffs protruding from the sea.

Crewmen starting milling around on deck and sails were quickly hoisted in an effort to harness the light wind wafting out of the east.

"We should go back," I said.

"We can't go now. Someone will see us."

Both of them repositioned themselves, making sure that they were well out of the sight of passing crewmen. As the cool wind blew in their faces, they could see waves crashing into the cliffs of what they assumed would be their new homeland. While Chandu should have been excited at the thought of once again setting foot on land, his heart grew heavy. He couldn't help but think that he had seen his grandparents for the last time.

"Where're you from, Imran?"

"Secunderabad."

"You miss it?"

"Mmm—no."

"Why not?"

"Nothing to miss."

"Don't you miss your grandparents?"

He looked at me for several seconds before answering. "More than ever."

"Where are they?"

"Dead," he replied without any emotion.

"Oh—all of them?"

"Yeah, all of them—killed—along with my mother."

Chandu's reply was awkward, "I'm sorry."

He took a deep breath, sighing heavily. "It's been two years. Two long years."

"How did they die?" he asked.

"Hindus," he said, pursing his lips. "Hindus came through our village one night going house to house, killing us Muslims."

"But why?"

He shrugged. "We're different, I guess. My father says that people fear others who are different."

"Hmm," he replied, pondering his father's wisdom. "Why do you think people are afraid of those who are different?"

"Don't know, Chandu. I think it's a grown-up thing."

He chuckled, "Something to look forward to, huh?"

"Suppose so. What about you? You have grandparents back where you came from?"

"Just Ammamma and Thathiyya. But my father wouldn't allow us to see them after they stopped being Hindus."

Imran turned his gaze toward the water. "But that didn't stop us from seeing them," Chandu continued. "Every day after school, Ammamma had hot *parathas* waiting for us."

"Ooh," said Imran, his eyes rolled up in his head, "hot parathas."

"Along with tamarind rice, pickles, and chutneys, her famous *gangoora*—"

"Stop," said Imran. "I don't want to hear about food."

"Oh, and her *ka-meetha*."

"What's that?"

"The best cashew nut pudding you ever had in your life."

"Why did I ask?" he chuckled.

*****

As the wind filled in, the ship tilted slightly starboard. The deck started thumping with activity as the captain started barking orders. The ship began cresting and pitching over the windblown waves, each time sending sheets of ocean spray over the bow. The captain yelled again, and a sailor scuttled over, grabbing the coil of rope that had been hiding Chandu from plain view. He quickly slid over and nestled himself beside Imran, desperately hoping they wouldn't be discovered.

Suddenly the ship turned leeward as the crew let out the sails. It was as though the captain surrendered his upwind battle and was now at the mercy of where the wind and waves wanted to take them. There was quiet except for the creaking of the masts. The waves that had been battering the sides of the boat were now rolling along side of them.

"Hey, look—no crew in sight," Chandu said.

Imran looked high and low and then said, "Yeah, but I don't want to go back down in that hole."

"Neither do I."

"Then let's stay here till we get to Natal."

"At least till morning rice."

"I'm not hungry," said Imran.

"I'm starving."

"Hey, what do you want to do when you grow up?" he asked.

"Don't know," Chandu answered. "I all I know is that I don't want to be a farmer."

"Why not?"

"I want to go to school and learn English."

"That's it?"

"No, that's not it. I just know that I don't want to work on a farm for the rest of my life."

*****

Siva eventually made his way below deck, but he looked weak and thin. The stress of the voyage was clearly taking a toll on him.

"What is all the commotion about?" he asked. His voice was strained and scratchy.

"Land!" one passenger exclaimed.

Siva trudged over to the porthole, politely brushing passengers aside. "Land? I don't see land."

"To the far left."

Siva poked his head out the porthole and looked downwind. "Ah, Madagascar." Expressionless, he headed back toward his cabin. "We're still days away from Natal," he was heard mumbling before he disappeared.

Moans of disappointment echoed as word passed through the lower deck. Imran raced over to our bunk.

"I guess those charts *were* right," he said.

"I guess so."

"Hey," he said softly, "Is your mother well?"

"Why do you ask?"

"Oh, just asking."

"You're asking for a reason."

He shrugged. "Just heard people talking—that's all."

"About what?"

"People are saying that your she's not right."

"Not right?"

"Crazy," he whispered.

"Who's saying that about my Amma?"

Imran tried to quiet his friend by putting his hand over his mouth, but Chandu pulled it away and asked, "What about you? You say my Amma's crazy?"

Nayadu sat up and said, "Enough, Chandu! Send your friend away."

"Leave!" he told Imran.

"Chandu, I didn't—"

"Go back to your family," said Nayadu.

Imran lowered his head, slowly got up and walked away.

*****

The next day, Siva failed to appear for his usual rounds. Mrs. Weatherly showed in his stead, but she looked like she hadn't slept for days. It was difficult for her to communicate with the passengers, but few words were needed. Dozens had fallen ill overnight. The captain's wife knew there was little Dr. Wigglesworth was going to be able to do with so many needing medical attention. She wasted no time enlisting the help of those who were still healthy to tend to those who were ailing. She then took one young man who was especially ill to the doctor for a diagnosis.

Dr. Wigglesworth recognized the symptoms all too well: diarrhea, vomiting, leg cramps. "I'm afraid this is not good, Mrs. Weatherly. I just sent Siva back to his quarters with the same diagnosis and with little I could do."

She lifted both hands to her mouth, "It's cholera, isn't it?"

The doctor nodded. "A particularly acute strain."

She lowered her head. She knew well the devastating effects of the disease. An outbreak of cholera on a similar voyage to Mauritius three years earlier nearly ended her life. Many of the passengers, as well as crew members, died before reaching the island colony. When she finally recovered weeks later in the home of the island's governor, Lord Spencer, Captain Weatherly decided that she had sailed her last voyage. No longer would he put his wife's life at risk on such perilous journeys.

But the captain's resolve was no match for the indomitable will of his wife. She would rather risk the perils of seafaring than sit at home tending gardens and knitting tapestries. Besides, she would never stand for such extended durations apart from her mate.

"Don't get too close to these coolies," said the doctor. "It's your only chance of surviving."

"How can I stay away from these people? They need someone to see after them."

The doctor shook his head. "Madam, I don't know whether they should commit you to an asylum or make you a saint."

She chuckled. "An asylum would be preferable to the conditions we're living with on this ship."

The spirit of Death slithered through the nether regions of the *Chadwick*, picking its victims seemingly at random and without mercy. Laying alone and shivering, the young girl pulled her knees into her chest trying to keep warm, but it was no use.

Prema caught sight of the pitiable young girl from her bunk and guessed that there was little hope for her. Nevertheless, she took her blanket and covered her trembling body leaving only her head exposed. She opened her eyes and smiled slightly. "Thank you, Aunty." Her voice was weak and quivering.

Prema pressed her hands on the young girl's cheeks and forehead. "You poor thing," she said softly.

"I'm thirsty, Aunty."

"Here, drink this," said Prema tilting a small cup of tepid water over the young girls parched open mouth. The girl reached up and pulled the cup to her lips.

"Some more?" Prema asked.

The girl nodded and then smiled.

"What's your name?" she asked before refilling the cup.

"Arti."

"Arti." She nodded in approval. "Where are you from, Arti?"

"A small village near Secunderabad."

Prema gave Arti another cup of water, and she quickly gulped it down.

"You are such a pretty young girl. So where's your mother and father?"

Arti turned her light-brown eyes toward the rays of light coming through the portholes and then lowered her head. "They're gone," she said softly.

"Oh, I'm sorry, Arti."

"They died in a fire."

"That's terrible. Any brothers or sisters?"

"A brother, but he died too—in the fire." Arti's face suddenly grimaced. "My legs, Aunty, they're cramping."

Prema gently placed Arti's head on the deck and started massaging her legs. Arti closed her eyes, and her body became limp. After several minutes, she was asleep. As Prema gently stroked the young girl's legs, she wondered how such a beautiful young girl wound up alone and deathly ill on a ship headed to a foreign land.

*****

Mrs. Weatherly poked her head into the crew's quarters to find Siva sleeping. His whole body was drenched with sweat, and she felt helpless. She was fond of him and dreaded the thought of his succumbing to the deadly effects of the virus. She remembered well when Siva showed up on the docks in Madras three years earlier looking for work. He had traveled from Bangalore after hearing about the abundance of work around the shipyards.

As Siva inquired with the captain about the availability of work, she recalled how well he spoke English and how well dressed he was. It seemed odd to her that he was interested in working aboard a ship. Sailors and crewmen were a distinct breed—rough-hewn and often unrefined.

"Sorry, laddie, I don't see you cut out for this kind of work," said Captain Weatherly.

"Please, Captain! I have a wife and two young girls and another on the way. I can do anything."

"Have you ever set foot on a ship before?" he asked.

"No, but—"

"You won't last a week 'board this ship."

Standing several feet behind the captain, Mrs. Weatherly interrupted, "Do you speak any other languages, young man?"

"I do, madam."

"Well?"

"I speak Tamil, Kannada, Telugu, Malayalam, and a little bit of Hindi."

Mrs. Weatherly pulled the captain to the side. "He speaks all the South Indian languages. We could use him as a purser."

"But what about Mr. Pickles?" he asked.

"What about that drunken good-for-nothing?"

"But I can't get rid of him. He's done too many favors for me in the past, and I owe him."

"Fine," she said. "Make this young man his assistant. It will make our lives much easier having someone aboard this ship who can speak to these Indian passengers."

He contemplated the idea while tugging on his beard, and after a brief moment, he said, "Well, I can't pay him very much—perhaps two percent of our profit." He turned to Siva. "What's your name, young man?"

"Sivasambarao, but everyone calls me Siva."

"Siva, you've made quite an impression on my wife, and so I'm going to bring you aboard as an assistant to our purser, Mr. Pickles. I'll pay you two percent of our profit."

"What can I expect to make, sir?" he asked.

He raised his eyebrows and replied, "Depends. You might walk away with thirty shillings, and you might not make anything. It's as a much a gamble for you, and it is for me."

Siva pursed his lips. "I'm a very optimistic man, Captain."

The captain smiled and said, "Very well. But let me warn you right now. Mr. Pickles is not an easy man to work with, and life aboard this ship has broken many a good man. Are you sure you're up to it?"

"I am, sir, you'll see."

"Very well, lad. Come aboard."

*****

Mrs. Weatherly took her own handkerchief and gently dabbed the moisture on Siva's face.

Siva cried out, "Deepa."

"No, Siva, it's me, Mrs. Weatherly."

"I thought you were my wife," he said after looking around the room. He reached for his eyeglasses.

"It's okay, Siva, just rest. Is there anything I can get you?"

"Water."

"Sure, anything else?"

"Just water," he whispered.

*****

When Prema saw Arti squirming violently in her sleep, she awakened her. "What's wrong, Arti?"

"Aunty," she said, suddenly aware of her surroundings. "Oh, I had a bad dream."

"It's okay, Arti," she said, stroking her head.

"Aunty, don't you have a family?"

"I do. I have my husband and daughter, Manisha, right there," she said, pointing over to the two as they napped.

"Oh yes, I've seen them before. You're lucky," said Arti.

Prema paused, never considering how lucky she was in light of Arti's circumstances. She smiled.

"I want to tell you something, Aunty."

"Anything."

"But I don't want you to leave me."

"I won't, Arti. What is it?"

She hesitated for a moment. "I don't know why, but I feel I need to tell you."

"Tell me what?"

"I'm a temple dancer."

Prema felt a little embarrassed because she had never heard of a temple dancer. She didn't know how to respond.

"I danced for men," said Arti, sensing Prema's bewilderment. "They paid me to be with them—you know."

"But why, Arti? Why would you do that?"

"Please, Aunty, don't hate me."

"I don't hate you, Arti. But tell me—why?"

"It's a long story."

"I'm listening."

"My older brother molested me from the time I was seven years old."

"The one who died in the fire?"

Arti lowered her eyes. "Nobody died in a fire, Aunty. I lied about that."

Prema was silent for a moment and then responded, "So you never told your father or mother about your brother?"

"I did, but they never believed me. Not until they caught him one day. Then they sent him away. But then my father became ill and died. After my father died, my brother came back to our home and started—you know. Then I became pregnant, and my mother sent me away. She said that the family would be disgraced if the village came to know. So I left our village for Secunderabad and went to the

94

biggest temple I could find. There I begged for money. The temple priest told me that I was a *Devadasi*. That means I was to be a wife of god."

"The priest knew you were pregnant?"

"No! I told him that I had never been with a man."

"Why, Arti?"

"I was ashamed." She continued, "He had his way with me and then told me that it was my duty to serve other temple patrons— whatever they wanted."

"And your baby?"

"I lost it after the second month," she replied with no emotion.

Prema wanted to somehow console Arti with wise counsel but hardly felt qualified. She had never traveled out of Korlakota except once when her mother and father took her and her older brother to Rajahmundry for a *Bonalu* festival. The family walked the entire way carrying their offering to goddess *Gangamma*—cooked rice with milk and sugar.

Prema recalled the many women in attendance dressed in their finest silk *saris* dancing to the rhythmic beat of the drums while balancing their pots on their heads. Often tranced, it was believed that they possessed the spirit of Gangamma. But Prema knew nothing about temple dancers. The only girls lingering around the small Shiva temple in Korlakota were those threading garlands of marigolds for worshippers.

Arti couldn't have been more than twelve years old, thirteen at the oldest, she thought to herself. With her fair complexion and light-brown eyes, Arti was the prettiest girl that she had ever seen. She shuddered, thinking how the young girl had become a piece of flesh to be used and discarded. How her dreams of getting married and having children had been stolen. The irony was cruel. Her fate was perpetuated by those seeking the attention of god.

Prema stroked Arti's cheek. "So how did you end up here—on this boat?"

"Some man came to the temple one day and kept telling me how pretty I was. We spoke for a while, and then he asked me if I ever wanted to get married one day and have children. I told him that I was a Devadasi and that I couldn't leave. He asked me if I was happy as a Devadasi, and I said no. He told me that he would come and fetch me that evening and take me away where my future husband would be waiting for me. So..."

Arti's voice trailed off, and her face suddenly writhed in pain. "Please, Aunty, help me to the loo."

Fortunately, there were few waiting, and Prema was able to get her in before it was too late. She was lucky. For many, the constant and sudden need to visit the loo was both humbling and horrific. Arti emerged minutes later looking even thinner and hunched over. The circles around her eyes were dark. Prema held her arm, ushering her back to her small space in the middle of the deck.

"They're saying it was contaminated food or water," said Prema while massaging Arti's legs.

"Do you think I'm going to be well again?" she asked, with an innocence that had long been lost.

Prema hesitated for a moment. "Of course, you're going to be well again."

"But I can't keep anything down, and my whole body is starting to pain."

"I know, but we will arrive very soon, and you will be able to get help there."

"But—"

"But nothing! You are going to get better, you hear me? Repeat after me! I am going to get better."

"I am going to get better."

"Again," she said.

"I'm going to get better."

"You see, you're already looking better."

"You're so kind to me," she said before her eyes closed.

CHAPTER 9

Sai Komdaari, the temple priest, warned Nayadu that he was forbidden to cross the black waters that surrounded their homeland but never said why. Now he knew. Anyone who dared would be cursed. He considered those who seemingly escaped without sickness or death and believed that theirs was simply a curse delayed.

As the *Chadwick* neared the shores of Natal, it was impossible to escape the smell of Death. The captain stopped all sea burials when land was sighted for fear of dead bodies washing ashore. Then he realized that it would be far thornier to arrive with a stack of dead immigrants. His first lieutenant suggested that lead weights be tied to the dead before sending them overboard, and with this, the captain agreed.

Then the captain made another decision that caused great consternation among the crew. *None of the sick passengers should be allowed to leave the ship,* he declared. He was sure that if it were discovered that the *Chadwick* was bringing Death to the shores of Natal, it would surely be turned away.

When Dr. Wigglesworth learned of the captain's decision, he made it clear that this was a disease borne from the consumption of contaminated water. There was no danger of it spreading once on shore. But the captain was concerned that Natal officials would pay little heed to his onboard physician. The debate went on till the boat docked when the captain finally conceded.

He said to the doctor, "I'll leave it to you to convince them there is no danger of an epidemic with our sick coolies."

He also realized that there was little chance of passengers leaving loved ones behind lest there be an uprising. This was perhaps the more compelling reason for his ultimate decision, and so it was that the new but weary arrivals were allowed to carry their sick relatives off the ship.

*****

Prema was relieved to see Arti open her eyes, but her gaze was distant and her breathing shallow. She lifted the young girl's head and poured some water into her mouth.

"Hang on, Arti," she said, "we've reached land."

She smiled slightly, and Prema took her hand and squeezed it. "We're going to get you off this dreadful boat, but you must stay alive. Do you hear me?"

She nodded and, with a hint of a smile, closed her eyes.

*****

The fatigued passengers filed slowly down the gangway with tears and somberness. The scourge of Death had vanquished the joy of arriving safely in the promised land. For every five or six able-bodied passengers, there was a sick one that had to be carried off. The captain stood stern with his first lieutenant at the bottom of the gangway counting passengers as they passed. No doubt he had grossly underestimated the amount of casualties by the end of the voyage and his face grew increasingly distressed.

Death was at Arti's doorstep, so it was that Velu, Nayadu, and Chandu would carry her out of the damp foul-smelling hole that had been their home for six dreadful weeks. The captain pursed his lips and shook his head side to side when he saw yet another limp body descending the gangplank. "For the love of God," he said to his first lieutenant, "how many bloody coolies did we lose?"

"All together?" he asked.

"Yes," the captain rejoined sharply, "all together!"

"Let's see," he said, looking at his papers. "We started with 325 but only delivered 186, that will fetch our fee of four shillings."

The captain cursed.

Eighty-nine Indian passengers had died en route. Some had chosen to end their misery by simply stepping off the side of the boat while others had little choice. It was the Kala Pani, the black waters that separated the unsuspecting passengers from their homeland, that would become the final resting place for so many.

For the captain, it was an unprofitable voyage. Not since the winter of 1879 had there been such a high number of casualties aboard a human cargo ship. The SS *Chadwick* would become infamous for its deadly voyage that year and would make only one more crossing before being retired—the captain along with her.

*****

When the captain's wife saw Prema and Arti, she directed them along with the two families to a piece of ground that was being shaded by the bow of the ship. While the sun provided relief to the damp bones of most, it would only dehydrate the likes of Arti. Mrs. Wigglesworth stroked the young woman's pale face with a look of hopelessness and then reluctantly returned to her duty of directing passengers. Prema, however, refused to leave her side. Arti's story had pierced her heart, and she was going to do everything she could to make her last days, if not hours, as comfortable as possible.

Velu put his hands on his hips and shook his head side to side. "Don't you know this is her karma."

Prema looked up at her husband and said, "She doesn't deserve to die."

Then, seemingly out of nowhere, a neatly coiffed Indian man dressed in black pants and shirt appeared holding clean blankets under one arm. He took a blanket and covered Arti then dropped to his knees and proceeded to pray.

"Why is this man praying to this girl?" Velu asked.

Prema shot her husband an indignant glare and sounded, "Shh!"

"He's speaking our language," said Nayadu.

The man stopped and looked up at Velu. His face was kind but serious. "I'm not praying *to* this poor young girl. I'm praying *for* her." His eyes moistened with tears. "To the God in heaven that he will heal her from her sickness."

Mrs. Weatherly reappeared and, with a sympathetic smile, gestured that they join the rest of the passengers.

"Don't worry," said the man, "she's in God's hands."

Velu took his wife by the hand and said, "You heard the man."

She nodded and, with hesitancy, let go of Arti's hand. She had become attached to the young girl whose life had read like a Greek tragedy. As they walked away, she turned to her husband. The tears had dried, but her voice was still emotional. "That poor girl does not deserve to die."

*****

"This way!" yelled a White man who had emerged from a large, newly constructed brick building just yards from where we had assembled. It was clean sturdy-looking structure with a round window near the apex of the roof.

"This way!" the man yelled again.

"Where's Siva garu?" Chandu asked his father.

"I don't know," he answered.

Siva's absence for the last week had been a concern for all of them, and they were now starting to fear that he too may have succumbed to the dreadful epidemic that had taken so many.

Inside the building, the air was dry and cool, and there was a smell of freshly dried mortar. There was nothing inside except a handful of White men sitting at a table.

They were quickly corralled into a long queue where the processing would begin. Nayadu was now 79258, Archana became 79259, and so on. Then their photos were taken. For most, if not all, this was a novel experience. There were *oohs* and *ahs* as the large black box let loose with an explosion of light. And when it was explained to them it would capture their image onto a piece of paper, this was more than the average immigrant could comprehend.

*****

Nayadu looked over the document that Rao had given him back in Rajahmundry. Some of the words were smudged, but it didn't matter; he was unable to decipher any of them. Now scribed on the top of the paper was the number by which he would be identified: 79258.

He turned to his wife and held the document in front of her face. "This is our ticket, Archana. With this I'm going to be the top agricultural specialist in this land."

She smiled and replied, "Okay."

He looked the document over again as if a second glance might enable him to read it. But alas, it was no use. Written in English was basic information denoting his name, age, height, his father's name, and the village whence he had come. Also noted was that he was a Hindu of the Kapu caste and that he was married with two sons. But nowhere on the document was it stated that Nayadu was more qualified than anyone else when it came to agriculture, although it was understood among Indians from Andhra Pradesh that Kapus were farmers.

By now, several hours had passed, and a majority of the single male passengers had been contracted to Phoenix Sugar Ltd. and Natal Railways. Among them was number 79284, the merchant whom Nayadu and Velu encountered before boarding the ship, and his son, number 79285.

There was no small commotion when an agent from Natal Railways bought the merchant's contract. He hadn't even bothered to look over the man's document.

When the interpreter said to the merchant, number 79284, "Okay you—go with this lahnee," he replied, "Go where?"

"You've been contracted to work for Natal Railways, now go!"

"But I'm here for business. I'm a merchant!"

The interpreter laughed. "You best not keep these people waiting. They don't have much patience."

"But what about my son?"

"He goes with you."

Suddenly the man dropped to his knees. "But you people are making a mistake. We're not low caste, we're businessmen."

"You better go with this lahnee before he gets angry."

The merchant's son, who was approximately eighteen years of age, said, "Let's leave, Father, why should we stay here?"

The interpreter smirked. "You've no choice in this matter. You were brought to this colony to work as indentured labor—not as free passengers as you suppose."

"And if we leave?" the merchant asked.

At that moment, the agent from Natal Railways interrupted. "Enough of this coolie banter! I don't have time for you to be negotiating with my new help," he said to the interpreter.

"You better go with him now," said the interpreter.

The merchant looked at his son and saw a certain defiant determination in his eye and knew what he had to do. He turned back to the interpreter and said, "We're not going anywhere with that man."

The interpreter turned to the agent and reported what the merchant had told him.

The agent's face reddened, and his eyebrows narrowed down toward his nose. "You tell that bloody coolie if doesn't want me to yank him out of here by his ear, then he better well change his—never mind. This one needs to learn a lesson right now." At that moment, the agent reared back and, with all his strength, struck the merchant square on his jaw. The merchant was out before he hit the ground. That was what it took to make the merchant realize that he was no longer in control. For the next five years, he and his son would be bonded to Natal Railways. The only command he would have over his destiny would be whether he chose to go on living or not.

It was shortly thereafter that a large White man with a thick beard, thinning black hair, and eyes that were dark and deep set walked slowly past the immigrants as if inspecting a garrison of soldiers. Two steps behind was a Muslim Indian man. He wore a white, loose-fitting throbe that extended to his ankles and a kufi typical of his coreligionists. His beard was long and streaked with gray while his moustache was neatly trimmed.

The White man stopped in front of Velu and held out his hand. The Muslim man stepped between the two men and smiled at Velu. "Greetings. The lahnee here would like to see your document."

The man took the paper from Velu and gave it but a brief glance then shifted his eyes to Prema. Then he said to the Muslim man, "What is Kapu?"

The Muslim man whose name was Farooq turned to Velu and asked him the same question in his best Telugu.

Velu stood erect with his chest slightly puffed and said, "Kapus are a proud people who are skilled at working the land,"

He laughed and rejoined. "You're farmers."

But the White man seemed less interested in the information on Velu's document and more interested in Prema. This wasn't lost on Farooq. He said to Velu, "You are just what this lahnee is looking for—a farmer with a pretty wife."

Velu's eyebrows rose high into his forehead. "What do you mean?"

"Don't become distressed about this. We don't want him to know that we are on to him."

Velu glared at the man with bewilderment.

"This man is my boss, and I have seen him have his way with women who don't belong to him too many times."

"I won't let him touch my wife," Velu growled.

"Easy, my friend. We don't want my boss here to start asking questions. I'm going to tell him a story that will cause him to pass on you."

Velu's face softened. "What will you tell him?"

"Don't you worry, my friend. I'll tell him something."

Farooq then turned and spoke to his boss in English. The man's eyes opened wide, and he quickly handed Velu's document back to him. Again, he moved slowly past the remaining immigrants, and when he approached Nayadu, Farooq said, "What about this one? He has two sons."

Archana retreated behind her husband in an almost childlike manner, coiling her hair around her finger. "What's wrong with the wife?" the man asked Farooq.

Farooq said to Nayadu, "Greetings, my friend, is this your wife hiding behind you?"

Nayadu was hesitant to answer but then replied, "Yes, she is my wife."

"And is she okay?"

"Yes, garu—she's shy, that's all."

"Are you sure? She doesn't look good."

"The voyage was hard for her, garu, but she'll be okay. She's a strong woman."

Farooq smiled and said, "Very well," but before he could turn and tell his boss, Nayadu held out his document and said, "Don't you want to see this?"

Farooq instead turned to his boss, and they conferred for several moments. Afterward, he asked Nayadu, "Do you take alcohol?"

Nayadu shook his head side to side.

"This lahnee, Mr. Cozen likes you. He is going to buy your contract."

Nayadu replied, "But you didn't look at my paper."

"You're a Kapu, aren't you?"

"How did you know that?" asked Nayadu.

Because you speak just like that man there with the pretty wife," he said, pointing toward Velu. "So I already know that you're a farmer. And we both agree that you look honest."

Nayadu smiled and pressed his hands together. "Thank you, garu. Thank you."

"Let's have that document you wanted us to look at. Mr. Cozen will need it to purchase your contract," said Farooq. He unfolded it and looked at it, though he was unable to read English. "And what would be your good name, number 79258?"

"Nayadu," he answered.

"Naidu?"

"No, I am Nay-a-du."

"Okay, okay, Naidu. I am Farooq-al-Sirdar. I am in charge of the coolies."

Mr. Cozen took the document so that he could purchase Nayadu's contract then said to Farooq, "Go ahead and load them on the back of the wagon. This is all we'll take today."

"Come," Farooq said to Nayadu and his family, "we will be taking a sugarcane cart back to the estate—your new home for the next five years."

Nayadu grabbed the satchel containing their goods and other belongings then noticed that the Velus were not going with them. When the Velus saw that the Nayadus had been contracted, they quickly made their way over to bid farewell. It was hard to imagine that they would part company after all they had been through. Prema embraced Archana and whispered in her ear. She only nodded.

"Keep well," Velu said to Nayadu. "And watch out for this man you're going with."

"For what?" Nayadu asked.

"Don't trust him, Nayadu. That's all."

Nayadu shrugged and said, "Very well," then dismissed his friend's admonition. He saw that Velu had been rejected by the man and attributed his friend's stern warning to sour grapes. Nonetheless, Nayadu extended his hand and said, "Our family will miss your family."

Velu took Nayadu's hand and said, "I hope we will meet again. You're a good man."

Farooq interrupted, "Okay, now we must go." As the sirdar led the way to the sugarcane cart, he said, "You are a very lucky man, Naidu."

Nayadu gave the man a puzzled look and replied, "I am?"

"Of course, you are, my friend." Farooq smiled easily, and when he did, his large cheeks protruded, forcing his eyes to squint. "I am a very nice man and treat all my coolies fairly."

Nayadu's eyes widened. "So you are my boss?"

Farooq nodded. "But Mr. Cozen is the big lahnee. He is the estate manager."

Nayadu asked, "Is he also a nice man?"

Farooq hesitated. "Depends."

"On what?" Nayadu asked.

When they arrived at the sugarcane cart, Farooq turned to see that Mr. Cozen was fast approaching from behind. "Let's not give this lahnee the notion that we are speaking of him. There will be plenty of time to speak later."

Just as they prepared to climb aboard the cart, Chandu spotted Imran and his father climbing onto the back of another sugarcane cart that would take them to their new home. Until that moment, he hadn't realized how close he and his Muslim friend had become. No longer did he feel resentment toward him. A small lump formed in his throat as Imran held up his hand. His face was cheerless. Now there was regret that he hadn't mended things with him before going separate ways. His thoughts went back to the conversation they had underneath the lifeboat where Imran assured him that they would always be friends, but Chandu was unsure if he would ever see his friend again.

*****

Mr. Cozen's last words before riding ahead of them on horseback were, "Get my new coolies back to the estate safely, Farooq. And don't take long. You should be there in three hours."

When he was well out of sight, Farooq said, "I do all the cooking for Mr. Cozen and his family. His wife and two girls really like my food, and this has given me great favor. He made me a sirdar last year, and now I have a nice place to live with my two wives."

Nayadu scratched his head and asked, "Why did you take my family and not our friends?"

"Mr. Cozen would have liked very much to take your friends but for the wrong reason. You see, he had his eyes on your friend's wife. I saw this and made up a lie to keep that lahnee from getting his hands on her."

"What did you say?" asked Nayadu.

"I told him that she was into witchcraft. Mr. Cozen's not afraid of many things, but witchcraft is one thing he runs from. You see, we always find dead animals around the estate from witchcraft these Africans do, and this troubles him greatly."

"So you chose us instead."

"Of course. Mr. Sykes, the owner of the estate, likes workers like you who are married, have a couple of hardworking sons, and stay away from the drink."

Nayadu glanced over at his wife, who was preoccupied with Pradip. He turned back to Farooq and asked, "Must I worry about my wife?"

"No, I don't think so, Naidu. He doesn't go for the bony ones." He smiled and added, "No offense to you, Naidu."

Nayadu was pleased with what he heard. If there was more to know, he wasn't interested. He leaned back on the satchel and set his gaze on the ocean off to the right. Large waves crested high—well above the height of a man and curled over with a mighty crash. A salty mist reached over the sandy shore while flocks of seagulls hovered overhead. They traversed a well-worn dirt road that kept the sea in sight until they reached the Umgeni River, which forced them to turn inland toward the hills.

Archana had drifted off to sleep and Pradip along with her. They traveled some distance away from the sea alongside the Umgeni River until they came to a wooden bridge. Farooq jumped off the cart and carefully stepped out onto the bridge, making sure there were no loose timbers.

When he was satisfied that the bridge was safe, he walked confidently back to the cart and said, "Did I mention that you are a very lucky man?"

Nayadu just smiled.

Farooq laughed. "No, really. You are very lucky. The owner of this estate we are going to is unlike any other in this province. His name is T. Everett Sykes, and he is the nicest White man you'll ever know. Too bad there aren't more like him."

He jumped back up on the cart and tugged on the horse's rein. The river moved slowly underneath the bridge en route to the sea. "I don't much like bridges," said the sirdar. "They make me nervous."

After crossing it, Farooq said, "One more bridge and about two hours to go before we arrive."

*****

The Sykes Estate was like nothing they had ever seen. They were greeted with beautifully gilded wrought-iron gates that opened up to a long trail fringed with majestic palm trees. At the end of the drive was a double-storied Victorian manor. The grounds were impeccably manicured. The estate itself was surrounded by green rolling hills. Almost as far as the eye could see was sugarcane, the colony's answer to the insatiable British appetite for sweet tea. The giant green stalks that carpeted the hills danced with the sea breeze coming off the Indian Ocean.

To the east of the estate, Indians labored under the hot sun. With nothing more than a turban-like covering on their heads and a pancha wrapped around their waists, they wielded their cane knives with precision as if pushing back an encroaching green menace. Behind them, Indian women dutifully gathered the felled stalks and stacked them on a waiting cart.

Mr. Sykes was there to greet them as they offloaded from the cart. Well advanced in years, he had a slow and careful stride, and his fingers were swollen from arthritis. Nevertheless, his smile was warm. He greeted each one, making sure that he was able to pronounce their names, and with this, Nayadu was impressed. As he looked around at the vastness of Mr. Sykes' land, he was sure that this was a man who embodied good karma.

*****

But T. Everett Sykes wasn't a religious man. He did, however, gird his family with a moral code that had been handed down to him by his missionary parents, William and Tilly Sykes. He believed that all would go well for those who treat others with respect.

T. Everett grew up as an only child who spent his youth cling-ing to the bootstraps of his adventurous parents while they trekked deep into the heart of Zululand. They lived in the back of a covered wagon; their mission had been to convert Dingane, king of the Zulus, to Christianity. They reckoned that if the king surrendered his life to the real King, then the whole Zulu kingdom would follow suit.

The couple never succeeded in converting King Dingane, but they did gain immeasurable favor with the Zulu king when they nursed him back to health from a near mortal wound that he received at the hand of his half brother, Umthlangana. As a token of his appreciation, he gave the missionary couple nearly 2000 acres of land, part of on which the Sykes Estate now lay.

*****

After Mr. Sykes welcomed them to the estate, Farooq led them behind the manor and down the hill where there stood a long single storied building. The sirdar extended his hand toward the building. "These barracks will be your new home. Welcome to Coolieville," he said with a hearty laugh.

They picked up their belongings and followed Farooq into the building that would be their new home.

"Big," said Nayadu.

"This place?" asked Farooq.

"Yes, we don't need such a big place."

Farooq laughed. "You don't, but the eleven other families living under this roof do. Gets a little noisy in here when they all come in from the fields."

He walked them to the very end and pointed to the only empty space. "Here you go." Then he smiled. "You're lucky you get some privacy on one side."

The only thing separating one family from the other was wooden slats, crudely erected, with large gaps in between. "Ramsamy and Asha live here," he said, pointing to the small space to the left. "They'll soon know all your business, and you'll know theirs. On the other side, you have the Chettys. But as you can see," he said, glancing around the barracks, "most hang blankets for extra privacy."

Nayadu dropped the satchels he'd been carrying in the corner of their new living space.

"You will start working tomorrow at sunrise—an hour break for lunch and another half hour for tea. Your day ends at sunset. Okay? Any questions before I leave you people?"

"Our pay?" asked Nayadu.

"I told you that Mr. Sykes is a generous man. He pays a shilling per month to be paid every second month. I hear coolies on other estates get nothing, so you are lucky. No work on Sundays. You miss a day of work, you will be charged one shilling, so don't get sick. Oh, and rations of rice and *mealie meal*, fruits, and vegetables will be given, but you must cook outside. If you must leave the estate, then you will need permission from Mr. Cozen. Any more questions?"

"Yes, Sirdar garu, what about my two boys?"

"What about them?"

Nayadu put his hand on his older son's head and said, "Well, this one is interested in school."

The sirdar snickered. "We need laborers around here, not scholars. Besides, the only schoolhouse for Indians around here is Hindi. Does your boy speak Hindi?"

"No, garu."

"Then there's no use speaking of it any further. He'll be expected to start work tomorrow morning like the rest."

Nayadu felt Chandu's shoulders slump and pulled him close to his side.

"Then how much pay for the boys, garu?" Nayadu asked.

"Hey, you shouldn't ask me such questions. Boys on other estates don't get paid till they start shaving. This lahnee, Mr. Sykes is a very fair man. You be thankful you landed here and not on some other estate."

Pradip cried out, "I don't mind working, Nana. I want to help you."

Chandu, however, did mind. He was sure that the gods in charge of karmic fate got things wrong. He wasn't born to be a farmer. He looked over to his mother for support, but she was quietly unpacking their belongings. Nayadu was well aware that Chandu was more interested in reading books than tilling the earth. But it would seem that there was little he could do. He looked at his son with sorrowful eyes waiting for him to say something.

Chandu sighed heavily. "Okay, Nana."

"Good boy."

*****

As the weeks passed, Nayadu's reputation as a hard worker grew. The long hard hours of toiling in the fields didn't seem to bother Nayadu, or Pradip, for that matter. As for Chandu, the beauty of the green rolling hills had lost its luster. He despised the break of day as one might loathe rancid milk. It held nothing for him but anguish.

Every day as they gathered stalks of sugarcane off the ground, he asked Pradip the same question: "How can you like doing this work?"

His answer was always the same, "Nana said that this is what we were born to do."

Finally, one day Chandu asked him, "Do you believe that, Pradip?"

"Why would Nana lie?"

"Are you happy to work like farm animals for the rest of our lives?"

Pradip mimicked the sound of a bullock and then laughed.

Chandu grumbled, "I can't do this for the rest of my life."

"Hey, you!" the sirdar yelled. "Less talk, more work."

"Sorry, garu," Chandu replied sheepishly.

Farooq Sirdar walked over and put his hands on his hips and pointed toward Pradip. "This little one works good, but you…" He shook his head side to side. "You are a different story."

He lowered his head and again said, "Sorry, garu." Though, deep down, he really wasn't.

"Let me tell you something. On any other estate, they would have already taken a *sjambok* to your backside."

He bent over a picked up a stalk lying next his feet. "I'm working, Sirdar garu—see?"

*****

That evening before dinner, Nayadu took Chandu aside and said, "You're bringing dishonor to this family." He knew that Farooq-al-Sirdar had spoken with him. "Why are you embarrassing me, boy?"

"It's not fair, Nana. Hindi-speaking Indians have a school, but we don't."

"Who said life is fair?"

"Nobody."

"Then why don't you work when you're supposed to?"

"Nana, can I ask you something?"

"What?"

"Do you really believe that because we're Kapus, we have to be farmers?"

He hesitated, looking down at the ground. "Yes, I do."

Hearing a hint of uncertainty in his voice, he pressed further, "Really, Nana?"

"It's our duty as Hindus to do what we were born to do," he said with a burst of confidence.

"Back home, I heard you telling Amma that if we crossed the Kala Pani, we would be defiled. Is that true?"

"Is what true?"

"Are we defiled?"

Nayadu pondered the question when suddenly Farooq Sirdar appeared. "Getting that boy in line?" he asked.

"He's a good boy, Sirdar garu."

"Of course, he is, Naidu. Come, let's walk." Nayadu jumped up and followed Farooq up the hill toward the sirdar's bungalow. "The boy just needs a little pushing."

"He wants to be schooled like the Hindi boys," said Nayadu.

"Likes to learn, does he?"

"He's only ten, but I sometimes think he's smarter than me."

Farooq laughed. "Can't have that, Naidu. Nothing worse than a boy who thinks he's too smart." His face then turned serious. "There's something else, Naidu."

"What is it?"

"Your neighbor, Ramsamy—he's dead."

Nayadu's eyes widened. "Dead?"

"We found him hanging in the barn a few hours ago."

Though dismayed to hear of such news, Nayadu wasn't completely surprised. Ramsamy had sunken into a deep depression from the time of his wife's death just weeks earlier. It would seem to most that the man had little to live for and had simply given up on life.

His wife, Asha, was pregnant when she died. She was young and portly with smooth dark skin. Some would say that she was attractive with her bright eyes and luminous white teeth. But everyone agreed that her husband doted on her and was excited about becoming a father.

As neighbors, they found it hard to keep secrets, and Nayadu knew that there were discussions about her quitting the fields. By then she was well into her pregnancy. But Mr. Cozen insisted that she continue working. It was assumed that he would work her until she gave birth.

Nayadu remembered well the morning she died. She was in good spirits as was her husband, Ramsamy. Then she suddenly complained of being fatigued. She went and sat down, propping herself against the wheel of the cart. When Mr. Cozen appeared, he scolded her for sitting down, and she returned to work. Minutes later, she was thrown to the ground by violent convulsions. Those that were present looked on in horror as she writhed in an uncontrollable fit. Ramsamy knelt by his wife's side and cried out her name in frantic desperation until her body went limp. He pulled her lifeless body close to his. He knew that she and the unborn child were gone, and he wept bitterly.

*****

"Let me tell you that I saw Mr. Cozen's face when that woman died. He smiled—and this made me wonder." Nayadu gradually stepped backward as the sirdar's tone grew angrier. "Why would an estate manager find satisfaction in losing a laborer, though she was a woman?"

Nayadu's brows narrowed toward his nose. He wasn't sure where the sirdar was going with the conversation. Farooq sensed his bewilderment and said, "Listen, Naidu, I know our talks never go deeper than harvesting quotas and cane grubs, but you were neighbors, and I think you know something."

Nayadu shrugged his shoulders and replied, "All I know is that Ramsamy was broken after his wife died. He was drinking every day and night."

"We know that, Naidu. But did you ever see the wife with another man?"

Nayadu shrugged. "Asha?" He shook his head side to side. "Never."

"All right then," Farooq said pensively, "I'll leave you now."

But Nayadu's curiosity had been piqued. "You think the wife had another man?"

"I overheard the doctor when he talking to Mr. Cozen after she died. He told him he was unable to find the cause of death."

Nayadu looked at him blankly.

"And," he continued, "he said that the baby inside of her was White."

"White!" Nayadu exclaimed.

"Shhh!" The sirdar looked around to make sure nobody was within an earshot of their conversation. "Nobody can know that we are speaking of this, you hear?"

"Of course," said Nayadu. He scratched his head and asked, "How could she possibly have a White baby?"

"Well, we know it wasn't Ramsamy's. He was blacker than a lump of coal, and his wife wasn't much lighter. So the only answer is that a White man was visiting with that wife when Ramsamy wasn't around."

"There are only two White men on the farm," Nayadu said contemplatively.

Farooq Sirdar gave Nayadu a glare as if the answer were obvious.

Nayadu's eyebrows rose slowly into his forehead. "Mr. Cozen?"

"You're quick Naidu. And I think he poisoned the poor girl because he knew that child was his."

Nayadu shook his head side to side. "I don't think Mr. Cozen could do something like this."

The sirdar scoffed, "Don't be so naive, Naidu. I've known this man for seven years now. Trust me when I say he could do something like this."

Nayadu shrugged and replied, "Okay, so what do you want from me?"

"Nothing, Naidu. I just wanted to know if you saw Cozen with your neighbor's wife?"

"No. I never saw Mr. Cozen with Ramsamy's wife."

The sirdar's brows furrowed. "You sound like your defending Mr. Cozen. Is he paying you to keep quiet?"

"Never. You want me to believe he's a bad man when he's been good to me."

"Ah, that's it. He's won you over, and now you're blind. Very well," he said with a certain disappointment and continued up the hill toward his bungalow.

Nayadu thought back to the day they first arrived when Velu Uncle warned him about Mr. Cozen. He told him that the man wasn't to be trusted. Nayadu wondered how Velu was able to say such a thing about a man he didn't even know.

Mr. Cozen was demanding and often unyielding, but that was to be expected as a lahnee. But he was also fair, and Nayadu found that he had great favor with the man often thanking him at the end of the day for his hard work.

Now he felt a sudden uneasiness in his stomach. It seemed that Farooq Sirdar was on a mission to seek justice for the deaths of Ramsamy and his wife. Nayadu, however, wanted no part of it. He just wanted to live and work in peace.

CHAPTER 10

It was the first Sunday following the death of Ramsamy, and the fields were at rest along with the workers. But there wasn't the usual chatter among the many families living side by side in the barracks. Instead, there was a depressing quietness.

Ramsamy had been well liked. He always had a kind word for those he knew and a disarming smile for those he didn't. Above all, he was excited about becoming a father. Asha's sudden death ruined him. Nobody knew why she died. She was young and robust and never missed a day of work. Some suspected that she labored too long into her pregnancy and worked herself to death though nobody knew for sure. Ramsamy's death only added to the senselessness of it all.

Nayadu needed to get away and decided to find his morning solitude on the other side of the estate. There was a wall that separated the Sykes Estate from the neighboring manor, and it was there where hardly any grass grew and where he would occasionally enjoy time alone, sipping masala tea or chewing betel nut and etching with his fingers in the hard ground.

Pradip was troubled on this morning and insisted on joining him. Nayadu was reluctant at first but could see that his youngest son wasn't going to relent. So together they walked through the dew-covered grass toward the east where the morning sun was hidden by gray-and-purple clouds.

"Nana, how long before five years is finished?"

Nayadu smiled. "Are you ready to go back home already?"

"Yes, Nana! I miss Ammamma and Thathiyya."

"I know you do."

"And I think if we go back home, Amma will get better."

Nayadu stopped and asked, "How do you know that?"

"Well, she never got sick back home."

Nayadu's eyes moistened, and he was lost for words. He was never known to be affectionate, but he put his arm around Pradip and pulled him close. He was trying desperately to make sense of the things going on around him which included his long-held understanding of the world around him.

He pulled Pradip's chin up only to see a sad and forlorn face. And while he wanted to assure his son that he would one day be reunited with his beloved grandparents he grew increasingly unsure.

Nayadu had always asserted that he would return to India after his five-year term of indenture. It was his homeland, and he believed it was his duty as a Hindu to die in the land of his birth so that the cycle of rebirths would not be interrupted.

He wanted to believe that he would make enough money to pay his debt to the Zamindar, get his farm back, and that his family would live happily ever after. But each passing day seemed to dim the aspirations of returning to Korlakota. After all, a shilling per month would not add up to much. He reckoned he would be lucky if he had enough to cover his family's passage back to India.

They resumed walking and Nayadu considered what Pradip said about his mother. She had always been a strong woman and was the backbone of the family. It wasn't until they crossed the Kala Pani when that all changed. This was never lost on Nayadu, but there seemed little he could do about it now. Returning home was not an option.

*****

Later that day Farooq Sirdar spotted Nayadu and his boys from his bungalow washing pots down in the stream. He quickly waddled his way down the hill and with a glower of disapproval said, "Why are you doing the woman's work?"

"The boys' mother isn't well today, Sirdar garu."

"You *must* take her to see a medical man, Naidu," he said sternly. It was clear to many that Archana's health was deteriorating, and Farooq had repeatedly suggested this to Nayadu over the weeks, but he was stubborn. He rejected the notion that Western medicine was better than their traditional medicines. With one hand on his hip, he wagged his forefinger at Nayadu and said, "She'll be no good to us or you if she doesn't get treatment."

Nayadu nodded in assent although the sirdar knew he had no intention of taking his advice.

He resumed scrubbing the remains of rice that had burnt in the bottom of Archana's favorite pot and asked, "Anything else I can do for you, Sirdar, garu?"

"Oh, nothing, I suppose." His face softened slightly. "Mr. Cozen has me going to Port Shepstone to buy..."—he furrowed his brows—"chaff cutters. That means I won't be back until tomorrow." His eyes rolled to the top of his head. "How many bridges there must be along the way."

Nayadu wondered why he needed to travel so far when tools were readily available in Verulam and Phoenix but said nothing regarding this. Perhaps it was a special tool that could only be obtained in Port Shepstone. He was just glad there were no sore feelings between them.

The sirdar started laboring up the hill but turned suddenly and said, "Hey, I know a man who left here a few years ago and went down to Port Shepstone to start his new life as a free man. He was considered by many here to be a healer. I'm going to find him when I get there and see if he can give me something for your wife."

Nayadu's eyes brightened. "Thank you, lahnee! I would be much obliged to you."

He dismissed Nayadu's praise with a wave of his hand. "I'm happy to do it."

They finished rinsing the pots and dishes and started up Bunglo Hill. It was called this by the laborers for the two bungalows that were perched on top. And though the climb to reach the top was not without effort the view from its summit was the reward: green hills as far as the eye could see and the balmy breezes sent in from the vast Indian Ocean.

Every trek over Bunglo Hill for Nayadu included a momentary respite at its apex finished by a covetous glance toward the bungalows.

Today was no different. Nayadu stopped with the rice pot tucked under his right arm while Pradip and Chandu held fast to the dishes and cups.

"Come Nana," said Chandu, "these things are heavy."

He pulled some betel nut out his pocket and pushed it into his mouth. "Carry on without me," he said, motioning them down the hill with his hand.

It was at that moment they heard the voice of Mr. Cozen. Unmistakable—deep with a breathy hoarseness that crackled when his ire was raised. Surely, this was from years of barking commands and smoking tobacco. It was a voice that was capable of rousing fear in the indolent and respect from the likes of Nayadu.

But his voice was noticeably softer with a sheepish lilt, and it was coming from inside the sirdar's bungalow.

Nayadu looked over at his sons and motioned for them to keep walking while he inched closer to the bungalow. They ignored him knowing he was in no position to scold them. He gave them a stern look and whispered, "Shh."

"I'm offering you each five shillings," said Mr. Cozen. "Where else can you make this kind of money in one hour's time?"

They heard the sirdar's first wife, Azara, respond with bewilderment: "What do you think Farooq would say about your proposal, Mr. Cozen?"

"Farooq doesn't need to know about our business. This is just between us."

Farooq's second wife, whose name was Farida, was still standing by the door after having let the estate manager enter. She was considerably younger than Azara and had yet to bear any children for her husband. She blurted out, "Five *pounds* or nothing."

There was several long seconds of silence before Mr. Cozen said, "I see." His voice was more forceful now. "Soliciting me for your little sex business. We'll see what Farooq thinks about this."

"Not true!" Farida cried out.

"We'll let Farooq judge for himself."

Nayadu gave Chandu an abrupt shove, almost knocking the dishes from his hand. "Let's go," he said with a forced whisper. They started walking down the hill when Mr. Cozen exited the bungalow.

"Naidu!"

Nayadu stopped along with the two boys. "Yes, lahnee?" His heart started thumping rapidly in his chest.

Mr. Cozen's eyebrows narrowed in over his dark, penetrating eyes. "What are you doing up here?"

"Uh...coming from the creek, lahnee."

"Going back to the barracks," Chandu added.

Mr. Cozen eyed them suspiciously then nodded slowly. "Carry on then."

As they descended Bunglo Hill, Pradip asked, "What was that lady selling, Nana?"

"Nothing, boy. Just keep walking."

Pradip's face shrunk into a sulking pout, but Nayadu was more concerned with what he had just heard. *Could it be that Mr. Cozen was up to no good?* he wondered.

He had been warned repeatedly that the estate manager made a sport of using women for his pleasure. He'd been told that this was a man not to be trusted. But he chose to dismiss such counsel. He refused to believe the stories. In his heart he knew Mr. Cozen held the keys to his future on the estate.

Then Nayadu stopped dead in his tracks. He suddenly realized that Mr. Cozen must have surely impregnated Asha. Now she and Ramsamy were dead. A chill ran the length of his spine. "Why did I even stop on the hill?" he mumbled to himself. *I would have been better off not knowing anything.*

They reached the entrance of the barracks when Farida came running down Bunglo Hill. She was barely twenty years of age, and though not beautiful in a classical sense, her soft voice and coy smile made her attractive.

"Please, wait!" She was winded and desperate.

Nayadu opened the door and shooed the two boys in with a sweeping motion of his hand, but again they didn't move. Then he snapped: "Get inside!"

With that they promptly scuttled through the entry only to paste their ears to the door once inside.

"Please help me. I know you must have heard what that evil Mr. Cozen said to us up there."

Nayadu hesitated. "Why do you say that?"

"Please! I saw you and your two boys standing outside the bungalow. You must have heard what was said."

Nayadu started to feel some pangs of sympathy for the young wife, knowing that Farooq Sirdar might be inclined to believe Mr. Cozen's story.

"This man is going to tell my husband that I propositioned him, which is a lie. I was never serious. I knew he would never pay us five pounds," she added. "You can tell Farooq what you heard, Mr. Naidu."

But all Nayadu could foresee at that moment was the dreadful consequences of betraying Mr. Cozen. He now knew that the estate manager would do anything to protect his own interests—and that meant anything.

He nodded and said, "I didn't hear anything."

Pradip whispered, "But we did hear. We heard everything."

"I know we did," Chandu replied.

"So why did he lie to her?"

"He must have a good reason. Come, let's go before we're found out."

*****

The following day Farooq Sirdar returned to the estate as planned. Mr. Cozen, who was patrolling the estate on horseback, spotted the sirdar as he rode through the gate and up the long trail. He intercepted the sirdar at the junction leading down and around the rear of the manor where the barracks were located.

"Welcome back, Farooq." Mr. Cozen glanced toward the rear of the cart and noticed it was empty. "Where are the chaff cutters I asked you to get?"

"This place you sent me doesn't sell chaff cutters. This man said that he was surprised you sent me such a long distance for a tool more likely to be purchased in Durban or even Phoenix."

Mr. Cozen's glare burned into the sirdar like hot coals on dry grass. "Do I hear insolence in your voice, Farooq?"

"No, lahnee." His head lowered in shame. "It was just a long, hard trip with many bridges. You know how I hate to cross bridges."

"Yes, I do, Farooq," he said musingly and added, "I also know how you hate undisciplined women."

"What do you mean by that, lahnee?"

"That young wife of yours, she's nothing but trouble."

"Tell me, lahnee, what did Farida do to trouble you?"

"She offered to sell her services to me for five pounds."

The sirdar's eyes opened wide as walnuts. "When was this?" he asked indignantly.

"Yesterday, just after you left. I went to offer those wives of yours some work around my home, and that's when that young one started acting up."

Farooq Sirdar's face turned red. "That little..." he grumbled. "Please, lahnee, you'll need to excuse me while I tend to her."

"Of course, Farooq. Do what you need to do."

*****

When the sirdar arrived home, only Azara and his two young daughters were there to greet him. "Where's Farida?" he asked impatiently.

"Gone," Azara replied.

"What do you mean she's gone?"

"She took all her belongings and left last night. She must have gone back to her mother and father."

"But why?"

"Who knows why except her. But surely it has something to do with Mr. Cozen."

"Is it true that she offered herself to him for five pounds?"

She nodded slightly and replied, "I suppose she did."

The sirdar stormed out the front door and down the hill toward the creek. He crossed over the footbridge and up the narrow path leading to Ahmed Khan's bungalow. Ahmed Khan was on old friend of Farooq's and a fellow sirdar. He was also Farida's father.

He banged on the door, hoping that Farida would answer, but it was Ahmed who opened the door to greet him.

"Where is my wife?" he snapped.

"She is here, Farooq," he replied calmly. "She came here last night because she was afraid."

He interrupted, "That little...she should be afraid!"

Ahmed put his hand up to quiet his friend down. "Farooq, I don't believe you know the whole truth."

The sirdar's face changed to one of curiosity. "The *whole* truth?" he asked.

The water running down the creek was enough to muffle their conversation, but Ahmed still looked around before continuing. "Mr. Cozen told you Farida tried to proposition him, did he not?"

"That's right."

"But did he tell you he first propositioned them?"

The sirdar's eyebrows narrowed down toward his nose. "No."

"He offered both your wives five shillings. Did Azara not tell you?"

"She didn't."

"This doesn't surprise me, Farooq. Azara never liked Farida. I'm sure she would love to see you get rid of my daughter."

"But why would she offer herself to Mr. Cozen for five pounds?"

"She said she knew Mr. Cozen would never agree to such a shocking amount of money and that he would hopefully leave them alone. But she realizes now what she did was a mistake."

The sirdar was still incensed, but no longer was he irate with Farida. "I've never trusted that man, Ahmed. He's vermin!"

"What to do?" Ahmed said with a slow nod. "Take your wife home and let it go. These are battles that we can't win."

Farooq Sirdar hesitated for a moment then said, "Send her home, Ahmed. I have something to do right now."

"You're not going where I think you're going?" Ahmed asked.

"I cannot let this go," he said determinedly.

"Farooq, you're making a mistake. Justice will be served in due time."

But Farooq Sirdar was undeterred. He left Ahmed Khan without another word and proceeded to Mr. Cozen's small home, which was situated on the west side of the estate near the horse stables.

As the sirdar made his way through the fields, he realized that a confrontation with Mr. Cozen might not end well. But it was a matter of honor now. It was a matter of defending the brazen affront to his manhood. Not only did the estate manager try to seduce his wives, but he tried to make him the fool along the way. *Chaff cutters* he muttered to himself. *This was just a ruse to remove me from the estate while he moved in on my wives.*

He spotted Mr. Cozen riding his horse into the stable, and he started walking faster.

The estate manager was surprised to see his sirdar and could see that he was troubled. He considered that the truth surrounding his visit with Farooq's wives might have surfaced and that this was not going to be a civil discourse.

"Farooq," Mr. Cozen said calmly.

"Don't I work hard for you, lahnee?" His emotions caused his voice to crack.

Mr. Cozen pursed his lips in a nonchalant manner and said, "I suppose you do, Farooq. What's this all about?"

"I think you know what this is about, Mr. Cozen. I'm wise to you and your evil deeds."

"Wait a minute here. Have you bloody forgotten who you're talking to?"

"I know exactly who I'm talking to!" he roared.

No longer was the sirdar in control of his actions. His raw emotions were now fueled by a lethal mix of rage and adrenaline. Mr.

Cozen noticed the veins in Farooq's forehead bulging and instinctively took a step backward and found himself against the stable wall.

"People like you don't deserve to live!" he bellowed.

"You've gone mad!" Mr. Cozen retorted.

Farooq saw a pitchfork leaning against a post and grabbed it.

"Put that down, Farooq!"

But the only sound to come out of the sirdar's mouth was a primeval shriek as he thrust the pitchfork at the estate manager. Mr. Cozen tried to move out of the way but was pinned against the wall. He let out a pitiful moan as two of the three prongs pierced his abdomen. He looked down in disbelief as he put his hands over the wounds. His shirt was soaked with blood.

"Farooq," he said between labored breaths. "Get help." Then he fell to the ground.

But Farooq prepared to finish what he started. He wasn't going to let Mr. Cozen live to tell of a near-death experience at the hand of his sirdar. The only stories to be told from this day forward would be of Farooq-al-Sirdar's heroism and how he exorcized evil incarnate from this earth.

He dropped the pitchfork and picked up a shovel. He would finish him off by smashing his skull with the blunt end of the shovel. Farooq Sirdar lifted the shovel high over his head, ready to unleash every ounce of his fury.

Bang!

A single shot rang out. The sirdar felt a painful sting in his back, causing him to drop the shovel. He found it hard to breathe and knew he'd been shot. He turned to see the smoke that was trickling from the end of a gun barrel. The gun barrel was still squarely aimed at him.

Bang!

CHAPTER 11

"Perhaps," she said with a sigh a resignation, "you should consider bringing her to a medical man. I can do nothing more for her."

Nayadu anguished at Chetty Aunty's advice. He hated to go against his principles, but he desperately wanted his wife to be cured. He nodded, and a tear ran down his cheek. "Do you think she'll ever be well again?"

The elderly woman consoled Nayadu with a warm smile and said, "There's always hope, young man. There's always hope."

Nayadu was thankful for her who, along with her husband, had become like adoptive parents to his family. Unlike most workers, they had no ambitions of leaving the estate and were now on their eleventh year. No longer indentured, they worked at will for Mr. Sykes for a small wage, food, and shelter.

They too had come to regard the Kala Pani crossing as a bad omen when their only daughter died during their voyage to the colony. Going back to India was not an option for them since it would mean tempting fate yet again. But neither did they see themselves pursuing gain as residents of the colony since they had no descendants.

So it was that they decided there was a certain security within the confines of the estate and that Mr. Sykes was a decent and fair man to work for. While every other laborer ticked down the days until they would be free from their contracts, the Chetty's were different. They had found contentment.

When Chetty Aunty had observed from their modest living space across the passage that Archana wasn't well, she started taking a keen interest in her welfare. She helped with cooking and routinely brought over her homespun elixirs. Over time, however, she grew weaker until finally she was unable to lift herself out of bed. That's when Nayadu went to Chetty Aunty and implored her to come up with something stronger—something that would fix her. But she knew of nothing other than what she had been giving her.

Nayadu finally decided that it was time to forsake his principles if it meant the possibility of seeing his wife well again. He went to tell Archana of his plan to take her to the estate's medical man. He knew she would go along with whatever he decided; nonetheless, he wanted her to know. But now she was sweating profusely, and he knew something was seriously wrong.

"Ammandi," she cried.

"What is it?" he replied while using his shirt to wipe the beads of sweat from her face. "What's wrong with you, Archana?"

She pulled her sari up to reveal large lesions on her inner thighs.

Nayadu's eyes widened. "My god!" he exclaimed. He rushed out of the barracks and quickly made his way toward the other side of the estate where Mr. Cozen resided. At first he was hesitant to disturb the estate manager at such an early hour but considered delaying his wife's treatment as the greater cost.

*****

Workers saw little of Mr. Cozen in the weeks following his near fatal encounter with Farooq Sirdar. He spent most of his time convalescing and only made an occasional appearance in the fields to make sure things were getting done. It was rare to glimpse him before the lunch hour.

Nayadu knocked on the door, causing Rex, Mr. Cozen's German shepherd, to start barking. He heard him yell at the dog and noticed that his voice lacked the resonance it once had. No doubt he was still weak from the wounds he suffered at the hands of his former sirdar.

Several more minutes passed before Mr. Cozen finally opened the door, his hair was still tousled from his sleep.

"Sorry to disturb you, lahnee, but my wife needs a medical man. I need to take her right away."

"Jeez, man, can it not wait till after breakfast?"

"Please, lahnee. I didn't want to trouble you, but she has sores all over her legs, and she's in pain. There's nothing more I can do for her."

He frowned with displeasure but could see that Nayadu was beside himself. "Okay, Naidu, hitch the wagon and we'll take her to Dr. Muller."

*****

Sitting on the back of the cart, Nayadu cradled his wife's tender body while Mr. Cozen skillfully negotiated the asperity of the pock-marked road. It was cold and overcast that day, and Nayadu desperately hoped that it wouldn't rain.

Archana talked to herself saying things of little relevance while Nayadu stroked her head. He looked up toward the sky and in a hushed, desperate tone said, "Please—spare her."

Dr. Muller arrived at his office at the same time they pulled up. When the doctor saw Mr. Cozen, he said to him, "What in the devil are you doing, Cozen? You should be home nursing that wound of yours."

"Emergency, Doc. One of my women coolies has fallen ill."

"You're putting a coolie's life over your own—a female coolie?"

"You don't understand, Doc," he said while straining to lower himself from the wagon. "I owe her husband my life."

The doctor's eyebrows rose high into his forehead. "Ohhh, he's the one."

"He's the one," Mr. Cozen replied. "If it weren't for him, I'd probably be in hell right now."

"Probably?"

"Okay, okay, I would *definitely* be in hell right now."

Dr. Muller walked toward the back of the cart and could immediately see that she was in a bad way. "Why did you wait so long to bring her in?" he asked Mr. Cozen.

He shrugged, "I only came to know how bad she was this morning."

The doctor pulled her right eyelid up and looked close into her eye. "She's very sick. Okay, bring her in so I can examine her."

Nayadu carried her into the doctor's office and set her on the table. The doctor washed his hands, "Why did the husband wait so long to get help for his wife?" Dr. Muller asked again in disbelief.

"You know these coolies," said Mr. Cozen. "They do their own hocus-pocus on themselves."

Mr. Cozen turned to Nayadu. "Do you speak English?"

Nayadu replied, "A little." His English was better than he liked to admit.

What were you giving your wife for her sickness?"

"Chetty's wife was helping me," he said, looking over at Mr. Cozen.

"What was she giving her?" the doctor asked.

Nayadu shrugged and grinned sheepishly. "Garlic, lemon, some herbs."

The look on the doctor's face grew with concern as he examined the sores on her thighs. He cleared his throat and peered over the rim of his glasses. "I'm going to have to examine her further."

Nayadu looked at the doctor and then at Mr. Cozen.

"Maybe you would like to wait in the other room," the doctor said finally.

"Why?" asked Nayadu.

"Maybe your wife would like a little privacy."

Archana lay on the table, oblivious to what was going on around her.

Mr. Cozen turned to Nayadu. "The doctor needs to examine your wife, Naidu. We should wait in the other room."

"I have to examine her reproductive organs to confirm my prognosis?" said Dr. Muller.

Nayadu shook his head violently. "No! That's not right, garu."

"He's a doctor, Naidu. He sees women every day."

Nayadu drew a large breath, clasping his hands behind his head.

"Do you want your wife better, Naidu?"

Nayadu looked up awkwardly. "Yes."

"Let the doctor do his job."

Nayadu dropped his head, his hands dropping to his side in resignation. He nodded with a faltering approval.

*****

The doctor emerged from his office minutes later, his face was serious. He pulled a chair over so he was able to sit across from the two men.

"I'm afraid it's not good," he said, his eyes darting back and forth between the two men.

"What's not good?" asked Mr. Cozen.

"His wife has syphilis. I should examine him before you leave here because it's transmittable. He may also have the disease."

"Syphilis?" said Mr. Cozen. His face went pale. "Isn't that from—"

The doctor nodded. "Yes, that's the only way." He took a deep breath. "There's no treatment for it, I'm afraid."

Nayadu looked at Mr. Cozen for an answer and then back at the doctor. "What does that mean?"

"It means that your wife will eventually—die."

Nayadu felt a hard lump in his throat, and tears started streaming down his cheeks. "No!" he cried. "Please—help her."

"I'm sorry," said the doctor, shaking his head, "there's no treatment for this disease. Come, Mr. Naidu, and let me examine you."

Dr. Muller ushered Nayadu back into the examination room while Archana was still lying on the table. "What's wrong with me, Ammandi?" she asked, her voice was weak.

Nayadu looked into her dark, sad eyes but couldn't speak.

"You don't show any symptoms of this disease," said Dr. Muller. He pulled Nayadu toward the window and spoke softly, "Have you not had relations with your wife?"

Nayadu's bemused look prompted the doctor to explain. "Syphilis can only be contracted through sexual contact."

Nayadu was embarrassed to answer and lowered his head. Then he nodded and replied, "She's not let me near her."

"Then she must have contracted it from someone other than yourself."

Nayadu glanced back over at Archana, confused. He didn't know whether he was supposed to be angry or sympathetic. Her doe-like eyes disarmed him. He knew his wife. He was sure the doctor's finding had to be wrong. Nayadu walked over to the examining table and explained to her what the doctor had diagnosed but told her that it was probably a mistake. Tears streamed down Archana's face, and Nayadu realized that she understood what he was saying. She had kept her secret for long enough and had nothing to lose now.

"It's true, Ammandi," she sobbed. "It was Mr. Pickles."

"Mr. Pickles!"

"He came behind me one morning when I was bathing and pushed me into the loo. He said he would kill the boys if I said anything. I am sorry that I didn't tell you."

Nayadu wept, and Archana embraced him. Nayadu, in turn, wrapped his arms around Archana and held her tight. There was no explanation as to how she was suddenly able to communicate what happened that fateful day aboard the *Chadwick*. Her thoughts and speech had grown increasingly incoherent during the weeks prior, and the family started to lose hope that she, as they knew her, would ever return.

Her lucid admission in Dr. Muller's office that morning gave Nayadu a glimpse of the Archana he used to know and a brief moment of intimacy that he so desperately missed. But he realized that there was no more hoping.

As days wore on, she continued to weaken until she was hardly able to lift her head off the dirty worn pillow that the two of them shared. He would never repeat what she told him.

Nayadu and the boys wept as her spirit slowly and peacefully drained out of her body on the seventeenth of July 1889, almost eight months to the day they had arrived in the colony.

She was only twenty-eight years of age.

*****

In the days following Archana's death, there were many tears and few words. They wept and they wept as if a part of their hearts had been ripped out of their chest. Chetty Aunty brought them food, but none of them had appetites. And then when the pain of losing Archana started to subside, they were hit with the reality that their lives would never be the same. Though she became only a shell of her former self in recent months, she was still Amma, and they never imagined life without her.

Then Nayadu announced to the boys one Saturday evening while eating dinner that they were moving.

"Where?" they both asked.

With a sly smile, he replied, "Bunglo Hill."

"Bunglo Hill," they retorted. "That's where the sirdars live."

"That's right. Your Nana has been promoted to sirdar."

Pradip squealed with delight, while Chandu was more dumbfounded. It was no secret that Nayadu aspired to becoming a sirdar, but everyone knew that he would have to wait until his term of indenture was completed.

"How were you able to become sirdar so quickly, Nana?" Chandu asked.

Nayadu's head jerked back as if that were the last thing he expected his son to ask. "Because I'm a hard worker!" he snapped. "What's wrong, you don't want to live in the bungalow?"

"No, I do, Nana, I do!"

Pradip chimed in, "I want to live in the bungalow, Nana."

"Then be thankful and don't ask questions."

*****

Chandu never asked again. Instead, he decided that the gods must have had pity on them. Moving out of the cramped and dingy barracks into the sumptuous living quarters found on top of the hill would be just the panacea to mend their ailing hearts. It would mean a fresh start to their difficult and troubled lives.

*****

The following morning, they proceeded to move what little belongings they had into Farooq-al-Sirdar's old bungalow. Farida moved back into her father's bungalow across the creek while Azara took her two daughters and left the estate. Nobody was able to say for sure what became of her.

In the adjacent bungalow, lived Sirdar Moonsamy Govender and his wife. Of the two remaining sirdars, he was considered the meanest, and therefore, they steered clear of him at every corner. But now it would be hard to avoid him living just feet apart.

Sirdar Govender had little patience for either of the two boys. He detested Chandu's perceived laziness out in the fields and threatened to lash his backside on a number of occasions. But Chandu was always quick to straighten out before the sjambok appeared.

Pradip, on the other hand, was a diligent worker but extremely impulsive. He wasn't prone to thinking through the consequences of his deeds or words, and this often landed him in hot water. He often disrespected the lahnees with his sharp tongue, and this caused Sirdar Govender to dislike him intensely.

The next morning, they started moving—Chandu with their one-armed Ganesha in one hand and the Shiva lingam in the other. Pradip was convinced that the amputated god had been rendered powerless with only one arm.

"He didn't keep evil away from Amma," he claimed as they walked up Bunglo Hill.

"But he *did* keep us three safe, didn't he?" Chandu replied. "And look at the favor we have now. How many get to move into a bungalow so quickly?"

Pradip glanced up toward the top of the hill and said, "Since he listens to you then can you ask him to poke Sirdar Govender's eyes out?"

Standing in front of the door of their bungalow was Sirdar Moonsamy Govender, and he didn't appear pleased that they were moving in. Nayadu, however, greeted him with a warm smile as they neared their new abode.

Most agreed that it was the sirdar's temperament and size that earned him his position. He was Mr. Cozen's right-hand man and was, in many ways, more intimidating.

As he stood in front of the entrance with his arms crossed, he replied, "How does someone like you become a sirdar without paying your dues, Naidu?"

Nayadu cleared his throat and said, "I'm just a lucky man, Sirdar."

Govender snickered, "Is that what you call it?"

Pradip stepped forward, still holding onto the rice pot he carried up the hill. He stuck his chin out and said, "You're not Nana's boss anymore, so move out of our way."

"Pradip!" Nayadu bellowed. "Show respect!"

He lowered his head in shame but said nothing.

"Pradip!" Nayadu yelled again.

Only his eyes rose as he reluctantly muttered, "Sorry."

Govender pursed his lips and shook his head side to side in disapproval.

Nayadu apologized again for Pradip's outburst and then asked if there was anything else. They were all standing with their hands full waiting to enter into their new home.

"I can name a half dozen men more fit for this job than you, Naidu. You haven't been here a year, and here you are. So tell me, what you did to become one of us sirdars?"

"He saved my life. That's what he did," said Mr. Cozen, appearing seemingly out of nowhere. He had come up the hill from the creek side and heard the sirdar's cross questioning. "And it was my pleasure to make Naidu a sirdar. I'm sure he'll do a fine job."

Sirdar Govender was startled and shocked by Mr. Cozen's revelation. "Naidu saved your life, sir?"

"That's right."

"But—" Govender was rendered speechless.

Pradip looked at his father with bewilderment. "How did you save the lahnee's life, Nana?"

But Nayadu was embarrassed by the sudden attention and dismissed Pradip's query with a wave of his hand.

"This man came into the barn when I was just seconds away from losing my life at the hands of that lunatic Farooq."

Sirdar Govender's eyes opened wide. "You mean it was Naidu who killed Farooq?"

"It was Naidu who saved my life. If it were not for his quick thinking, I would be—well, I wouldn't be standing here right now."

Mr. Cozen had gained back some of the weight that he had lost but was still gaunt. His voice also was hollow and weak. "So I don't want to hear any false rumors running around this estate, you hear. The constable ruled the homicide as justifiable."

There was awkward silence for several seconds until Mr. Cozen said, "So I want you to show Naidu the ropes, Govender. He has a lot to learn."

"Very good, lahnee," Govender replied but still confused. "It'll be my pleasure."

With hardly a smile, the estate manager turned and started down the hill toward the Sykes Estate. Govender narrowed his eyes, studying each of them for several seconds, then with a slow nod, said, "I guess you are lucky, Naidu."

They were relieved when he turned to make his way back toward his own bungalow, but then he stopped. He turned back and, with a sinister smile, said, "I wonder if Mr. Cozen is worried you might kill him to get his job."

The two boys both looked at their father and saw the hurt on his face.

"Come, Nana," Chandu said, pushing the door open and entering first. He set the relics down and ran to the rear window. Nayadu and Pradip followed, and when Nayadu saw the view, he smiled. It was as if they were all seeing the view from atop Bunglo Hill for the first time.

They gazed silently upon the rolling hills of sugarcane while the cool ocean breeze swept across their sweaty faces. The bubbling waters of the crystalline stream below provided a tranquil reminder that we were far from their native land and the muddy waters of the Godavari River.

A tear streamed down Nayadu's cheek.

"What's wrong, Nana?" Pradip asked.

He drew a deep sigh. "Amma would have liked this place."

"Especially the kitchen, Nana. It's bigger than the one back home," said Pradip.

"Come," Nayadu said, wiping his face, "we have more things to bring up from the barracks."

"Nana," Pradip said. His tone was curious and somber. "Did you have to kill the sirdar?"

"Sit down," he said.

The two boys sat down on the floor from right where they were standing, and Nayadu sat across from them.

"I need to tell you what happened that day. You see," his eyes darted back and forth between them, "there was much excitement in my heart that day when I saw Farooq Sirdar had returned from Port Shepstone because of what he promised."

Pradip interrupted, "What, Nana, what did he promise?"

"He promised that he would bring with him a potion that would cure Amma. So when I caught sight of him riding toward the barn, I followed. But when I got there, I saw something terrible. There was the sirdar pushing a pitchfork into Mr. Cozen. What to do?" he said abruptly. "I was confused. I know that there are many who do not like Mr. Cozen, but I knew what the sirdar was doing was not right."

"So what happened next, Nana?" Chandu asked.

"Mr. Cozen dropped to the ground, and his shirt was soaked with blood. He was begging for help, but I could see that the sirdar was angry. He was going to finish him off. Then Mr. Cozen looked over and saw me. He didn't say any words, but I knew what he was saying to me. His eyes spoke for him, saying, *You're my only hope.*

"Then I saw the sirdar drop the pitchfork and grab a shovel." Nayadu's tone intensified with each word as if he was suddenly reliving the whole event. "Mr. Cozen's horse became distressed, and that's when I noticed his rifle holstered to the saddle."

He shrugged. "I didn't think about it. I grabbed the rifle and pointed it at the sirdar just as he was ready to hit Mr. Cozen over the head with the shovel. Then I pulled the trigger.

"The explosion made the horse run scared and nearly knocked me from my feet. Farooq dropped the shovel and turned around. His eyes were as round as walnuts. I tell you, boys, that I was scared. I thought my heart was going to burst from my chest."

"Did you miss, Nana?"

"Didn't know if I hit him or not. I thought he was going to come after me. So"—Nayadu lowered his head, and with an emotional sigh, his eyes began to water; he shook his head slowly side to side and said, "I saved one life but took another."

"What about the potion, Nana? What happened to it?" Pradip asked.

Again, Nayadu shook his head side to side. "Don't know," he said. "Mr. Cozen was near death and told me I must go to Mr. Sykes for help. So I did. Mr. Sykes told me to go back to the barracks and stay there. So I did. I never saw the sirdar again."

"What if he had the cure for Amma?" Pradip asked.

A look of sorrow came over Nayadu. "I think about that every day."

Pradip stood up and pointed his finger at his father. "You killed Amma!" he bellowed. "You're responsible for taking my mother away!" Then he ran out the door and down toward the creek.

"Pradip!" Chandu yelled.

"Let him go," said Nayadu. "He's right. I *am* responsible for taking his mother away. We should have never come to this place. We should have never crossed the Kala Pani. We don't belong here, Chandu. We're strangers here. We don't even have a temple to worship our gods." A tear rolled down Nayadu's cheek. "I'd rather be starving back in Korlakota, still working for the Zamindar if it meant having Amma back."

*****

Outside the barracks, Chetty Aunty was cooking lunch, and when she saw Chandu, she asked him if they had eaten.

"No," he replied. He thanked her and went inside to retrieve what little belongings were still left in the little stall that had been their home for the last nine months. There, sitting peacefully across the sandy passage was Chetty Uncle. Most workers spent their

Sundays relaxing and doing mostly nothing, and Chetty Uncle was no different.

He smiled and said, "We're going to miss you, boy."

"I'll still come around, Uncle. You and Aunty are like family to us."

"We feel the same," he replied with a gravelly laugh.

Chandu gathered some clothes and books and started back.

"Did you finish reading those books?" Chetty Uncle asked.

"All of them except this one," he replied, indicating with his chin the book that was on top of the stack he was carrying. It was *Tale of Two Cities* by Charles Dickens and, by far, the most difficult book he had read. It made him realize how poor his English skills truly were. Nevertheless, he plowed through it as a farmer might till fallow ground.

"I think those are the key to getting off this farm, boy. Don't stop reading."

"No, I won't, Uncle," he replied with a courteous nod.

As Chandu started walking away, he asked, "Hey, where's your father and brother?"

"Oh…," he replied hesitantly, wondering whether he should lie. But if Chetty Uncle was one thing it was intuitive. He knew by the tone of Chandu's voice that something was awry.

"Troubles?" he interrupted.

"Well, Pradip thinks Nana killed Amma. And Nana doesn't disagree."

Chetty Uncle's eyebrows rose high into his forehead. "Sounds serious—and confusing. Sit down and tell me about this. I want to hear."

Chandu set his books down and sat down next to the old man. "Do you remember when Mr. Cozen was nearly killed by Farooq Sirdar?"

"Of course, I do, boy. I'm not so old that my memory is going."

"Yes, but everyone thinks that Mr. Cozen killed the sirdar in self-defense."

Chetty Uncle's brows furrowed. "Didn't he?"

With a slow shake of his head side to side, Chandu replied, "No, it was Nana who killed Sirdar Farooq."

"What?" the older man gasped.

"He killed him to save Mr. Cozen's life."

"Hard to imagine your father harming a stray dog, let alone Farooq. Hmm," he said, scratching the back of his head. With a sudden look of bewilderment, he asked, "So what does this have to do with your Amma?"

"The sirdar was supposed to have returned from Port Shepstone with a cure for Amma. But after the shooting, Mr. Cozen ordered him to get help—so he did. He went to Mr. Sykes, who told him to go back to the barracks. He never saw the sirdar again and was never able to know if he had brought with him a cure for Amma."

"Ahh, this is why the young one thinks your father killed your Amma."

He nodded. "And," he added, "Sirdar Govender thinks that Nana killed Farooq Sirdar to get his job."

"Well," he said, biting his lower lip, "I can see how he would think such a thing."

"Chetty Uncle!" he barked. "You don't think that Nana killed the sirdar to get his job, do you?"

"Oh no. Of course not, boy. I know your father well enough to know that he would never do such a thing. As for the young boy, you must tell him that it was not your father's fault that your Amma died."

"But Nana's blaming himself, Uncle. He thinks bringing us across the Kala Pani was why Amma died."

"Perhaps," he said with a slight nod. "But I believe it was fated to happen."

With a curious look, Chandu asked, "You mean it was his karma?"

"No, not karma," he replied with a quick nod side to side. "Fate is something we have no control over. It's what has already been decided."

"By who?" he asked. "The gods?"

Chetty Uncle shrugged slightly. "Perhaps."

"So we are not responsible for what happens."

"Not exactly, my boy. We are all responsible for our actions. It's just that everything we do has been—fated. It was meant to be."

Chandu pondered the concept for several seconds before Chetty Uncle finally said, "So go and tell your father to stop blaming himself, and tell your brother to stop blaming your father. Let them both know that your Amma's death was already decided long ago. Just like you coming here and speaking with me this morning was your destiny—and mine," he added with a smile.

"Did you know that I was going to come here this morning, Uncle?"

"No, my boy. I don't know the future." His face suddenly turned serious. "But I do know that there is going to be some big changes around here before long. Changes that will have an effect on everyone."

"What kind of changes," he asked.

The older man leaned forward and glanced down the passageway to see if anyone might be listening. With a softer tone, he said, "I don't think Mr. Sykes is going to live much longer."

"What do you mean?" Chandu exclaimed.

"Shh—not so loud, boy. We don't want rumors to get started around here. Mr. Sykes is old and very sick, is all. I'm concerned when he dies, who'll take over the estate."

"Won't Mr. Cozen take over?"

Chetty Uncle chuckled. "I'm afraid not, boy. Mr. Cozen is nothing more than a hired hand. No, I'm afraid this estate is going to fall into the hands of one of Mr. Sykes's two children. Either way, things are going to change."

CHAPTER 12

Chetty Uncle would have said that it was his fate to die the way he did, but the irony didn't go unnoticed. He was alone that afternoon as he led a team of oxen to the Tongaat Sugar Mill. Behind the beasts of burden was a cart overflowing with stalks of cane ready to be milled. Nobody knew for certain what caused the older man to fall.

Some speculated that his heart might have failed while others claimed that he simply tripped and was unable to move in time. Everyone hoped, for mercy's sake, that he died before the hooves of the oxen and the wheels of that heavy cart rolled over his body.

Why? Chandu wondered to himself. *Why would the gods determine that this kind man would die such a horrible death?* This notion of everything being fated to happen started to trouble him. All he could do was hope he would meet a much kinder fate than that of so many of his fellow Hindus.

Mr. Sykes, on the other hand, managed to hang on for another six months before losing his battle with diabetes and high blood pressure.

As Chetty Uncle had all but predicted, a battle for ownership of the estate erupted between the two children. On one side was Emily Heinz, daughter of T. Everett and wife of Rupert Heinz. The Heinz family was part of a large German community that had settled in the fertile hills north of Pietermaritzburg. Besides sugarcane and maize, the Heinz's were successful in cultivating black wattle and eucalyptus trees, which made them prosperous.

On the other side was Edward Sykes, the only son and heir apparent to the T. Everett Sykes Estate. Edward was, in fact, legal heir as indicated by the will of his father. But Edward's wild lifestyle began to erode T. Everett's confidence in his son.

Edward's frequent sojourns in Johannesburg were cause for grave concern among his family, especially his ailing father. There he mixed with the seediest crowd the city had to offer. Edward's lack of interest in the affairs of the estate and his apparent lack of interest in women were enough to eventually cause T. Everett to reconsider his will. When T. Everett confronted Edward with his intention, Edward responded by simply packing up and moving to Johannesburg.

T. Everett was heartbroken that his only son had gone wayward and that the estate, which he had worked so hard to establish, might end up in the hands of a different dynasty. Sykes left his will unchanged for years in hopes that his son would return. It wasn't until his health started to deteriorate that his daughter, Emily, grew concerned over the fate of the estate. She knew as well as anybody that Edward was not fit to inherit such a responsibility. She, along with Rupert, urged T. Everett to change the will so that they would become the legal heirs. T. Everett finally agreed just days before his death. His hope of passing his estate on to his son had withered away.

When Edward learned of his father's passing, he raced back to Natal to claim his inheritance. Little did he know that his birthright had been nullified with the feeble stroke of a pen. Edward's barrister would argue that T. Everett Sykes was not of sound mind when he changed the will and that Rupert and Emily had coerced her father to alter his expressed intention. The defense would contend that Edward abrogated his responsibilities, which led T. Everett to change heirs.

Caught in the middle of this bitter feud was the Elizabeth Sykes, mother of the two litigants.

She was well aware of her husband's dilemma and could testify that he was coherent right up to his last breath, but she stopped there. She refused to bolster any argument that would effectively leave her only son without a legacy.

Mr. Cozen desperately hoped that Edward Sykes would win the estate. He was confident that if the young man were to take over the plantation, he would let him run the land as he saw fit. He might even talk the young heir into giving him a raise.

Such would not be the case if Emily's husband, Rupert, were to take over. He was a hard-nosed man who ran a tight ship. Everyone, including Mr. Cozen, would be on a short tether.

As the litigation between the two siblings languished on into its tenth month, the future of the estate became more uncertain. Large numbers of laborers had reached the end of their five-year term of indenture and left the estate. Mr. Cozen had no one to turn to but Mrs. Sykes. He explained to her that production had slowed severely with so few laborers left on the estate, but she claimed that she was powerless to do anything while the will was still in probate.

As remaining laborers were forced to work on Sundays to make up for the labor shortage, dissension among the ranks came to a boiling point.

It was a Saturday afternoon, and heavy rains forced work to a halt in the fields. The downpour was a welcome respite for the overworked laborers but did little to quell their growing disgruntlement.

Workers had only been paid pennies on the shilling for over three months, and Mr. Cozen suspected that they would not tolerate much more. In large part, he relied on Nayadu and Sirdar Govender to pacify laborers with promises of bonuses once the profits returned.

But there were other factors contributing to the dissatisfaction among the ranks. This was learned when Pradip overheard a half dozen of them colluding outside the barracks after dinner one evening.

"Moodley garu was really angry," said Pradip. "He said that this is not what he was promised back in India. Some of the other men were saying the same thing."

Nithin Moodley was one of the newer workers on the plantation. He, along with five others, was brought over just before Mr. Sykes passed away. And from the onset, it was recognized that he was a malcontent. Nayadu found him to be insufferable.

On the other hand, it was easy to see why these men might be upset. They were no different than the unsuspecting merchant who was led to believe that he would come here free to live his life as a businessman. Fate was cruel as the father and son were unwillingly bonded for five years toiling under the hot sun.

Pradip continued, "He was telling the rest of them that they should all stop working."

Nayadu sat up. "Stop working! They can't do that."

He jumped up from the mat on which he was reclining and headed for the door. He knew that these men were upset and rightfully so. But striking would only make things worse. If production on the plantation came to a halt, then the estate would never recover.

He went next door to Sirdar Govender's bungalow to let him know of the plan. Govender was none too pleased to be disturbed, but Nayadu was sure that this was important and there was no room for delay.

"So what do you want me to do?" the sirdar replied with indifference.

Nayadu was taken aback. "Shouldn't we do something to stop them?"

Govender's face scrunched up. "Who can blame these men," he said with a shrug. "They're overworked and underpaid. And so are we." Then he backed up several steps and closed the door.

But Nayadu was still convinced that production needed to continue in spite of the hardships. He knew the only way that workers would see their wages restored was to keep the estate producing sugar. He headed down the hill to see Mr. Cozen.

*****

"Moodley, huh," Mr. Cozen replied with his lip curled upward. He stroked his unshaven chin and said, "I'm going to have to sleep on this." He patted Nayadu on the shoulder. "Thanks, Naidu. Now go home and get some sleep."

*****

Nayadu awoke long before the sun rose. As was his custom, especially when he was feeling uneasy about things, he made himself some masala tea and headed down the hill to the eastern border of the estate and the wall that separated the Sykes property from the Tillman Estate. The ground was muddy from the heavy rain the day prior so Nayadu stood and leaned against the wall and pushed some betel nut into his mouth.

It was a moonless sky, and everything was still. The only sound was that of the soggy twigs crunching limply under his bare feet. He started to wonder whether he had done the right thing by going to Mr. Cozen. He felt a certain sympathy toward the plight of his kinsmen and the hardships they faced. On the other hand, he knew what trouble a strike would bring upon all the workers.

As the black sky slowly gave way to the encroaching sunlight, Nayadu made his way back to the bungalow to awake his two boys then headed straight to the fields. He saw Moodley walking to the field alongside another laborer and felt a sense of relief. As he got closer, he even heard Moodley joking and laughing. Nayadu felt confident that there would be no strike today.

At 6:00 a.m. Nayadu did a head count, and when they were all accounted for, he breathed a sigh of relief. He knew tensions were running high among the laborers but desperately hoped that the ownership issue would soon be resolved so that things would return to normal.

Mr. Cozen arrived shortly thereafter on horseback. Instead of dismounting and meeting with the sirdars, as was his custom, he sat and glared icily at the men. Nayadu knew that the estate manager was troubled by what he had revealed to him the evening prior but had no idea what he planned to do.

Nayadu's heart started to race. He wanted to grab some betel nut and shove it into his mouth, but he was too nervous to move.

Then the manager barked, "Moodley! Come here now!"

If perhaps Mr. Cozen were not straddled on top of his horse with his rifle holstered in plain sight by his side, the notorious new recruit would have resisted the manager's directive. But he didn't. Instead, he pushed his way through the men without emotion and looked Mr. Cozen straight in the eye.

"You've got a damn cheek, Moodley, stirring up my men."

Moodley shrugged his shoulders not out of disrespect but because he understood little of what Mr. Cozen said to him. The estate manager, however, had already made up his mind as to what he was going to do with his alleged troublemaker. He started to unfasten the sjambok secured onto the side of his saddle, and the workers started to murmur loudly. While Nayadu had hoped for a little diplomacy, Mr. Cozen took a different approach.

"Come here, Naidu!" Mr. Cozen yelled out.

Nayadu froze with fear. He wondered if he had somehow angered his boss.

"Now, Naidu! Don't keep me waiting."

Nayadu scurried over and stood next to Moodley. Then Mr. Cozen handed Nayadu the whip and said, "I want you to teach this fellow a lesson he won't soon forget."

Nayadu held the whip up with incredulity. He had never held one before and was astounded at how heavy it was with its thick braided leather. But more shocking was what he was expected to do with it. He could scarcely imagine inflicting harm on even the least of his Indian brothers—even if they were rabble-rousers.

He looked up at Mr. Cozen and said, "Why me, lahnee?"

The manager laughed. "Why not you, Naidu? Aren't you the one who told me of this troublemaker's plans to go on strike?"

At that moment, Nayadu could feel every eye on him. He felt betrayed by Mr. Cozen that he would be shown in front of everyone to be an informer. Shame washed over him like a midsummer rain squall. "I can't flog this man, lahnee. He's here to work this morning."

As he said this, he looked over at the condemned man. While his posture and face reflected his defiant nature, Nayadu could see the anguish in his eyes. Nayadu knew deep in his heart that this man did not deserve to be flogged. As he saw it, Moodley's only offense was that he was outspoken concerning all the injustices that were facing the Indian laborers. He, like all the rest, had already suffered enough. Working like animals in these fields with so little pay was a few steps short of hell.

Nayadu felt a surge of immense pity for the man.

"I'm not giving you a choice, Naidu. You give him ten lashes with that whip, or I'll flog both of you."

Nayadu knew by the tone of his voice that he wasn't joking. What he couldn't figure out was why he had turned on him. After all, Nayadu had saved his life. He was a hard worker and loyal to Mr. Cozen. Without speaking, Nayadu's eyes did the pleading. They implored the mercy of his boss. But Mr. Cozen sat on his saddle without expression or emotion.

Sirdar Govender stared intently, waiting to see how Nayadu would answer to the directive.

Then Nayadu remembered how Velu had so bravely chosen the whip rather than spending time in the brig during their infamous voyage aboard the *Chadwick*. Though Mrs. Wigglesworth intervened after one lash, Velu's courage had left an indelible impression on all of them.

But Nayadu knew that he didn't have that kind of courage. The thought of the rigid leather whip ripping into his flesh made his knees buckle.

He looked again over at Moodley, but this time, he avoided looking him in the eyes. He tried desperately to rid himself of the pity that he was feeling just moments earlier.

Nayadu took a deep breath. *I am a sirdar*, he reasoned to himself. *Like it or not, this is my job.*

Nayadu pointed to the ground indicating that Moodley should lie down prone on his stomach. That was the custom in which workers on the Sykes Estate were flogged. That way they couldn't move so easily.

Moodley, however, didn't move.

"On the ground, Moodley," Nayadu said in his best Tamil.

The man's eyes glared with defiance toward Nayadu and then toward Mr. Cozen. Then he turned to the workers, who stood dumbfounded.

"Are you going to let them flog me?" he yelled out. "Do I deserve this?"

The men, however, murmured among themselves.

"What's he saying?" Mr. Cozen bellowed.

Nayadu replied, "He wants these men to help him."

Mr. Cozen then pulled out his rifle and cocked the trigger. His face reddened, and he yelled at Moodley with the gun pointed squarely at him. "On the ground now, coolie!"

But Moodley only stared at him with cold insolence.

The estate manager shoved his rifle back into its holster and climbed down from his horse. Then he yanked the sjambok from Nayadu and swung it with brute force at Moodley's dark thin legs. The sheer power of the whip knocked the defiant laborer's feet out from underneath him, and he hit the ground with a resounding thud. The man didn't even have a chance to cry out in pain before Mr. Cozen landed another blow in the same spot. Moodley let out a sickening scream as blood trickled out of his wounds.

He held his hand up in resignation, but the estate manager swung once again, this time cutting him across his wrists. He bellowed out in agony as he recoiled his hand into his chest and then curled up into a fetal position.

There would be no mercy from Mr. Cozen. He determined that the source of all the growing dissension on the estate was going to be rooted out once and for all. Nobody dared to intervene as he continued to unleash a dozen more lashes upon the helpless laborer. When he was finished, he turned to the men and offered a stern warning: "The next one who wants to cause trouble around here won't have it as easy as this one."

Moodley lay whimpering like wounded animal.

"Now get to work!" Mr. Cozen snapped.

The ruthless beating that was inflicted upon Moodley had a profound effect on Nayadu. He bore an underlying sense of responsibility for the incident and wondered whether it was all worth it. To his Indian brothers, he was a traitor. As far as they were concerned, he had sold his soul to the Sahibs. And Nayadu wasn't so sure that he hadn't.

When Moodley took his own life the following week, Nayadu took it hard and didn't speak for two days. On the third day, he told Mr. Cozen that he was resigning his position as sirdar, but Mr. Cozen wouldn't hear it. He threatened to make him and his boys sleep with the horses in the barn. Because Nayadu didn't want to subject his sons to such harsh conditions, he reluctantly stayed on as sirdar.

"This is the loneliest job in the world," Nayadu would lament night after night. "How I miss your mother," he would say with sadness in his eyes.

Living on Bunglo Hill had come with a steep price: loneliness. Not only was Nayadu shunned by the Indian community but the boys as well. Chandu made himself care little about being excluded from games that others Indian boys and girls played on Sundays by reading books.

Pradip, on the other hand, befriended a warmhearted Zulu boy named Siyabonga. He was the son of Mrs. Sykes's housemaid and was fond of bouncing around the estate with hardly a stitch of clothing. And though Nayadu had little affection for the natives, he couldn't help but smile when he saw the two together. Always by their sides was an old dog that was surely older than either of them. With cataracts in both eyes, the old canine would bump into an object and then proceed to run around in a circle chasing after his tail. The senile old dog would keep them laughing for hours at a time.

At least the boy wasn't lonely, Nayadu thought to himself.

*****

It was early Sunday morning, and Nayadu was preparing to walk into town when Sirdar Govender knocked on the door. Nayadu was surprised yet pleased to have a visitor and quickly invited him in. When Nayadu offered him tea, he managed a slight smile but declined.

"Have you heard the news?" Sirdar Govender asked without hesitation.

Nayadu shrugged. "What news?"

"I overheard the lady Mrs. Sykes speaking with her daughter just yesterday. It seems that the daughter's husband is taking over the estate."

Nayadu's eyes widened with wonder. "That's good—isn't it?"

With a shrug, he replied, "He's no Mr. Sykes, but he's what the estate needs right now. I heard the daughter say that he would have this farm back in top form in no time."

"But we don't have enough workers, and the ones we have aren't getting paid," Nayadu lamented. What do you think he's going to do, Govender?"

"I don't know, but this might be your last Sunday off for a long time."

Sirdar Govender left without another word, leaving Nayadu with more questions than answers. From the top of Bunglo Hill, he could see through the trees that canopied the Sykes Estate, where Mr. Cozen was engaged in what appeared to be a serious conversation with the frail matron and her daughter. No doubt, changes were on the horizon for all who lived and worked on the estate.

His Sunday walks into town always took him alongside the palm-fringed drive and through the gilded gates. It was one of the more ostentatious estates by anyone's standard, but Nayadu paused on this occasion as he neared the area where the three were still engaged in conversation. He hid himself behind some bushes and noticed Mrs. Sykes was crying while her daughter tried to console her.

It was Edward of whom they were speaking. He died in Johannesburg from his excesses. He was known to overindulge himself in every bad habit known to man, and it didn't seem to surprise his sister. At least she didn't seem bothered by the news. She and her husband had been entangled in a battle over ownership of the estate, and it would appear now that the battle was over.

While the elderly matron patted her teary eyes, Emily turned to Mr. Cozen and said, "Mr. Heinz will be arriving from New Hanover tomorrow morning. If you expect to keep your position, Mr. Cozen, then you better start putting your coolies to work."

Nayadu recoiled at the woman's sharp renouncement and tried to make sure he wouldn't be spotted by either of them. He was determined to have his day of rest and take a stroll into Verulam's town center.

Mr. Cozen replied, "With all due respect, Mrs. Heinz, today is the first day off my workers have had off in several months. These coolies have been working hard every day, sunrise to sunset. Most haven't seen a wage in weeks."

"Well," she replied sharply, "there will be some changes around here when Mr. Heinz arrives here on the estate. You can be sure of that, Mr. Cozen."

The estate manager cleared his throat and replied, "I hope so, madam. Can I be of any more assistance to you or Mrs. Sykes?"

"No, thank you, Mr. Cozen. That will be all."

When Mr. Cozen headed back to his house and the two ladies disappeared into the manor, Nayadu made his break toward gate, which he feared might become impassable in the very near future. Sirdar Govender wasn't lying. By all appearances, Mr. Heinz was going to extract every last ounce of life from his laborers.

"Nana!" Chandu yelled as he scurried quickly toward the dirt road passing in front of the estate.

Nayadu turned and shot his son an unsympathetic glance. He quickly caught up with him and said, "I'm coming with you." Nayadu cherished his trips to Verulam alone where he could gather his thoughts, but his son's forlorn grin softened his heart. "Okay, where's your brother?" he asked.

"He must be with Siyabonga."

"Oh, we'll be back before he even misses us," he replied with a half smile.

Verulam was a bustling little town that had two hotels, three churches, and several dozen Indian-owned markets. A small temple had also been recently built just outside the town center. Nayadu liked to believe that it was his request to Mr. Sykes years earlier for a place to worship their gods that initiated the structure.

Whether true or not, Nayadu was glad to have a place to go that bore some resemblance to home and would often spend hours outside the temple just talking.

He was careful not to tell others of his station. Sirdars were largely looked down upon by Indians as quislings.

As the two of them passed through town center where merchants busied themselves selling produce and various sundries, Chandu was struck by a familiar face. The fair skin, large hooked nose, and undersized bifocals were unmistakable. He had hardly changed over the last three years. With unbridled excitement, he darted over to their old friend from the *Chadwick* who was shopping for vegetables and exclaimed, "Siva garu!"

He didn't immediately recognize Chandu until Nayadu walked up, and then a broad smile stretched across his face. "Nayadu!" he exclaimed. "And you must be the older boy."

"That's right," he replied eagerly. "I'm Chandu."

"Chandu, of course," he said pensively. "And where is the younger one and his mother?"

Nayadu quickly replied, "My younger one, Pradip, stayed back. He likes to play with other boys when we're not working."

"Ah," he said, smiling, "If we could only bottle the vigor that comes with youth." Then his face turned serious. "And your wife?"

Nayadu lowered his head. More than two years had gone by, and he still found it difficult to speak of his wife's passing.

"Amma died, garu," Chandu answered.

"Oh," he replied somberly. "I'm sorry to hear that."

Nayadu cleared his throat. "What about you, Siva garu? We thought you—uh—"

"Died?" he replied with a wry smile.

"Uh—yes."

"Nearly did"—he grinned—"but I survived."

"We really missed you," said Nayadu.

"Thank you, friend—you're kind," he replied while paying the merchant for some brinjals and tomatoes.

"And, uh, how's your friend, the one who talks big?" Siva asked.

"Hah, Velu—don't know—oh, we miss them too."

Siva grinned. "I'm sure he bought a big farm somewhere."

"You think?"

Siva just smiled. "And you? What are you doing here in the colony?"

"I'm a sirdar on the Sykes Estate."

"Sirdar? How did you become a sirdar so quickly?"

He hesitated before replying, "Just liked by the lahnees over there."

"Well, what's not to like, Nayadu?"

"And your family?" Nayadu asked.

"Back in Bangalore. My girls are getting big."

"Thought you were finished with crossing the Kala Pani."

Siva chuckled, "You have a good memory."

"You said you missed your family."

"Terribly. But it was working under that rogue, Mr. Pickles, that really made me homesick."

Nayadu shook his head side to side. "He was a very bad man."

Chandu blurted out, "Did they find who killed Mr. Pickles?"

He reached over and tousled his hair. "Don't believe they did. I was one of their suspects, but they never had any evidence against me."

It was all Chandu could do to keep himself from telling the little secret that he had been sitting on for so long. He wondered if there would be any harm in finally telling his secret—that he and his friend, Imran, found Mr. Pickles breathing his last breath. But the more he thought about it, the more it seemed to be a bad idea.

"So why did you come back?" asked Nayadu

"When I returned home to my family I was unable to find work. I eventually left to find work in Bombay. It was there that I met Govindas Mahendhi, a young Gujarati barrister who'd been hired to defend a wealthy Muslim here in the colony. He told me of his plans to come here and asked if I would join him."

"How will you manage without your wife and children?"

"Oh—I'll either send for them or I'll go home—it depends."

"On what?" Chandu asked.

He smiled. "Mr. Mahendhi."

CHAPTER 13

Mohammed Deedad was a wealthy Muslim merchant who had been in the colony for thirty-five years. He and his brother, Aziz, started a family business by importing various goods and fabrics from Bombay and his native province of Gujarat. Eventually, they opened a number of retail businesses in close proximity to the large mosque on Grey Street, which was a short distance from Natal Harbor.

As his wealth grew, so did the attention of the district tax collector. With a little probing, the collector discovered that the businessman had not been paying all his taxes. Mr. Deedad was arrested and jailed. As a Muslim, he had little hope of defending the charges against him with European counsel. When his brother-in-law back in Bombay alerted him of a young firebrand Hindu lawyer who had won some impressive judgments, he had him make the young lawyer an offer he couldn't refuse.

As a barrister, Govindas Mahendhi never dreamed of traveling over four thousand miles to represent a client, especially a Muslim. There was little love lost between Hindus and Muslims in the small village of Dasnagar where Mahendhi grew up. Tensions had existed between the two groups from the time the Mughals had swept through India several centuries earlier, conquering the Hindus and destroying many of their temples. It was only after the British had moved into India that Muslims and Hindus found common ground in their fight against British rule.

But Mahendhi wasn't altogether opposed to the British. A long-standing fascination with the British monarchy and their customs inspired him to pursue his higher education in London. It was there that he not only earned his law degree with honors but refined his English skills and acquired a taste for fine clothing.

Though he had already started to make a name for himself as a skilled and tenacious lawyer, he believed Bombay to be a jungle full of lawyers all clawing for clients and success. He was sure that lawyers would be the ruin of Bombay and the thought of it left him sleepless at night. When Habib Mansouri, Deedad's brother-in-law informed him that this burgeoning colony in the Natal province of South Africa was desperately in need of Indian barristers he knew that he was supposed to go.

His initial meeting with Sivasambarao had been brief and hurried but the timing was kismet. He was optimistic about his new associate who had departed for Natal a week earlier and that everything was coming together.

*****

Rupert Heinz was a second-generation German whose parents had come to Natal in 1843. They were enticed to leave their homeland in the Kingdom of Hanover in Germany in an effort to help settle the newly British annexed colony. Originally, they settled in Port Natal, which would later be renamed Durban. They attempted to grow cotton but when this failed, they uprooted and moved inland to Pietermaritzburg. The Heinzes didn't stay long, however. They along with the Küsel family pioneered north and settled in an area they would call New Hanover.

Both families became prosperous farming sugarcane and maize. The Heinzes, however, foresaw the need for wood in this new colony and started growing black wattle and eucalyptus trees and this made them wealthy.

Of the three Heinz brothers, Rupert was the oldest and most driven. Some would argue that he was also the handsomest of the three. He was reasonably tall with blond hair and piercing blue eyes. He also spoke four languages: German, Afrikaans, English, and Zulu. But perhaps what defined him most was his no nonsense way of doing business. He and his brothers had developed a reputation in the colony for keeping their workers on a short leash within the law and sometimes outside of the law. They had little tolerance for laziness or sham sickness, and laborers on the Heinz farm came to know that hard and fast.

Mr. Cozen sat across Mr. Heinz in the same leather chair he had sat in so many times before. This time the man sitting behind the desk was much younger—even younger than himself. And the room was filled with the smoke of burning tobacco, something Mr. Sykes would have never permitted.

Mr. Heinz put his cigar down in the ashtray and smiled. "Mr. Cozen, I don't blame you for the situation in which this estate has landed. I realize that there were and continue to be circumstances that you have no control over. We've faced similar circumstances in New Hanover. As this colony grows, there is more demand for Indian labor. All the while, very few, if any, renew their contracts. So we're faced with a dilemma."

He took another pull from his cigar. "And I know that you've been unable to purchase more laborers while control of the estate was being contested."

Mr. Cozen nodded slowly.

"Well, first thing we're going to do is pay these coolies all they're due. That will bring back some morale. I'm even willing to throw each coolie an extra shilling as a consolation. That should boost their productivity."

Mr. Cozen nodded. "They will be very happy."

Mr. Heinz let out a sigh. "Next thing is to get more laborers. There isn't another ship coming in till next week. But we'll both be there to see what we can get. In the meantime, I've been thinking about bringing some of my *Kaffirs* over from New Hanover."

He paused and lowered his head while maintaining eye contact. "Ever work with our beloved Zulus Mr. Cozen?"

"No and don't care to Mr. Heinz. Can't imagine they make good workers."

"They're all we had till the Indians started to arrive. You're right though. They aren't the best of workers, but they'll work. You just have to push them. You and your sirdars will have to get used to them."

*****

The SS *Punjab* sailed out of Bombay and arrived in Durban with mostly Indian merchants and copious amounts of goods and spices. Mr. Mahendhi was among the passengers, and Siva was there to greet him.

The enthusiastic barrister called out to his new associate as soon as he caught sight of him. "Siva!" He descended quickly down the gangway with a bag in each hand and promptly dropped them when he stepped onto the wharf. "He extended his arms wide to hug his new colleague as if they were long lost friends. "I've been looking forward to this moment for weeks. I can't tell you how glad I am to be here."

Though Siva found the gesture awkward, he obliged his new boss with a quick hug and replied, "The feeling is mutual, sir. May I take your bags for you?"

The barrister replied, "Under one condition—that you now call me Govindas. I consider you a colleague, my friend, so let's not be so formal."

Siva pursed his lips and said, "Very well—Govindas." He grabbed both bags and led the way while the barrister followed.

"Were you able to purchase a buggy?"

"Right there in front of you," Siva said, pointing toward the mud-covered, two-wheeled carriage. "Please excuse the mud. It did rain last night. But I believe you'll be pleased with way she glides over these roads."

"I'm sure it will be fine, my friend." Then he glanced over at the horse and his expression changed. "But I'm not so sure about her."

Siva shook his head side to side. "This old mare was all I could find, sir. But the owner assured me that she had a lot of good years left in her."

The barrister chuckled. "As long as she gets us home." With just enough room for Mr. Mahendhi's bags on the floor panel in front of their feet, they were quickly on their way. "Speaking of home," he said, settling into the cushioned leather, "where are you taking me?"

"To our office, of course."

"And where is this office of ours, may I ask?"

"Well," he said hesitantly, "it's in Phoenix."

The barrister's brows raised into his forehead. "Not in Durban?"

"I couldn't afford an office in Durban after purchasing this horse and carriage. The horse was fifty shillings and…"

"Fifty shillings for that old mare," the barrister interrupted.

"It was her or nothing," Siva rebutted. "But I believe I got a good price on this buggy at thirty shillings."

"It seems that I underestimated your start-up costs. Not to worry, we'll make the best of whatever you found for us."

Siva smiled. "I'm glad you feel that way, sir. We have a little bit of a journey ahead of us."

"And what about my accommodations?"

"You'll be staying with me, of course. That is until you find a place to your liking."

It was several hours later that the tired old horse turned off North Coast Road and onto Stonebridge Street. The barrister had fallen asleep along the way, and Siva didn't wake him till they reached the office which sat on the corner of Stonebridge and Southgate Street.

Siva nudged the barrister out of his slumber. "We're here, Govindas."

The barrister sat up and looked around bewildered at the various shops and markets that lined the dirt road. Everywhere he turned he saw Indians staring curiously at him and Siva. He quickly turned to Siva with widened eyes. "Are we back in India?" he asked half seriously.

Siva let out an uncharacteristic chuckle. "This is Phoenix… or Little India, as I've heard it called. And this," he said, gesturing toward a small stand-alone brick building with a large window, "is our new office." It was far and above the nicest building on the street, but that wasn't saying much. Most of the hovels lining the road were put together with wood and corrugated metal.

Siva had hoped that his new boss would like the new office that he had worked so hard to find. But the look of incredulity still pasted on the barrister's face said it all. "You don't like it," Siva said with a noticeable lilt of disappointment.

The barrister smiled disingenuously and furrowed his brows. "It's just not what I envisioned for us, my friend. But," he said, quickly jumping down from the buggy, "it will have to do for now."

The front room was large enough and that was where Siva situated his desk. An adjacent smaller room that had a door for privacy was where he put the barrister's desk. It was sparse yet clean and organized.

"Well, how do you like it?" Siva asked again, hoping his boss had a renewed perspective.

He smiled out of the side of his mouth. "It'll do, my friend. Shall we go? I should like to get some rest before I start in on this Deedad case tomorrow. I expect that we will have to travel back to Durban to speak with my client."

As they were about to leave, the barrister glanced down at the newspaper sitting on Siva's desk and glimpsed the headline. "What's this?" he asked, picking up the paper for a closer look. He read slowly:

Coolies Claim Bait and Switch

"Interesting," said the barrister as he read further. "Listen to this, '*The Protector of Indian Immigrants has filed complaints with the governor. The Protector claims that coolies are being brought into the colony under false pretenses.*' The article goes on to say, '*Recruiters in the coolies' native country of India use whatever means necessary to coerce naive immigrants, often lying about conditions, pay and job position that will be waiting for them. Many immigrants are stunned and dismayed to find out that they have unwittingly become part of a bonded labor system with all their freedoms stripped away.*'

"Listen to this, my friend," he continued, "'*the last several years have seen alarmingly high rates of depression and suicide among coolie immigrants leading to demands for immigration reform.*' Immigration reform," the barrister scoffed. This indentured labor system sounds like it's one degree short of slavery."

"Yes, I'm surprised they printed the story in the paper," said Siva. "But this isn't news. This has been happening for many years now."

"They're mocking this whole situation, my friend. These Europeans obviously don't believe that Indians are British subjects and entitled to the same rights. These deceptive practices are an affront—even to the least of Her Majesty's subjects. Where's my quill?"

*****

Over the next several months, the barrister would send out a barrage of editorials lambasting the indentured labor system. He sent letters to the local *Natal Times* and overseas to the *London Times*. Often pointed and sometimes satirical, he argued repeatedly that the British had effectively traded in one form of slavery and replaced it with another.

The barrister's opinions on the matter proved him to be wise beyond his years but did nothing to turn the tide in favor of the immigrants. Not until fellow countryman and former classmate Lal Chandra caught sight of his editorials in the *London Times*. Chandra, a London resident, held a high position in the British Embassy and hobnobbed with the likes of England's Viceroy, Lord Hildebrand. Chandra convinced the Viceroy that Great Britain needed to court the public's unfavorable opinion on slavery or any institution that even resembled slavery. Lord Hildebrand conceded and promised to suspend the indentured labor system until its imperfections could be modified. But the barrister's grievances were heard around the world and pressure mounted until a law was finally legislated from Great Britain barring the familiar practice of recruiting unsuspecting Indians into a five-year term of servitude.

The ruling didn't win the barrister any friends among the European community in Natal, especially those who depended on Indian labor. Mahendhi had effectively become a thorn in the sides of estate owners across the Natal province. The young barrister could have never guessed that his taunts would awaken a goliath.

*****

"Excuse me, Cozen," said Mr. Heinz. His was tone irritable. "Have you heard the news?"

"About what—no more coolies?

"Yeah, I want to know who this Mahendhi fellow is—and where he came from."

"Back to work you two," Cozen said to Nayadu and Sirdar Govender. He and Mr. Heinz started walking back up to the house. "I've heard that this Mahendhi chap is a coolie lawyer who recently arrived here from India."

"What else do you know about him?" asked Mr. Heinz.

Mr. Cozen paused. "Not much. I did hear that he has a small office in Phoenix."

"See what else you can find out about him, Cozen. We don't need troublemakers like him in our colony."

"What are you thinking, boss?"

"I'm thinking we can't survive without new labor. These coolies don't stick around after their term is up. They either go back to India, or they go and start their own business."

"Yeah, in a few years there'll be no more laborers to work the fields."

"Well, I have an idea, Cozen."

"What is it, boss?"

"They may have severed a major artery, but we can still keep this beast alive."

"You have a way of getting more coolies?"

"I believe I do, Cozen. We send one of our own to go back and round some up."

Mr. Cozen scratched his head in confusion. "One of our coolies?" he replied.

"Yeah, we send one whom we can trust will go and convince others to come back with him. We offer him an incentive for every coolie he recruits."

The men stopped walking once they reached the shade of one on the many jacaranda trees surrounding the manor. "The question is," Mr. Heinz continued, "who can we trust with this kind of job?"

Mr. Cozen tugged on his moustache as contemplated. "I can't think of any coolies I would trust with such a job. Not one is likely to ever come back."

"What about that new sirdar? Is it Naidu?"

Mr. Cozen nodded. "Yeah, I suppose out of all our workers he would be…but he still might not come back."

"He will if we keep his boys here with us," Mr. Heinz replied with a sly grin.

"He would never leave his boys behind, boss. They're all he has."

"Bring him up to my office," Mr. Heinz ordered. "We'll see if we can't entice our loyal Sirdar."

*****

Cozen escorted Nayadu up to the office where Mr. Heinz awaited the two men, reclining in his desk chair and puffing on his favorite tobacco pipe.

"Come in, Naidu, and have a seat," said Mr. Heinz, pointing to a nearby chair.

Nayadu smiled tentatively, unsure of why he had been summoned to the big boss's office. He sank into the cushioning under the soft leather, and a smile swept across his face. He bounced up and down several times.

"You like that chair, huh, Naidu?"

Nayadu nodded and smiled. "Very nice, lahnee."

Mr. Heinz exhaled, sending a plume of thick, hazy smoke into the light fixture hanging in the center of the room. "Naidu, Mr. Cozen here says you're the best worker we got here on this plantation. I just want to tell you how happy I am to hear that."

"Thank you, lahnee."

"Mr. Cozen here says you're the best we got, so I want to give you an opportunity to make a lot of money."

Nayadu's eyebrows rose.

"Are you interested, Naidu?"

"Yes, lahnee."

"Good—well, here's the plan. We're going to send you to your native place so you can bring back workers like yourself to come work for us."

Nayadu paused for a moment and then replied, "How can I do this, lahnee?"

"We'll put you on a steamer so that you can go back to your family and your friends and anyone else who you know and let them know what kind of money can be earned here in Natal." Nayadu still hadn't grown accustomed to Mr. Heinz's German accent and strained to understand him. "Here's the good part, Naidu. I'll pay you one shilling—wait, make it two shillings and six pence for every coolie you're able to get work on this estate. And I'll pay you one shilling per month for every worker until his indenture expires. But," he said, pointing his finger at Nayadu, "you need to bring back no less than fifty workers."

"Fifteen workers?" asked Nayadu.

"Fifty! Five zero."

Nayadu started adding the numbers in his head and realized that he could become a very rich man if only he could convince fifty villagers to immigrate. Then he thought some more.

"How do I tell a villager that he can earn good money here?"

Mr. Heinz abruptly stood up from behind his desk and said, "I plan to pay you coolies well once we get the production levels back where they should be. Take my word for it."

"Sounds good, lahnee, but what about my boys?"

"How old are your boys now?"

"Chandu's fourteen and Pradip's eleven."

"They're practically men, Naidu. Can't you leave them in ' care of another family until you return?"

"I should like them to come with me, lahnee."

"Well, Naidu, I can't afford to send all of you. Besides, I need their hands here on the plantation."

Disappointment swept across Nayadu's face. He had no words.

Mr. Cozen interjected, "Listen, Naidu, I know you will miss your boys, but the money you'll make will be well worth the sacrifice."

Nayadu's eyes darted back and forth between the two men. He didn't want to disappoint either of his bosses, but the thought of leaving his boys weighed heavy on him. He took a deep breath and exhaled. "Okay, I'll go and get more workers from my native place."

Mr. Heinz looked over at his underling, Mr. Cozen, and smiled wryly. "You've made a smart decision, Naidu. We'll start making arrangements for your passage to India."

*****

Late that afternoon, Nayadu sat his two boys down and explained to them what Mr. Heinz had offered. He assured them that the last thing he wanted to do was leave them but that a lot of money was at stake.

"I want to go with you, Nana," said Pradip.

Nayadu smiled sadly. "You boys have to stay."

"How can you leave us?" he said, fighting back tears. "You're all we have left!"

"Pradip, Nana's just trying to earn enough money so he can buy us our own farm," Chandu said, unsure whether that was their father's true motive. He wondered, deep down, whether he agreed to ` out of blind loyalty to these lahnees.

"But what if he doesn't come back?"

will come back," said Nayadu.

where will we stay while you're gone?" Pradip asked.

" said Nayadu, pulling on the thin, straggling whiskers `s chin, "maybe you can stay with the Chetty Aunty."

`adip.

`ellowed. "I don't want to go back to those

`aid Nayadu.

Just then there was a loud knock on the door. On the other side was Mr. Cozen with timely news: "Naidu, I've arranged for your boys to stay with Sirdar Govender."

Nayadu's eyes widened. "Uh, lahnee, Sirdar Govender doesn't like my boys. I'm afraid—"

"Nonsense, Naidu! He told me he would be glad to keep them while you're gone."

*****

That evening the boys lay awake, deeply troubled they would be staying with Sirdar Govendar. They both begged their father to let them stay with Chetty Aunty, but Nayadu wasn't going to go against what his boss had already ordained.

"Who do you think is meaner," Pradip asked, "the Zamindar or Sirdar Govender?"

"The Zamindar wanted to kill us, Pradip. I don't think Sirdar Govender wants to kill us."

"But he doesn't like us, Chandu."

"Why do you say that?"

"I can feel it."

"We'll make him like us."

"But why doesn't he and his wife have any children?"

"I don't know. Maybe they don't want any."

"I thought everybody was supposed to have children when they get married."

"Who told you that?"

"Nobody."

"It's not true. Now let's go to sleep."

"Maybe the wife is cursed."

"Go to sleep, Pradip."

*****

"Show respect for Sirdar Govender while I'm gone," said Nay as he loaded his satchel onto the back of the cart.

"When are you coming back, Nana?" Pradip whined, tugging mercilessly on his father's brand-new pressed white shirt. Mr. Heinz had purchased new clothes for Nayadu's recruiting mission and he looked smart.

"Leave him be," Chandu scolded.

Pradip didn't relent, "Are you gonna see Ammamma and Thathiyya, Nana?"

"I don't know, boy, but I'll bring you something back with me, okay?"

"What are you gonna bring?"

"Let's go, Naidu!" Cozen yelled from the driver's seat of the cart. "We need to move, man."

Nayadu hugged them tight before jumping onto the back of the cart while Pradip wept until they were well out of sight.

*****

"You'll sleep here," said Sirdar Govender, pointing to an empty space of floor in the corner.

"But Nana let us sleep in our own beds in our—" Chandu quickly wrapped his arm around Pradip's neck and cupped his hand over his mouth.

"I'm not your Nana, am I?" Govender snapped. "You're going to live by my rules while staying here. I have many chores for you every day," he said. "You don't work, you don't eat."

"Uh, excuse me, Sirdar Govender," Chandu interrupted. "When 're we supposed to do these chores?"

"When you're done in the fields," he snapped. "If you're going 'nder my roof and eat my food, you're going to work!"

'vas too scared to say another word. Pradip whispered into still wanna stay here?"

*****

lar Govender walked outside to find the two 'n between chores. He pointed to a stain on one of his shirts, dark red—possibly a bloodstain. In a very cross tone, he demanded to know why the stain had not been removed.

"We did our best, garu. This spot cannot come off your shirt," Chandu replied.

"This is not your best! Otherwise, this spot would not be here!" Pradip jumped up. "This was our best!"

The sirdar threw the shirt at Pradip, grazing his head and landing behind him.

"Clean it again!"

Pradip picked up the shirt and threw it back at Govender. "Clean it yourself!"

Chandu's heart started beating rapidly, and his mouth went dry. He knew that Pradip had crossed the line. The sirdar reached over and grabbed Pradip by his ear and dragged him into the bungalow. His brother stood, watching in terror Pradip wailed in utter helplessness. As the door of the bungalow slammed behind them, Chandu heard him crying out his name. A sudden sensation of guilt coursed through his veins.

He questioned whether he should have tried rescuing him from the clutches of the sirdar. Then he visualized himself jumping on the man's back, choking him with one skinny arm and gouging his eyes out with the other. Guilt turned to trepidation as he began to fear for Pradip's safety. He ran to the door, but it was locked. Inside he could hear each thwack of the rubber sjambok against his brother's body. Pradip wailed.

*****

From that point, the two boys plotted their escape. Though it was no small decision, they believed that staying was more dangerous than leaving.

"But where are we gonna go, Chandu?"

"I don't know—anywhere away from here."

"I know," said Pradip, his eyes wide as saucers, "let's go back to India and find Nana."

"We can't go to India," he replied dismissively.

"Then where?"

He pondered momentarily but knew of nowhere. Pradip could sense his uncertainty. He lowered his head and said, "Maybe we shouldn't go."

Chandu looked at his little brother's sad face and suddenly felt an overwhelming sense of responsibility for his well-being. "Pull your shirt up." Pradip lifted his shirt, revealing the dark bruises Govender had inflicted. "We're going tonight—after everyone's asleep."

"But where are we going?"

"I don't know."

*****

It seemed natural that they would gravitate toward town. There they would easily blend in with the throngs of people engaged in commerce. For two days they managed to exist on the fringe of activity without so much as being questioned. They snatched fruit and nuts from unsuspecting vendors along the way and slept under the stars. Their experience on the ship, slinking around undetected served them well, but they knew they wouldn't survive long under such conditions.

By the third day, their luck turned around when they spotted Siva walking through Verulam's town center. He was as surprised to see them as they were happy to see him.

"What are you boys doing here alone—where's your father?"

"He's gone back home to bring back more workers. We were staying with another sirdar who was beating Pradip. See, look here!" Chandu said, showing him the marks that covered Pradip's body. "We ran away three days ago."

"Should we get a doctor for you?" he asked Pradip.

"No," he replied awkwardly.

"So where've you been staying?" asked Siva.

"Nowhere," Chandu replied. "We've been sleeping over there behind that empty building. We've eaten only some fruit that was given to us by some kind store owners."

"Well, what should I do with you?"

"I don't know, Siva garu, but please don't make us go back to the estate," he pleaded.

Siva drew a slow deep breath, staring intently at Pradip and then Chandu. "Very well, come along with me. I know who may be able to help you."

CHAPTER 14

"Aahhh!" Pradip exclaimed as they ascended the steps leading up to the weathered yet stately house. "Is this our new home?"

Before Siva could answer, the barrister appeared, standing with open arms on his verandah. "Welcome, my friends. Welcome to my new home."

The double-storied house bore resemblance to the Sykes Manor with its portal windows and patterned shingles, but the similarities ended there. The once elegant dwelling and former residence of Ira and Emma de Villiers had long ago relinquished its dignity to time and neglect. With no legal heirs, the grand house, along with its several guesthouses and maid's quarters, had become a ward of the municipality. While most Europeans would have been happy to allow the empty abode to continue decaying into eventual demolition, the barrister saw the old house's potential and recognized it as an avenue into White society.

"Well, who do we have here, my friend?" the barrister asked Siva.

"This is Chandu and his brother, Pradip," said Siva, nudging the two boys up the creaking stairs. "They have nowhere to sleep."

The barrister shot a bemused look over the top of his bifocals.

"I know the boys and their father," he said, resting a hand on each of their shoulders. "I was purser on the voyage that brought them here some four or five years ago."

"They look like they haven't eaten in days," said the barrister. "So where's the father now?"

"Back in India recruiting laborers for the Sykes plantation. They're Telugu, but this one speaks English," Siva said, tousling Chandu's hair.

"Speaks English, does he," the barrister replied with raised eyebrows. He smiled and gestured them toward the door. "Welcome, boys, to Villa Pravina. I named the house after my wife, who is back in Gujarat with my three boys."

Except for the gold chandelier hanging from the frescoed ceiling, was an interior that was dark and brooding. A magnificent wooden stairway with worn, wooden steps, and dust covered balustrade ascended into the shadowy upper reaches of the manor. Covered furniture was pushed up against walls lined with blackish, graying wallpaper ornamented with fleur-de-lis.

"Yes, she needs some work," he said, glancing around as if he knew what everyone was thinking. "Mrs. Mahendhi would have wanted me to wait till I had the place cleaned up before attaching her name to it," he grinned widely, "but she's not here."

To the right through French-styled doors was a parlor where rows of shelves filled with leather bound books reached to the ceiling. Chandu was awestruck.

"Boys, why don't we get you cleaned up and fed before we—"

"You like to read, Mahendhi garu?" Chandu asked.

He smiled. "Call me *Mr.* Mahendhi, my young inquisitor. And yes, I love to read, but these," he said, gesturing at the vast array of books, "came with the house. What about you, my little friend, do you like to read?"

"Yes, Mr. Mahendhi, I love to read."

"Well, I have everything here—English literature, Hindu philosophy, Tolstoy—"

"You have Tolstoy?" asked Siva.

"Yes, but I haven't read any of his writings yet."

"The man's brilliant," said Siva as he browsed through the book titles, "especially his religious works. Brilliant how he combines the moral teachings of Jesus with the asceticism we find in our religion."

"Well, I have read quite a bit of the Christian Bible. There's definitely a lot of virtue to be found in Jesus's teachings," said the barrister. "But I don't believe that he's the only way to heaven. I tend to believe we're all on different trains heading to the same station."

"Oh, I agree," said Siva, pulling out one of Tolstoy's books: *The Teachings of Jesus.* "But this Jesus *was* the quintessential pacifist. If only the whole world could get ahold of his teachings, there'd be untold peace throughout the earth."

The barrister turned toward Chandu, smiling. "What do you think, my young friend, do you think Jesus was the 'quintessential pacifist'?"

His brows instinctively narrowed toward my nose. "What's a 'quintessential pacifist'?"

"The peacemaker of peacemakers," Siva answered.

Chandu knew nothing about Jesus except what he heard from his father. "Isn't this Jesus the White man's god?"

Siva and the barrister looked at each other not knowing exactly how to answer the question, so he continued, "If this Jesus is such a 'peacemaker,' then why do all these Whites who worship him make so much war?"

The barrister laughed. "Hey, this young man has a point. Maybe we should hire him to work in the firm."

Siva changed the subject, "More importantly, what are we going to do with these boys right now?" I didn't tell you that the younger one was beaten quite severely by one of the sirdars on the Sykes Estate, where they've been living. That's why they ran away."

"Tomorrow we can bring them to the Protector of Indian Immigrants. If we're lucky, they'll bring a case against the estate."

"But I don't think these boys can go back, Govindas. It's too dangerous."

"Are you willing to take them in?"

"Well, sure, I can take them. There's room at my place."

"Very well, we'll petition for custody. But when did you say the father is coming back?"

"I don't know."

"You said he's in India recruiting laborers for the estate?"

"That's what the boys told me."

The barrister snickered. "These Whites have already found a loophole in the new ordinance barring labor recruitment. They're using laborers to—"

"Sirdars."

"Oh, the father's a sirdar. Okay, they're using sirdars to go back and recruit more unsuspecting Indians into indentured slavery."

*****

The two boys sat anxiously behind the barrister and Mr. Thomason, Protector of Indian Immigrants, waiting for the magistrate to emerge from his chambers. Across the aisle was Mr. Heinz and Mr. Cozen. After several tense minutes of silence, Mr. Heinz looked over, directing his stare toward the barrister. "So you're the coolie lawyer who's making trouble for us farmers."

Mr. Thomason whispered into the barrister's ear, "Best just to ignore him, Mahendhi."

The estate owner continued, "Hey, you think you're so smart wearing that fancy suit. You're still a—"

Just then the magistrate entered, and the courtroom went silent. He sat down, looked over his brief of the case, and then looked down at the plaintiff. "You again, Mr. Heinz," he said.

"It was one of my sirdars, Your Honor. He was beating on one of his own."

"Then what are you doing here?"

"The protectorate wants to take these two coolie boys away from me," he said, pointing to the two boys. "Their family is still under legal contract, Your Honor."

The barrister stood up. "Your Honor, if I may."

"Who are you?" asked the magistrate.

"Govindas Mahendhi, Esquire."

"Esquire? I've heard of you, Mahendhi."

"Thank you, Your Honor."

"Sit down! I want to hear from Mr. Thomason."

The protectorate rose slowly and cleared his throat. "Your Honor, I think you know Mr. Heinz's record concerning laborers.

I have here behind me, Pradip Nayadu. The young lad was savagely beaten by one of Mr. Heinz's sirdars without cause, leaving him badly injured. I believe it would be irresponsible of the court to send either of these boys back into the custody of these men."

"I would like to know where the boy's parents are," said the magistrate.

"Apparently the boys' mother is dead while the father is back in India on some sort of recruiting mission," said Mr. Thomason.

"Recruiting mission! What is he recruiting?" asked the magistrate.

"I'll let Mr. Heinz speak for himself, Your Honor."

"What is the boys' father recruiting, Mr. Heinz?"

"Your Honor, the father isn't recruiting anybody. He's gone back to his native country to tell some of his friends and family about prospects here on my estate, that's all."

The magistrate shook his head side to side. "Does the young boy in question speak English?"

"Uh, very little, Your Honor."

"Do you have a guardian in mind for these boys, Mr. Thomason?"

"Yes, Your Honor. Mr. Mahendhi's associate, Sivasambarao."

"Very well. If you believe he is willing and able, then I'll award custody of these boys over to Simbasa...uh, Mr. Mahendhi's associate."

Mr. Heinz's anger flared. He stood up and bellowed, "If it wasn't for that coolie lawyer sitting over there, these two boys would still have their father here with them." He pointed his finger at Mr. Mahendhi. "He's the one causing all the problems around here."

"I understand, Mr. Heinz. Now, sit down. We're adjourned."

*****

Though the skies unleashed torrents of rain in the hours following the magistrate's ruling, it would have been impossible to dampen the spirits of the two boys. Siva was waiting for them on the steps outside the courthouse, and by the smiles on their faces, he knew the outcome.

"They're all yours, my esteemed colleague," said the barrister.

"Congratulations, boys," said Siva, holding out his umbrella over the two of them, "you no longer have anything to fear."

"But you might," Mr. Thomason said to Mr. Mahendhi. "I'd watch your back if I was you."

The barrister, who was diminutive in size only, looked up at the protectorate. His bifocals were hanging low on his nose. "It looks like I've made a few enemies taking a stand for my oppressed brothers and sisters."

"Your actions have put a lot of livelihoods at stake. Don't get me wrong, Mr. Mahendhi, I support what you've done, bringing so much attention to the problems inherent in this bonded labor system. I've seen more abuses over the years than I care to remember. I just hope you don't become the sacrificial lamb for this cause."

"I have faith in the justice system, Mr. Thomason. But thank you for your concern. I'll certainly stay vigilant."

Mr. Thomason headed off to his carriage, and Siva walked up to the barrister, took his hand, and said, "Congratulations, yet another victory."

"I did nothing, really. The circumstances spoke for themselves. Let's bring these boys to their new home, and you can drop me off at the office on the way."

"You seem troubled, Govindas. Anything wrong?"

The rain let up, giving the barrister an opportunity to deflect the question. "Let's go," he said, leading the way to his carriage.

"Concerned about what Mr. Thomason said?" Siva asked.

With his hand, the barrister swiped the rain droplets that had managed to slip through the carriage canopy and settle on the leather seat. "Well, I certainly don't take his admonition without consideration, my friend, but it was the boys I was thinking about. I'm concerned that we may have cut them off from their father."

"How so?"

"The father is still under employ of this Mr. Heinz, but the boys, as well as us, are now estranged from the estate."

"Oh, I see what you mean. We may have just complicated things for this family."

*****

While Villa Pravina sat high on a lonely hilltop in Sydenham, Siva lived modestly in a rented three-bedroom house in Phoenix not far from the law office. Three bedrooms were more than he needed but he anticipated that his wife and three daughters would join him if things worked out in the colony. And while Sydenham was a quiet and clean Durban suburb with its mostly White residents, Phoenix had already become the most densely populated Indian settlement outside of the Indian subcontinent.

By 1894, there were already more than forty thousand Indians in Natal compared to a mere five thousand just fifteen years earlier. The Indian population was quickly catching up with the Whites, who numbered around fifty thousand, and the Whites were getting nervous. It wasn't the bonded Indian laborers that worried the Whites so much as it was the growing influx of Indian merchants and laborers who were choosing to stay in the colony after their term of indenture.

Believing that the Indians would eventually outnumber them, the European community responded by proposing the Disenfranchise Act. The desired outcome, of course, was to denude every Indian of every right due him or her as British subjects. This only served to fuel the barrister's mission to bring equity to his adopted brothers and sisters.

Lord Falmouth, governor of Natal Province, was all too familiar with the barrister's ability to find a sympathetic audience and quickly summonsed him into a private meeting.

Barely over five feet in height, Lord Falmouth's stature belied his status and determination to see that Natal would become one of Great Britain's most prized colonies. He had little patience for anything or anyone who stood in the way of that objective, and it was well understood that Lord Falmouth harbored nothing but absolute contempt for the Indians.

"You've been rather forthright with your opinions of how we govern our colony, Mr. Mahendhi," said Lord Falmouth. "I thought it best that we transcend the growing war with words and see if we can't learn to understand each other. I know that your people are disappointed with the proposed Disenfranchise Act, Mr. Mahendhi. It's most unfortunate." The governor paced slowly and with precision the length of his desk and back. "But you must understand something," his voice grew louder. "We are cultivating a colony here in Natal that is befitting of her Majesty the Queen. We cannot let the growing population of your people continue without putting controls into place."

Mr. Mahendhi responded calmly, "I have nothing but respect for Her Majesty, Your Lordship. But we are all British subjects and entitled to be treated as such. Is not this act to disenfranchise us Indians nothing more than a disguised attempt to rid the colony of us Indians?"

"Mr. Mahendhi," said Lord Falmouth with an unctuous smile, "do your people really care so much about having franchise here in the colony? You people have no history of voting, so why do you want to start now."

"You're right about one thing, Your Lordship. Our people don't know what it is to vote. They are simple in their ways. But it's not about voting, Your Excellency, it's about being afforded the rights due us as British subjects. We are being discriminated against because of our race."

"Well, we have afforded franchise to your people. Those who are able to pay the ten-pound poll tax just like everybody else in this colony, Mr. Mahendhi. There are plenty of Muslims who are able to pay, but they've chosen not to." Lord Falmouth pulled his cigar from his mouth while his eyes burned into the barrister. "So why *now* are you people so bent on retaining franchise?"

Mr. Mahendhi was unmoved by Lord Falmouth's not-so-subtle attempt to intimidate him. "Because," he replied, "if franchise is taken from us, then what will be next? Even educated Zulus are given the right to vote. If we are denied the right, then you will have lowered our status beneath that of the raw natives. It would be an insult to the nation of India."

"Listen, Mahendhi. The fact is that your people are mostly uneducated and unaware of what is going on in this colony. Most don't even speak English. Frankly, they are unfit to vote. If we were to grant them the right, your people could collectively shift the power base of this colony and bring it to utter ruin."

The barrister grinned slyly, stood up, and walked around to the back of his chair. "So that's what this Disenfranchise Act is all about. The Europeans are fearful that the Indians are going to take over the colony."

Lord Falmouth steered his gaze away from him toward the window. "We won't take that chance. This is a British colony, Mr. Mahendhi, not an Indian colony. We will do everything necessary to keep it that way."

"But, Your Lordship, you've already seen from past experience that Indians don't care about voting."

"We cannot take that chance, Mr. Mahendhi."

*****

Siva arrived home midafternoon to find Chandu reading one of the books he had borrowed from the barrister. "Where's your brother?" he asked. He was in a good mood but serious at the same time.

"Outside somewhere," Chandu replied. "Why, is he in trouble?"

"No, not at all. I just enrolled you two in Phoenix Primary School."

Chandu jumped up with a shriek of excitement and hugged Siva garu until he finally had to push him away. It was what he had always hoped for since arriving in the colony.

"But I'm concerned that your brother might not fare so well sitting in a classroom."

"Don't worry, Siva garu. I'll watch over him."

He took a deep breath and said, "Okay, but I think this will be easier said than done."

And with little time this became evident. Chandu coaxed and prodded but to no avail. Pradip cared little for learning and even less that he was an enormous distraction to the other learners. Mrs. Reddy was a patient woman with a passion for teaching, but her resolve had been unwittingly tested by Pradip's inability to sit still for more than several minutes. She respectfully likened him to a caged animal and suggested that he was perhaps better suited for something more physical than that of sitting in a classroom for hours on end.

*****

"Well, now we know for sure that Pradip isn't cut out for school," said Siva. He stroked his chin as he tried to figure out what to do with him.

"Hey!" he exclaimed suddenly. "I saw a Help Wanted sign posted in front of Boya's Offal Shop. How do you think he would take to that?"

"Doing what?" Chandu asked.

"I suppose he would be cleaning the innards of the sheep and goats that he sells."

"But we're Hindus, Siva garu. We don't eat that stuff."

"Who said anything about eating it? Besides, Boya's a Hindu, and he doesn't seem to mind selling the stuff."

Chandu shrugged in resignation. "If it keeps him busy."

"Very well," said Siva. "I'll take him down to Boya's tomorrow morning."

*****

"Look at this!" said the barrister, reading the headline on the bottom of the front page of the *Times*. "*'**Apathetic and Apolitical Nature of Indians Renders Them Unqualified for Franchise**.'* Can you believe this," he said, throwing the paper onto his desk.

Siva walked over from his desk and picked up the paper to see for himself. The barrister continued, "These people are determined to strip us of every last morsel of dignity."

"More than you know," said Siva. "Listen to this, 'It is incumbent upon the colony to preserve our European traditions. The growing Asiatic blight replete with their underhanded business dealings and unsanitary habits are a serious threat to the European way of life.'"

The barrister snickered and shook his head side to side. "They're a bunch of scared chickens. Not only are they afraid that we are going to take over the colony politically but economically as well."

Siva quietly folded the paper and stared pensively out the window.

"What do think, my friend?" asked the barrister.

"Huh, about what?"

"About these Europeans and what they're saying about us."

"Uh, well, I was just thinking that I should wait before bringing my wife and girls over to the colony."

"Why? Not sure you're going to survive here in the colony or do you anticipate trouble?"

"Both."

"Well, what do you think we should do?"

"Maybe we shouldn't rouse trouble for ourselves," Siva said.

"Would you prefer that we shrink back like withering flowers?"

"I'm concerned that if we continue to antagonize them, they will make things worse for us."

"Maybe you still don't know me very well, my colleague—I'm no shrinking violet."

"But aren't you concerned about what Mr. Thomason told you about watching your back?"

"I refuse to live in fear, my friend. I believe God has already numbered my days and nothing I do or don't do is going to change that. Now, if you don't mind, I have some editorials to write."

The barrister sat down and titled the first one "*Why should the greatest Empire in the world fear losing one of their jewels to a bunch of dirty and illiterate Indians?*" But he suspected the irony would be lost on his adversaries.

*****

Pradip was pushing his rice and dhal around the plate with his fingers but eating very little. Finally, he asked, "Have you ever eaten trotters Siva garu?"

Siva snickered, "Getting tired of rice and dhal, are you?"

"Aren't you tired of eating the same thing every meal?"

Chandu asked him, "What are trotters?"

"Pig's feet," he replied with a smile. "They're really good."

"Pradip!" he snapped with indignation. "You can't...you aren't supposed to eat meat. Don't you know that?"

"Why not?" he snapped back.

"Because," Chandu replied sharply, "we're Hindus, and Hindus don't eat meat."

"Hindus aren't supposed to cross the Kala Pani, but we did." He shrugged his shoulders dismissively.

"Perhaps," said Siva, "but that pig's foot that you were gnawing on might have belonged to your reincarnated uncle."

Pradip's eyes darted back and forth between his brother and Siva. "Then why does Boya garu eat them? He's a Hindu."

"You have to ask him," said Siva. He stood up and walked over to his desk to finish up some work. Pradip pushed his plate away with a look of defeat on his face.

"If Amma was reincarnated what is she now?" Pradip asked with a hint of skepticism.

Chandu pondered momentarily, "Well, she's surely been born into a royal family."

"In India?"

"Of course, where else?"

"Then I want to go back to India and find her," he said sternly.

"You can't. She's a different person now."

"But won't she recognize me when she sees me."

"Uh, well, do you recognize anyone from your previous life?"

"No, I guess not."

"Chandu, how do you know Amma is in a royal family?"

"Because she was a good person. If you're good, then you're born into a better life until finally—"

"You become one with the Brahman," Siva chimed in.

"And what if you're not good?"

"Then you come back as a—pig. Or worse," Chandu said with a chuckle, "a cockroach!"

Pradip nodded pensively. "There's going to be a lot of cockroaches in the next life."

"Yes, there will be."

CHAPTER 15

Mr. Cozen poked his head in the door of the law office and asked, "Where's Mahendhi?"

With a curious gaze, Siva answered, "He's not here right now. May I help you with something, sir?"

Mr. Cozen closed the door behind him and asked, "Who are you?"

"I'm Sivasambarao, Mr. Mahendhi's associate."

"Associate," he mumbled.

"I beg your pardon, sir."

"You mean you're helping Mahendhi cripple our farming business?"

"Sir, maybe you would like to come back when Mr. Mahendhi is here," Siva replied nervously.

"When will he be back?"

"Can't say for sure, but I'll gladly give him a message."

"Mahendhi took possession of two of our coolie boys some months back. You know who I'm talking about?"

"Of course," said Siva, suddenly aware of to whom he was talking, "you're from the Sykes Estate."

"That's right."

"Is there a problem?"

"I need to know if Mahendhi still has the two boys."

"Uh, they're with me now," he replied hesitantly.

"Oh, they're with you now," he said derisively. He reached into his pocket and took out a telegraphed message and tossed it on Siva's desk. "Here you go," he said. He opened the door and started to leave. Then he turned around and said, "Just remember that it's you people who are causing all these problems!"

Siva waited till Mr. Cozen was well on his way before picking up the message. It was from Nayadu.

*****

The barrister arrived back to the office later that afternoon saying nothing as he walked by Siva's desk.

"That bad?" Siva asked.

He turned around and took three enveloped editorials that he had written out of his coat pocket. "Worse!" he said, throwing them down on Siva's desk. "The *Times* refuses to publish anything I've written. They all but threw me out of the building, saying I'm nothing but a rabble rouser."

Siva cleared his throat and said, "Mr. Cozen stopped by today."

The barrister stopped in his tracks and turned around. "What did he want?"

"He dropped off this wire from the boy's father."

The barrister took the telegraph from Siva and studied it closely. "Hmm," he said, placing the note back on Siva's desk. "Just says that the boy's father has run into trouble—nothing else. What do you suppose happened to him?"

Siva shook his head side to side. "Could be anything. I just hope that poor man is able to find his way back home."

"Well, we have to tell the boys something."

"I say that we tell them that he's been delayed in returning home. Let's not dampen their spirits by telling them that he's run into trouble."

The barrister nodded. "Good idea, my friend. Now what else did this Mr. Cozen have to say?"

"He was looking for you."

"Of course, he was looking for me."

"And he says we are to blame for all the problems. He even suggested that we are to blame for the boy's father being in trouble," Siva stood and started pacing back and forth. "That Cozen chap scares me."

The barrister's eyebrows narrowed toward his nose. "Did he threaten you?"

"Threaten, no. He just scares me—that's all."

"We're making a lot of Whites angry, my friend. We just have to keep our eye on the prize, and that's equality for our Indian brethren."

"But I didn't come to Natal to become a freedom fighter, Govindas."

He smiled and said, "Perhaps not, but this is what we've become." He shrugged. "So to speak. With all due respect, maybe you should decide if this is where you should be."

*****

Pradip barged through the door perspiring and gasping for air. "Chandu!" he bellowed. "Siva Uncle! Come!"

Siva was busy proofreading a petition that the barrister had just written. Slightly annoyed by the interruption, he asked, "What is it, boy?"

"Come look!" he said, motioning with his hand.

Chandu ran to the door to see what stirred his brother into such a frenzy. Sitting high on a rickety old horse-drawn cart was a couple with a young girl whom they all knew well. The scene was reminiscent of the first time the two families met. They were the only two families from Korlakota daring enough to leave everything behind for a promised land. Manisha was at least ten by now and already starting to bear resemblance to her mother. It was apparent that she was going to be a very attractive young woman.

He ran out to greet them with Siva close behind. "How did you know where to find us?" Chandu asked.

"We didn't," replied Velu while disembarking from the cart. "We spotted Pradip as we were—"

"No, Nana!" Manisha interrupted. "It was me who saw Pradip."

Velu chuckled. "Okay, it was this one who saw him coming out of the offal shop up the road. I wouldn't have made him out. The boy's grown tall and handsome."

Pradip grinned with embarrassment. He had already grown as tall as Chandu but clearly more physical. No doubt, he had taken after Archana's side of the family with his angular features and thick wavy hair.

Velu turned to Pradip and asked, "What are you doing in an offal shop?"

"I work there," he replied proudly.

"And he eats there," Chandu added mockingly.

Prema's eyes opened wide with surprise. "You're eating meat, Pradip?" she exclaimed.

"No!" he replied emphatically. "How do I know if I'm eating someone's—"

"That's true, my boy," said Velu. "You don't know." Then he changed the subject and asked, "Now where is your Nana and Amma?"

Eyes darted back and forth as nobody was sure what to say.

Then Siva spoke up, "The boys' mother passed away about four years ago due to an illness, and the father has traveled back to India to do business."

Prema gasped. "No," she cried out in disbelief. She ran over and pulled both boys into her fleshy bosom. "Don't you poor boys worry. We'll make sure that you're taken care of."

They both looked up at her and, in unison, asked, "You're moving here?"

"We are," Velu replied, his voice no less abrasive than the last time they were together.

Siva overheard and said, "So you'll be staying on in the colony?"

Velu grinned. "What will we go back to in India?"

Prema interrupted, "Just look at how thin you are. When was the last time you had a properly cooked meal?"

Siva smiled and answered, "It's been quite awhile. Please help yourself to the kitchen." He then turned to Velu and asked, "So where are you coming from?"

"Port Shepstone."

Siva replied, "Never heard of it."

"But we're here now," said Velu. "Heard that there were many Indians here and good business."

"What business?" Siva asked.

Velu shrugged and said, "Trading."

Siva grinned. "No shortage of Indian traders here in Phoenix."

"True," Velu replied. "They're everywhere."

Siva walked back over to his desk and said, "Please excuse me. I have to finish revising this petition before tomorrow."

Velu followed Siva and gazed curiously over the documents spread out on the desk. Siva tolerated Velu's prying eyes for several moments before asking, "Do you read, Velu?"

Velu grinned coyly. "Uh, no. What does this say?"

Siva leaned back in his chair and clasped his hands behind his head. He looked at Velu over the top of his spectacles and asked, "Have you heard of the Disenfranchise Bill?"

Velu returned a blank stare.

"The Whites in this colony are trying to pass this bill so that we Indians will never have the right to vote."

Siva shrugged his shoulders and with raised eyebrows asked, "So why do we care?"

"Well, my boss, Mr. Mahendhi will argue that we Indians deserve the same rights as any British subject. So that's what this petition is for. He believes that enough Indian signatures will keep the bill from being approved."

Overhearing the conversation, Chandu asked, "How are you going to get people to sign, Siva Uncle?"

"Good question."

"I can help," Chandu offered.

Siva pondered for a moment then nodded. "Perhaps, you can."

*****

A month had yet to pass before Velu was able to open the business he dreamed of having. Situated in the front portion of their rented home, it was the only provisional store on their street. He sold everything from cigarettes to sweets. If he didn't have it, he promised to have it within two days. Velu was a good trader.

Chandu and Pradip were elated to have the Velus close by. Prema insisted that they as well as Siva join them for dinner every night. "Men have no business in the kitchen," she said. For months they'd been making do with mealy rice, dhal and sour milk. Though they'd been improving with their cooking skills, even experimenting with different types of curries, it was obvious that it was a skill that didn't come naturally for any of them.

*****

"How's business, Velu," Siva asked over dinner one evening.

"Good."

"No problems?"

"No, why do you ask?"

"You haven't heard about all the Indian businesses that are being looted or burned to the ground?"

Velu nodded slowly and said, "No, it's very quiet on this street."

"The Whites are angry because a parliamentary injunction has stalled legislation to disenfranchise the Indians."

Velu's brows furrowed. "A what?"

"They want to get rid of us," Chandu blurted out.

"It seems that the Whites are taking out their anger on Indian-owned businesses," said Siva.

"What do these people have against us?" Velu asked. "I'm just a hardworking man minding my own business."

"Aren't they scared that Indians are putting them out of business, Siva Uncle?" Chandu asked.

"That and they fear we'll outnumber them in a few years," he answered. "That's why they don't want us voting."

"I see," said Velu. "We could vote for Mahendhi garu."

Siva laughed. "These Whites would quit the colony if that ever happened."

Velu's face turned serious. "So what can we do garu?"

"In my opinion, we need to rise above these things we are being accused of."

"What things?"

Siva cleared his throat. "Well, illiteracy, for one. Indians need to learn how to read and write."

Velu lowered his head, but his eyes were still fixed on Siva.

"This is a colony pioneered and dominated by Europeans. If we want to get ahead, we have to conform. We have to learn English and we have to learn the culture."

"But, Siva garu," Chandu interrupted, "won't we become more of a threat to these Whites if we all start learning to read and write and speak English?"

Siva shrugged. "Of course, there's no winning with these people. But I believe the best thing for us to do is learn their ways and not make trouble."

"You mean like Mr. Mahendhi?" he asked.

"I'm not mentioning any names. All I know is that these people don't like to be challenged. Just today there was a nasty editorial in the *Natal Times* targeting Indian business owners. They've accused them of receiving stolen goods, tipping scales, and unfair business practices. What's more is that we Indians have been labeled as vile creatures with dirty habits living in shabby conditions. They even made mention of the widespread practice of living and trading on the same premises calling it unsanitary."

"I never tip my scales," said Velu.

"The word going around now is that the Europeans are going to use these charges as grounds for not renewing business licenses. If licenses aren't granted, then businesses will be forced to shut down."

"Business license?"

Siva glared at Velu. "You do have a business license, don't you?"

Velu's eyebrows raised. "Didn't know I needed one."

Siva shook his head in disbelief. "You better go down and apply for one first thing tomorrow before you get yourself in trouble. Don't tell them that you're already operating a business, and don't tell them that you live on the premises."

*****

Siva slid a stack of dog-eared pages onto the barrister's desk. "What's this?" he asked.

"These are signatures for the petition—almost two thousand."

The barrister looked up, his eyes as wide as saucers. "Two thousand! In two days?"

"Our boy, Chandu," Siva mused.

"I guess you were right about him, my friend. But how was it possible for him to get so many signatures?"

"Well, he decided to tell the people that if they didn't sign, the Whites were gonna come and ship them back to India."

His mouth gaped open. "You mean he didn't explain the purpose of the petition."

"To some, yes, but to most, no."

"Why not?"

"He said he knew they wouldn't understand, so he didn't want to waste his time or theirs."

"Okay," the barrister said, scratching his head, "but I still don't see how he managed to get so many signatures in such a short period of time."

"I asked him the same thing. After a little prodding, he admitted to me that he added a few signatures himself."

"You mean he forged signatures?"

"Well, not exactly."

"What do you mean 'not exactly'?"

"Forgery is signing someone else's signature, is it not?"

"Yes, of course."

"The boy made up names."

He looked down at the signatures and read aloud some of the names. He raised his eyebrows. "I can never approve of what he's done, but I have to admit that he's, well, clever."

"Think we should punish him?"

"Punish him? I'm ready to hire him."

*****

In spite of the thousands of signatures that were ultimately submitted, the petition fell flat. The Colonial Secretary contended that given the Indians' overall political awareness or lack thereof, it was highly unlikely that a majority of the signatories even knew what they were signing. He wasn't far from the truth. Nevertheless, there was no more sympathy to elicit just short of beseeching the Queen herself.

But the spark that was the petition gave birth to a political and social activism within the Indian community. The Indian National Congress was formed with Govindas Mahendhi at its helm. At his side was the capable, if not reluctant, Sivasambarao.

And Chandu's apparent aptitude in producing signatures for the petition prompted the barrister to recruit him as an apprentice and errand boy. It was an opportunity that would befall few, if any, of his peers, and he was elated. The barrister was fast becoming renowned throughout the colony as an agitator among the European community, but to the Indians, he was their champion.

*****

As the weeks went by, Chandu's efforts and cleverness didn't go unnoticed. He sat him down one afternoon and said to him, "You've impressed me with your smarts, my young apprentice."

"I wasn't trying to impress you, Mr. Mahendhi."

"Of course not," he replied. "But I'm concerned that your potential will be wasted if you aren't afforded a proper education."

"Working under you and Siva Uncle is a proper education."

"That's very flattering, my young prodigy, but working with us won't gain you any credentials. You must be properly educated in a university. Then I can make you one of my colleagues."

"You mean a barrister?"

"Why not?" he shrugged.

"But universities cost a lot of money, don't they?"

"They do, but that shouldn't concern you."

"Why not?" he asked.

"Because I would like to sponsor your education."

"Mr. Mahendhi, I don't know what to say."

"Don't say anything. You can think about it if you like."

"But what university is going to accept someone like me?"

"How would you feel about going overseas?"

His eyes widened. "Overseas?

"I have contacts at my alma mater, the University of London. It wouldn't be difficult to get you in."

"In England?"

He chuckled, "Yes, in England."

He paused for a moment, pondering the gravity of Mr. Mahendhi's offer, then asked, "Do you think I'm ready for this?"

"No, that's why I want to send you to a preparatory school first. There you will get everything you need to succeed at the university."

"Mr. Mahendhi, I don't know what to say."

"Don't say anything. You go home and think about it and let me know tomorrow."

*****

That evening as they ate supper with the Velus, Chandu was hardly able to contain the news.

"Hey, that's wonderful, my boy," said Siva. "You shouldn't pass up this opportunity."

But there was no smile on Pradip's face when he asked, "Where's London?"

Chandu knew London was in England but had no idea where England was. All he knew for sure was that it was far from Natal and not much closer to India. It was an answer that he sensed was not going to bode well with his little brother.

Siva answered, "London is where the Queen lives—in a huge castle."

"Does she like Indians?" Pradip asked.

"I think she does," Siva replied.

"Then can I go?" he asked.

There was silence until Prema inched over to Pradip and put her arm around him. She hugged him just as his mother would have and said, "We would all like to go with Chandu, but we can't. So we have to be happy for him and send him with best wishes."

Pradip was hardly a little boy, but his lower lip extended out like that of a pouting five-year-old.

"Must I not go?" Chandu asked.

He looked up and said, "Huh?"

"I'll stay if you want me to."

He smiled. "You will?"

"Of course. I don't want you to be sad."

All eyes were on him and he knew it. "No," his voice was barely audible. "You must go."

"Are you sure?" he asked.

He nodded. "Besides, Nana should be coming home any day now."

Siva cleared his throat. He felt a sudden pang of guilt that he hadn't told them of their father's ominous message sooner. "Uh, I need to tell you boys something."

"What is it?" Chandu asked.

"Your father sent a wire to the estate, and it was delivered to the office by our friend, Mr. Cozen. Your father said that he had been delayed and that he wasn't sure when he was going to return."

"That's it?" Chandu asked. "He didn't say anything else?"

"Oh, that he missed you both very much."

CHAPTER 16

"Why have you not eaten this morning?" Siva asked.

"Not hungry," Chandu answered.

"Nervous, I suppose?"

He nodded. The thought of braving the biggest city in the world put his stomach in knots. And he dreaded the thought of saying good-bye.

"Not having second thoughts, are you?"

He smiled coyly.

"Just remember my boy that you will never get another chance like this again."

In that instance Chandu recalled similar words spoken to his father and mother by Rao sitting on the floor of their small home in Korlakota. It was a revelation that radically altered the course of their lives. He could only imagine what would have been had they chosen to stay back in Korlakota. He contemplated the raw courage that it must have taken for his parents to leave everything that was familiar and journey across the perilous Kala Pani for a land that was unfamiliar, even forbidden.

By the time the barrister arrived to fetch him, everyone who meant anything to him had already gathered to bid a somber farewell. But it was Pradip who was most overcome with emotion, and understandably so. Chandu was the only family he had left to hold onto. He latched on to his older brother and held him tight, and in between muted sobs, he uttered, "Please don't forget about me, Chandu."

The barrister pulled out his handkerchief and handed to Chandu. "Here, I don't want you messing up your new suit before you board the ship."

"You look smart, my young friend," he said, putting a final adjustment on his necktie. He took ten pounds and held it in front of his face. Chandu had never seen so much money at one time. "This should cover your needs until summer," he said before shoving the notes into his pocket.

Chandu squirmed in discomfort as the stiff collar of his tailored shirt caused his neck to itch. "You'll get used to the clothes after some time," he said, smiling. "You can't look like you're from the farm, or they'll treat you like a farmer."

The SS *Sycamore* belched a thick plume of steam and sounded a final warning to those passengers who had yet to board. Chandu picked up his bag and felt his heart thumping inside his chest.

"Represent us well, my young friend," he said, gently pushing him up the gangplank. "Walk tall!" he yelled. Chandu pushed his shoulders back. "And don't worry, my future colleague, Mr. Kingsford will find you when you arrive in London."

At the top of the gangplank stood the purser, thick and menacing. With his fat, hairy fingers, he snatched the ticket from Chandu's hand.

"First class!" he growled. "Where did you get this ticket?"

He pointed down to the barrister, who was still standing at the bottom of the gangplank.

"Coolies don't travel first class on this ship," and he pushed the ticket into Chandu's chest. "I don't care how they're dressed."

Mr. Mahendhi quickly ascended the gangway and asked the purser why he was refusing the ticket.

"Who are you?" he asked.

"Govindas Mahendhi, Esquire."

The man snickered. "You look like a coolie in a fancy suit to me."

Mr. Mahendhi pushed his glasses up high on his nose and stuck his chest out. "This young man is holding a first-class ticket and has every right to travel as such."

"And I just told you that we don't allow coolies to travel first class on this ship."

Chandu shrunk back several steps, expecting that any second that the barrister might be tossed over the railing into the water.

"Problem, Mr. Newton," asked the second officer, appearing suddenly and out of nowhere.

"No problem, sir. Just have a coolie trying board as a first-class passenger."

"Sir," said the barrister, "this young man is not a coolie. He's on his way to London to attend school, and he holds here a first-class ticket to travel aboard this steamer."

The second officer took a look at the ticket then handed it to the purser. "This is a perfectly good ticket, Mr. Newton. Have a steward come and show this young man to his cabin." He turned quickly toward the barrister. "My apologies." Then he was gone.

The barrister whispered in Chandu's ear, "Don't worry, my lad, they've evolved way beyond this nonsense in London." He hurried down to the bottom of the gangway and then yelled, "Be sure to write!"

*****

Chandu tossed his bag onto the small cushioned berth that he was sure he would likely outgrow before reaching London. Between his berth and the cabin door was a petite writing desk and, on the desk, a well of black ink and a goose feather quill. He sat down and opened the desk's drawer. On the left was a Bible. *I have no use for this*, he thought to himself. Underneath the Bible, however, was a small stack of stationery embossed with the name of the ship, SS *Sycamore*. He decided he wouldn't delay his promise to write, and so he began.

He dipped the quill into the ink and wrote: "It's not every day that a boy from a small village in India is able to travel to London to get schooled. How did such a thing come to pass?"

And thus commenced what would turn into a chronicle of his family's journey. He recorded the highs and the lows and everything in between, and before he reached London, he managed to exhaust an entire well of ink.

*****

"You open for business?" the man asked while stomping the mud off the bottom of his shoes. It had been raining hard all day, and Velu was preparing to close the shop early. Pradip, who was now working for Velu, was startled at the sight of a White man in the small shop.

"Yes, sir?" Pradip asked the man.

"Who's the owner of this shop?" the man asked.

Pradip pointed to Velu, who was now making his way to the front.

"Your name?" the man asked Velu.

"He doesn't speak good English," Pradip replied.

"What does this man want with me?" Velu asked.

"Your name," Pradip said softly.

"Ramsamy Velu," he said, loud enough for the man to hear.

"And his number?" the man asked.

"The man wants your number, Uncle."

Velu had been trying to forget the number that was symbolic of his bondage, but it was still etched in his memory. "79242."

The man perused his notes and then said, "I would like to see Mr. Velu's trader's license."

Pradip again turned to Velu. "The man wants to see your trader's license."

"Not yet. I paid, but they haven't given it to me yet."

Pradip turned to tell the man what he was told, but Velu stopped him.

"Wait. Tell him I've lost it. No, wait, tell him that it was stolen the other day. Tell him someone broke into this shop and stole the license off the wall here."

When Pradip told the man Velu's story, he laughed.

"Is that so," he said. "My records say that no license has been issued to Mr. Velu. That means this shop is illegal and no longer open for business."

Pradip pleaded, "But, sir, he has paid for the license. They haven't given it to him yet."

"That's not my problem, boy. He should have waited, and he should have told me the truth. I have no patience for lawbreakers and no mercy for liars. Good day!" he said as he popped open his umbrella and then disappeared down the street.

*****

Nearly seven weeks had passed before the *Sycamore* reached the English Channel. Nobody cared to brave the chilly gray drizzle that would try desperately to hide the emerging land masses on either side of the ship except a young British couple hiding under an umbrella and Chandu. With the monotony of the long voyage nearly behind them came a sudden surge of excitement.

"This is my first time to England!" he yelled across the deck.

The couple turned in unison and the wife smiled. She said, "I didn't know anybody else was out here."

"It's the dapper young Indian chap that we've been curious about but had yet to meet. Come, lad, tell us who you are?" said the husband.

He walked over and extended his hand. "I'm Chandu. I'm going to be studying in London."

"How utterly fortunate for you, Chandu. You couldn't have picked a better place to get your education. Oh, I'm Miles Addison, and this is my lovely new bride, Nelly. We're returning from an absolutely adventurous honeymoon in Capetown."

"Congratulations," he replied. "So you're going back home?"

"Yes, we live considerably north of London in Nottingham."

"Look at those magnificent white cliffs, darling," said Nelly, pointing out into the distance.

"Ah, yes, the White Cliffs of Dover. Aren't they grand, Chandu?" Miles remarked.

"Amazing," he replied and walked over to the port side of the boat that faced England. The ship turned north hugging the English coastline and then west into the wide mouth of the Thames River. The swift current of the rising tide moved the boat rapidly along the narrowing and meandering waterway. The gray sky darkened and lights began to twinkle along the misty banks.

Chandu was lost in his thoughts of what life in London might be like for a young Indian lad like himself when Miles interrupted, "Where are you going to stay while your studying, Chandu?" By now, his wife had returned to their cabin while Miles stayed behind to smoke his pipe.

"Oh, I have a friend. Well, he's not a friend—yet. He's a friend of a friend back home in South Africa. Mr. Mahendhi."

"You're staying with a Mr. Mahendhi?"

"No, he's my friend back in South Africa. I'm staying with a Mr. Kingsford. He's a friend of Mr. Mahendhi."

He chuckled. "I think I understand."

They both stood staring out ahead of the ship as the Victorian city splendor neared. In the distance was a large bridge that posed as large gate. Ships with large masts like the *Sycamore's* would not pass without consent.

"That's the Tower Bridge," Miles said as if he read Chandu's mind. Just then the ship slowed, and a shrill steam whistle sounded repeatedly to alert the bridge tender of their approach.

"See those two red lights?" Miles said, pointing to the upper window of the left tower. "That means the bridge is closed." Just then, the enormous steam engines hissed loudly, and within seconds, the spans began to slowly rise. "It's all hydraulics," Miles said, almost as if he were himself responsible for the engineering feat.

When the spans had reached their apex, the lights turned green and the *Sycamore* moved slowly into the lair of the city. Suddenly the smell of the River routed their senses causing Miles to jest: "Welcome to London!" he went on to say. "You must know that this great city of ours has become so overcrowded with immigrants in recent years that we are struggling to cope with all the growth. That's why they built this bridge. It was only finished last year. My grandfather, Horatio Jones, was the architect," he said proudly. "But now we have to figure out how to restrict what flows into this mighty River of ours, don't we?"

"Do people wash their clothes in this river?" he asked.

"Heavens no, my lad. The servants use proper dolly tubs to wash clothes in this part of the world. Well," he paused with contemplation, "not everyone has servants, do they?" His face turned serious, and he pointed his index finger just inches from Chandu's nose. "Promise me, Chandu, that you won't so much as put your bloody big toe in that nasty river." He put his hand on his shoulder and said determinedly, "This river is one the greatest and most important rivers in the world, but you don't want to go in it. You have to stay above it. This great city of ours isn't much different, Chandu. If you stay above it, you'll be fine."

*****

"I don't think you realize how serious this is," Siva said to Velu in regard to the unexpected visitor he had that afternoon. "Lying to that White man was unwise."

Velu lashed out. "What more can they do to me! They've already closed me down!"

"Listen to me when I tell you that you mustn't reopen your shop until you have a license."

"Do you think these people are going to give me a license now?"

Siva pursed his lips and nodded. "I don't know."

Velu took his plate and threw it against the wall. Everyone recoiled as pieces of plate and food exploded in different directions. "Damn these Whites!" he yelled at the top of his lungs.

*****

"You're sure you've got a place to go?" Miles asked as he and his wife prepared to descend the gangplank. He looked along the wharf for anyone resembling Mr. Kingsford. Chandu remembered the barrister's description of his old friend and former landlord: *tall, light-brown skin, and black wavy hair, but it will be his thick, bushy eyebrows that will catch your attention.* But nothing. His chest tightened at the thought he might not appear. That perhaps there was some great big misunderstanding.

"I'm sure he'll be here," he answered.

"Very well, Chandu," he replied with a broad smile. "I do wish you great success with your studies. And remember what I told you. Don't let this city beguile you."

Chandu shook his hand and thanked him and then walked slowly down the gangplank hoping that Mr. Kingsford would suddenly appear, but he was nowhere in sight. It was already dark, and a thick cold fog had settled in over the wharf. The trench coat that Mr. Mahendhi lent him was warm, but the London chill was starting to find its way to his bones.

The great steamer ship had emptied of all her passengers and was now at rest. He wanted desperately to go back to the warmth of his small cabin aboard ship but knew Mr. Kingsley would never find him were he to show up.

He bundled his coat tight around his thin frame and propped himself on his bag under one of the two gas lamps keeping the wharf from total darkness. *Mr. Mahendhi said it would get cold here, but how does one know cold unless one experiences it,* Chandu thought to himself. Now he knew and could say that he was not suited for this type of weather.

As a matter of survival, he knew the gas lamp looming high over his head would do little to keep him warm and he had to make a decision—risk leaving to find shelter and perhaps getting lost or staying and shivering to death.

He wasn't ready to die yet, so he picked up his bag and started walking. He walked up along the cobble stone road that bore the most light. Pubs on each side of the way teemed with life as rowdy patrons spilled out into sidewalks undaunted by the cold weather.

Smithwick's Galley and Grog sat quietly just up the hill, and it was there that he decided he would find warmth and a hot meal. He would worry about finding Mr. Kingsford afterward.

Just then a horse and carriage appeared out of the fog. The driver had the bushiest eyebrows he had ever seen, and he knew that it was Mr. Kingsford. He called out to him as he almost passed by, and he quickly brought the carriage to a halt.

"Chandu?"

"Yes, it's me," he answered with a renewed excitement.

"I'm so sorry, lad. I had some problems with this carriage, and… well, here I am, and here you are. I'm so glad that you were able to recognize me. Tell me, how did you make me out?"

He smiled with some embarrassment and lied, "I wasn't sure if it was you. I took a chance."

He chuckled. "Thank God, or I would have ridden right past you." He jumped down and threw his bag in the back seat of the beautiful four-wheeled carriage. "My wife has a hot bath and warm meal awaiting you back at the house."

*****

It was Byron Kingsford's small boarding house in which the barrister had stayed eight years earlier when he attended London University. During that time the two had become good friends, and there was little that the barrister didn't know about the man before he graduated.

The boarding house had been handed down to him by his father, Bradley Kingsford. But it was Bradley's father, Captain William Kingsford, who had proved to be most unconventional and noteworthy.

When he was stationed in Calcutta, India, as a British officer, he found himself irresistibly attracted to the daughter of one of his servants. Amorous involvements with servants were forbidden, but Nirusha's smooth mocha skin tone and almond-shaped eyes made Captain Kingsford leave all sensibility aside.

Nirusha was barely eighteen years of age compared to the captain's thirty-seven. But the captain's biggest breach of ethics was the fact that he had a wife back in Scotland. The British officer pursued a relationship with Nirusha behind closed doors, which eventually led to Nirusha falling pregnant. It was a scandal that sent shock waves throughout the Indian community.

Eventually, his infatuation with Nirusha blossomed into a deep abiding love that ultimately put his military career in jeopardy. In spite of orders to leave the young Indian girl, he remained devoted to her. He decided to resign from his post in the British Army rather than leave the Indian maiden with whom he had now fallen deeply in love.

The British, however, were not going to let the captain off so easily. He was arrested for violating the laws and ethics of the British Empire, which included adultery. He was tried and sentenced to five years in prison. When he was finally released, he found Nirusha and his five-year-old son, Bradley, waiting for him. They married and continued to live out their lives in Calcutta while eventually having four more children.

Growing up as an Anglo-Indian in India at that time was difficult. Neither the Whites nor the Indians were willing to accept them. They were misfits that were forced to live on the fringe of society. When Bradley reached the age of twenty-two, he left the color-conscious country of his birth and immigrated to the land of his father. Eventually he moved down to London, where individuality was the rule. There he found a large Anglo-Indian community that blended in with the rest of English society.

Bradley's son, Byron, was a proper Englishman. Aside from dark eyes and thick black eyebrows, he bore little resemblance to his Indian heritage. His wife, Anne, also an Anglo-Indian, bore him three children. The oldest, Annabelle, was in her first year at London University.

*****

The acrid smell of smoke awakened Manisha from her sleep. She jumped out of her small bed and ran over to where her father and mother lay sleeping.

"Nana!" she screamed, pulling violently on his nightshirt. "Wake up, Nana! There's a fire in our house!"

Both Velu and his wife awoke in horror to find black smoke starting to fill the small room. The roar of the fire could be heard coming from the direction of their small storefront, which had been closed for several weeks now.

"Must be all the cooking oil!" he yelled. "This place is going to burn quick!"

Flames blocked the only door leading out of the small rented house. Velu grabbed Manisha by the arm while Prema followed. Velu lifted his daughter through the window easily enough, but with Prema, he struggled. The narrow window would not allow her to pass.

"I'm stuck!" she yelled.

Velu pushed as hard as his slight frame would allow but only seemed to wedge her in tighter."

In the meantime, the flames were nearing, and the room was filling with smoke. Velu desperately gasped for fresh air while continuing his effort to push his wife through the window.

Looking on in horror, Manisha ran next door to see if she could find help. Several small explosions from within the store had already awakened Rajesh Singh, who was already abounding through his front door.

"Please help, Rajesh Uncle, she can't get out!"

Mr. Singh ran swiftly around to the side of the house where Prema was stuck like a cork in a bottle. She screamed hysterically, "Help me, please, help me!"

He grabbed her sweaty hands but was unable to get a firm grip.

"Please hurry!" she bellowed. "I don't want to die."

He quickly removed his shirt and wrapped it around her right arm. Then, with his feet braced against the wall, he pulled with every last ounce of strength he had left. She slid through, landing on top of her rescuer. Smoke started billowing out of the small window but Velu didn't follow.

"Ammandi!" Prema cried out.

Mr. Singh's eyes widened. "Velu's still inside?"

"Yes, he was behind me. Please," she wailed, "you have to save him."

He took the shirt he used to save Prema and wrapped it around his face. From the window, flames were visible, and he wondered if Velu could still be alive. He took two deep breaths and started to pull himself through the window. To his amazement, he saw Velu's hand clutching desperately to the sill of the window. Without hesitating, he grabbed his hand and pulled. As Singh struggled with his remaining strength to pull Velu from the encroaching flames, Prema jumped up and grabbed hold of her husband's other hand. Together they managed to pull him out with only seconds to spare.

"Ammandi," was the only word she could utter.

Velu coughed violently and struggled to regain his breath.

"He's taken in a lot of smoke," said Mr. Singh. "We should get him to a doctor."

Prema pulled Manisha to her right side and stroked her husband's forehead with her left hand. She looked up at Singh with tears streaming down her face. "Thank you, Singh garu. You saved our lives."

*****

Chandu quickly learned that English society had a way of casting a glaring light on his shortcomings. He became keenly aware of his English skills or lack thereof. But never was he more aware of them than when he was in the company of Mr. Kingsford's oldest daughter, Annabelle.

Her striking hazel eyes were framed with long, thick eyelashes, and her cheeks dimpled with the easiness of her smile. When she walked, her chestnut curls danced delicately on her soft shoulders while the rest of the world seemed to stand still. And when she spoke, each word shot an arrow straight into his heart.

But to her, he was a curiosity. She was intrigued by how he and his family were taken to Natal and all the events that eventually landed him in London. He was an uneducated, uncultured Indian lad dressed in the finest clothes money could buy. The silk shirt, the showy tie, along with a double-breasted vest and morning coat, were all meant to hide his humble upbringing, and she knew it. Every day he wore the same pretentious outfit until one day she joked he was impersonating a peacock. He laughed along with her, but swore to never wear the clothes again.

*****

Annabelle was also a vegetarian. But her vegetarianism was rooted in philosophical depths that were beyond Chandu's realm of experience. In fact, there was a vast subculture of vegetarians whose movement combined elements of humanitarianism, idealism, and spirituality. At least that was how it was explained to him. He found nothing revolutionary about vegetarianism. To him it was tradition and lifestyle. But he could see that this fascinated Annabelle. She often commented that she admired his simplicity. Nevertheless, she coerced him into joining a group of high-minded individuals who espoused all things opposing to culture.

The Essex Vegetarian Society was a motley group of pseudo-intellectuals representing every sphere of antiestablishment. Chandu politely listened to the different speakers share their passions for social reforms while his activism was limited to benign nods and picking up literature at the end of the meetings.

Annabelle liked to dine at the numerous vegetarian restaurants that were springing up all around London. She often invited Chandu, along with her society friends, as a sort of talisman, but Chandu was oblivious. To say that he was beguiled would have been an understatement. Nevertheless, it didn't take long for his spending to catch up with him. After two months, his pockets were empty. Mr. Mahendhi had entrusted him with enough money to last for six months, and he managed to exhaust it in two.

*****

"Sorry to wake you," said Singh, "these good people have just lost their home to fire and asked me to bring them here."

Siva didn't have his glasses on and squinted to see who was riding on the back of the man's wagon.

"You are Sivasambarao?"

"Yes, I am?" he replied still confused.

"Velu's wife said that you would be able to help them, so I offered to bring them here."

"Velu?" he said, making his way up the small makeshift steps leading up to the road. There, Velu lay on his back with his head nestled in his wife's lap.

"Please, garu, we've just lost everything and have nowhere to go," she said tearfully.

Siva grasped Velu's leg. "What happened?"

"I don't know," Prema's voice cracked with emotion. "We barely got out of our home before it burned to the ground."

"Velu here took in a lot of smoke," said Singh.

Siva lifted Velu's right eyelid. "We should get him to a doctor."

"No, garu," Prema replied, "he just needs rest."

Siva backed away and said softly to Singh, "Any idea how the fire started?"

"No, but I have my suspicions."

Siva nodded. "So do I."

He walked back over to the cart where Manisha rested her head on her father's chest. "I've not much room here, but you're welcome to stay for now."

"Thank you, garu, we are indebted to you," said Prema.

*****

The following Monday Chandu skipped out on his classes and went searching for a job. He was confident that he could earn back the money he squandered, leaving nobody the wiser. Several days of frantic searching, however, yielded nothing. So in his desperation, he put on the fancy clothes that he said he would never wear again.

Then he started looking off the main streets and down the narrower, twisting cobblestone alleys east of the city.

By late afternoon, dusk had settled, and flickering gas lamps were attempting to make up for the lack of sunlight. It was down those alleys that the inescapable smell of decaying horse manure lay rotting between the cobblestones. And it was down one particularly dark alley that he chanced upon a Help Wanted sign hanging in the window of the Pig & Whistle pub. He walked in, pulled the sign out of the window, and set it on the bar.

Behind the bar was an older chap whose features reminded him of his mentor, Mr. Mahendhi—short, round head—except this bloke's teeth were yellow, almost brown, and of course, he was White.

By now Chandu was convinced that Londoners weren't very fond of dark chaps like himself working for them. But here, in this part of town, there were lots of non-Whites coming and going and he had a good feeling that his luck was going to change.

Besides the barman, the place was mostly empty save for a few crusty patrons sitting at a nearby table tipping pints and belching puffs of smoke.

The barman appeared annoyed that he had taken the sign down and promptly put it back. "What are you supposed to be?" he asked with his thick, cockney accent.

"Looking for a job, sir."

His brows furrowed, and he asked, "Are you sure you're in the right place?"

"Aren't you looking for help?" he asked.

He nodded. "How old are you?"

"Sixteen, sir," he replied.

"You Indian?"

"Yes, sir."

"So what can you do?"

"I can do anything, sir," he answered, not really sure of what he might be getting himself into.

"How long you been here, lad?"

"A couple of months," he replied. "I've been studying at Kensington Boys School."

"So why aren't you in school?"

"I've run out of money, sir, and I'm desperate for a job."

He walked around to the front of the bar to size him up. "Very well, I can start you out cleaning the floors and tables, and then we will see from there. Come back tomorrow at 10 a.m. Oh, by the way, what's your name, lad?"

"Chandu."

"Chandu, leave the white gloves at home."

"Oh, okay, yes sir."

"And the tie."

"Leave the tie at home, sir?"

"Yeah, you won't need to wear a tie here."

"Yes, sir."

"In fact, you can leave that entire bloody outfit at home."

"Okay sir, I can do that."

"We're simple in this part of town, lad. Sweeping floors while dressed like a penguin will get you some peculiar looks."

"I understand, sir. I'll be sure to wear my—uh—not so finest."

"Oh, and one more thing, lad."

"Yes, sir."

"Don't be late."

CHAPTER 17

The growing hostilities toward Indians and especially Indian merchants gave birth to the Indian Natal Congress. The objectives of the INC were to not only defend against the mounting discriminations, but to bring unity to the splintered Indian community. Caste and language created wedges among the Hindus and Muslim Indians looked down upon Hindu Indians. The fractures were many and threatened to make the Indians their own worst enemy.

Membership swelled to over 450 members, while wealthy Muslim merchants would make up a majority of the members. The barrister capitalized by imposing a three-pound annual subscription on its members. The dues, he decided, would cover administration costs, while the rest would go into a relief fund. He also used the subscription as a means of maintaining a certain caliber among its members. Past experience proved that there were plenty of low-class trouble makers who had nothing better to do than to disrupt public proceedings.

The Whites, however, saw it differently. To them, the INC was a surging political beast whose growth knew no limits. The barrister responded to all criticisms by simply extending an invitation to any and all Europeans so they could see for themselves that nothing subversive or clandestine was taking place.

But the ongoing months of unrelenting pressures inherent in the role the barrister was now playing were taking a visible toll on him.

Siva commented, "Govindas, you're looking very tired. You should take some time to rest."

"You may be right, my friend, but the work must continue."

"If you work yourself to death, you won't be of use to anybody."

"I'm afraid I don't know how to rest. It's just not in my spirit to lay idle."

"Can I make a suggestion?" asked Siva.

"Of course, my friend."

"Take some time off from all this and return to India. There you'll be able to recruit some more barristers. This is what we desperately need. But there you will also be able to see your family. This will also do you much good."

The barrister's eyebrows rose high into his forehead as he considered Siva's suggestion. "I'll think about it, my friend."

*****

"So where do you stay, lad?" the barman, Mr. Hood, asked Chandu at the end of his second day on the job.

"Oh, I rent a room on the other side, close to school."

"No family here?"

"No, sir, I'm here alone."

He scratched his beard, and his brows furrowed. "So your folks are in India?"

"Well, my father's in India."

"Your mother?"

"She died when I was ten."

"Sorry, lad."

"It's okay, sir."

"Then your father sent you here to get an education."

"Not exactly, sir. It's complicated."

"Okay, okay, you don't want to tell me. Nevertheless, you came here to get schooled did, you not?"

"Yes, sir, I did."

"And right now, you're not going to your classes because you're working here trying to earn some money."

"That's right, sir."

"What if I put you to work at night so you can still go to your classes during the day?"

"I would be grateful, sir."

"Well, I need a night watchman from seven to eleven, five nights a week. Are you sure you want it?"

"Yes, I'm sure."

Mr. Hood opened the cash register, pulled out a shilling, and handed it to him. "Here you go, lad. Now be here tomorrow night at half past six, and don't be late."

*****

The barrister was packing some documents into his briefcase when Siva arrived to the office on Monday morning. "You look like you're going somewhere."

"I'm taking your advice, my friend, and going to India."

"Good, you need some rest, and you need to see your family."

"I've alerted all my clients that I'll be gone for several months, and I've emptied my schedule. There's an INC meeting on Friday and which Ali Kader will facilitate. I need you to collect dues as well as—"

"What are those?" asked Siva, his eyes fixed on the stacks of pamphlets that the barrister was stuffing into his briefcase.

"Oh, these—just some literature I put together outlining the grievances we have with the colony."

"And what are you going to do with the literature, Govindas?"

He walked over and peered out the window before responding in a hushed tone. "I'm going to Madras to speak with some key leaders in the government. But please, my associate, you mustn't speak about this to anyone. If these Europeans receive word of what I'm doing, they will bar me from returning to the colony."

"But what are you doing?"

He grinned. "What I do best, my faithful colleague. I'm going to stir up Indian opinion against the colony's policies regarding our people."

Siva picked one of the pamphlets up and started reading it. "But what good are these going to do in India?"

The barrister sat down in his chair and removed his bifocals. "What's driving the economy of this colony right now, my friend?"

"Sugar," Siva responded with a shrug.

"And what is the backbone of the sugar industry?"

"Indian labor?"

"Exactly, and these Europeans are doing everything within their power to reopen the flow of indentured labor into the colony."

"Well, if the colony becomes self-governing, that may well happen," Siva replied.

"I know, that's why I believe it's important that I stir up some indignation among Indian leaders."

"But, Govindas, Indian leaders will hardly care about the hordes of low-caste Indians who sold themselves into bondage."

"You're right. But they will care about the way we free Indians are being treated."

"Are you suggesting that they use the supply of Indian labor as a means to change the colony's attitude towards us free Indians."

The barrister grinned slyly. "Why not? Indian labor is the Achilles' heel of this colony. No labor supply, no colony. We have many battles to fight, my friend, and we have to use whatever means possible."

"But what about the rights of the indentured laborers?"

"The fight goes on."

*****

"This is where I want you to stand," said Mr. Hood, positioning Chandu in front of an obscure door in the rear of the pub. "Now, if you see anyone with a dark-blue uniform, large gold-plated buttons, and a fancy rounded-off top hat with a spike on it, I want you to knock twice and then one more time. Like this, *bam, bam—bam.* Understand?"

"I understand, sir."

He repeated, "What's the secret knock?"

He rapped on the door, *bam, bam—bam.*

"And who are you looking for?"

"A constable?"

His face turned red as he cleared his throat. "That's right, lad. Not that we're up to no good around here. Constables don't like us getting too loud, you see."

"I see, sir."

"That's a good lad."

Behind the door, Chandu would eventually learn, was a high-stakes gambling operation and that Mr. Hood lost his previous watchman to the scorn of a neglected wife. And so it was that he was able to strike a tenuous balance between his studies looking *into* the law and his night watchman's job looking *out* for the law.

His only regret was that he now saw very little of Annabelle. He convinced her that his studies were getting more intense and that he was studying late every night in the library. Though she was his only confidant, he feared she would look down on his circumstance, and he hesitated being forthright. But his story wasn't completely untrue. His studies were intensifying, and he was slipping further and further behind. He just needed to hold on until the summer break when Mr. Mahendhi promised to send more money.

*****

Days turned into weeks with nary an opportunity to use the secret knock when finally, one evening two uniformed constables entered the pub. It was his cue. This was the moment that he had been anticipating for weeks. Then his mind suddenly went blank. He couldn't remember whether it was one knock followed by two knocks or two knocks followed by one. He replayed the knock in his head, *bam, bam—bam.* Or was it, *bam—bam, bam.* He knocked and then he knocked again twice. The door opened, and Mr. Hood peered out. "What is it, lad?"

Without saying a word, he pointed to the two constables who were already heading in their direction.

"Oh, for the love of—!" Mr. Hood exclaimed before bolting the door shut. One of the constables brushed Chandu aside like a gnat and pounded on the door.

"Open up, police!"

Nothing. Again, they pounded, demanding that the door be opened. Still nothing. They took a few steps backward and then rammed the door with their sides knocking it to the ground, but everyone had escaped through the rear window. Everyone—that is, except one very large fellow who sat quietly, scooping chips into his pocket.

Chandu escaped out the front door unnoticed and walked briskly down the narrow street, turning around every odd step to see if one or both of the constables were pursuing him. Finally, when he was blocks away, he slowed and realized that his unremarkable career as a night watchman was over. Now it was time to come clean.

*****

The barrister landed in Madras, where he was invited to speak before a small gathering of Indian leaders who had grown increasingly hostile toward British rule. His rhetoric was welcomed as reinforcement to what they already suspected: The British were on a mission to subjugate the entire undeveloped world.

One invitation to speak led to others until he rallied his way up the subcontinent through Calcutta, Delhi, and over to Bombay. It was there that he found himself back on familiar ground, the place where his career as a barrister had begun. It was also there that he found himself on the brink of exhaustion. His pace had been relentless, and his former colleague and mentor, Vinod Sharma, was concerned.

"I believe you need to take some rest, Govindas."

The barrister sat cross-legged, holding his tea with both hands. "I *am* resting, my friend. Can't you see?"

"How do you feel?"

He shrugged dismissively. "Don't worry about me. I'll be okay."

But the barrister's voice was listless, and Mr. Sharma kept pressing. "I've not seen you look so thin, and there's no white left in your eyes. Please, Govindas, let me cancel the meeting tonight so you can take an extra day to rest."

The barrister smiled in a manner familiar to his friend. Without words, Mr. Sharma knew that his proposal would go unheeded.

"There was once a time when you used to listen to my advice."

He let out a sigh. "You're right, Vinod. You've always given me wise counsel. But I have so little time left here before I return to Natal."

"I think your efforts are misguided."

"Why do you say that?" he asked.

"The hysteria you're creating is what keeps you going. But what do you think will come from all these meetings at the end of the day?"

The barrister cocked his head back abruptly. "You think I'm wasting my time?"

"Maybe."

"Maybe?" the barrister replied incredulously.

"Once you've gotten on that boat and sailed off, Govindas, we'll go back to fighting our own battles, and you'll become a mere memory."

"How can you say that?"

"Easy. You can stand up in front of these people and rant all you want about how evil these Whites are down there in Natal. Don't misunderstand me, Govindas, your speech last night was brilliant and very provocative. But the Raj here is no different. They'll scream and yell and even agree to your proposal of not allowing any labor to leave our harbors. At the end of the day, though, these Britishers know well that rupees trump ethics in this country. I believe you've overestimated the moral standards of our people."

"I disagree with you," replied the barrister before rising to his feet. "I have something to show you." He took several steps in the direction of his briefcase then turned and looked at Mr. Sharma. His gaze was distant and unfocused.

"Are you all right?" Mr. Sharma asked.

"Yeah, I'm…" he continued several more steps before collapsing.

*****

Mr. Kingsford was wiser than Chandu ever suspected. Though, he rarely saw the man with his private entrance into the guesthouse, somehow, Mr. Kingsford knew that his deeds were mischievous. In fact, it seemed he was already prepared for his visit with him on the first day of his unemployment.

He sat Chandu down and lectured him on how privileged he was to have such a wonderful opportunity to be schooled in London. But he didn't stop there. He moved closer and Chandu could tell he wasn't comfortable with what he was about to tell him. Annabelle, he said finally, had a way over unsuspecting boys and that he needed to be careful.

"I like your daughter just fine."

"Of course, you do. Just don't lose focus of why you're here."

He didn't know if he was telling him this because he knew that he had already fallen prey to his daughter's beguiling charm or if he was trying to spare him some future anguish.

Chandu contemplated that Mr. Kingsford had seen him in his daughter's company, and it was likely very obvious that he was smitten with her. Perhaps, he thought, there were boarders before him who had squandered all their money trying to impress Annabelle, and he was no different from the rest. He felt embarrassed that he had to tell him that he had fallen—hard and that he was broke.

He smiled knowingly at his confession. "Have you learned anything?"

"I have, Mr. Kingsford. I need to be myself."

"It was a ten-pound lesson," he laughed.

"What now, Mr. Kingsford?" he asked.

"Mr. Mahendhi sent a telegraph several weeks ago to inquire how you were doing?"

"Did you tell him?"

"I wired back that you were learning a lot, that's all."

"So you've known all along?"

"You forget that Mrs. Kingsford does your laundry, young man. You brought the pub home with you every night on your clothing."

"I didn't know what to do, Mr. Kingsford."

"I trust Mr. Mahendhi saw something very promising in you. I'm going to trust his judgment, and I'm going to trust that you've learned your lesson, young man. Therefore, I'll cover your expenses until summer."

"Oh, thank you, Mr. Kingsford."

*****

When the barrister awoke almost thirty-six hours after collapsing in Mr. Sharma's office, he found himself in a small bed with his wife, Pravina, and three young sons by his side. Mr. Sharma had managed to get his old friend to his home and summons his family from Gujarat hoping that the sight of his loved ones would adjust his priorities.

Mr. Sharma knew well his former colleague's drive and ambition and that it had the potential of being his undoing. "Don't lose focus of the more important things in life," he often told the young upstart. But he also recognized him as the firebrand he was and that he was a man destined to leave his mark on history.

His wife, however, recognized only that she was raising her sons without their father and desperately hoped that this incident would serve to open her husband's eyes. She cared little whether he became wealthy or successful as an advocate. She especially had little concern for the issues surrounding Indians half a world away. But she wasn't going to voice her feelings now.

The barrister was too weak to even lift his head, but the sight of his wife and boys brought a wide smile to his face.

"Where am I?" he asked.

"Mr. Sharma's home," she answered. "A doctor came and looked you over and said you've overworked yourself."

"How long have I been here?" he asked, struggling to push himself up from the small bed.

"Almost two days," she answered softly and gently resisted his attempts to get up.

"I've missed my meeting."

Mr. Sharma interjected from the doorway. "The meeting came and went without you, Govindas. The doctor said you need to rest."

The barrister's body went limp, and he stared up at the ceiling pondering his next move. "I'm glad you're here," he said after a few minutes. "I believe it's time we all go back to Natal together."

"No, Appa," said his eldest son, Baba, who was eight. "Come back home with us."

"Come," he said, extending his feeble arm out, and all three boys crowded in close to their father. "Sometimes when you want to see a difference in this world, you have to be that difference."

"Can't you be that difference at home," said Baba.

"Yeah, Appa, can't you do that at home," said his six-year-old.

He smiled. "Right now I'm needed down in Natal, and I need you boys to be with me and support me. Do you think you can do that?"

The boys lowered their heads. "Yes, Appa, we can do that."

"Okay, let your father rest," said the boys' mother so the barrister was left to sleep some more.

*****

They retreated to the main room where Mr. Sharma's cook had already prepared lunch for the guests. "He's a man who won't be stopped," Mr. Sharma noted while washing his hands. "But leaving India maybe a smart thing to do right now."

"Why's that, Mr. Sharma?" asked the barrister's wife.

"The doctor who examined your husband said a bubonic plague is sweeping across the country."

"Bubonic plague?"

"The black death," he said before sitting down. "The plague swept through Bombay about twenty years ago, killing hundreds and thousands."

The wife put her hand over her mouth. "No!"

"I'm afraid so."

*****

Annabelle knocked twice on the door before peering in, "Hi, Chandu, are you busy?" Her smile was no less intoxicating then the first time he laid eyes on her. Even her father's admonition to him several days earlier did little to change his feelings about her.

"Just doing some writing."

"I thought you might like to join me and some friends."

"Oh?" he replied.

"We're going down to Manchester Hall to hear this man speak," she said, handing him a pamphlet.

"About what?" he asked, though it didn't really matter.

"Theosophy."

With raised eyebrows, he answered, "Okay."

Her eyes squinted slightly, and the tone of her voice sharpened, "You know about theosophy?"

He shrugged. "No."

"Shall I tell you?" she asked.

He could tell she was itching to enlighten him, though he was sure it was just another one the many revolutionary ideas that were sweeping through London at that time. Men like Leo Tolstoy, Karl Marx, and Charles Darwin had already agitated the conservative way of life making the city and especially the campuses ferment for debates, but Chandu always stayed on the periphery.

He read the bold words on the top of the pamphlet aloud: *Man's Spiritual Evolution into a Higher Consciousness.*

Her face lit up. "Doesn't that sound absolutely grand, Chandu?"

He could only offer a smile. "Are you still a member of the Essex Vegetarian Society?"

She curled her lip and shook her head side to side. "I came home one day last week while Mummy was making shepherd's pie." She smiled coyly. "I couldn't resist, Chandu. She's such a good cook."

Even her shallow convictions did little to abate his infatuation. "When are you going, Annabelle?"

"Meet us in front of the hall in one hour. There's someone I want you to meet."

*****

Vinod Sharma waited till the Mahendhis were boarding the SS *Fairlady* before handing him the telegraph. It was a tough decision for him to make. Held therein was an ominous message from Siva alerting the barrister of the rumors that were now circulating around the colony.

One rumor was that the barrister was intent on bringing a shipload of artisans, merchants, and professionals such as lawyers, accountants, and doctors. Though he had every intention of recruiting some lawyers to help alleviate his growing burden, his intense speaking schedule never allowed for it. What's more is that the few lawyers he did offer jobs had little interest in moving to a place that was become notoriously anti-Indian.

The other was less rumor and more fact. News of the barrister's crusade to dissuade future shipments of labor to the burgeoning colony had been reported by the *London Times* and had made news down in Natal. Interestingly, the Europeans were bothered little by the accusations the barrister was making—allegations that Europeans were suppressing the rights of Indians. They were livid, however, that this Indian advocate was attempting to bring the colony to its knees by strangulating future labor supply.

Mr. Sharma knew that his former colleague was sailing into a proverbial storm, but he also knew that the colony needed him. What's more is that Bombay was on the brink of quarantine because of the plague. He was sure that if the family didn't make it out on the *Fairlady*, then they may never get out.

CHAPTER 18

Mr. Heinz stood outside his small office affixed to the side of the Sykes Manor and gazed out at the green hills surrounding the estate. Production had slowed to a crawl, and there was nothing he could do. He thought about all the money he'd invested into his sirdar, Nayadu, with hopes that he would return with workers. But many months had now passed, and it seemed unlikely that he would ever return.

The more Mr. Heinz thought about the situation, the angrier he became. He smashed his fist into the door and let out a guttural wail. There was a root cause of his and every other Natal plantation owner's problem, and he was determined to make it go away.

*****

Chandu raced up the steps of Manchester Hall because he was late. Annabelle and several of her friends were at the top of the stairs waiting, and she smiled as he approached. The chilled air pinkened her round cheeks.

"I didn't think you were going to make it, Chandu."

"Sorry, I'm late," he replied, embarrassed that he kept everyone waiting.

"Don't you own a coat?" asked the fellow standing next to Annabelle. Before Chandu could answer, he continued, "Probably don't need coats in India, do they?" His tone was sarcastic, and Chandu quickly realized he wasn't looking to be his friend.

Annabelle jumped in, "He came from South Africa, Charles, and I'm sure that Chandu just forgot his coat."

"How do you forget a coat?" he asked. "It's cold enough to snow."

"I had to have it cleaned," Chandu lied through his teeth. "But I didn't want a little chill in the air to keep me from this lecture."

The truth was that he swore off the ostentatious apparel he'd been wearing since he had hardly a penny to support such a facade. He decided he would rather experience the numbing chill of London's unsympathetic weather than live as an imposter.

Annabelle chimed in, "Chandu, you haven't met Charles yet?"

He extended his hand. "How do you do, Charles?"

He begrudgingly shook Chandu's hand but said nothing.

"Charles is president of the Young Marxist League, Chandu."

Chandu nodded slowly. "Must be quite a responsibility."

"It is," he replied arrogantly.

"So," Chandu asked with some hesitance, "why are you here?"

His freckled face reddened at his query. "What do you mean 'what am I doing here'?"

"Marxists are supposed to be atheists, and this is a talk on theosophy."

His brows furrowed. "Atheist?"

"Someone who doesn't believe in God."

"I know what it means, you obnoxious little twit," his words were caustic. "For your information, young Marxists like myself don't fret over the humanistic dimensions of Marxist theory. We are agents of change. Our movement will change the existing state of being."

"The existing state of being?" Chandu echoed in curiosity.

"The struggle between the classes, you fool! Why should all the power and wealth in this world lie in the hands of the privileged few? Does that seem fair to you?"

He shrugged. "I don't think you can change fate."

Charles scoffed, "That's where you're wrong, little brown man. We can and will change the way things are!"

Annabelle interrupted, "We're already late. Can we please go inside before all the seats are taken?"

"Of course, my love," Charles replied. "Let us go before this boy further cross-examines me."

"Please be nice to him, Charles. He's a friend of mine."

Chandu stood, cold and defeated, on the large granite step while Charles escorted Annabelle up the few remaining steps leading into the hall. It was then that he realized he was Annabelle's friend and that he would never be anything more than that.

Annabelle looked over her shoulder. "You coming, Chandu?"

"Uh, you go on, Annabelle. I really need to catch up on some studying."

"You sure, Chandu?"

"I'm sure."

"Okay then, I'll see you later," she replied sweetly before disappearing into the hall on Charles's arm.

*****

Nana would have never approved of Annabelle, he thought to himself as he made his way back home. *Not only is she not full-blooded Indian, she's not even Hindu,* he rationalized to himself. But something inside of him hurt, and he didn't know what it was.

"When it comes to marriage, we first consider the family," he recalled his father saying to him and Pradip years earlier one evening during dinner. "The family has to be of the same caste with the same values," he said, holding his two hands out like scales. "Otherwise," he said wagging his finger, "the marriage will never work." He told them not to worry whether you love the girl or not—love grows over time.

Chandu wondered whether time would heal his broken heart.

*****

It was summertime in the southern hemisphere, and the days were long and hot. Mr. Cozen was as tired as Mr. Heinz was exasperated. He'd been working long, hard hours to make up for the lack of laborers. But he had no choice. This work was all he knew.

Mr. Sykes had been a friend of Mr. Cozen's father and, as a favor, agreed to take on his troubled son as a laborer. The younger Cozen had failed miserably in school and had some minor scrapes with the law. Working outdoors on the estate suited him and gave him the stability he needed. Several years later, Mr. Sykes made him the manager and allowed him to move onto the estate. That was over twenty years ago.

Mr. Heinz knew that Mr. Cozen was as dependent on the estate as the British were dependent on sugar, and he was going to capitalize on that. He pulled him into his office one evening after much contemplation and reasoned with him.

"I think it's time for drastic action, Cozen. We can't expect that our situation is going to improve as long as that coolie lawyer is allowed to cause us problems."

Mr. Cozen sat slumped in the cushioned chair and nodded. "What did you have in mind, boss?"

Mr. Heinz leaned forward and said, "We need to eliminate Mahendhi."

Mr. Cozen sat up. "You mean—?"

"Shh!" he said with a forefinger in front of his lips. "I've been thinking about this for a while, and I don't see any other way."

Mr. Cozen didn't say anything for fear of what was coming next.

Mr. Heinz's piercing blue eyes almost spoke for him when he said, "I want you to see that this gets done."

"You want me to go and kill this man?" he asked incredulously.

"I didn't say that *you* had to do the job. I said I want you to see that it gets done. And news is that he is coming back to the colony from India with more of his kind. Let's send these people a message."

*****

Chandu's head swirled with thoughts as he walked home from Manchester Hall. Strangely, he found meeting Annabelle's new beau a liberating experience. No longer was he concerned about how Annabelle perceived him. His preoccupation with conformity and being accepted had become a yoke of bondage. As far as he was concerned, Annabelle didn't even know the real Chandu. But neither did he know Annabelle. No doubt, he'd been captivated by her beauty and charm and was flattered that she had included him in her circle of friends. But at the end of the day, he would have been hard pressed to clearly define what motivated her to get out of bed in the morning. She was sincere in her convictions, but he wondered if perhaps she wet her finger each morning and lifted it to the sky, seeking from which direction the latest revolutionary fad was coming.

As he got closer to the Kingsford guesthouse, he realized that he wasn't really home. Never did he feel so far from home. He desperately missed his family. Tears welled up in his eyes, and he hid his face from a boy his age walking toward him from the opposite direction.

He thought about the prelaw courses he'd been studying and wondered why he was devoting himself to something that did little to motivate him. He naively believed that he would grow to like law, but such was not the case. With each passing day, he realized that it was for Mr. Mahendhi that he was studying law, so in a sense, he was still a prisoner—Mr. Mahendhi's prisoner.

*****

Mr. Kingsford wasn't surprised when he came to see him in his den after dinner. He knew he was disturbed during dinner and even asked him if things were all right, but Chandu knew that then was not the time.

Flames crackled in the fireplace as Mr. Kingsford invited him to sit in his guest chair. The black leather was warm on one side—the side close to the fire—and he slid to that side of the chair.

"So," he said, removing his reading glasses, "what's been bothering you, Chandu?"

He took a deep breath. "I'm dropping out of school."

He pondered his statement with one arm of his glasses between his teeth. "Studies too difficult?" he asked finally.

He lied, "Yes."

"So you're going to quit?"

"I don't want to, Mr. Kingsford, but I don't want to waste your money or Mr. Mahendhi's money."

"So you want to go home?"

He nodded.

"And what will you do when you get there?"

He felt beads of sweat on his eyebrows and shifted to the other side of the chair. "Well," he said hesitantly, "I can work for Mr. Mahendhi."

"Doing what?"

He shrugged. "Anything, I suppose."

He smiled. "Yes, he will probably need someone to clean his office at the end of each day. And you'll probably do fine delivering important documents. There's no need for an education to do such things."

His wisdom dismantled Chandu's flimsy argument, leaving him without a response. Finally, he said, "I don't like studying law, Mr. Kingsford. It's boring."

He thought for a second. "What would you rather study?"

"Well, I like to write."

He snickered in a polite sort of way. "You want to write? What would you like to write?"

"I hadn't considered what I would like to write, and again"—he shrugged—"I just like writing. I've been keeping a journal ever since I left Natal."

"I'm sure you're a fine writer, Chandu, but it's very difficult to earn a living as a writer."

But writing for money wasn't Chandu's motivation. All he knew was that he enjoyed it a lot more than studying law. Neither of them said a word, and Chandu sat with his eyes following the patterns stitched into the Persian rug beneath him.

"Don't give up your dream to be a writer, Chandu," Mr. Kingsford said after some minutes passed, "but don't give up your studies either. If you fulfill your obligation to get your education, I believe you will one day realize your dream to be a writer."

"You think so, Mr. Kingsford?"

"I do."

*****

"Quarantine!" exclaimed the captain of the SS *Fairlady*. "I have passengers and cargo to deliver to Mauritius."

"You've come from a plague zone, sir, and we cannot allow for the possibility of spreading any diseases here in our colony," replied the lieutenant governor.

"We've had no incident of sickness, and everyone on board is in good spirits, I assure you, sir."

"I'm sorry, Captain, but the governor has already issued a decree that your passengers be quarantined for ten days until it can be ascertained that no disease is present."

"Ten days! I can't wait here for ten days. I have thirteen passengers needing to get off here, sir. I'd rather choose to sail off and throw them overboard than wait here for ten days."

The lieutenant governor raised an eyebrow. "Thirteen passengers? That's all?"

The captain turned to the purser to confirm. "That's it, sir."

"And do you have a passenger Mahendhi aboard this ship, Captain?"

The purser replied, "One Govindas Mahendhi, wife Pravina, and three sons."

"What is this all about, sir?" the captain asked. "As the commander of this ship, I would like to know why you are inquiring about my passengers and why there's a mob of people along the dock who look ready to lynch the first person who steps off this boat."

The lieutenant governor glanced out at the varied throngs of onlookers. Among them were Siva and Ali Kader, who had taken over the leadership of the INC in the barrister's absence. Maintaining a safe distance from the crowd, they waited anxiously to welcome the barrister back into the colony. It was apparent, however, that the rest of the crowd didn't share the same sentiments.

As epithets and threats were hurled toward the boat, the lieutenant governor turned back to the captain, "Your cargo isn't welcome here in this colony."

"What's wrong with my cargo, sir?"

The captain knew nothing of the political turmoil and controversy surrounding the growing population of free Indians in the colony. Nor did he know the press had reported that the SS *Fairlady* was arriving with hordes of artisans, merchants, and professionals bent on tilting Natal's demography.

"Captain, you've brought with you one of the biggest nuisances this colony has ever had the displeasure of hosting. And now he's trying to bring in more of his ilk."

"Well, that's not my problem, is it? Now," he said, putting his hands firmly on his hips, "am I being detained for quarantine, or am I being detained because I'm carrying a passenger that's given you a rash or two?"

*****

Also growing impatient was Tinus de Groot. He mixed inconspicuously among the malcontents dockside, but his mission far exceeded that of jeering and demonstrating. He'd been hired by Mr. Cozen to bring an end to the source of one of the colony's biggest headaches—Govindas Mahendhi. Now he was just ready to get the job over with.

Mr. de Groot was an easy hire. Tall and thin with a passion dedicated to preserving the European standard of living, he shuddered at the thought of sharing even a fraction of the rights for which his forefathers had worked so hard. He accepted the notion that Indian labor was a necessary evil in the colony, but as far as he was concerned, they were not welcomed to stay in the colony beyond their term of indenture. Even viler were the free Indians. "We should make them all swim back to India," he was fond of saying.

Mr. Cozen's instructions were clear: "There'll be plenty of commotion surrounding the arrival of these coolie immigrants, especially Mahendhi. Wait until he makes his way through the mob and get as close to him as possible—real close. Then, quickly push that six-inch blade between his ribs. There should be enough confusion that your deed will go unnoticed. That is, until he's lying in a pool of blood. And whatever you do, don't get caught."

Mr. de Groot's fee was one pound.

But the only one to descend the gangway was the lieutenant governor, along with several officers.

"No passengers are leaving this ship until the governor signs an order lifting the quarantine on this vessel. If you have loved ones aboard, go home. If you don't have loved ones aboard, go home. There is no reason to remain here."

*****

Late that afternoon, all passengers hoping to land on Durban soil were ordered to bring their blankets and bedding where it was carefully gathered by crewmembers into a heap and set ablaze. Then the passengers were subjected to humiliating fumigations. The barrister humbly accepted the order but was mortified that his wife had to endure such treatment. He now wondered whether his crusade through India was a mistake. *Perhaps it had done more harm than good*, he thought to himself.

The captain showed up at the barrister's cabin. "I really don't know what to make of this nonsense, but I assure that this is not my doing. It seems as if there's some politicking going on here and that you are at the center of it all."

"Think nothing of it, Captain. They may have stripped away our blankets, but they haven't stripped away our dignity."

"Maybe not, but if I were you, I'd be a little nervous about stepping off this ship."

Mrs. Mahendhi and the boys sat quietly listening. While the boys knew a little English, their mother spoke none and could only guess what the men were speaking about. The barrister was thankful she was unable to understand.

"And just when will we be able to leave this ship, Captain?"

"Sorry, but I have to leave tomorrow irrespective of this quarantine. I know we came from a plague zone, but this is purely political, it appears. If they don't lift this thing by tomorrow, you'll have two choices: sail on to Mauritius or jump overboard."

*****

Siva and Ali Kader showed up the following morning, as did the demonstrators, but they were fewer in number than the day before. Tinus de Groot had arrived early and grew nervous with each passing hour. There were fewer people, which meant that his deed would be less obscured.

When the lieutenant governor rode up on horseback, the mob went silent. Would the quarantine be extended, or would the passengers be released? Most were hoping for an indefinite quarantine and that the ship would be turned away along with its passengers. Mr. de Groot, however, stood to profit and hoped that the quarantine had been lifted. While Mr. Kader stood calmly waiting for his friend, Siva paced nervously, wondering what bedlam might ensue once the barrister set foot on dry ground.

"Look, here they come," said Mr. Kader, nudging his elbow into Siva's side.

Several jeered at the tall slender Indian man who was followed by his young bride, confusing him for the barrister, and it was apparent that the waiting mob had no idea what Govindas Mahendhi looked like. Each successive passenger was taunted—eight in all. But Mr. Mahendhi and his family were not among them and the crowd grew restless.

"Where is he?" the crowd yelled.

"Send him out!" some others cried.

"These people are looking for blood. Maybe we should distance ourselves from this whole thing?"

"We've done nothing wrong, Siva. Let's see what happens."

The captain appeared at the top of the gangway and barked at the rioters, "The man you're looking for isn't aboard this ship, so back away from here. We're getting ready to sail."

Several of the rioters yelled out, "Where is he?"

"I don't get paid enough to give out that kind of information," he said. "And even if I did know, I wouldn't tell you bunch of hooligans."

Siva and Mr. Kader were as dumbfounded as the rioters to find out that Mr. Mahendhi wasn't aboard the ship.

"Govindas and his family are safe at my home," the man said discreetly.

Siva recognized the man as the barrister's friend and confidant. The Reverend George Stadelmaier was a Wesleyan Methodist minister with whom the barrister had become friends shortly after the young barrister first arrived in the colony. The reverend had dinner at Villa Pravina on a number of occasions where they would often discuss Christianity and other religious philosophies. The two had a deep respect for each other.

"He told me that you would likely be here waiting and was concerned that you would be worried about him. He and his family will stay with me for a few days until this foolishness subsides."

"Can we visit with him?" asked Siva.

"It's not a good idea right now. I don't want to draw any unwanted attention to my home. Besides being a little weak and thin from his recent illness, he's fine. In fact, he wanted to face these people, but I told him it wasn't wise."

"When did you take him off the ship, sir?" asked Mr. Kader.

"Late last night. I awoke with an overwhelming sense that his life would be in danger if he were to face this mob today."

"But why, sir?" Mr. Kader asked. "Why do all these people want to bring harm upon Mahendhi?"

"Well," said the reverend, crossing his arms, "I would consider your colleague a revolutionary of sorts, and revolutionaries will always face fierce opposition."

Both Siva and Mr. Kader nodded.

"You should go home now. Govindas will be fine at my home," the minister departed, heading west toward his home in Glenwood. Siva turned the horse and carriage around, and the two were on their way north toward Phoenix. The men, however, were being followed.

*****

Siva and Mr. Kader hadn't traveled very far before Tinus de Groot had overtaken them on a lonely stretch of road connecting the wharf with the busy streets of Durban proper. The two men were startled when the lone horseman veered into their path, bringing their horse and carriage to an abrupt halt.

"What were you two doing down at the docks," he asked.

The two men looked at each other, and then Ali Kader answered, "We were there to greet a colleague, sir. Why do you ask?"

"Who is this colleague you were waiting for?"

Again, the two glanced at each other, confused. "What business would this be of yours, sir?" Mr. Kader replied.

Tinus de Groot unholstered his knife, revealing the length of the blade to the two Indian men. "Step out of that carriage," he said, his words were slow and menacing.

Without hesitating, Siva dropped the reins and stepped out of the carriage. Mr. Kader, who was much older, moved slower, and this irritated de Groot. He then reached over and jabbed the tip of his blade into the haunch of the yoked beast, sending it into a frenzied dash down the road. Holding the knife in front of his face, he said, "You were saying?"

Fearful for his life, Siva stammered, "Uh, it was Mahendhi... Govindas Mahendhi we were waiting for."

"And where is he?" the man barked.

Siva wondered whether this would be a moment of truth. He knew his fear was about to force his hand and divulge the where-abouts of his boss.

But Mr. Kader replied, "We don't know, sir. He never showed."

The man let out a frustrated sigh and sheathed his knife. He then veered his horse around and galloped off back in the direction from whence he came. The two men stood in disbelief and silence, waiting till the man disappeared before speaking.

"I'm afraid for Govindas," said Mr. Kader, his eyes round like saucers.

"I'm afraid for all of us," said Siva.

CHAPTER 19

Siva was stunned to find the barrister in the office the morning following the harrowing incident down at the wharf. In fact, Siva considered staying away from the office himself but decided that he had too much work to do with his boss away.

"Good morning, my friend," he said with a cheerful smile and seemingly oblivious to the commotion his activities were causing. "How have you managed in my absence?"

Siva was incredulous. "Uh, Govindas, are you aware that there are—are European louts looking to lynch you?"

"That wasn't the kind of greeting I was expecting from you, my friend."

He replied with a disingenuous smile, "I'm sorry, but Ali and I were accosted yesterday morning by some rogue fixed on cutting you into pieces."

The barrister scoffed, "I've told you this before, my friend, I'm not going to live my life in fear. As I've said many times, God has already numbered my days, and when it's done—well, it's done."

"Perhaps, but does that mean you shouldn't use a little caution or good sense?"

The barrister laughed. "So what do you suggest I do, my concerned colleague?"

"Go into hiding for a while—back to the reverend's house—a least until these Whites cool down. And stop writing inflammatory editorials to the *Times*. You're only making things worse for yourself and the rest of us."

The barrister's face turned serious. "I'm surprised at you, my friend. I thought that you had more fortitude than this."

"But we're outsiders, Govindas—foreigners in this—"

"We're all British subjects," the barrister interrupted, "and we deserve to be treated as such. I know that you didn't follow me to this colony to become an activist for Indian liberties, my friend, but this is our fate, and you have to choose whether you want to be a part of it or not."

*****

The barrister was not going to be quieted or intimidated. He quickly resumed his war on European injustice. Knowing that the *Times* had grown weary of his incessant attacks on the colony's oppression of his people, he adopted the European pseudonym Grover Madison. Knowing that his editorials would be no less inflammatory, he knew it was possible that his diatribes would never see print, but it was a chance he would take.

*****

"Any idea who Grover Madison is?" Mr. Heinz asked his estate manager early morning just after the workers headed out to the cane fields.

Mr. Cozen shrugged. "Never heard of him, boss."

Mr. Heinz opened the paper that had been folded under his arm. "Listen to this," he said, reading from the editorial section of the *Times*. "'*How a citizenry could possibly allow a lynch mob to lay in wait for an innocent man is the mark of an uncivilized society.*'" He scoffed, "We're uncivilized?"

Mr. Cozen's brows furrowed. "That sounds like something that coolie lawyer Mahendhi would say."

"They're probably friends," Mr. Heinz replied. "Obviously, this chap has no stake in the welfare of this colony. And he calls us uncivilized."

"Should I have de Groot finish the job he started?"

Mr. Heinz shook his head. "He missed his opportunity. I can't chance having my name being dragged into anything if he was to get caught. But forget de Groot and that coolie lawyer for now." Mr. Heinz pulled a telegram out of his pocket and handed it to Mr. Cozen. "Read this."

Mr. Cozen took a quick glance at it and handed it back to his boss. "You read it, boss. I—I don't have my glasses." The real reason was that Mr. Cozen hadn't progressed beyond grade five and was slow to read.

"Very well," said Mr. Heinz, snatching the paper back into his hand. "It reads:

'Dear sons,

I am writing to you with the help of this kind fellow who has come to my aid, and I hope that this message is able to reach you. I have had a lot of problems since I arrived back in India. I believed that there would be a lot of our people who would be happy to come to Natal if they knew that there was much money to be earned. But when the people came to know why I was here, they became hostile toward me. They believed that I came here to kidnap their children and their daughters to bring back to Natal. They heard these kinds of stories. I was arrested and put in jail. They took my money and wouldn't allow me to contact anybody. All I could do was look forward to the day that I would be free and to see you two boys again. After 963 days in the jail, I was set free. They told me I must leave the village and not return. But now I have no money to return to you. Please give this message to the lahnees so they can know I am still alive and that I am needing help to return.

Nana.'"

"So the mystery's solved," said Mr. Cozen. "We know what happened to our long-lost sirdar."

"He's asking for help to return, Cozen."

"And?"

Mr. Heinz crumpled the paper inside his fist. "I refuse to invest one more penny into this—this sirdar."

"Aww, boss, where's your compassion?"

"What do you know about compassion, Cozen? It's your lack of compassion that keeps you employed here."

"But Naidu didn't deserve to rot in some jail for nine hundred-something days, boss. He's a good, hardworking man."

"Well then, I'll go ahead and wire the poor chap some money and take it out of your pay if you feel so strong about it."

"Wait a minute, boss. I don't feel *that* strong about it."

"You have to remember something, Cozen. I'm a businessman first, and I find that being profitable and being charitable are incongruent propositions."

"What?"

"In other words, Naidu is going to have to find his own way back here."

Mr. Cozen shrugged. "And what about his boys? Don't you want to pass this message on to them?"

Mr. Heinz took the telegram and ripped it into little, indecipherable pieces. "And let it become known that Mr. Heinz was refusing to help one of his sirdars reunite with his sons—never! Nobody will ever know that Naidu made contact with us."

*****

It had been nearly six years since Nayadu had set foot in his home village of Korlakota, and he considered the occasion bittersweet. The neighboring village of Lakshmipuram had not been kind to him, but he was going to keep that to himself. In fact, the only person he wanted to see was the temple priest, Sai Komdaari.

A young woman sat outside the Shiva temple stringing garlands, and Nayadu believed her to be the same young girl who had always been there. He poked his head inside before entering, and there, sitting next to the Hanuman shrine was Sai Komdaari. With his legs crossed and his eyes closed, he sat motionless. Nayadu wondered how long he'd been in that position and wondered further how someone could possibly sit for so long without moving, eating or even relieving himself. No wonder so many considered him to be a god.

Nayadu rang the bell and entered, but the priest didn't move. He went back out and rang the bell again, this time longer, but still no movement. *He probably hears the bell so often that he doesn't hear it anymore,* Nayadu thought to himself. He inched closer to the priest, looking for the slightest movement, and then became convinced: *This man isn't breathing. He's even stilled his heart.*

He now wondered what consequences he might face if he were to disturb the guru. Nayadu supposed that the priest was no longer present in his body—that his intense meditation had allowed him to transcend the physical realm into some other spiritual dominion. He imagined that a sudden disturbance might wreak some sort of celestial havoc causing the guru to return with a cosmic thud.

But with nowhere else to go Nayadu was desperate. He needed money to get home, but from Sai Komdaari, he needed sage advice. He cleared his throat, and Komdaari slowly opened his eyes. At first, he wasn't sure if the priest was looking at him or looking through him. He waved his hand in front of the priest's face.

"It's you, Nayadu," he said slowly and without expression.

Nayadu let out a sigh of relief. "Yes, Komdaari, garu, it's me."

"You've gone very thin. Jail has not been kind to you."

Nayadu's brow's furrowed. "You knew I was in jail?"

"Does it surprise you that I can know such a thing?"

"You knew I was there and—"

"Compose yourself, Nayadu," he said calmly. "As a priest I never interfere with one's karma. And you know that I warned you not to cross the Kala Pani. You chose to ignore my advice."

Nayadu's head sank low. "You did warn me. But I have to go back. My two sons are there."

"Nayadu, why don't you send for your sons and settle down here where you belong? Things are better now that the rains have returned."

"I've been told that I must leave. If they know that I'm still here, then they will put me back in jail."

"I understand," he said, his body still poised and motionless. "So the best advice I can give you is to go see your wife's mother. I believe it would be worth your while."

"And her father? You didn't mention him."

"He died—about a year back. That aunty has been by herself. Go see her, Nayadu."

Nayadu dreaded the idea of visiting his mother-in-law. Not because she had become a Christian but because he would have to tell her what had happened to her daughter. It would be especially difficult because he was aware that she never wanted her family to leave Korlakota. But Nayadu trusted the guru's wisdom.

"Okay," he said with a nod, "I'll go to her."

*****

The small, thatched roof home was almost completely enveloped by overgrown grass and shrubs. By all appearances, the place looked abandoned. Nayadu's first thought was that perhaps the old woman had moved on. *But to where?* he wondered. She had nowhere to go. As he moved down the path closer to the front entrance, he started to wonder what he might find inside. There didn't appear to be any sign of life on the property.

"Hello!" he yelled just feet from the front entrance. "Amma!" he yelled again.

"Hello," came the faint cry from within the rundown dwelling. "Yes, come in."

Even after all the years of being apart, she recognized the voice. She pulled herself out of her small, worn bed and shuffled over to her long-lost son-in-law. She took his thin hands and looked up to him, and tears streamed down her cheeks.

She looked out to see if anyone was behind him. "My baby?" she said, looking back up at Nayadu's forlorn face. "She's gone, isn't she?"

Nayadu was suddenly overcome with emotion; his head fell into his chest, and he began to weep. "I'm sorry I didn't tell you sooner." The years of separation melted away as the two sobbed in each other's arms.

"How did she die, son?" she said finally, ushering him over to the straw mat by her bed.

"A disease," he said, still overcome with emotion, "while we were sailing to Natal."

"Archana's father died last year," she said, shaking her head, "and I've been alone here."

"I'm sorry," said Nayadu.

"It's okay," she said, barely audible.

So you're not angry with me?" he asked, wiping the dampness from around his eyes with his dirty sleeves.

"I'm too old to get angry," she replied. "Besides, what good would it do? I have a God who has forgiven every bad thing I've done. I know that I have to do the same."

Nayadu didn't know what to say.

"Where are the two boys?" she asked.

"They're back in Natal, Amma."

"So where is this place, Natal, and why are my two boys there while you are here?"

"It's a long story, Amma..." And after Nayadu spent the next hour telling her his tale of woe, he said, "And now I need to get back to Natal so that I can see the boys again."

"But you have no money," she said, "and you must be very hungry."

"I am."

"Good," she said, "I will make you something."

She had always considered Nayadu the son that she and her husband never had. They had lost their only son to a drowning accident in the Godavari when he was just five years of age. So the couple doted on their son-in-law and were utterly heartbroken when he decided to cut them out of their lives.

But they never wavered in what they had come to believe and boldly proclaimed their religion to anyone who would listen. Few did. Most of the villagers were indifferent to the old couple's new-found religion, thinking it perhaps odd but in no way a threat, so they left them to themselves.

Nayadu, however, took exception. To him, this new religion was an affront to the Hindu way of life and the traditions handed down to him by his forefathers. He drew a line in the sand and forbade them as well as his young family to cross it. It was the cause of much tension in their home, but he was steadfast. Chandu and Pradip, however, found ways to get around their father's mandate, and he was never the wiser.

The older woman was breaking some firewood into smaller pieces when she paused. "Son, I have some money stashed away, and I would like to give it to you. I don't know how much you need, but it should help."

"Amma, I can't take your money. You need it for yourself."

"I have enough to get by. We managed to save enough over the years."

"Amma, why don't you come with me back to Natal so you can see the boys? We can take care of you."

"Ha! Do you really think I'm up to sailing over the Kala Pani? I'm not even up to traveling to church anymore. Oh," she said with a distant look in her eyes, "how I do want to see those boys again. No, you go with my blessings, son. Stay here tonight, and you can leave tomorrow. And don't waste any time in leaving this place."

The next morning, he said an emotional goodbye and headed in the direction of Rajahmundry. She had given him more than enough money for passage back to Natal. He pondered his good fortune and reckoned the gods were being good to him for a change. Nevertheless, he wasn't going to waste any more time in Korlakota. He was determined that he would catch a ride on the next ox cart headed east.

The familiar road took Nayadu down and alongside the Godavari. He knew that in another few months, the monsoon rains would arrive and that the river would swell into a tempestuous beast. For Nayadu, she was a beast that demanded respect. He prayed to her more than he prayed to Shiva. The River's mood meant life or death to villages that fringed her banks, and Nayadu had always been her staunchest devotee.

Today, she was ambling slowly along, and Nayadu stepped up his pace to keep up.

*****

But Nayadu would soon pass a familiar landmark—his farm, and curiosity would not allow him to pass without stopping.

He was surprised to see that a family had taken residence on the property and that the land was being farmed. Though the rains hadn't yet reached these parts, the land was still verdant. *The place looks good*, he thought to himself. He traversed down the steep grade and found a young man yoking a pair of oxen. He smiled as soon as the young man noticed him approaching and said, "I'm Nayadu."

"Nayadu? You're the man who used to live here. Do you know who I am?" he asked.

He squinted and replied, "Should I?"

"I'm Sangam Bukkaya's grandson, Sunish."

"Bukkaya! How did you land on my farm?" Nayadu lashed out.

The young man recoiled. "Don't be angry with me. The farm was given to me by my grandfather."

"I didn't know that Bukkaya had the right to give away my farm."

"It was the Zamindar who asked Tata if he knew of anyone who could take over the farm. Tata asked me if I was interested, and I said yes. But he's gone now." His head lowered. "Died several years ago."

"Oh, I'm sorry," said Nayadu.

"He'd been ill for some time."

"So what about the Zamindar?" asked Nayadu.

"What about the Zamindar?"

242

"Do you pay him to farm this land?"

"Very little. He and Tata were good friends."

"I know. So I wonder who's good friends with the Zamindar now, now that your Tata is no longer around," said Nayadu.

"I don't know what you mean, but you can ask him yourself. Here he comes now."

The last two people on earth that he would have wanted to see again were descending slowly down the steep trail on horseback. Riding behind R. K. Chouderey was his agent and right-hand man, Chandra Sudhakar. Nayadu considered running but realized that there was nowhere to flee except into the Godavari.

"Greetings, Chouderey garu, Sudhakar garu," said Sunish.

"Yes, greetings to you. You have company, I see," said Chouderey.

Nayadu tried not to make eye contact with the two men, hoping they would not stay.

"Yes, this is Nayadu. He used to live on this land," said Sunish, completely oblivious to the tensions that existed between Nayadu and the two men.

Nayadu didn't know what else to do except smile and greet the two men. He could only hope that the years had softened them. Chouderey and Sudhakar looked at each other and then started laughing. Nayadu wasn't sure if he should laugh along with them. He smiled awkwardly from the side of his mouth.

"Nayadu, did you come back to claim your farm?" Chouderey asked.

"Uh, no, Chouderey garu, I just stopped to greet this young man."

"Going somewhere?" he asked.

"I was just leaving, yes," Nayadu replied with a slight quiver in his voice.

"Don't we still have some unfinished business?" Chouderey asked as he spit betel nut just inches from his bare feet.

Nayadu was cornered. He had no clever answers and nowhere to turn.

"Please just let me go on my way", he pleaded. "You have already taken my farm."

"I didn't want to take your farm away from you, Nayadu. You borrowed money from me and didn't pay me back," Chouderey said.

Sudhakar nodded.

"What do you reckon the interest on that loan is by now, Sudhakar?" asked Chouderey.

"More than he has, I'm sure," Sudhakar answered wryly.

"I'm going to make you a deal, Nayadu," said Chouderey. "I'll take all the money you have on you, and you are free to go to wherever you are going."

"But I don't have any money?" said Nayadu.

"If I find that you are lying to me, then there is no deal."

"What does that mean?" Nayadu asked.

"It means that you are asking too many questions," Chouderey growled. "I should turn you upside down and shake all the money out of you and then throw you into the Godavari. Is that what you want?"

Nayadu knew that if he handed over all the money that Ammamma had given him, he would have no way of getting back to Natal. Suddenly Sunish appeared in the doorway of the small house holding an old hunting rifle.

"Okay, okay, I'll give you what I have," said Nayadu.

As Nayadu slowly reached into his pocket, Sunish took aim and pointed the barrel of the gun squarely at Chouderey.

"Wait a minute. What are you doing? Put that gun down right now!" said Chouderey, pointing his finger at Sunish.

"If you two don't get off this property, you will never be seen again by your families," said Sunish while cocking the trigger into firing position.

"You'll regret this, boy!" yelled Chouderey as the two men turned their horses around and dashed away.

Nayadu couldn't believe what had just happened. Again, he was able to dodge the wrath of the Zamindar.

"Thank you," he said with a sigh of relief.

"I was happy to do that. I've never liked that man or his friend, Sudhakar. They have been bullying and stealing from the villagers for too many years now. I should have finished them off right there."

"What stopped you?" asked Nayadu.

"No gunpowder," he said with a broad smile.

Nayadu laughed.

"I inherited this old rifle from Tata, but I've never used it. I'm not sure it even works."

"So what will you do when the Zamindar comes back with his thugs?"

"I guess I'll cross that river when I come to it. But you should get going. Where are you heading?"

"To Rajahmundry train station."

"Okay, I'll give you a ride there. My oxen are already yoked and ready to go."

CHAPTER 20

When Siva marched into the office without taking off his hat or coat, the barrister knew something was awry. Siva placed the keys to the office on his boss's desk and said, "I'm going back to India."

He leaned back in his chair and, with a bemused glance, replied, "But why, my friend?"

"I've been away from my family for too long, Govindas. It's time I go to them."

He nodded and replied, "I understand. You've been away from your wife and girls for some time, my friend." He cleared his throat and continued, "But something tells me that this is not the only reason you're leaving."

Siva hesitated ever so slightly before saying, "No, that's it." But the barrister knew he was lying. He knew well that Siva had grown uncomfortable with his bold editorials to the *Times* and his daring crusade to gain equal rights for Indians. It was no secret that Siva wanted to simply live in peace and earn his wage—regardless of the existing conditions.

"Well," the barrister said haltingly. He never expected that Siva would up and leave on him. "We'll certainly miss you, my friend. I really had hopes for you around here."

"I had hopes too, Govindas, or is it Grover now?" He shook his head disappointingly. "I suppose my hopes were a little more selfish than yours." He turned and walked toward the door.

"Wait, what's to become of that Nayadu boy and that family staying with you?"

"Oh, they're moving."

"Can I ask where?"

"Back to the cane fields."

The barrister let out a sigh of disappointment. "Which one?"

"The Sykes Estate."

The barrister's eyebrows rose high into his forehead. "Will the boy be safe there?"

"I trust the Velus will look out for him."

The barrister rose from his chair and shook his head. "That's a real shame."

Siva nodded. "Yes, it is." Then he left.

*****

Chandu had grown quite used to being invited into Mr. Kingsford's den for sit-downs and usually had an inclination as to the direction it was going to take. But tonight, he hadn't a clue. His conscience for the most part was clear yet there was a nag of apprehension as he sunk into the familiar cushioning of the black leather chair.

"I read some of your writing, and I must say that I was impressed," said Mr. Kingsford. "You very well may want to compile all these experiences you've written about into a book one day."

He hardly considered his rantings book worthy but was flattered by Mr. Kingsford's remark.

"There are so many things I never knew about you, Chandu. You never told me that your mother died while rescuing you and your brother from the clutches of a wild lion or that your father was traveling around the world in search of the lost city of Nirvana."

"Oh," he lowered his head in embarrassment. He'd forgotten that he embellished some parts of his writings. "I thought it would be more interesting than—than the truth."

His eyebrows narrowed down toward his nose. "What's wrong with the truth?"

Chandu shrugged. "I was ashamed." He took another deep breath. "I was ashamed to write that my mother died of some strange disease and that my father cuts down sugarcane for the Whites and that they sent him to India to get more laborers but hasn't been heard from for several years now."

Mr. Kingsford's face relaxed. "Is that the truth?"

He nodded. "Yes."

"Well, I would have to say that what you just told me is no less interesting than being rescued from the clutches of a lion or finding the lost city of Nirvana, young man. Certainly, it's more believable. But I must admit, you have a colorful imagination and a real gift for writing."

He walked over to his desk, picked up his newspaper, and started scanning the front page. "Ah, here we go," he said, before handing Chandu the paper and pointing, "Read there."

He read the headline, "'*Lord Hildebrand rejects Natal bid for self-governance.*'"

"Do you see who wrote this article?" he asked.

"Oh, it says here, Winston Attleboro."

He smiled. "He's one of the *London Times* top newsmen, and he happens to be an old friend of mine. I spoke to him yesterday about taking you on as a weekend apprentice."

Chandu moved to the edge of the seat. "And?"

"He said he would think about it."

His body deflated like a ruptured dirigible.

"If he says he will think about it, then there's a good chance he will take you on."

"Thank you, Mr. Kingsford. That would be a dream come true."

"Just keep up your studies, lad."

*****

When Velu finished his term of indenture several years earlier, he vowed to never pick up another cane knife for as long as he lived. Five long arduous years of cutting and stripping stalks of cane from sunrise to sunset had hardened him. But the fire that nearly took his life along with his family had humbled him.

As they were ushered down the sandy corridor separating the stalls, he looked down at his pretty young daughter and could only hope that he would one day see her as a beautiful young bride. He was just happy to be alive.

"There are many empty spaces because we are short on labor," said Sirdar Govender. "Choose any empty space you see."

"We'll take this one," said Velu, pointing to the space on the very end.

"Good choice," said the sirdar. "At least this one has some privacy on one side."

Prema suddenly noticed that Pradip was nowhere in sight and called out for him.

"This Pradip is your son?" asked the sirdar.

"He's like our son," Velu answered. "His father was sent back to our country to get more workers. I'm sure you know of Nayadu."

The sirdar's eyes widened with surprise. "Pradip Nayadu?"

*****

Pradip slipped off without being noticed to the one familiar place on the estate that represented good memories—the creek. And it was there that he found his old friend Siyabonga. They embraced each other, and with the few English words that the two had in common, Pradip was able to learn that Siyabonga's old, blind dog had finally died. Nevertheless, the mood was far from somber, and they frolicked for an hour both in and out of the creek then rested underneath the large infamous willow tree that they jokingly referred to as the *gallow tree*. Not one, not two, but three laborers had hanged themselves from one particular limb that had since been cut down by Mr. Cozen, but the two boys gave little thought to the tree's history.

As they parted ways, Pradip realized that the only way back to the barracks was a well-worn trail that crossed over Bunglo Hill and within feet of where he was sure evil lurked—Sirdar Govender's bungalow.

Memories of his last days on the estate replayed in his mind. He shuddered as the vivid details of his beating flashed before him. He could still remember the stinging pain of the sjambok's leather straps and how the sirdar showed him so little mercy.

His heart started racing, and without hesitation, he sprinted up the trail desperately hoping for a pass. As he neared the bungalow just feet to the left of the trail, he imagined the sirdar leaping out and into his path and he ran even faster.

Safely over the hill, past the two bungalows, Pradip slowed his pace as the barracks came into view. Then it dawned on him and he stopped in his tracks. It would be sooner than later before the sirdar would corner him and take him to task for running away all those years ago. His hope was that time would have dulled the memory of those days and that there could be a new start.

Pradip turned around and looked up at the small bungalow. His heart started racing, and his palms started sweating. He decided it wasn't going to be today that he would face his nemesis. He wasn't ready. He turned to resume his trek down Bunglo Hill when he heard a familiar voice.

"Is that you Pradip?"

Sirdar Govender stood in his doorway with an uncharacteristic smile on his face, but Pradip still felt pangs of apprehension course through him.

"Come," he said, motioning with his hand. "I can hardly recognize you from the last time I saw you."

Pradip wondered whether this man was putting on an act to lure him into his lair to beat him once more. He contemplated running down the hill and to the safety of the barracks. But as he studied the sirdar's face, he could tell this was no act. This didn't even seem like the same man.

"The Velu's are concerned for you, boy. But I told them that you had likely gone down to the creek where you used to spend so much of your time. Was I right?"

He nodded and replied, "Yes, I saw my friend Siyabonga down there."

"Ahh, Siyabonga," he replied fondly. "Please, come inside my home, Pradip. There is something I want to tell you." The sirdar sensed Pradip's apprehension and said, "Don't be afraid. I'm not going to hurt you."

Pradip smiled out of the side of his mouth and proceeded into the bungalow.

"Honestly, I don't know how I recognized you. You've become a young man. Please, have a seat."

The first thing Pradip noticed was that the numerous shrines and lamps were now gone, and he was tempted to ask the sirdar about this. Then he noticed a Christian Bible on a small table, and he knew that this man had gone the way of his grandparents. As his father would have put it: He abandoned the traditions of our forefathers and was following the White man's religion.

The sirdar cleared his throat and looked Pradip straight in the eye. "Pradip, I believe your coming here was an answer to prayer."

Pradip was now convinced that this was not the same man. His face had softened. Even his voice was different.

Pradip answered, "You prayed I would come here?"

"Often." He paused and then his eyes moistened with emotion. "You need to know how sorry I am for how I treated you when you stayed here."

Pradip fought back the emotions he felt welling up.

"Do you think you can forgive me," the sirdar asked.

Pradip pursed his lips and nodded.

Just then Mr. Govender's wife came into the room with their baby boy, and he recalled the gossip about the childless couple—that they were under a curse.

"This is Matthew," he said, taking hold of the small child. "His name means *God's gift*. Would you like to hold him?"

Pradip smiled and extended his arms to receive the small child when suddenly he heard the shrill beckoning, "Pradiiiip!" It was Manisha.

"Ah, these people are worried about you," said the sirdar. "Go to them, and we'll meet again."

*****

Chandu arrived home late from school one afternoon and was summoned by Mr. Kingsford's middle daughter, Elizabeth to join her father in his den. There, sitting across from him was a youngish man, rather unkempt, bouncing the youngest Kingsford daughter, Gertie on his knee.

"Chandu," said Mr. Kingsford. "We've been waiting for you."

Gertie continued to giggle wildly though the man had already set her down, and her father dismissed her from the room. "This is Winston Attleboro."

"From the *London Times*? he asked, and both men chuckled.

"The same," he replied, extending his hand. Chandu determined that this man's smooth face and simple appearance belied the sophisticated prose attributed to him in the paper. No frock coat, no ascot, not even a tobacco pipe—just gray wool trousers and a tieless white shirt.

The newsman said, "You're interested in journalism, I'm told." His words were swift, leaving him to assume he needed to get back to the office to make a deadline.

"I do like to write," he replied.

"Mr. Kingsford says you have some writing talent and a colorful imagination."

Chandu shrugged and revealed a bashful smile.

"But it takes more than that to do what I do. You have to see the unusual and the ironic in the everyday. And you have to be curious." He suddenly stopped and looked him straight in the eye. "Are you curious?"

"I *am* curious," he replied.

"Good. It's an exciting time to be in this line of work. We turn out mass quantities of papers with linotype machines and rotary presses. Within minutes, we can send stories overseas with telegraph and inter-ocean cables. It's absolutely shocking how influential a talented newsman can be," he said in a single breath.

"Mr. Attleboro was the one who broke the story about Jack the Ripper," said Mr. Kingsford.

The newsman snickered, "Made the bloke a bloody celebrity—no pun, of course."

Mr. Kingsford chuckled at the newsman's little play on words, and Chandu smiled along.

"So," said Mr. Kingsford as if he were preparing to sell his old friend a new suit, "would you like Chandu to come see you this Saturday?"

The newsman stood up and turned to Chandu. "Come by Saturday at nine, and we'll talk some more."

*****

The barrister's case file was as diverse as it was deep. He was representing the spectrum of Indian immigrants ranging from wealthy Muslims to illiterate laborers as well as defending all the disproportionate allegations that were being leveled against the Indian community.

But with Siva gone, he found the growing workload unbearable. No longer could he take on new cases and he maintained that position even when an Indian pastor came knocking on his door late one Friday afternoon.

"Sir, I've traveled a full day's journey from Stanger on behalf of a young girl in desperate need of your help."

The barrister was already preparing to leave the office and asked, "Your name, sir?"

"Pastor Gopal Thomas."

"Pastor, I'm not taking on any more cases right now."

"Please, sir, allow me to tell you her story before you say no."

The barrister hesitated momentarily before answering, "Since you're a man of God, it's my honor to listen. But it won't change my ability to take her case. Please sit," he said, gesturing toward a nearby chair.

"This girl I speak of works on a tea plantation in Stanger. She finished her indenture several years back, you see, and had intentions of leaving the estate to find work in the city."

"How old is this girl?"

"At that time, she was about eighteen. The plantation owner told her that she would have to pay a three-pound tax if she were to continue living in Natal."

The barrister interrupted, "Only true if she came here after 1895."

"That's right, sir. She came here in 1888. But this young girl didn't know any better, you see, and she agreed to reindenture with this owner because she didn't have the three-pounds."

The barrister nodded. "I don't think there's anything I can do for this girl, Pastor."

"There's more, sir. That plantation owner just went and sold this girl for the purpose of marriage to one of the laborers on the estate for twelve-pounds.

The barrister's countenance changed. "How do you know all this, Pastor?"

"One of my church members works on the same plantation. She was greatly concerned and asked me to pray for that young woman."

His fingers tapped rhythmically on the desk, and the pastor knew the barrister was contemplating what to do.

"What's this owner's name?"

"It's the DeWitt plantation."

The barrister nodded as if he already knew the answer. Mr. DeWitt owned the largest tea plantation on the North Coast and had a reputation for mistreating Indian labor—the most serious of which was murder. But even the Protector of Indian Immigrants was able to do nothing more than fine the owner, and the barrister knew that justice might be elusive.

"Any witnesses?"

The pastor nodded. "I think so."

He pursed his lips and shook his head side to side. "I don't have the time to pursue this." Then he slammed his fist on the desk and said, "But I'm going to make time."

*****

Within weeks, the barrister, with the help of the Protector of Indian Immigrants, brought a suit against the plantation owner on a number of charges including slavery, fraud, and exploitation. The case went quickly to trial, and the estate owner pled innocent of the charges maintaining that the girl had manufactured the story to discredit him and to free herself from her term of indenture. Under ordinary circumstances, the word of a coolie girl would carry little weight against that of a White plantation owner.

The barrister, however, corroborated the girl's story with the testimony of the man to whom she was sold. The man was disinclined to testify against his master but even more reluctant to lose out on the twelve-pounds that he had paid for the girl. The barrister convinced him that a fair trial would allow him to recoup his twelve-pounds.

The trial was over before the end of the day but not without a fair amount of legal wrangling, a decision was granted in favor of the girl. Not only was she granted her freedom from the fraudulent marriage but from the second term of indenture as well. Not surprisingly, the plantation owner avoided jail but did have to pay some large fines, including the reimbursement of twelve pounds to the jilted laborer.

For the barrister, victory was sweet, but for the pretty yet demure twenty-year-old, it was bittersweet. With no place to live and no means to provide for herself, she turned to the pastor, who had already invested some interest into her well-being.

Pastor Gopal Thomas was as kind as he was passionate and was devoted to his God. He arrived into the colony in 1886 a broken and desperate man. He lost his young wife and child while she was giving premature birth aboard ship. After he served out his term of indenture working for the Natal Government Railways, he bought a small plot of land in Stanger, where he started a church.

He now had a flock of twenty-six faithful congregants, and when he wasn't leading the Sunday worship service, he was visiting the different homes of his church members to encourage and pray for them.

The pastor beseeched the same woman who had alerted him of the girl to now take her in as a temporary border and she was happy to acquiesce. She had a daughter that was close in age and believed it to be a privilege to come to the aid of this young girl.

Pastor Thomas made it a point to check in during the girl's first week with the family. He also wanted to invite the girl to church on

Sunday morning. He knew that she wasn't a Christian, but he wasn't going to let that stop him from at least extending an invitation.

"Good morning, Pastor," she said. Her smile was radiant but revealed her awkwardness. The pastor looked at her and then looked at her again. He had briefly met with her on several occasions before and during the court hearing, but now he seemed sure that he had met her on another occasion. There was a familiarity about her that he hadn't noticed before.

"Good morning, Arti," he replied in Arti's native language of Telugu. The pastor was from the northern region of Tamil Nadu but knew a bit of Telugu. "How are you getting on?"

"Good," she said with a soft smile.

"Very good," he said. "These are wonderful people you are staying with. They will take good care of you."

"They are, and I am getting on well with Nirusha. She is very nice to me."

"Arti," he said, clearing his throat. "I want to invite you to my church this Sunday. Will you come and join us?"

"Sure," she said. "But I'm not Christian."

He laughed. "It doesn't matter. We welcome everybody."

She smiled bashfully. "Okay then."

The pastor's face lit up. "Great!" he exclaimed.

"One more thing, Arti," he said, his fingers interlocked as if he were getting ready to pray.

"What is it, Pastor?" she asked innocently.

"I feel that we have met somewhere before, perhaps many years ago. Do you feel the same?" he asked.

She shook her head slowly side to side. "If we've met, Pastor, then maybe it was in a previous life."

He laughed. "No, I'm sure it was in this lifetime."

*****

Chandu was unaware of Winston Attleboro's rising celebrity largely because of his disinterest in reading the daily news. But the newsman's sensationalized stories surrounding this mysterious murderer, whom he'd dubbed Jack the Ripper, had brought him renown. His penchant for recounting, with vivid detail, what he believed occurred based on his examination of a crime scene left readers spellbound. While his peers considered him unorthodox and speculative, his editor believed him to be the reason newspapers were selling better than ever.

Chandu wondered why the man would even consider hiring someone like himself as an apprentice? Then he learned that the newsman had been following the events surrounding the Indian question down in Natal. He had become keenly aware of this firebrand barrister who was a thorn in the flesh of every European bent on maintaining a certain status quo in the colony.

When Mr. Kingsford casually mentioned to Mr. Attleboro that Govindas Mahendhi had been sponsoring Chandu's schooling efforts, he suddenly took an interest in the young man's prospects. So it was that he spent an inordinate amount of time probing Chandu about the barrister—his likes, his dislikes, his habits, what he liked to eat, even the company he kept.

Chandu was happy to oblige. After all, he was being mentored by one of London's favorite newsmen. What's more is that he had no reason to suspect his interest in the barrister's personal life to be anything more than human curiosity.

Then he read Mr. Attleboro's piece on Mr. Mahendhi, and everything became clear. The newsman was as cunning as he was gifted at writing. Chandu felt betrayed and disillusioned. Mr. Attleboro used information that he shared with him to misrepresent and even slander the barrister. Chandu's stomach turned as he read how Mr. Mahendhi had greedily clawed his way to social prominence on the backs of his oppressed Indian brothers. Chandu read of the barrister's lavish spending and frequent galas, entertaining women of questionable character, and he felt nauseous.

Everything that he told the newsman about the barrister was exaggerated and taken out of context, and when he confronted Mr. Attleboro with his objections, his curt reply was: "I'm here to sell newspapers, old sport."

Chandu, however, was not. It was time to go home.

CHAPTER 21

Nayadu walked out onto the deck of the SS *Courtesan* when the Natal coastline came into sight and suddenly felt anxious. *Had his wire been received or had he been written off as deceased? Would Mr. Heinz and Mr. Cozen be angry with him since he was returning alone? Would he even have a job or place to live?*

All these questions swirled around in his head.

Never mind that he had spent most of that time unjustly imprisoned in a small, rat-infested hole with bars. Forget that he was nearly lynched by an unforgiving Zamindar and his agent. These are things that Nayadu would blame on his karma—events of which Nayadu knew Mr. Heinz would care very little.

*****

As Chandu knelt over his suitcase, trying to squeeze in the various mementos from his time in London, Mr. Kingsford said, "Any room for this?" In his hand was a photograph of Chandu surrounded by the Kingsford family shortly after he arrived in London. Annabelle stood next to him while Mr. Kingsford stood behind him. He truly felt like he became a part of the family, yet he dreadfully missed his own.

Mr. Kingsford's smile masked his disappointment that he had not finished what he started. But deep down he knew that he was not destined to become a lawyer. Mr. Kingsford watched with fatherly concern as Chandu gradually lost interest in his studies. His admonishments to persevere ultimately came to naught.

He, too, was disappointed that Winston Attleboro had used his relationship with Mr. Mahendhi to source information that he would use to misrepresent his dear friend. He could hardly blame Chandu for cutting his apprenticeship short under such circumstances.

"You became the son we never had," he said fondly. Chandu felt his emotions start to well up and decided that he would tuck the photo away between two pairs of knickers. He continued, "Don't feel like you failed, lad. I believe you'll find your purpose back home in Natal. You're bright, and that will illuminate the way for you."

"Thank you, Mr. Kingsford. That means a lot to me."

"Don't give up on your writing," he continued. "Perhaps that talent and imagination you have will make room for you."

"Perhaps," he replied, but Mr. Kingsford knew that there were other things on his mind.

"So what's got your joy, lad? Is it Annabelle? Are you disappointed about how things turned out with her?"

"No," he replied with a slight chuckle, "nothing to do with Annabelle—though I'm disappointed that she's not here to say good-bye. I thought we were friends."

He snickered. "Probably Charles' doing. You know that he's quite jealous of you."

"Jealous? Of me?"

"Oh yes, he is."

"But why would he be jealous of me?"

"Well, because—you're bright and you're—you're a man of the world." He smiled and then added, "So to speak."

He snickered, "But Annabelle didn't see me that way."

"Oh, I think she did. She's just a bit whimsical right now."

"You think she and Charles will marry someday?"

He rolled his eyes and said, "I can only hope. But I believe your father has already picked out a nice girl for you back home."

"You think?"

He pursed his lips and grinned. "I think so."

He pulled the suitcase shut, but it was overstuffed. "Move over," he said, and then he sat down on the bag, compressing it enough so it was able to latch shut. He grinned satisfactorily, put his hand on

Chandu's shoulder, and said, "So then, what is it? What's got your joy?"

"Mr. Mahendhi thinks I'm coming home for a break from my studies. He doesn't know that I'm going home to stay."

Mr. Kingsford lowered his head momentarily and then looked up sheepishly. "He knows, lad. It was my duty to tell him since he has entrusted you into my care."

Chandu's chest tightened with his words, knowing that the barrister had put so much hope in him becoming an associate.

"Should I be worried?" he asked.

With a nod, he replied, "Yes, I was going to give you this later, but now is a good time."

The wire read: "*Come to my office when you arrive so we can discuss your future with G. K. Mahendhi and Associates.*"

"What do you think this means?" he asked.

He paused for a moment and then said, "My old friend is a reasonable man. I believe he'll consider everything you've been through before making a decision. I believe your experiences here in London will serve you well."

"I'm sure you're right, Mr. Kingsford. You always are. But I can't think of any experiences at the moment that will benefit me back home."

He cleared his throat. "Well, I happen to know that relations between the Indians and Whites are only getting worse in Natal."

He lowered his head and mumbled, "The Whites just don't like us."

Mr. Kingsford drew a deep breath and shook his head side to side. "Racialism." Then he laughed and said, "As if God made some sort of mistake. If you ask me, it was the Whites who were at the end of the line when God was handing out skin pigment. Don't you think?"

"Hey, that means I was ahead of you."

He replied with a smile, "You were—way ahead." Then the smile left his face, and he said, "But you became quite adept during your time here in dealing with those who did not like the color of your skin. You learned to avoid those who antagonize and walk away from trouble."

"That's easy."

"Not at first, it wasn't. You had to endure a few cuts and bruises before learning some diplomacy. And this is a skill that will serve you well back home. I believe that the God up there uses the events of our lives to prepare us for future events. That seems to be how it works, Chandu. I wouldn't worry if I was you. Consider yourself prepared for things to come. What's more is that I know Natal Indians could use a young man like you." He picked his bag up for him and said, "Come, it's time to go."

*****

As Nayadu prepared to descend the gangway, he looked around the quayside, hoping that somebody—anybody he knew had somehow received word of his arrival and was waiting to welcome him back into the colony. But there was nobody except two rough and ready dockers who had been assigned to check documents. They stood expectantly on each side of the lower gangplank.

The one on Nayadu's right held out his hand. "Where's your papers?"

"Papers?" Nayadu replied, and he suddenly realized that he had forgotten a lot of his English.

"Immigration papers, man!" he retorted impatiently. "All coolies need papers."

"Sir, I'm not a coolie."

"Not a coolie!" the man said mockingly. He glanced across to his partner and, with a snicker, said, "This coolie says he's not a coolie, and he doesn't have any papers with him. What should we do with him?"

The second man looked around before answering, "I gotta friend who needs coolies real bad. He'll pay good money for 'em."

The first man replied, "You'll have to split the money with me."

Nayadu implored the two men, "Please, sirs, I work for Mr. Heinz."

The second man hesitated for a second and then blurted out, "Never heard of him!"

Nayadu grabbed a hold of the second man's arm and said, "But, sir, I'm a sirdar."

"Unhand me!" he said, yanking his arm away.

The first man cocked his head slightly and squinted his eyes. "Then where are you coming from?"

"India," Nayadu replied, "to get more workers for Mr. Heinz."

The first man snickered. "And where are these workers?"

Nayadu knew his explanation would do little to satisfy the men. He looked back up the gangplank hoping somebody would be coming behind him, but he was one of the last to debark.

The two dockers looked at each other and then each shook their head side to side, grinning slyly. The first man grabbed Nayadu by the back of his shirt and said, "Come with me, Mr. Coolie."

Nayadu was tied up and thrown into a small holding cell until the sun settled low in the sky. It was then that both men came and retrieved Nayadu, throwing him onto the back of a flatbed wagon and covering him with several empty burlap sacks.

As the two set out heading north, the first man asked, "How much will this coolie fetch?"

"Seven, maybe eight shillings."

The first man smiled. "Not bad for a day's work."

By the time they arrived at the estate, it was late, and several dogs started barking at the sound of the approaching wagon. The estate manager appeared with his Brown Bess musket at his side, and he immediately recognized the second man in the light of a three-quarter moon.

"You have something back there for me?" he said, wasting no time with formalities.

Hearing the estate manager's gravelly voice, Nayadu sat up at once. "Mr. Cozen! It's me—Nayadu."

A stunned Mr. Cozen moved closer to the wagon and said, "Nayadu?"

A smile swept across Nayadu's face. "It's me, lahnee."

He turned to the two men and, with a bewildered look, asked, "Where did you find *him*?"

The two men looked at each other, puzzled, and then the second man said, "Uh, he came in on the *Courtesan* this afternoon. Told me that he worked for you and that you would pay me if I delivered 'em here to you."

"But why is he tied up?" asked Mr. Cozen.

The man cleared his throat. "Well, he doesn't have any papers, so I didn't want to take a chance that he was—uh—sneaking into our colony."

Mr. Cozen untied Nayadu's hands and helped him down from the wagon. Nayadu had nothing but the clothes on his back, and Mr. Cozen kept his long-lost sirdar at an arm's length. "My god, Nayadu, what the hell happened to you?"

"They locked me up, lahnee," said Nayadu as the two of them started walking toward the barracks.

"Wait a minute, Cozen," said the docker, "aren't you forgetting something?"

"Oh," said Mr. Cozen, reaching into his pocket. He walked back and handed the man a shilling and said, "Thanks for bringing back my sirdar."

*****

The estate manager glanced over at his bedraggled sirdar with an awkward smile and said, "I can't believe you're back, Naidu. I'd given up on you."

Nayadu fought back his emotions, and with clinched lips, he simply nodded.

Mr. Cozen smiled, "Naidu, you need to get some rest. Go find a place to sleep in barracks for now, and we'll meet up in the morning. I want to hear everything that happened to you."

As Nayadu retraced the old familiar trail leading behind the estate down to the barracks, he started counting all his recent good fortune. What were the odds that those two dockers, with their evil intentions, would try and sell him to the very estate which he was destined? He looked up at the moon and smiled, thankful for the light that it was shedding on the trail. It was warm that evening, and Nayadu was glad for he had nothing to cover himself while he would sleep.

He started whistling a tune—a tune that he only whistled when luck seemed to be chasing after him. It was a tune that his boys knew well with their father's trademark style of whistling off key, usually flat. And when Pradip heard the familiar tune, there was no mistaking that their long-lost father had returned. He jumped hastily off a lower tree branch in front of the barracks.

"Nana!"

Nayadu was both elated and stunned at the sight of Pradip. Even in the dim light, he could see that his younger son had grown tall and handsome and decided then that Pradip's features—his thick, wavy hair and pronounced cheeks—would serve well to keep Archana's memory alive. When the two hugged, Nayadu had to look up at his youngest son, who was now sixteen years old.

Then a sudden bristling of some branches on the tree startled Nayadu. It was a windless night, and he said, "What was that?" Pradip turned toward the tree and replied, "Probably a monkey." The branches stirred again, and a shadowy figure fell suddenly to the ground landing with a dull thud. Nayadu cautiously backed away while Pradip ran over and lowered himself onto one knee. "Are you okay, Manisha?" he asked, taking her hand into his. She smiled. "I'm okay, Pradip," and he helped her to her feet.

Nayadu walked over and set his hands on his hips. "Manisha?"

She smiled bashfully, "Yes, Uncle."

"The Velus are here, Nana," said Pradip. "I've been staying with them."

"The Velus are here?"

"Yes, Nana, they're living here—in the barracks."

Overwhelmed and confused, Nayadu scratched the side of his stubbled face and then said, "And Chandu—where is he?"

"London, Nana—getting schooled."

Nayadu's eyes widened as big as saucers, "London!" After Pradip explained to his father how this barrister, Govindas Mahendhi decided to sponsor Chandu's education overseas, he raised his eyebrows and said, "My luck is really turning."

*****

Tomasz was from Poland and had left his homeland ten years earlier looking for untamed frontiers. He was a jack-of-all-trades and had spent those years moving around Europe and the United Kingdom but failed to find what he was looking for. It was only after several weeks at sea that he finally divulged the true purpose of his quest, and that was to find a wife.

Now he was in his thirties and became convinced that he would have to travel to a distant land to find the wife he was looking for—as he put it, "where the women have high cheek bones and the sun has kissed their skin."

When Chandu told his roommate, Tomasz that there was no shortage of dark-skinned women in Natal, he was pleased. But Chandu found it strange that he would desire women who were considered inferior in his society, and when he expressed this to him, he scoffed.

He asked, "Where you come from, are you inferior?"

"Sadly, yes." he answered. "If you're not White, then you are a second-class citizen."

This greatly distressed Tomasz, and they talked at great length about the dynamics that were shaping the ever-changing society in Natal. And when he explained to Tomasz how the barrister had sent him to London to study law so that he might assist him in his practice but that he failed miserably, he disagreed.

"You are a writer, no?"

Chandu nodded tentatively.

"Yes, you are, and you were a newsman in London?"

"Well," he replied hesitantly, "I interned for a short period of time."

He smiled broadly. "Good enough." He smacked his open hand on the table and said, "You go home and start your own newspaper." He leaned over, close enough that Chandu could smell the pickled sardines he'd eaten earlier. "And I want to help you, my friend."

"A newspaper?" he thought out loud.

"Of course," he said assuredly. "You get this barrister to buy a printing press, and you are soon to change the way people think."

*****

Nayadu rose early the next morning as he was accustomed to doing. It was Sunday, and all was quiet at the first light of dawn. He gazed contently upon his son as he slept. He crossed his legs and sat, thinking about the meeting he would have with Mr. Heinz and Mr. Cozen. The estate manager had referred to him as Sirdar and that comforted him. Perhaps his job was secure, he thought to himself. But he still worried how Mr. Heinz would receive him.

Then he poked his head out and looked down the wide, sandy corridor that separated the north- and south-facing stalls. Soiled blankets were strung from wall to wall offering each family a thin veil of privacy. Curious, Nayadu peered between the slats of wood separating him from his neighbor, but there was yet enough light to make out faces.

He knew the Velus were living on the very end, several stalls away on the same side because Pradip had informed him the previous evening. He was anxious to reunite with his old friend.

He thought about Manisha and how beautiful she had become. At fourteen, she was practically a woman now, and surely, there were families that were eyeing her as a future daughter-in-law. He lay back and tucked his clasped fingers behind his head, waiting for some more signs of life before he would start reacquainting himself with the estate.

"So what's a sirdar doing here in the barracks?" came the familiar scratchy voice, startling Nayadu from his hazy thoughts. Without hesitating, Nayadu jumped up from his resting place and threw his arms around his long-lost friend. He stepped back, nodded, and grinned with a broad smile. "Fate has brought us together again."

"My daughter woke me early this morning and told me that you came here last night. I had to see for myself," he said with a reserved smile.

"Walk with me to the creek," said Nayadu, motioning toward the door. "I've not bathed for days."

Once outside, Velu patted Nayadu on the back and said, "Glad you made it back." Nayadu smiled, and the two said nothing as they walked up the hill separating them and the creek. No other words were needed. The stories could wait for another time when everyone was gathered. For now, it was just good to be in the quiet company of an old and trusted friend.

As they approached the top of the hill where two of the sirdars' bungalows sat overlooking the entire estate, Velu said, "The boy says that you were living here."

Nayadu hardly glanced at the bungalows but rather feasted his eyes on the cool water of the creek at the bottom of the hill. He shrugged his shoulders and said, "I lived in a jail for more than nine hundred days."

*****

The creek was lower than usual, and Nayadu stepped carefully across the smooth, sun-blanched boulders before lowering himself into the water. He forgot how refreshing its waters were. He scooped a rounded stone off the bottom of the creek and started scrubbing the grime off his arms and legs. "Here," said Velu Uncle, taking a small piece of soap wedged in between two branches and tossing it to Nayadu.

After scouring himself clean, he dabbed himself dry with his sullied pancha and then proceeded to put on his only shirt. "Here," said Velu Uncle, taking off his shirt and handing it to Nayadu, "wear this."

Nayadu smiled as he took the shirt. "You're a good friend, Velu." Nayadu pulled the sleeve of the shirt to his nose and said, "I forgot what a clean shirt smelled like."

Velu smiled and said, "Come and join us for breakfast." Nayadu was convinced at that moment that the Velus were destined to be in-laws. Whether Velu felt the same way or not, he wasn't sure. He cleared his throat and said, "Manisha has grown."

Velu gave Nayadu a curious look and then replied sarcastically, "Children do that."

"She's blossomed into a beautiful flower," said Nayadu, and the two started walking slowly up the hill.

Velu nodded. "Yes, she takes after her mother."

Nayadu cleared his throat again before saying, "She'd make a good wife for my son."

Velu Uncle stopped in his tracks and turned to Nayadu. "I've been thinking the same."

A smile swept across Nayadu's face. "Really? You've been thinking the same?"

"Of course. I think Pradip is a fine boy. He reminds me of myself."

The smile suddenly disappeared from Nayadu's face. "Pradip?"

"Yes, he's got a strong spirit, Nayadu. I like that."

"Wait a minute, Velu. I was speaking of my older boy, Chandu. I can't go marrying off the younger one first."

"Chandu?" Velu replied, scratching his head. "And Manisha?"

"Soon, he'll be home from overseas, Velu—schooled."

The concept and value of being educated was lost on Velu, and Nayadu as well for he was lost for words when Velu replied, "But the boy doesn't like to work." Nayadu lowered his head before he added, "Besides, Manisha and Pradip get along nicely."

Nayadu couldn't deny what he'd seen the night before when Manisha tumbled out of the tree. Had he not just returned from overseas and had, perhaps, less important things occupied his mind; he might have been more inclined to ask some embarrassing questions. The childhood relationship between Pradip and Manisha had obviously evolved.

But Nayadu always told his boys when they were younger: "First, we'll find a good and respectable wife for Chandu, then for Pradip." Though marriage was far from their minds at that time, it made sense. With age comes precedence.

Nayadu lifted his head toward Velu and said, "Chandu is a smart boy, you know. He'll be a lahnee when he comes back."

"A lahnee? What kind of lahnee?"

Nayadu shrugged. "I don't know what kind of lahnee, but getting schooled makes you smarter and more important. You watch."

Velu pursed his lips. "I don't know, Nayadu."

He negotiated further, "And since I don't have any daughters for whom I would have to pay dowry, I won't demand any from you."

Velu's eyebrows rose high into his forehead. "Let me speak with her mother before making a decision." And as the two started making their way toward the barracks, Velu added, "After breakfast."

*****

Chandu was no longer apprehensive about the barrister. In fact, he was excited about telling him what he planned to do. He convinced himself that he too, would be pleased with the idea of starting up a newspaper. But first they had to find their way back home, wherever that was.

The streets were quiet, and it was then that Chandu realized it was Sunday. Finding a ride on the back of an oxen cart was easy as industrious Indian boys made it their duty to drive by the wharf after dropping a load of cane at the mill. A newly arrived ship was rarely on schedule, and that meant passengers would be looking for transportation. It was a great way to earn a few extra pence.

But the mill was closed on Sundays and the streets were quiet. So Tomasz and Chandu started walking, hoping that a traveler would pass by. They walked for nearly an hour when a young Tamil boy driving an ox cart approached. The boy knew rides were few and far between and tried to take advantage of the two travelers. But when Tomasz threatened to take his cart, he quickly settled on three pence.

Tomasz, in fact, ordered the lad to take them to the barrister's office in spite of the fact that nobody knew where it was.

Mr. Mahendhi's message to Chandu before leaving London was clear: "Come to my office when you arrive so we can discuss your future with G. K. Mahendhi and Associates." What wasn't clear was whether he had a job or not.

Chandu wasn't even sure where he was going to lay his head that evening. Tomasz, on the other hand, was a seasoned wanderer and showed little concern about what lay ahead. He lived in the moment and was confident that the future would take care of itself.

It was late afternoon when they finally arrived at the law office of Mr. Mahendhi. Tomasz and Chandu spent the last few hours of the journey talking about the Indian struggle for dignity in the colony let alone equality and what it was going to take to achieve that. Tomasz was convinced that an Indian newspaper was a starting place in helping to establish a sense of community among the Indians.

As they debarked from the cart Tomasz pointed toward the front of the building and said, "Look there!"

Chandu turned abruptly and was shocked to see that the large paned window fronting the office had been shattered. As they moved closer to inspect the damage, it was clear what had happened. Someone hurled a brick through the window, and there was nobody to be found.

*****

Prema listened quietly as her husband told her of what Nayadu had proposed. She responded, "I think the boy's father makes a good point, Ammandi. Chandu *will* be a good provider for our daughter. We need to consider what is best for Manisha, not what the boy looks like or whether he has a strong spirit. These things won't get him far in life."

Manisha, who was washing dishes outside of the barracks, was able to hear her parents' conversation and came running inside. "No!" she yelled, startling them both.

"Manisha!" her mother responded. "What's wrong with you?"

Her sudden burst of rage turned to sulking. "You can't marry me to Chandu."

"Why not?" asked her mother.

Manisha put her head in her hands and sobbed. Her father put his arm around her and after some time said, "What about Pradip?" She didn't answer but stopped, weeping, and leaned her head on her father's chest.

"How can we marry her off to someone she doesn't like?"

"She doesn't know what's best for her. She's still a young girl. That's why we need to decide what is best for her. She will learn to love Chandu."

Manisha pulled away from her father and ran out of the barracks toward the creek.

*****

Underneath the gallow tree sat Pradip, and when Manisha approached, she said nothing about what transpired back in the barracks. She walked down to the creek, picked up a stone, and hurled it with awkward fury into the water.

"Something troubling you, Manisha?"

She ignored him and instead picked up another stone to toss into the water. Pradip sprang from his resting spot and caught Manisha's arm before she could fling the second stone. "Let go of me!" she whined.

Still holding her arm, he looked into her eyes and said, "Something *is* troubling you. Why don't you tell me?"

She turned her gaze away from Pradip's eyes, and the stone fell from her limp hand. She shook her head side to side, and a tear streamed down her face. "There's nothing to tell," she mumbled, barely audible.

Pradip put his hands firmly on her shoulders, gently squeezing them, and said, "Please—tell me what's troubling you."

She hesitated for a moment and then told him, "My parents are going to marry me off to your brother, Chandu."

Pradip's arms fell to his side, and he went silent.

"What are we going to do, Pradip?" she sobbed.

He pulled her close and angled his head so that it rested on hers. "I don't know," he answered. "But we have to do something."

CHAPTER 22

Mr. Heinz's office extended out from the side of the Sykes Manor and had windows on three sides. Mr. Sykes added the room onto the house only several years before he died but did so so that he might better see who was coming and going around the compound. He also wanted to be easily accessible to workers. That was the kind of man Mr. Sykes was. On the other hand, Mr. Heinz tended to be more private and was prone to keeping the curtains drawn, and today was no different.

Nayadu was able to hear Mr. Heinz's deep resonant voice as neared the door of the office. He supposed that the two men were discussing his future as sirdar and hesitated to see if he might hear what the men were saying.

Suddenly, the door flung open. Mr. Cozen smiled and said, "Come in, Naidu. We've been waiting for you."

Mr. Heinz pointed to a small wooden chair facing his desk and, before he was seated, asked, "I hear you ran into a bit of trouble back in your native land."

Nayadu nodded and contemplated what he might say in response. Then he blurted out, "I was jailed."

Mr. Heinz feigned a look of distress. "But why were you jailed, Naidu?"

Nayadu replied, "Because, lahnee, they thought I was going to steal their women."

Mr. Heinz couldn't help but chuckle, and Mr. Cozen followed suit.

Nayadu continued, "Then the Zamindar tried to steal the only money I had to get back here."

Mr. Heinz glanced quickly over at Mr. Cozen with a puzzled look and then asked, "What is a Zamindar?"

"Oh," Nayadu's face lit up, "he's this high-caste fellow who came in and became the big lahnee of all the farmland in Korlakota. We had to pay him taxes every month to protect us from foreigners."

Mr. Heinz looked again over to his estate manager with incredulity. He turned back to Nayadu and said, "You paid this chap to protect you?"

"We had no choice. If we didn't pay, he would send his men to force us."

The two men listened with astonishment as Nayadu unfolded the entire tale of how his family narrowly escaped from the Zamindar and his men before their trip over the Kala Pani and how a strange twist of fate had crossed their paths once again. When Nayadu finished Mr. Heinz said, "You're either the luckiest man alive or the unluckiest man alive."

Nayadu grinned. "I'm alive, lahnee, so I must be lucky."

Mr. Heinz took a deep breath and leaned back in his chair. "Well," he said before clearing his throat, "Cozen and I are glad you're back with us though we had high hopes you would've returned with workers. I spent a lot of money to send you, you know."

Nayadu lowered his head shamefully. "I know, lahnee, I'm really sorry."

"You still want to be sirdar, don't you?"

"Of course, lahnee."

"Good, good," he replied. "We like having you as a sirdar. But a lot has happened since you were gone." His eyebrows narrowed down toward his nose as he asked, "What do you know of this Mahendhi fellow?"

Nayadu tightened his lips. "I don't know him, lahnee. But he must be a good man. He sent my oldest boy to London to get schooled."

Mr. Heinz snickered. "This 'good man' as you call him is a troublemaker, Naidu! If he gets his way, you'll be out of a job. In fact, we'll all be out of jobs."

Nayadu grew increasingly confused as to where Mr. Heinz was leading him. "I don't understand, lahnee," he replied.

"Naidu, did you like living up there in that bungalow overlooking the entire estate?"

Nayadu's eyes lit up. "Yes, lahnee, very much."

Mr. Heinz smiled. "Do you want to move back up there?"

"Of course, lahnee."

"It's a nice way of life for you, isn't it, Naidu?"

Nayadu nodded and smiled. "I liked it very much."

"Well, this Mahendhi fellow doesn't want you to have that, Naidu. He wants to change everything about the way we run our farms. And if he succeeds, we'll all be out of business."

Nayadu was no less confused and stroked the stubble on his chin. "So what do you want from me, lahnee?"

"Mahendhi has sponsored your boy's education, has he not?"

Nayadu nodded.

"Though you don't know this chap you have a connection with him. And I suspect that you're interested in knowing how things are going with your boy, are you not?"

"Yes, I miss him very much, lahnee."

"Good. Then this is what I want you to do."

*****

There was nothing to be found other than the brick and a spattering of broken shards of glass. Nothing else seemed to be disturbed. Either it was a random act of vandalism or a not-so-subtle message to the barrister. But with all the feathers the barrister had been ruffling as of late, it was likely the latter.

Chandu exited through the front door still holding the brick when he and Mr. Kader rode up in the carriage. Before the horses even stopped, Mr. Kader yelled out, "What have you rogues done?"

Tomasz took several steps backward and was poised to flee the scene. Chandu quickly responded, "Mr. Mahendhi, it's me!"

*****

With Siva gone, the barrister was working more than ever. But as his activism for the plight of Indians in the colony increased, he was taking fewer cases for the wealthier Muslim Indians.

The greed and haughtiness of his more privileged clients contrasted sharply with lower caste Indians. Back home in India, he might not have had the same awakening. But here, it incensed him that his Indian brothers were afforded less dignity than the natives. And it wasn't only the Whites who treated the lower caste Indians with disdain. The wealthier Indians who had managed to come to the colony on their own volition made it their duty to distance themselves from the Indians who had entered the colony as indentured labor.

But Ali Kader was different. Though he was a Muslim and had a lucrative import business, he also sought to see that all Indians are treated with dignity. As long as he was able to run a profitable business, he considered it a privilege to help the INC with its mission.

*****

The two men jumped down from the carriage with bewildered expressions. "What's the meaning of this, boy?" the barrister asked. "And who is this fellow?"

"This is my friend Tomasz. We shared a cabin on the voyage home." But neither of the two men looked convinced that they had come in peace. "We just arrived here ourselves, Mr. Mahendhi, and found this inside your office."

The barrister managed a slight smile when he took the brick and set it inside the door. "One less brick I have to buy when I seal off this window, I suppose."

Mr. Kader, however, looked around nervously, wondering if someone might still be lurking nearby.

The barrister put his hands on his hips and quickly looked Chandu over from head to toe. "So you're back," he said with a hint of disdain.

"I am, sir, and I have some pleasing news for you."

He raised his eyebrows in a mocking sort of gesture and replied, "Oh, you do. Please tell me as I could really use some good news right now."

"Well, I, uh—I," and suddenly he found it difficult to say to the barrister what he had been dying to tell him for the last several weeks.

"Chandu is starting a newspaper," Tomasz announced in his stead.

"Uh, yes," he rejoined with a sudden burst of confidence. "I'm going to start Natal Province's first Indian newspaper."

The barrister showed no emotion as he asked, "Oh, you are? And how do you plan on funding this capitalist venture of yours?"

"Isn't this what your people need to bring them together?" Tomasz asked fearlessly.

"Perhaps," he replied. "But that doesn't answer my question."

"Well, I was thinking you could help us buy a printing press, Mr. Mahendhi."

When he didn't immediately respond, Chandu knew he was willing to at least consider the idea. He looked over to Mr. Kader, who responded, "Where does one buy a printing press?"

The barrister responded, "So you think this is a good idea, Ali?"

He shrugged. "Sure, why not? This could be a way to help educate our people about what is going on in our colony."

"That's right," Tomasz chimed in with his thick Polish accent. "The Indian people need their own newspaper."

The barrister nodded slowly and then smiled.

*****

Nayadu emerged from his meeting with Mr. Heinz and Mr. Cozen with mixed emotions. On the one hand he was promised that his position as a sirdar was secure and that he would be allowed to move back into his old bungalow within weeks. They would simply move the other sirdar out and into a smaller cottage at the bottom of the hill near the barracks. But it would come at a price.

He retreated to the same spot that he had always gone when he needed to think, and it was there next to the wall that separated the Sykes Estate from the Mills Estate that he sat for several hours.

He was under strict orders not to say anything to anybody about what had been discussed behind the doors of Mr. Heinz's office. But he'd been away for so long he had no idea what had been transpiring in his absence. Nor did he care quite frankly. He had already endured more than his fair share of traumatic events and only wanted to live in peace.

*****

The Velus were relaxing in their stall when Nayadu stopped by. Velu could tell that he was troubled.

"Do you know this Mr. Mahendhi?" Nayadu asked.

Velu nodded. "Wealthy bania lawyer, but a good man [*bania* was a term used by Natal Indians for Gujaratis]. Sent your boy to school, didn't he?"

Nayadu nodded pensively. "Yes, he did." And that meant a lot to Nayadu. How could a man who spent so much money on a kid he hardly knew to get an education overseas be considered a rogue?

"Why do you ask?"

Nayadu ignored the question and asked, "Why else is he a good man?"

Velu's eyebrows rose high. "I hear he's been fighting these Whites so we can have a better life." He glanced quickly at his wife and then added, "He's not like other high-caste Indians."

Nayadu again nodded thoughtfully and then made his way back to his own stall. He sat and pondered what was said about Mr. Mahendhi, both good and bad. Then he considered what he knew to be true about the man. He glanced around at the slats that barely concealed his neighbor's most personal business and considered that it was surely better than jail. How he hoped he might move back into the comfort and prestige that the bungalow on top of the hill offered. But he wasn't willing to pay the price.

*****

The notion of starting an Indian newspaper grew quickly on the barrister. "I'll look into seeing where I might buy a printing press tomorrow," he said. "But this day is nearing its end, and I'm guessing that you've not even seen your loved ones yet."

A sudden feeling of anxiety swept over Chandu as he was now being forced to confront the fate of his family. "Where's my brother, Mr. Mahendhi?"

The barrister glared sorrowfully over his bifocals and said, "I'm afraid the boy's back on the Sykes Estate. I haven't heard any other reports regarding his welfare. Shall I take you to him?"

His heart sank. "I don't understand. What happened? How did he end up back on the Sykes Estate?"

"A lot of things have transpired while you were away, lad. Siva left us and went back to his family in India. In the meantime, your old friends, the Velus came up from Port Shepstone and took your brother in. They too, however, ran into a bit of bad luck when their business burned to the ground. They were lucky to survive, but they lost everything they owned. With nowhere to turn, they went back to the cane fields."

"I have to say," the barrister continued, "I was quite distressed to learn of this news. I should like to see every Indian move up and out of these slave camps.

"And Nana?" he asked.

The barrister shook his head. "I'm afraid not lad."

This was not how things were supposed to have gone, he thought to himself. *Nana was a good man. Was the curse of the Kala Pani still upon us?*

"Come, lad," said the barrister. "Let me take you to the estate so you can see your brother and your old friends."

"But what about Tomasz?"

"He can stay with me for the time being."

278

"Yes, don't worry about me, friend. I can sleep anywhere," said Tomasz.

"Mr. Mahendhi, you wired that you wanted to speak with me about something as soon as I arrived back. What is it?"

"Oh," he replied, "we'll chat about that on the way to the Sykes Estate."

*****

The ride from Phoenix to the Sykes Estate was short, and the barrister wasted no time telling Chandu that he was disappointed that he squandered an opportunity most would never have. But he had been in contact with Mr. Kingsford and realized that being a lawyer wasn't his fate. He reckoned that perhaps his destiny was more purposeful than that of squabbling over points of law while wearing a silly powdered wig.

"I hadn't thought about this idea of starting an Indian newspaper, but the more I think about it, the more I like it," he said as he navigated the pockmarked dirt road. "Mr. Kingsford said you have a real talent for writing, so perhaps this is what you were destined to do."

Chandu nodded without speaking. But deep inside, there was an excitement that he was trying hard to contain.

"But," he continued, "it will take time to get this newspaper started. In the meantime, you're going to work for me until all the money that you misused is repaid. Is that fair, my young apprentice?"

"Yes," he replied eagerly. "That's fair! But what will I do for you?"

"Don't you worry. I'll have plenty of work for you to do. Oh, and since you don't seem to have a home, I expect that you'll be living with me."

They arrived in front of the gilded gates that fronted the Sykes Estate, and he felt a sudden pang of anxiety course through his veins. His last memory of the place was that of Sirdar Govender. He wondered whether he was still around.

"Mr. Mahendhi, I would like to stay here tonight with my brother, so you won't need to wait up."

He nodded slowly. "Are you sure?"

"Yes, I'm sure."

"Okay, I'll come back for you in the morning. We have a lot to accomplish."

*****

The smell of curry wafted up through the stale hot air, and his mouth began to water. He caught sight of a handful of women each cooking over small open fires. He stopped to see if he recognized anyone, but nobody looked familiar.

With his bag in hand, he moved slowly into the barracks. He carefully eyed each stall in eager anticipation that he would soon be reunited with his little brother and their long-lost friends—the Velus. He was already trying to envision what they might look like after all these years.

But with each measured step, his heart grew heavier thinking of the misery found in the barracks—where laborers were sheltered in no better conditions than the beasts of burden on the estate. He had now seen the world from a different lens, and this was no way for humans to exist.

He was beset with curious stares from families, most of whom had just finished dinner and had settled in for the evening. It appeared that a lot of the laborers that lived in the barracks before he left for London had moved on. Finally, he put his bag down and yelled, "Pradip! Where are you?"

Several stalls from the end, an all too familiar figure leaned out with a curious gaze, and before he could react, he bellowed, "Chandu! My son, you've come back to me!"

"Nana!"

"Am I dreaming?" he asked as they both embraced.

Nayadu stepped back, looked his son over, and then reached over and tugged on his moustache. "You couldn't grow this last time

I saw you." Then he looked up at his extended forehead. "And your hair, what happened to all your hair?"

Just then, Pradip appeared, and Chandu smiled with his arms open. "Come here, brother." He was now taller than both his father and older brother and, unlike either of them, bore a head of thick wavy hair.

"You're still my *little* brother, you know," he said, looking up to him.

He smiled and said, "I know." But his smile quickly faded, and he pulled away.

Chandu stood, staring at him, puzzled by his sudden coolness. Pradip responded with a disingenuous smile and said, "It's good to have you back, brother."

"And I hear the Velus are here."

From behind, a scratchy yet familiar voice replied, "That's right, boy."

They embraced, and Chandu rejoined, "Where's Aunty and Manisha?"

"Down at the creek washing the pots and dishes," he replied. Then a smile swept across his face. "Wait till you see Manisha. She's a beautiful young woman now."

Pradip backed slowly away and then dashed out the door. Nayadu winked dismissively at Chandu and said, "Tell you later."

"Everything okay?" he asked.

Velu said, "Maybe you should tell him now, Nayadu."

He nodded with a look of discomfort. "Okay, let's walk, son. I have something to tell you."

They walked toward the east side of the estate and stopped at a waist high stone wall that separated the Sykes Estate from the bordering Mills property.

"Your brother will be down by the creek," he said. "He's upset."

"What about?"

"You."

"Me?"

"And Manisha."

"And Manisha? What are you talking about, Nana?"

"The two of you in marriage."

"Marriage? To Manisha?"

"Of course, to Manisha. Why not? She is a beautiful young woman now who would make any father-in-law proud."

Chandu hadn't seen Manisha since returning and could only envision the whiney young girl who never left her mother's side. He objected, "But, Nana, Manisha's still a girl. She can't even—hold an intelligent conversation."

Incensed, Nayadu retorted, "You too good for us now that you're schooled? Did that place make you forget who you are? Where you come from? Your culture?"

Chandu slipped his hands into his pockets and lowered his head in shame. He could feel his father's eyes burning into the top of his skull while he etched with his foot in the dirt. He continued, "Do you know how many Indian men in this colony are suffering without wives?"

It was a problem that hadn't gotten any better during his time away from the colony. Chandu remembered one man during their early years on the estate who was known to them as Moon. He was well into his thirties and never married, and his desperation for a wife ultimately plunged him into the deepest recesses of depression and loneliness.

He pleaded first with Mr. Cozen and then Mr. Sykes for consent to return to India to find a wife but was denied permission. The lahnees failed to realize the gravity of Moon's state of mind. Moon, who was never a drinker, turned to alcohol as a means to drown his misery with calamitous effects. Emboldened by the alcohol, he started making unwanted comments and advances toward several of the wives working in the field.

One day, in a moment of drunken unrestraint, he forced himself on one of the laborers' wives, causing her to scream in utter terror. Her husband, who was cutting cane a short distance away, came running to her aid. When he saw Moon having his way with his wife, his used his cane knife to put an end to Moon's misery. In a blind rage, the woman's husband gutted her assailant and then severed his head.

In a strange twist of irony, the husband landed in prison for murder, and his wife ended up remarrying another worker on the estate.

When Chandu said nothing, Nayadu added, "How many of them would cut off their left foot for a girl like Manisha?"

Or someone's head, he wanted to say, but instead, he asked, "Can I think about it, Nana?"

"Think about it, son," he said, wagging his finger close to his face. "But don't forget what I said."

"You still didn't tell me why Pradip is upset about this whole thing."

Nayadu pursed his lips tight and drew a deep breath through his nose. "Those two have eyes for each other."

"Then," he answered with raised eyebrows, "why not marry them together?"

His brows furrowed. "I can't marry off the small one before the big one."

"But, Nana, if these two have eyes for each other—"

"They'll get over each other. I have to get you married first, and Manisha will make you a perfect wife."

*****

Back in the barracks, Nayadu and his son spent the next several hours trying to recapture all the years they spent apart. Chandu sat in awe, listening to his father's exploits in Korlakota—his time in jail and how he so narrowly escaped death at the hands of the Zamindar. By all reasonable expectations, Nayadu should not have been telling his story. He was surely going to live a long life.

And with the news of Thathiyya's passing, Chandu was moved to tears. He always believed that he was the stronger of his grandparents and that he would live for years to come. He felt it was unlikely that Ammamma would live much longer without her husband to care for her, and his heart grieved for her.

When the conversation turned toward his time in London, he had to be careful with his words. There were far too many incidents and experiments which a conservative Indian father would not understand. And though he never entered into an intimate relation-ship with Annabelle, he was reluctant to talk about her. Perhaps it was pride or maybe embarrassment. Whatever it was, he wanted to give his father the impression that he had his wits about him during his time abroad and that he wasn't so easily led astray by a girl.

And then he remembered Mr. Kingsford's uncanny admoni-tion as he was packing his suitcase: "I believe your father has already picked out a nice girl for you back home." He wondered how he could he have possibly known such a thing. *Surely,* he thought to himself, *this was my fate. The will of the gods revealed through Mr. Kingsford.*

*****

"Have you seen Manisha?" asked Velu. He had walked down to Nayadu's stall to find his daughter, and it suddenly occurred to them that Pradip had also not returned.

"Her mother left her down at the creek with Pradip hours ago. I thought she would have returned by now."

"Of course," Nayadu replied. "It's not like Pradip to stay away this late."

"Shall I go down to the creek to fetch them?" asked Chandu.

The two fathers looked at each other and then at Chandu. Then, almost simultaneously, they said, "No, you wait here." It was as though both of them realized at the same time why Pradip and Manisha were late in returning.

"Get some rest," Nayadu said. "Uncle and I will go together and get them."

Chandu didn't want to stay back, but he knew they wouldn't allow him to go. And though he was exhausted from his long jour-ney, he would not sleep easily. He was sure that something was awry.

CHAPTER 23

The moon and stars were hidden by clouds, making the night a montage of dark shadows. Even as Pradip and Manisha sat just feet apart on the bank of the creek, they were but silhouettes in each other's eyes. Manisha was warmed by Pradip's soft voice, and when he started stroking her arm with the back of his hand, she moved closer to him. Then she leaned back into Pradip's chest, and he nuzzled his nose in the softness of her silky black hair.

He took his hand and gently pulled Manisha's gaze toward his and said, "Are you sure you want me over my brother?"

She turned away from Pradip and replied, "How can you ask me that?"

"I have to know for sure."

"You're daft."

"Hey!"

"Well, you are."

"But Chandu is schooled now. He's going to make lots of money."

She looked at Pradip without saying a word, her look suggesting that she had little interest in anything but him. He gazed into her large round eyes then down at her lips, and he knew that he wanted to kiss her. He was sure that Manisha could hear his heart thumping in his chest as he moved his face toward hers.

"Maneeeeshaaa!" It was her father.

"Pradip, where are you?" Nayadu bellowed.

Both men were halfway down the hill when Pradip jumped to his feet. He extended his hand out to Manisha and pulled her to her feet. He put his hands on her cheeks as if he were going to kiss her and said, "Do you love me?"

She pulled close to him, her body firm against his and looked up into his handsome face. She nodded with a bashful smile.

"Then it's time."

"Time for what?" she asked.

He put his hand over her mouth. "Shhh! We have to go," he said in loud whisper. "If we go back, they are going to engage you to my brother."

"But where are we going to go?"

"I have an idea," he said, taking her by the hand.

"But, Pradip—"

"Shhh. Follow me."

*****

The two men returned to the barracks gravely concerned that Pradip and Manisha were nowhere to be found.

Prema started sobbing. "I didn't think they would run off when I left them."

"Where are they gonna go?" Velu scoffed. "They didn't even take anything with them. No clothes. No money." He snickered. "They'll be back as soon as they get hungry."

"What do you think, Nana?" Chandu whispered to his father. "You think they'll come back?"

He stared blankly and shook his head.

"You know where they went, Nayadu?" Velu asked.

Nayadu took a deep breath and then said, "I think Pradip is going to try and make his way back to India."

Prema gasped, "India!"

"How do you know this, Nayadu?"

"I know my son."

"How will they get back to India with no money, Nana?" Chandu asked.

"It's not hard to get aboard a steamer without being seen. All they have to do is get themselves to the docks and jump the next boat heading to India."

Prema leaned over and pulled on her husband's shirt. "We have to stop them, Ammandi."

Velu turned toward Nayadu and said, "Are you going to just sit here while your son tries to take my daughter to India?"

"How will we find them when there's no light? Besides, they're well on their way by now."

"We'll take horses, Nayadu."

Nayadu shot Velu a curious look. "Horses. Where are we going to get horses?"

"There are four good horses down in the stables. All we need is two."

"Are you mad, Velu? Cozen will lynch us for taking those horses."

"He doesn't have to know. If we go now, we'll be back before daylight."

"Those dogs will know. They bark when the wind changes direction."

Prema tugged on Velu's shirt again. "Then go tell Mr. Cozen our babies have run off. He'll help us."

Velu looked over at Nayadu and said, "You're a sirdar. Mr. Cozen will listen to you."

Nayadu pinched his lips together, contemplating the idea of waking up his boss. He wouldn't be happy. On the other hand, he reckoned Mr. Cozen as a fair man, in spite of his reputation. He recalled with bitter sweetness the concern Mr. Cozen showed for Archana and how he rushed the two of them to the doctor on the back of his wagon.

"Okay, Velu, we'll go."

"To tell Mr. Cozen?"

"No. We'll get a couple of horses and go find those two."

Velu smiled and said, "You sure?"

Nayadu's face was serious. He gave a quick nod and said, "I'm sure."

"Nana, must I come with you," Chandu offered.

"No," he replied without hesitation.

*****

Nayadu took the lock securing the stable door into his hand and whispered, "This is a different lock. Someone changed the lock."

Velu peered over his shoulder. "Are you sure? Try your key."

He tried to insert his key into the lock, but it didn't work.

Velu stepped onto the lower hinge of the door and pulled himself up so he was able to peer into the stable. "Hey, I can squeeze myself through here."

"Then what?" asked Nayadu.

"We take a couple of horses and go."

"How are you gonna get out?" Nayadu asked with a curious look.

Velu hesitated for a moment and then replied with raised eyebrows, "Didn't think about that." Frustrated, he stepped down and kicked the stable door with his bare foot.

"Shh, you're gonna wake up the whole farm."

Just then, Rex, Mr. Cozen's German shepherd started barking. Rex was harmless for the most part, but his snarl and long pointed teeth were enough to frighten even the bravest of souls. Velu let out an expletive before saying, "Let's go before that stupid dog finds us out."

Nayadu didn't need convincing. He had already started making his way back to the barracks before Velu had lowered himself down from the stable door.

*****

"I'm scared, Pradip," said Manisha as the two navigated the rocky dirt road without any help from the stars or moon. Pradip was barefoot and had already sliced the tender skin between the third and fourth toe of his right foot on a jagged stone. She considered whether his wound, which was causing him to favor his right foot, combined with the pitch-black night, were perhaps bad omens.

Pradip stopped and gently lifted her head by her chin. "Why are you scared when you're with me?"

"Let me see your foot," she said, lowering herself toward his wound.

He pulled her back up by her shoulders. "Don't worry about my foot, Manisha. I'll be fine."

"But you're laming. And—and I still don't know where we're going." She pouted.

"It shouldn't matter to you where we're going as long as we can be together."

"But—why can't you tell me?" she asked with an innocence that caused him to draw her into his arms. He tilted his head and rested his cheek on the top of her head and swayed gently side to side with his arms wrapped firmly around her.

"We're going home," he whispered.

She gently pushed away from his chest and looked up at him. "This is probably the best thing, Pradip. I don't like the way this feels."

He chuckled. "No, Manisha, we're going home—to India. That's where we belong. This place is not our home, and it never will be."

"India?" She furrowed her brows in bemusement. "You're being serious, aren't you?"

Pradip's eyebrows rose, crinkling his forehead. "Don't you miss your grandfather and grandmother. India's our home, Manisha. It's where we belong."

She took a step backward. "I hardly remember my grandparents, Pradip. And I barely remember India."

"Me neither, Manisha, but we don't belong here, and these people don't want us here."

She lowered her head and began to sob. Pradip pulled her close. Manisha sniffled and gazed up at Pradip with her misty eyes. "Why don't the people here like us, Pradip?"

He drew a deep breath through his nose. Shaking his head side to side, he said, "I guess because we're different."

Pradip lifted his head toward the sky suddenly and said, "Do you hear something?"

"What?" Manisha replied.

"Shh, listen," he whispered. "A horse—sounds like it's slowly moving in this direction."

"Oh, Pradip," she said, holding him tight, "what are we going to do? If we get caught away from the farm, they'll flog us."

By now, the clouds had broken and light from the crescent moon was illuminating the coarse road on which they were traveling. Pradip saw no place to conceal themselves except for the tall stalks of sugarcane that bordered both sides of the road. Without saying a word, he grabbed her hand.

Manisha held her ground and said, "Wait. Where are we going?"

"We have to hide, Manisha."

"But I'm scared," she whined.

"We have no choice," he said, this time pulling her by her bony wrist. As Pradip led the way toward the dense stalks, he stepped into a ditch. Before he could retract his forward momentum, he found himself lunging uncontrollably into waist-deep muck. Manisha let out a scream as Pradip inadvertently pulled her in with him. He put his hand over her mouth, and she promptly pulled it away.

"Stop that!" she growled.

He quickly pulled himself out on the other side and pulled her out with him. Wet and dirty, they scurried into the brush.

Pradip poked his head out to see a single horseman trotting slowly in their direction. He hid himself from view and held Manisha close to his side. He whispered, "Only one. He must be on his way home or something."

The rider halted and dismounted right where the two had left the roadside. Pradip knew that something had caught the man's attention. Then he recognized the familiar silhouette.

"It's Mr. Govender," Pradip whispered. "What is he doing here?"

Moonsamy Govender walked over to a shiny object glistening in the moonlight and picked it up. Pradip grabbed Manisha's right wrist and noticed that one of her three bangles had fallen off.

"He found one of your bangles," said Pradip, almost breaking a whisper. His tone was sharp. She looked at him innocently and said nothing.

Mr. Govender examined the bangle and then called out, "Manisha! Pradip! Can you hear me?"

Pradip placed his forefinger across his lips without making a sound.

"Pradip!" Mr. Govender seemed sure that the two were nearby. "You can't always run away from your problems."

Pradip whispered to Manisha, "Why does this man care about my problems?"

"Trust me when I tell you that it's best you two come back to the farm."

Manisha looked up at Pradip with her doe-like eyes. "I think he's right," she said, gently tugging on his arm. "It *is* best that we go back."

Pradip said nothing but instead stared blankly out toward the road where Mr. Govender was now preparing to remount his horse. He knew that going back would mean ultimately losing Manisha.

*****

"Why can't you just tell Mr. Cozen," Prema said on the verge of tears. "Our babies are out there somewhere alone. They must be scared."

Nayadu's face was etched with helplessness. Everyone knew he didn't want to awaken Mr. Cozen.

"Nayadu," said Velu, "if you don't go wake that lahnee, I will."

Nayadu looked toward Chandu as if to seek his approval. "Go, Nana," he said, gently nudging him toward the door, "before they reach the port."

He nodded and walked out the door.

Manisha's mother cried out, "Please hurry!"

*****

"How do you imagine they're going to get aboard a ship without being seen?" The irritation in Mr. Cozen's voice was mild, but Rex was barking again, and he snapped at the dog, "Hush up!"

"The boy is clever, lahnee."

"Well, go get them, Nayadu. I can't afford to be losing labor around here."

Mr. Cozen went back inside to retrieve the key to the stable when Mr. Govender arrived on horseback. On the back were Pradip and Manisha. Pradip slid off the side and then helped Manisha dismount. Rex barked furiously at the commotion while Nayadu walked over and slapped Pradip on the side of his head and said in Telugu, "Where did you two run off to?"

Both Pradip and Manisha lowered their heads in shame and Mr. Govender said, "I think they're both sorry for running off, Nayadu."

"They're gonna be sorrier when I'm done."

Mr. Cozen emerged from his home with the keys jingling by his side. "Shut up, Rex!" he yelled. Then his eyes widened. He looked up at Mr. Govender still sitting horseback. "You catch our runaways, Govender?"

"They're just confused, lahnee. They're sorry for what they did."

Mr. Cozen looked over at Nayadu and said, "Well, Nayadu, do you want me to mete out justice, or do you want to handle it?"

"Please, lahnee, I'll take care of it."

"Very well then. I'm going back to bed."

"Thank you, lahnee."

Mr. Cozen went back inside his home, and Nayadu grabbed Pradip by the ear. "Run home!" he said to Manisha. And though Pradip was now taller than Nayadu by several inches, he dared not cross him.

Govender called out to Nayadu as he was leading Pradip away, "Hey, Nayadu."

Nayadu turned without saying anything.

292

"Be merciful."

*****

Mr. Mahendhi arrived early the following morning in his buggy to pick up Chandu for his first day of work as his newest associate though it was still unclear as to what his duties were.

"We're going to get you a new suit today. I'm buying," said the barrister.

Chandu smiled and replied, "Sorry, Mr. Mahendhi, but I didn't get much sleep last night."

"Excited about your new job, I'm sure."

"Of course," he replied.

"It must have been moving to finally see your brother after so long?"

"Oh, it was—my father too."

The barrister turned his head abruptly and, with astonishment, replied, "Your father is back from India?"

He nodded. "Yes, he is. And it was a long night."

The barrister laughed. "You do look tired, my friend. But I'm afraid I have a busy day lined up for us, so rest will have to wait."

"Okay," he replied, then he slid forward on leather seat and rested his chin on his chest hoping to catch a quick nap.

"I don't think your friend Tomasz will be coming back anytime soon," said the barrister, rousing Chandu from his rest.

"He sat up and asked, "Oh, where did he go?"

"He left around the same time I did this morning but in the other direction. Said he was on a mission."

"What mission?"

"To find a wife."

Chandu chuckled. "I hope he comes back. I really like him."

They rode quietly for several minutes, and Chandu could tell the barrister had a lot on his mind, so he said nothing.

Knowing that he had been betrothed to Manisha and that she and Pradip had affections for one another, weighed heavily on him and kept him awake most of the night. But he wasn't ready to talk about it with his boss.

*****

The barrister broke the silence and said, "Are you aware that we are on the brink of war?"

"We?"

"We, meaning the colony."

"No," Chandu said, taking him half seriously.

"I'm quite serious my young cohort. I heard reports last night that thousands of Boer soldiers have breached the border descending down the Drakensburg Mountains."

"What do they have against us?" he asked.

"They've likely decided that it's better not to sit and wait for the British to move in on their territory in the Transvaal. Do you know that they're sitting on untold quantities of diamonds and gold?"

"No," Chandu said with a shrug, "but why would these Boers attack our colony?"

"But I just told you, my young associate. They've apparently decided that the best defense is a good offense."

"Do you think it will affect us," he asked.

"Us meaning our Indians?"

"I mean should we be concerned?"

"I don't know. I can't believe that the Boers will push the British all the way to the coast."

Several quiet minutes passed, and then Chandu posed a question: "What if we help the British?"

"Help them in what way?" the barrister replied.

"Help them fight those dirty Boers."

He chuckled. "I'm a barrister, and you're my associate. We're not soldiers."

"But what if we get all our Indians to enlist in the British Army?"

"You mean *try* to enlist."

"Don't you think it will show these Whites that we are loyal to the colony?"

The barrister paused and then nodded slowly. "I think it would, my young colleague. I think it would."

The barrister went silent again, and Chandu knew that he struck a nerve deep within his core. Natal Indians desperately needed validation in the colony, and this was perhaps the way they could do it. His pride caused him to sit a little straighter, and then a pit suddenly formed in his stomach.

"What if we're on the wrong side? I mean, what if the Boers are destined to win?"

"Let me tell you something, my young warrior." The barrister's face was serious. "I've spent some time in Pretoria, and I've seen the resolve of these Boers. They are a fearless and proud people. Every Boer you will ever meet will have some sort of battle wound to show you. But if there's anybody who hates Indians more than the British, it's the Boers. They are as racist as they come. And for that reason, they have to lose this war. It would be a fate worse than being reincarnated as an insect if the Boers were to come into control over this colony."

*****

One would never know that Govindas Mahendhi was Natal's most prolific and best-known Indian barrister by the appearance of his office. In place of a pane glass window was now a wooden board with G.K. Mahendhi & Associates painted on it. After the third broken window, the lawyer grew tired of replacing it. Inside was a small room with two desks facing each other and a door which led to his office.

"Make yourself at home," he said, gesturing toward the empty desk on the left.

Chandu walked behind the desk, pulled out the chair and sat down. "I'm one of your associates?"

"You work for me now, my young colleague."

The desk sitting across from him still bore Siva's name.

The barrister commented, "He'll be back you know."

"Siva's coming back?"

"That's right."

"That's nice."

"Yes, it is nice," he said with a smirk. "And now I need to leave you."

"But where are you going?"

"I'm going to pay the illustrious Lord Falmouth a visit. I shan't be too long. In the meantime, I've left letters that I've written to the editor of the *Times*, as well as motions I've filed so you can catch up with what has been happening to our brethren here in the colony."

"Where?"

"In the drawer in front of you."

The barrister pulled the door shut behind him, and Chandu immediately started leafing through the stack of papers. But his mind was elsewhere. All he could think of was the events from the previous night. They played over and over in his mind. He was sure that Pradip would have preferred he never returned from London.

CHAPTER 24

"You've gone mad, Mahendhi. You people have no military training," scoffed Lord Falmouth at the suggestion of Natal Indians helping to fight the encroaching Boers. "You would be more of a hindrance to our troops than anything else."

The barrister replied without hesitation, "That may be, Your Lordship, but I believe if you give our men a chance, they will prove themselves worthy subjects of Her Majesty."

Lord Falmouth laughed, his unlit cigar almost breaking loose from his thin, pale lips. "Listen, Mahendhi, if you people want to help us fight these Boers, then I have an idea. We will need stretcher bearers on the frontlines if the fighting gets fierce. You can enlist your men to carry our wounded off the battlefield and back to the infirmaries. Do you think you can do that?"

Lord Falmouth's tone was derisive, but the barrister was pleased with his offer. The capacity in which the Natal Indians would serve the Crown was inconsequential. Putting their lives on the line to remove dead or wounded soldiers from the battlefield would surely remove any questions of loyalty. He responded stoically, "If that is how we can best serve Her Majesty, then so be it. We would be honored."

"Fine," he said, motioning the barrister toward the door. "I'll speak to General Whitehead and let him know that you and your people will be available for service."

*****

297

If there was ever a time that Chandu felt nervous, it was during the ride home late that afternoon. Not only did he have to come to terms with the foolish idea of being on a battlefield without any means of protection, but he was going to have to tell his father of this crazy plan.

The mood was somber when Chandu and the barrister arrived to find Nayadu and Velu sitting alone outside of the barracks. Both men stood to their feet to greet Mr. Mahendhi.

Chandu instinctively knew something was wrong by the look on their faces. "Tell me what's wrong, Nana."

"Your brother has gone."

"Gone? Gone where?"

"To fight some war."

"You mean the war between the British and the Boers?"

Nayadu shrugged his shoulders. "How do I know who's fighting?"

Velu interrupted, "Your brother told us that India sent an army over to help the British fight against these farmers from the Highveld."

The barrister and Chandu looked at each other with bemusement. "I didn't know India sent over troops," said the barrister.

Nayadu just nodded. "I couldn't talk to him. Such a strong spirit that boy has."

The barrister cleared his throat. "Mr. Nayadu, your boys are young men now and—"

Nayadu interrupted, "Yes, garu, they are strong and smart young men, but this is not how their mother, and I raised them. We raised them to follow our rules and our culture."

The barrister took a deep breath and said softly, "I'll leave you, Chandu. I think you should spend some time with your father."

"You don't mind, Mr. Mahendhi?"

"No—no, of course not. I'll see you tomorrow morning." He pulled Chandu close and whispered in his ear, "Don't tell of the plans to volunteer in the war."

He nodded.

The barrister bid farewell, followed by Velu so that father and son were alone. Chandu anguished over the thought of telling his father about their proposal to serve the colonists as stretcher bearers. In his mind it was a task no less perilous than that of carrying a rifle. He wondered whether there would ever be a good time to tell him. Nayadu etched with his finger in the dirt, and Chandu knew he was at a loss for words.

Then he mumbled as if he were speaking to someone else, "The boys are grown now. I can't tell them what to do."

"Nana, are you talking to me?"

He looked up at his son and asked, "Why do you think Pradip went to fight in this war?"

Chandu hesitated a moment and asked, "Honestly?"

"Yes."

"I don't think he could stand Manisha and I getting married."

He nodded slowly. "I wonder if we made a mistake."

Chandu didn't say anything but began to wonder himself. It was tradition to marry the oldest first, but at what cost?

*****

Prema poked her head into the Nayadu's stall and said, "Come, you two. The food is ready."

"You go," said Nayadu, "I'm not hungry."

"Come, Nana, you have to eat to maintain your strength."

"No, please go without me," he insisted.

Chandu was also in no mood to eat but was not going to pass an opportunity to eat Aunty's cooking.

They ate quietly, except Manisha's brother, Arun, who had a lot to say about mostly nothing of importance. Chandu's eyes fixed upon Manisha, who sat with her back against the wall. With her legs crossed and her plate in her lap, she just sat slowly eating her food. He decided that somewhere in time Manisha had blossomed into a beautiful young woman, and he found it hard to look away. Then, for a brief instant, she looked up, and their eyes met, but just as quickly, she looked away.

Velu seized upon the moment and said, "You were smart, Chandu, to get out of these cane fields."

Chandu didn't know how to respond, so he didn't.

Velu turned to his daughter and said, "You know Chandu is working for that barrister now. What's his name, Chandu?"

"Mahendhi," he replied. "Govindas Mahendhi."

He turned back to Manisha, who showed little interest in what her father had to say. "He will be a good provider."

"Leave her be," said her mother. "You're embarrassing her and Chandu."

"Why am I embarrassing them? I'm just speaking the truth."

Manisha set her plate aside and walked toward the door.

"Where are you going?" her father asked, but she didn't answer.

"Let her be," said Prema. "Her emotions are high."

"Should I speak with her?" Chandu asked.

The two looked at each other as if unsure and then both agreed. "She has to talk to you sometime, Chandu. Go see what's bothering her," said Velu.

Chandu eventually found Manisha down by the creek. He had no words for her, so he sat just uphill from her and gazed upon her beauty. He found the feelings suddenly surging through him to be strange. He never imagined having any feelings toward this girl, whom he once considered annoying.

He picked up a stone and tossed it into the streaming water. She looked up and around to see him but looked back toward the water. *What do I say to her?* he asked himself. Finally, he went and sat next to her. He found another stone and tossed it into the stream. Then another and another.

Finally, he said to her, "I really like your mother's cooking."

When she didn't respond, he felt stupid. Then he asked her, "So—how do you feel about..." Before he finished his question, she put her head down and started sobbing. His heart sank, and he contemplated whether to say anything to console her. Finally, he got up and left her. He decided if she didn't want him, then he wasn't going to say anything more.

*****

The barrister opened the letter on his desk with nervous anticipation. It was from Lord Falmouth, and they both knew that their fate was held in the words inked on the paper he eagerly unfolded. It read:

Mr. Mahendhi,

As per our conversation last week, I have duly spoken with General Whitehead. He has agreed to the proposal. I should like for you and your band of recruits to report out in front of my office Monday, 26th of October, 1899, at 8:00 a.m. for further instructions.

Regards,

Lord Falmouth

The barrister smiled and said, "This could be the catalyst that would change how our Indians would forever be treated in this colony."

Chandu answered, "But what about the band of recruits he is talking about? He wants us to report in less than two weeks and we don't have any."

"Yet," he answered. "We'll announce this at our INC meeting this week. That will be the best way to get the word out."

*****

The recruiting efforts were a huge success as hundreds of free Indians committed to volunteer their services. Indians from every caste represented in the colony stood proud ready to do his part. Leaders were selected among the men who tended to be the wealthier or more educated among the ranks. Nobody objected as this was customary in Indian society. The barrister and Chandu, along with thirty-five other brave men, were selected and briefed on their mission. They would become the Indian Ambulance Corp.

*****

Chandu just happened to be looking out the window of the law office when he saw his father ride up on a horse that he borrowed from Mr. Cozen. He knew by the look on his face that he was distressed. Chandu made sure to meet him outside the office.

"What's wrong, Nana?"

"Is it true you're going to fight this war?"

"We're volunteering, Nana, as stretcher bearers. We won't be fighting."

"I don't know what this means."

"We'll be carrying wounded or dead soldiers off the battlefield. That's all. We're doing this for the sake of our Indians…so we can be treated more fairly."

He shook his head with disapproval and then said, "Why do you have to go? You're all I have left."

"I'll be safe, Nana. I promise."

Chandu could tell that his father wanted to hug him, but he didn't. Showing emotion was foreign to him. He turned as if to leave and then turned back, "Sirdar Reddy was killed yesterday. One of the workers took a cane knife to him."

"That's terrible," Chandu replied. He didn't ask about the circumstances surrounding the sirdar's death because he knew the sirdar had a reputation of dealing harshly with the workers. It seemed inevitable that someone would eventually turn on him.

"Mr. Cozen wants to make me the new sirdar."

"That's great, Nana. Do you get his bungalow?"

"Only if I do what they are asking of me."

Chandu's head lurched back. "What are they asking you to do?"

Nayadu leaned in and whispered, "They want me to spread a rumor about your boss. That he's secretly planning to lead all of us Indians to take over the colony."

Chandu recoiled sharply. "That's a lie, Nana!"

Nana raised his hand to calm his son's sudden outburst. "I know, I know."

"Did you agree to this, Nana?"

Disappointment swept across Nayadu's face. "I guess you don't know me, son."

Chandu smiled with one side of his face and said, "I do know you, Nana! You could never go against your conscience. I've always admired you for that."

Nana nodded bashfully. "So I turned it down," he said. "I'd rather live in the barracks for the rest of my life than betray a good man like your boss, Mr. Mahendhi."

A tear strolled down Chandu's cheek. "You're a good man, Nana."

Nayadu cleared his throat and said, "Okay, I must go, but you must come home tonight, and we will meet with the Velus."

"Nana, that girl doesn't want me. She wants Pradip."

"Nonsense, you come for dinner, and we will meet at the Velus'."
Then Nayadu promptly mounted up and rode away.

*****

Chandu convinced the barrister to leave him at the plantation, intimating that he and his father were to meet with his proposed future in-laws.

"You didn't tell me you were betrothed, my young colleague."

"I don't think this girl even likes me."

"Don't let that bother you. My wife detested me for the first year of our marriage." He chuckled. "Of course, we were both kids, and I had no understanding of what it was to be a husband. Nor did she know what it was to be a wife. But with time and the wise counsel of our parents we learned."

"I didn't tell you that she and my brother, Pradip, were taken with each other. That is until he ran off to the war. So I feel like I'm competing for her affection."

"Forget affection," he scoffed. "Any girl would be lucky to marry a fine young man like you. I just hope that your father is getting a handsome dowry."

"They're old family friends, Mr. Mahendhi, and they don't have any money."

"Well, if fate has destined this girl to be your wife, then I'm sure she'll be a good one."

Chandu knew there must be truth in the barrister's words. After all, he had been married for almost half his life, and he was only twenty-seven years old.

*****

That evening while the parents discussed such things as where and when the wedding would take place, Chandu was hoping to merely make eye contact with the girl who would soon become his wife. He knew he could learn to love her like the barrister said. But he seriously wondered if she would ever like him.

Nayadu turned to his son and said, "We're thinking after Diwali will be good to marry you two."

Chandu replied, "Don't know when I'll be returning from my war service."

Nayadu frowned. "You don't know when you'll be coming home?"

"No."

Nana and Velu looked at each other, unsure of how to respond. Then Velu said, "Then we'll wait for the boy to return before we make any more plans."

*****

With rifle fire sounding behind them and cannon fire in front of them, they found themselves perilously close to the firing line.

304

Day after day, Chandu led his ten men with every ounce of courage he was able to muster, picking up dead and wounded soldiers and retreating miles at a time to the nearest hospital base. The carnage was a test of his fortitude, and at times, he wondered where he would get the strength to continue.

The bigger test, however, was not one of physical endurance but one of the heart. One such trial that sought to strip his men of all dignity occurred when two of his men placed a wounded British soldier onto their stretcher. The soldier had been shot in the stomach and was losing a lot of blood.

"Where's your bandages?" he yelled at the two stretcher bearers. "Can't you see I'm bleeding to death?"

Chandu heard the soldier's complaint and knew both men spoke poor English. He explained to the soldier, "Sorry, sir, these men have exhausted all their bandages. But I'll have them move you swiftly to a hospital base."

"Of course," he scorned, "that's all you coolies are good for. Then hurry and get me to the infirmary!"

It was unlikely that the men who struggled to bear this soldier understood his insensitive and hateful words but knew well enough that he held them in utter contempt. And from that point, his heart wept no longer for the wounded or dead but for the thin, disheveled men who were laboring with all their might to carry the very men that would just as soon spit on them.

*****

"I spoke to one of the officers," said the barrister one evening at base camp. "He told me that he thought the Indian Army might be assisting the British troops in Colenso."

"Colenso? Where's that?"

"South of here," he replied.

Chandu's heart raced with a renewed hope that Pradip was well and that he would be able to speak to him. The closeness that they had as young boys had been splintered by a tradition that he was willing to forsake if it meant bringing them back together. He just wanted an opportunity to speak with him.

"Who's picking up their wounded soldiers?" he asked.

The barrister smiled and nodded. "Not us, my boy. It's too far, and we already have our marching orders."

*****

It was in the shade of one of the large majestic palms that fringed the trail leading to the Sykes Estate that Siva found his first familiar face since returning to Natal.

"Nayadu!"

He dropped the cane knife that he had been sharpening and jumped up to greet Siva. He pressed his hands together and bowed slightly. "You're back, garu."

"You as well," Siva replied. "I'm very happy you made it back safely."

Nayadu nodded and smiled.

"Come," he said, leading the way to his bungalow, "join me for some tea."

As the two made their way up Bunglo Hill, Nana said, "Many things are going on these days, garu. Both my boys are fighting in this battle with these Boers. I'm not sure if I will ever see them…" Nana's voice trailed off.

"Don't worry, Nayadu. They'll be back."

Nana struggled to hold back his emotions. "I hope so, garu. I hope so."

"I hear Govindas is also with your son fighting this war."

Nayadu looked blankly at Siva. "Govindas?"

"Mahendhi garu."

"Ah yes, Chandu's lahnee. I don't know if it was his idea to go fight this war, but I think he's been good to my son."

"Yes, he has, Nayadu. Not many people out there that will pay to send someone they hardly know to college."

Nayadu nodded. "The lahnees here don't like Mahendhi garu. They say he's going to hurt all the sugarcane farms here."

Siva smiled slightly. "I don't know if he has that much power."

The big lahnee, Mr. Heinz, told me that if I wanted to be a sirdar again, then I needed to start rumors that he was secretly planning on leading us Indians to take over this colony."

"And you agreed?"

Nayadu shook his scrunched face. "No, garu. I could never do this. I like the man."

They reached the top of the hill and were standing just feet from the entrance of one of the bungalows. Siva looked around curiously and asked, "Then what are we doing here?"

"Come inside," he said as they passed a young woman sweeping dirt away from the entrance. She was dark complexioned and not especially attractive with her beetle-nut stained teeth. Nayadu instructed her in English to bring him and his guest some tea. Instead, a girl bearing striking resemblance the first returned with the tea and some biscuits.

Siva turned to Nana and said, "So they made you a sirdar, anyway."

Nana smiled. "These are sisters, garu. Seeli, and this one here," he said, gesturing toward the one pouring tea, "is Sonali."

Siva thanked Sonali in her own language, "Dhanyavad."

Nana remarked, "You know she's Hindi?"

Siva nodded. "Only North Indians wear nose rings like that."

"Sonali is Sirdar Reddy's widow. They had nowhere to go so I let them stay."

With raised eyebrows, Siva said, "Seems like a good arrangement to me."

"It is, garu, it is. When Sirdar Reddy died, they needed another sirdar, but I was not willing if it meant telling lies about Mahendhi garu. Then he went to this war. They think he's dead." He shrugged. "So they made me sirdar."

The two men sipped their tea, and Siva listened with fascination as Nayadu recounted his exploits in India. "Unbelievable," was the only word Siva could utter as he relived the fantastic adventure. And when it was time for Nayadu to return to his duties in the cane fields the two men bid each other farewell.

As Siva walked down the hill leading to the front of the estate, he saw Mr. Cozen and Mr. Heinz talking to two constables. Mr. Cozen spotted Siva descending the hill and pointed. The attention of all four men turned toward Siva, and he sensed that something was awry.

As Siva neared, one of the constables called out, "Sivasambarao?"

Siva instinctively removed his eyeglasses and slipped them into his top pocket. The last time he was confronted by a group of angry White men, he was knocked on the side of the head.

"You pronounced my name correctly. Congratulations."

"A bloody wiseacre," said one of the constables.

Siva's face turned serious. "Am I in trouble?"

The other constable who appeared less threatening stepped forward and said, "Are you the same man who worked for this Indian barrister, Mahendhi?"

His brows furrowed. "I did work for the barrister, yes."

The other constable took Siva by the arm and said, "You're under arrest for the murder of William Pickles."

"But I didn't murder anyone!" he exclaimed as the two constables led him away.

"We're not the ones to decide whether you're innocent or not."

*****

As the weeks passed on the battlefield, many were weakened from exhaustion and poor nutrition. Chandu was no exception, and eventually he fell ill, requiring extended rest and medical treatment. He was given a cot in the hospital separated from the rest of the soldiers, and that was where the barrister found him as he lay recuperating.

"How are you doing, my boy?"

"Tired," he answered quietly.

"You've heard that we've been surrounded by these Boers?"

All he could do was nod. In fact, the Boers had surrounded their forces on three sides and had taken control of the railroad. Without a leader, his men had been relieved of their duty and spent their remaining time doing kitchen duty and other miscellaneous tasks.

"I overheard that there are more troops coming up from the South to bring relief."

Chandu didn't reply.

"Maybe your brother will be there among those troops who come to our rescue," he said, trying to lift Chandu's spirits.

"Maybe," he answered softly too tired to engage in any further conversation.

"Take rest, my boy," he said, patting him on his leg.

After the barrister left the room, his eyelids became heavy. In spite of the ongoing chaos, he fell off to sleep. His reality suddenly became a dreamscape in which he became an observer of all the frenetic activity taking place within the makeshift hospital room.

Doctors and nurses were running around frantically tending to the soldiers who lay wounded, some mortally. In the midst of everything, he watched an older man calmly make his way through the confusion and walk directly to a soldier who was sobbing and lay seriously wounded. It appeared that his right leg below the knee was missing.

As Chandu moved closer, it became obvious to him that this man was not a doctor. He leaned over and put his hand on the wounded soldier's chest. The soldier stopped sobbing. Then the older man whispered something into the soldier's ear, and the soldier smiled. When the nurse approached, the man left. The soldier closed his eyes and went to sleep.

Chandu awoke deeply moved by what he saw. He looked over to the cot where the wounded soldier in his dream had been lying, but the cot was now empty. Trying desperately to distinguish reality from reverie, he asked a nurse if there had been a soldier with a missing leg in the nearby cot.

"He didn't make it," she said coldly.

"You mean he died?"

"That's right, about an hour ago."

"Was that man in the white suit who spoke to the soldier a doctor?"

"I don't know who you are talking about," she replied impatiently.

"The tall, old man with the beard and white suit who was speaking to the soldier. You surely saw him," he said, trying not to be disrespectful.

"I think you need some more rest," she snickered. "There are no old men with white suits walking around here."

He put his head back down on the dirty pillow and contemplated the soldier's fate. By then he had seen scores of dead and wounded soldiers and had become numb to the smell of death. But whether what he witnessed was real or not, he was sure of one thing. Whatever that man had whispered into the young soldier's ear gave him peace and contentment. He wondered what kind of words could have taken away the tears and anguish of that frightened young man who must have known that death was knocking on his door.

*****

Relief soldiers under General Symons managed to force the Boers to retreat. Had they arrived any later, the British battalion, along with the small band from the Indian Ambulance Corps, would have died of starvation. Rumors throughout the camp intimated that it was General Whitehead's incompetence that allowed British troops to be encircled by the Boers. After the food supply was depleted, the horses had to be shot and used for food. They were down to their last portions when General Symon's forces rolled in.

Chandu looked intently for any sign that the Indian Army was allied with General Symon's men.

"Are there any Indians with you?" he asked a pair of soldiers walking through the camp. They looked at him as if he didn't speak English. "The Indian Army," he said slowly, "are they here with you?"

"It's *sir* to you", said one of the soldiers.

Chandu quickly realized they were in no mood to be interrogated.

"Yes, sir!" he replied.

Without answering, they walked away.

*****

The war would continue for several more years with many casualties on both sides, but the Indian Ambulance Corps would disband after what came to be known as The Battle at Ladysmith. Fighting eventually moved up into the Boer Republics of Transvaal and the Orange Free State, where there were few Indians. In the end, it would be the Boers who would eventually surrender to British troops.

There were no reports as to what became of the Indian Army, and it was up for speculation as to what happened to them. Some guessed that they went back to India. Others figured that they retired here in the colony and assimilated into the fabric of the interracial society. There were even some who believed that such an army never existed. One thing was sure, Pradip never returned home.

CHAPTER 25

The barrister felt good. He was sure that the volunteer efforts of his Ambulance Corps had earned them enough favor among the White community. If ever there was a favorable time to repeal this act that effectively disenfranchised all Indians living in Natal, it was now.

But there was another issue that threatened to undo every seed of goodwill that the Indian Ambulance Corps managed to sow, and that was Siva's arrest for murder. The barrister's instincts told him that this was just another desperate attempt to discredit him and rid the colony of its perceived antagonists.

*****

The barrister found Siva in a small holding cell reserved for the colony's worst criminals. With no window, it was dark, and the air was foul. Siva clung desperately to the bars that separated the two men.

Siva cried out, "How can they hold me here with no evidence."

"I just spoke to the magistrate. They believe that they have a case against you."

"What case?"

"Statements that were made by some of the crew aboard the ship incriminated you, my dear friend."

"They were lying. They were just trying to save their own necks."

"You needn't worry. I know this case against you has no merit. You're a good man, and I know you're innocent of this charge. Your defense shall be your good character. We will fight this with character witnesses and provide enough reasonable doubt." The barrister rested his chin in his hand as he pondered his next move. "Is there anyone who sailed with you that would testify on your behalf?"

"Of course, many of the Indian passengers. Nayadu, Chandu, Velu. The captain's wife, Mrs. Weatherly, was very fond of me."

"Is she here in the colony?" he asked. "Her testimony on your behest would be most helpful since she's European."

He lowered his head in discouragement. "No. The captain retired years ago."

"Hmm," said the barrister, rubbing his chin.

"They asked me if I worked for you when they came to arrest me."

The barrister lowered his head and peered slowly over the top of his spectacles. "I suspected as much. These people are looking for a scandal in order to bring disrepute upon me."

"Why are they doing this?"

"Because we are troublemakers, that's why," he replied. "The Colonial Office has been digging up anything they can find to use against us. Because you were a suspect in this murder case, they have decided to reopen it and try to scare you back to India. You watch, my conjecture is that they will offer to drop the case if you pack up and leave the colony."

"Do you think we can win this?"

"They're going to try you on evidence that carries little weight, my friend. They have no hard evidence. In any capital case such as murder, the prosecution has to prove its case beyond a reasonable doubt. We just have to push for a speedy trial. They are going to delay the trial as long as possible to try and break you."

"Please, Govindas, you have to get me out. They're talking about moving me out to the diamond mines."

"I'll do my best, my friend."

"And please go visit my wife to tell her that everything will be all right. I know she and my children are worried."

*****

The only sign of life on the Sykes Estate on Sundays was that of cast iron pots simmering a variety of tangy yet spicy curries over open fires. The women toiled while the men didn't. Even the dogs were good for nothing except the occasional yawn.

When Chandu arrived, he expected to find his father relaxing, if not napping in the stall he had chosen to call home since arriving back on the estate from India. He was returning without any news of his brother, and it was not going to be easy to tell his father. But he was nowhere to be found.

He nervously walked down to the Velus', unsure if he wanted to see Manisha, but they weren't there, and he felt somewhat relieved. Then he asked a laborer who was laying down in the stall next to the Velus' if he knew where his father might be.

"Oh, Naidu's up on the hill now. They made him sirdar."

"Sirdar?" He wondered whether his father gave in to the pressure of the lahnees and started spreading rumors about the barrister. He made his way up Bunglo Hill, and when he reached the top, he called out, "Nana!" He called out again, "Nana!"

Nayadu opened the door, still groggy from a midafternoon slumber.

"Chandu?"

"Yes, Nana! It's me. I'm home."

Nayadu embraced his son and held onto him. "You've come home to me."

Chandu hugged his father, trying to recall the last time his father showed so much affection and smiled.

Two young women appeared in the doorway and startled Chandu. "Oh, this is Sonali and her sister Seeli. They—uh, came with the bungalow."

"They came with the bungalow, Nana?"

"I'll tell you later. First, come inside and tell me everything. I want to know if you met up with your brother."

Chandu lowered his head, and Nayadu knew. Tears filled his eyes, but he didn't ask another question about the war. It would only raise more questions. He cleared his throat and said, "Velu Uncle tells me that this girl isn't ready yet."

Chandu's heart sank.

He nodded as he continued, "They don't want to force her into this marriage."

Chandu let out a sigh and said, "Maybe she's not the one, Nana."

Nayadu shrugged and said, "I don't know, son. Hopefully, she'll come around." He patted him on the back and smiled. Then he said, "Sit down." His face was serious. "There's something else I need to tell you."

"Something wrong?"

"No, nothing's wrong," he replied, smiling only slightly.

"Then what is it?"

"I married Sonali."

"Married! But—but—" He had no words.

"I've been very lonely since losing your mother, Chandu." He waited for a response, but Chandu still had no words. "She and Seeli have taken good care of me since I moved into the bungalow."

As Nayadu went on to tell his son about the small nondescript ceremony that was witnessed by Seeli and Mr. Cozen, Chandu could see a sparkle in his eyes, and his heart gradually filled with joy. Though he never imagined his father ever being married to anyone other than his mother, he was glad he found someone.

"What about the sister?"

"What about her?"

"Where will she go now that the other one is married?"

"Nowhere," he said calmly. "She'll never leave her sister."

"And?"

"That's fine."

The two sisters had never lived a day in their lives without the other. They had come to the colony as young girls with their father and mother from a small village in Uttar Pradesh in North India. There were no disillusionments for the girls' father upon arrival in the colony. He expected that he would work hard under harsh conditions but that it would be a means to an end. That end meant eventually gaining his freedom after his term of indenture and looking for a way to support his wife and two daughters. His hope was for an opportunity in this new land—a land that would not consider him as "untouchable."

On his first day as a free Indian, he told the three of them that he was going to go out and find work off the plantation. He was determined that there was an easier way to earn a living than cutting cane or working in the hot sun from dawn to dusk though he wasn't sure what. Perhaps he could be a trader as so many of his brethren had a knack for. But what would he trade and where, he wondered. Surely it would come to him if only he could explore the world outside the plantation.

So he set out early that morning with a day's worth of food rations and several shillings. He told them that if he didn't return that evening not to worry.

He never returned.

Weeks passed then months and still no word.

Mr. Cozen told them that they were welcome to stay in the barracks but that they would have to work out in the fields. They didn't see much of a choice for they had no real skills upon which to rely and didn't know anything about life outside of the Sykes Estate.

So fourteen-year-old Sonali and thirteen-year-old Seeli worked along with their mother each day in the fields gathering felled cane and stacking it on the cart for transport to the mill. The girls labored tirelessly at their mind-numbing task, though they were deeply depressed. They wondered if they would ever see their father again and would spontaneously break out in tears without warning.

Nevertheless, the girls were hard workers, and this caught the attention of Sirdar Sunil Reddy. He had a reputation as a taskmaster which didn't engender warm feelings among his own people. But he was more concerned with doing the job he was being paid to do, and that was to keep the laborers working.

He saw that either girl would make a fine wife, though he didn't think they were particularly attractive. When he determined that Sonali was the older of the two, he told her mother that he was intent on marrying her daughter, and she agreed. But there was a catch. Neither girl would consider leaving the other, so it was that Seeli would have to live with the married couple. Sirdar Reddy approved and, in fact, found the arrangement much to his liking. The sirdar then moved their mother into his bungalow, and he soon found himself being waited on hand and foot.

When word got around that Sirdar Reddy had his own bevy of servants, rumors started abounding. The most believable was that he had killed the father so he could have the mother and daughters as his personal slaves. But there was never any proof, and soon the rumors subsided.

So it was that the four lived under Sirdar Reddy's roof until the mother died after several years from an unknown illness. After the sirdar was killed by an irate laborer, the two sisters feared they would be moved back into the barracks and forced to earn their keep by working in the fields once more. But fate would have a different plan.

*****

The barrister ran into one stall after another. He pushed tirelessly for a speedy trial of Siva's murder case thought he had yet to secure any witnesses. But he was confident that the colony had no case and that they were merely stonewalling. They argued that they were waiting for the witnesses who made the allegations against Siva to arrive from India and that it would take at least another three weeks.

Mahendhi argued before the magistrate that the colony had only the flimsy words of a few sailors, hardly enough evidence to convict a man for murder. True to the barrister's prediction, the colony's prosecutor offered Siva a plea bargain. If Siva agreed to plead guilty to accidental murder, then the colony would simply deport him back to India. If he refused the plea bargain, they would push their case against him, holding him in jail until their witnesses arrived to testify.

"I'll plead guilty," Siva said upon learning of the prosecutor's offer.

The barrister's eyes widened. "What? You can't do that!"

"I can't stay here any longer, Govindas. I would rather go back to India than rot in this place."

"And sully your good name?"

"My name is already sullied."

"No, it's not. We're going to vindicate you, my good and dear friend. You just need to bear with this. It's no accident that you came back to this country, and it's no accident that you're going through this my friend. We'll get you through this."

*****

The last person Chandu expected to see walking through the door of Mahendhi & Associates was Manisha's mother. She walked several miles unsure whether she would even find him and for a woman of her size that was no small task. A broad smile swept across her face when she found him sitting behind his desk.

"Chandu," she said, using her sari to wipe away the sweat from her forehead. "I'm glad I found you."

"Please sit, Aunty," he said, pulling over a chair next to his desk. He brought her some water while she took several minutes to gain her composure.

She looked at him and smiled. "I'm so glad you made it back without harm."

"Me too, Aunty."

"And such fine clothes you have on," she added.

"Thank you. Mr. Mahendhi insists that I wear them."

"Did you see your brother?" she asked sheepishly.

"No—I didn't."

She let out a sigh and said, "Manisha thought he would be coming home with you."

"No…" His voice trailed off.

"I'm sorry," she said. Then her face changed. "I'm tired of my daughter's nonsense. And her father isn't much better. She has him in her pocket."

He was at a loss for words and offered none.

"Come home and have supper with us tonight, Chandu. When she sees that Pradip isn't coming home, then she will come to her senses."

"You don't think Pradip is coming home, Aunty?"

His question disarmed her, and she looked at him with sympathetic eyes. "Oh, I didn't mean he is never coming home, my dear. I do hope he does. But it's you we want for our daughter." She sat up on the edge of the chair. "So will you come?"

He didn't want to win Manisha under those conditions, but how he longed to set eyes on her again. So he agreed.

"I have to deliver some important papers to one of our clients, but I'll take you home if you like?"

"I'll ride with you, Chandu, and then you can take me home. I want to tell you about another problem we are having."

"Problem?"

"Concerning our business."

"Of course," he replied. "I still haven't heard what business you're doing. You can tell me on the way."

She smiled coyly and said, "It wasn't that long ago that you were climbing trees and playing tokudda billa, and now you're—all grown up—and important."

"I'm not important, Aunty."

"Well, maybe not yet. But you will be one day."

"The carriage is right out front," he said, changing the subject. He grabbed the legal documents that he needed to deliver to Mohammed Deedad and locked the door behind him. Mr. Deedad was the firm's wealthiest client and ran a large business importing various goods and fabrics from India. He also owned a number of retail businesses and buildings in close proximity to the large mosque on Grey Street. The legal documents he was delivering to him were for the purpose of evicting tenants of his who were not paying their rental fees.

He hastened the gait of his new horse with a quick snap of the whip so they would make it back before dusk. And after he reached a brisk pace, he said to Prema, "So tell me about your business."

"Well, we want to open another sundry shop, but we can't get a trader's license. Uncle applied and paid for the license, and then they told him that they weren't issuing new licenses, only renewing old ones."

He nodded. "You're not the only ones being denied a trader's license, Aunty."

"We're not?" she asked naively.

"Afraid not. If the colony can't ship all of us Indians back to India, then they are going to do whatever they can to make our lives miserable. Now they're trying to starve us out of the colony."

"But you and so many of our people volunteered, risking your lives for the British Army."

He shrugged. "And for that we'll get a pat on the back, I suppose."

"Why, Chandu? Why are these Whites doing this to us?"

"Fear. They see that we Indians have a real skill for trade and that they will lose control over it. They also see that we are growing, and this really scares them."

"What can we do except go back," she said.

"Back to what?" he asked. "The Zamindar?"

"But what can we do?"

He thought about it for several minutes and then asked, "Don't you do some stitching, Aunty?"

"I make all of our clothing."

"Do you like it?"

"You mean enough to start a business doing it?"

"Why not?"

She pursed her lips. "But what about Uncle?"

"He can sell the clothes for you."

She laughed, "Velu, selling clothes?"

"Sure, he's a good talker. Take your money and buy a couple of those sewing machines."

Her eyes narrowed. "But won't we still need a trader's license?"

"If you are working out of your home and selling wholesale to White businesses, then these people won't go after you because you're a part of their system. It's the Indian shops that these people go after."

She pursed her lips and, with an affirming nod, said, "Hmm, I do like to sew. I'm just not sure if Velu will go for it."

*****

In good time, they arrived at their destination and stopped the carriage where the road ended and the footpath began. Mr. Deedad's office was a hundred yards or so down the path.

"It won't take me long, Aunty." He took the several documents he needed out of his case and rolled them up then proceeded down the footpath. He hadn't walked twenty steps when all of a sudden, *Thwak!* He found himself lying on the side of the path with a numbing pain and loud ringing noise in his ear. The papers that he'd been carrying were taken by the stiff wind blowing out of the east while two menacing White men stood over him.

"Don't you know that coolies aren't allowed on these footpaths?" said the shorter one of the two.

He was too scared to open his mouth. As he looked up, he had trouble focusing on his assailants. He saw stars for several minutes.

"And what business do you have wearing these clothes?" said the taller one.

He said nothing.

"Stand up!" said the short one.

He slowly stood to his feet and started to brush the dirt off his suit. He looked back toward the carriage and saw Prema with her hands over her mouth. She was too frightened to say anything, and he didn't blame her.

"Don't let us catch you on this footpath or any other footpath again. They're for White people. You understand?"

He simply nodded and stood there until they went on their way. Never had he been so humiliated in his entire life. But besides having his dignity badly bruised, he lost the important documents that he'd been entrusted to deliver.

He walked slowly back to the carriage where Prema sat in disbelief. With her eyes as wide as saucers and her hand over her mouth, she didn't know what to say. He turned the carriage around and felt her arm around him.

"Mr. Mahendhi trusted me to deliver those documents," he said softly.

She pushed his hair back out of his face and said, "Who cares about a piece of paper. You were just assaulted by two—two criminals." She gasped and said, "Chandu, your face is swollen. Pull over right now."

He stopped the carriage on the side of the road, and she gently caressed the swollen area of his face between his left ear and cheekbone. "Does that hurt, my dear?" she asked.

"A little," he answered. In fact, her touch had a way of making it feel a lot better.

She leaned over and placed a light kiss on the tenderness of his cheek and said, "Better?"

He smiled awkwardly and nodded. Then she kissed his cheek again and said, "I'll make it better."

He didn't know what to make of her strange affections and rather attributed them to a maternal instinct. But when she put her one hand behind his head and the other on his chin, the line defining their relationship started to blur. She turned his face in her direction and pulled his head toward her so that his lips came in contact with hers. He found the softness of her lips against his strangely exhilarating. As awkward as it was, he didn't want her to stop. Then she quickly pulled away.

"Chandu, I—I don't know what to say."

Neither did he. Though he had always considered Manisha's mother attractive for an older woman, he never imagined any sort of romantic feelings toward her. It was the first time he ever kissed a woman, and he found the experience extraordinary.

Feeling emboldened, he reached up with his hand to stroke her cheek, but she pulled his hand away. "No, Chandu, please don't."

"But—why not?"

"You're going to be marrying my daughter. It wasn't right for me to kiss you like that."

"Then why did you do it?"

"I—I don't know. Can we forget about this and never speak about it again?"

"O—kay," he said reluctantly. But he knew it would be hard to forget that kiss. He tugged on the reins, and they were rolling back toward Phoenix. He gave little thought to the pain the White men had inflicted upon him or the documents that had been lost. He could only think of those few magical seconds during which time seemed to stand still.

*****

They traversed the rest of their journey in awkward silence and were both relieved to arrive while the sun was still visible. He jumped out of the carriage and ran to the other side to assist her, but she was already several steps down the walkway toward the front door. She turned around and said, "I think Manisha is going to be glad to see you."

By the time he tied off the horse, Prema had disappeared into the quaint, pale-green home with its corrugated tin roof, and he pondered whether he should follow. He stood for several moments staring at the house. *Why did she have to kiss me like she did?* he asked himself.

Manisha suddenly appeared in the doorway. "Chandu!" She put her hand over her mouth. "You're back."

He smiled and waved to her.

"When did you get back?"

"Two weeks ago."

"Well," she asked, "aren't you coming in?"

The confusion that he'd been feeling up to that point vanished at the sight of Manisha.

Her hair was pulled back into a single plait, revealing her flawless skin and long, slender neck. She was smiling as he walked toward her, and he wondered if she was going to ask about Pradip.

She gasped as he got close. "Chandu, what happened to your face?"

"Oh," he said, realizing his face was still swollen. He had already forgotten about it. "I, uh, had a run in with some Whites in town." He knew there was no use lying about it since her mother had witnessed the whole encounter.

Her mouth gaped. "You were in a brawl?"

"Not really," he answered somewhat embarrassed. "I was attacked."

She pulled her hands to her mouth, revealing an uncanny resemblance to her mother. "Are you okay?"

"I'm fine—just hungry."

"Well, I hope you don't mind that I cooked the supper today. I know how you love Amma's cooking."

His eyebrows rose into his forehead. "You cooked?"

"Are you surprised?"

"Uh—no, I'm sure your cooking is good." In truth, he wasn't really concerned about the quality of Manisha's cooking. She could have served him a bowl of curried shoe leather, and he would have smiled to the last bite.

She grinned and said, "I guess we'll find out."

*****

Velu arrived minutes later. He'd been working long days hawking betel nut, loose tobacco, and cigarettes—three for a penny. At this he was really good, and if he came home with less than one shilling fifty, it was considered a bad day. For now, it was putting food on the table.

Chandu's heart raced when he came in the door. He wondered whether it was possible that he could have found out about the kiss. Perhaps someone had spotted them and told him. He felt like he betrayed Velu. He was now glad that the affections stopped where they did. He didn't want to think about it ever again.

"Is the queen coming for dinner?" he asked, eyeing Chandu's tailored clothing from neck to toe.

"She's already here," Chandu replied, glancing over at Manisha. She smiled and lowered her head.

Arun scoffed, "Manisha? A queen?"

Manisha snapped back, "Quiet you!"

Velu narrowed his focus on his face and said, "Who knocked you?"

"Oh, it was—"

Prema interrupted, "Chandu has a wonderful idea for business, Ammandi."

Velu raised his eyebrows and asked, "What is it?"

She walked over and stood in front of her husband. She smiled widely and said, "Clothing."

His brows furrowed. "Clothing?"

Chandu interrupted, "I told Aunty that you must invest in some sewing machines and make clothing for wholesale. If you work out of your home, then nobody will be the wiser."

"But I don't stitch," said Velu.

"You must sell the clothing. You're a good trader."

He stroked his chin then grinned slyly. "I am, aren't I?" He turned to his wife and said, "Okay, let's consider it."

*****

As Chandu prepared to leave that evening, Manisha gave him a hug and asked, "Did you enjoy the meal?"

He lied, "It was the best I've had ever."

She smiled and gave him another hug. "Thank you for coming."

Her parents walked him out to the carriage, away from Manisha's hearing, and Velu said, "We'll be meeting with your Nana to start planning your marriage to our daughter."

Prema smiled and said, "I believe you've won her heart, Chandu."

He looked over their shoulders, and Manisha stood in the doorway of their small home. She waved goodbye one last time, and his heart melted. No longer was he Pradip's loathsome older brother but rather someone whom she had apparently come to respect.

CHAPTER 26

"I'm so glad you're here," he said to Chandu upon entering the office of Mahendhi & Associates. "Come, my young colleague, look and see what I've brought back from Johannesburg." On a flatbed cart just outside of the office sat a printing press.

He smiled and said, "Do you know what we are going to be able to do with this?"

Chandu walked around it as if he were an expert on printing presses and then glanced up with a sly smile. "We're going to make our voice heard, Mr. Mahendhi."

With a chuckle, he replied, "Indeed we are."

"But where are we going to put it?"

"You see this place," he said, pointing to the empty storefront next to their office. "I've already made a plan to buy it so that we can start our newspaper."

"Did you say *our* newspaper, Mr. Mahendhi?"

"Why do you sound so surprised? Did you not tell me that you came back here to start a newspaper?"

"I did."

"Well, I can't do this on my own, and you did work underneath the world's arguably best newsman, that rogue Winston Attleboro."

"Mr. Mahendhi, it was for only a short time."

He grinned and said, "Nevertheless, I have the utmost confidence in you. You'll make a fine newsman for the *Indian Observer*."

"*Indian Observer*. I like it."

*****

"And when we get Siva out of jail, he can help me edit in the different languages that are spoken among our—"

Before he could finish his sentence, Chandu's father and the Velus arrived unexpectedly. "Are we interrupting?"

"No, no. Please come in and sit down," said the barrister as they moved back into the office.

"You remember Nana, Mr. Mahendhi," Chandu said in English.

"Of course. And to what do we owe the pleasure?"

Nayadu's English had improved greatly over the months working at the plantation. "My son's to be married, and we're here to let him know of our plans."

The barrister smiled and extended his hand first to Nayadu and then Velu. "That's wonderful news."

"You and your family are invited," said Nayadu.

"Thank you. My family is honored."

"And we would like Siva garu and his family to come."

The barrister cleared his throat. "That might not be so easy."

Nayadu's eyes opened wide with curiosity. "Something wrong?"

"Do you remember that rogue purser on the *Chadwick*, Mr. Pickles?" Chandu asked.

The Velus nodded, and Nayadu replied, "Yes, someone killed him, I remember."

"Siva garu has been accused of that murder."

Prema gasped, then covered her mouth with her hand. She whispered something in her husband's ear, and he put his finger over his lips.

"Why did you not tell us, son?"

"I'm sorry, Nana. I've had so many things on my mind."

The barrister leaned over to Chandu. "They all know Siva quite well, do they not?"

"From the beginning of our voyage, he became a friend to us. All of us know that he could have never done such a thing."

"Then they won't mind testifying in court as character witnesses."

Nayadu asked, "What does this mean?"

"Mr. Mahendhi wants you to tell the magistrate what kind of person Siva garu was—if you thought he was a good person or someone who could have possibly killed Mr. Pickles."

Nayadu turned to the Velus and said, "We can do that, can't we?"

The Velus looked at each other and then agreed but with noticeable reticence.

*****

When they finally left, the barrister had taken note of the Velus' demeanor and said, "I think your future father-in-law may be hiding something."

Chandu also noticed. His stomach churned at the notion that he might have something to do with Mr. Pickles' murder.

The barrister asked him, "Do you think he's capable of murder?"

"Anyone could have been capable of murdering Mr. Pickles. He was a despicable person."

"Fair enough," he replied. "But do you think that Velu is capable of killing another human being?"

He paused for a moment and thought to himself that perhaps he was capable, but he certainly wasn't going to admit it now. He thought how such a thing might jeopardize his future wedding, and that was the last thing he wanted to do. "I don't know," he replied.

"We need to find out."

*****

Chandu knew that something was awry the moment he arrived for work the next morning when he found the barrister going through his desk.

"Mr. Deedad contacted me last night and said he never received the documents you were to deliver him. Can you tell me why?"

"I lost them," he answered sheepishly.

"You lost them?"

"Mr. Mahendhi, I was attacked by two White hooligans as I was delivering them, and the documents blew away in the wind."

"And why did you not tell me about this?"

His head lowered in shame. "I'm sorry, I've just had so much on my mind lately."

His eyes widened, and his tone softened. "Were you hurt?"

"They knocked me to the ground and bruised me up a bit, but it was mostly my ego that was hurt."

"Consider it a rite of passage," Mr. Mahendhi quipped with a slight smile. "Or better yet, consider it a primer for things to come."

"Things to come?" he replied incredulously. "Do you think things will get worse?"

"I believe so, my young friend. A rumor of a proposed ordinance to impose a compulsory registration of every Indian is looming large on the horizon. If they get their way, the status of every Indian will be nullified and subject to re-registration. Every personal detail will be documented. There's talk that they will even go so far as identifying marks on personal areas of our bodies."

"They're making us out to be criminals!"

"Worse," he replied. "They're making us out to be lower than the natives. I would prefer the sentence of a criminal then to submit to the humiliation of registration." He shook his head in disgust and snickered. "It just shows how much the Whites hate us and want to rid us from the colony."

"Our service in the war was—"

"For naught!" he said, shaking head. "For absolutely nothing."

"We can't win with these people," Chandu said.

"Well, it's obvious that the strategies we have been using up till now have been fruitless. I am ready to take extreme actions to show these Whites that we aren't going to just lie down and let them treat us like pariah dogs."

Chandu asked hesitantly, "What kind of extreme actions?"

"I'm talking about resisting their ordinances passively. That means being willing to go to jail for our cause."

"You want to go to jail, Mr. Mahendhi?"

"Willingness on the part of our people to go to jail rather than submit to the unjust and hate-filled laws of these Europeans would bring untold shame upon these people. Would you not agree? And if they lash out in violence as they did with you, you would rather turn to them the other cheek. By doing so, you heap burning coals on their head."

"Tolstoy?"

"Jesus," he replied. "Our gentle patron."

"Jesus? You didn't become a Christian did you, Mr. Mahendhi?"

He chuckled. "A Christian, no. But I do admire the man's teachings."

"I heard that Jesus commanded his followers to love their neighbors as themselves. Are we not neighbors, or do you think they meant to say White neighbors?" Chandu commented tongue-in-cheek.

The barrister laughed. "Yes, my observant young colleague, I too see very little evidence of Christianity displayed among those who call themselves Christians."

They climbed into the carriage and started their journey from Sydenham to Phoenix. It was a rather long journey, and Chandu constantly questioned the barrister's reasoning for living so far away from the law office. He'd fallen in love with the old manor that would become Villa Pravina, and the unique view it offered from its hilltop location. He would also contend that his spacious home was necessary for entertaining important clients. On the other hand, he'd grown to appreciate that his office was centered in the Indian community as Phoenix was quickly becoming the largest settlement of Indians outside of India.

Mahendhi & Associates, however, was losing its important clients because of two Muslim lawyers who had recently arrived into the colony from Gujarat. The barrister considered it fate. He knew that he had a bigger purpose in Natal than that of representing wealthy Muslim businessmen. Their conversations en route to the office were now more concerned with the welfare of Natal Indians.

But today would not be all business. The barrister said, "So soon you will be my *married* young associate. You must be very thrilled."

Chandu gushed, "Very."

"Has it been decided when?"

"Three weeks from Saturday."

"And the location?"

"Mrs. Sykes is allowing us to have the wedding on the estate."

"I would like to host it at my home if you think the families would agree," he rejoined.

"Are you sure?"

"Yes, of course. I already spoke with Pravina, and she says we must do this for you."

"Thank you, Mr. Mahendhi. I think everyone would agree that this would be better."

*****

Later that same afternoon, Prema came to the office alone to see Chandu. She sat down then got up and peered out of the window. "Manisha's father doesn't know I'm here."

"What is it, Aunty?"

"I didn't sleep last night, Chandu."

"Why not?"

She broke down, sobbing. "I have to tell somebody, or I am going to die."

The barrister came out of his office when he heard the commotion. He walked over and handed Prema a handkerchief. "What's upsetting her?" he asked Chandu.

"She wants to tell me something important."

"Tell her that anything said to either of us is not to be mentioned otherwise."

Chandu translated what the barrister said into Telugu, and she nodded. "But I've done something very bad."

"Couldn't be *that* bad, Aunty,"

"I'm the one," she sobbed.

"You're the one?"

"I'm the one who killed Mr. Pickles."

The gravity of her confession left Chandu wordless as he felt his heart sink deep into his chest. She wept bitterly. The barrister looked to Chandu with a puzzlement and said, "Something about Mr. Pickles?"

Chandu took a deep breath and told him, "She's confessed to killing him."

He furrowed his brows and said, "Her?"

Chandu also found it hard to believe but knew in his heart that she was telling the truth. He turned to her asked, "But why?"

"I had a horrible dream one night after I had learned that your Amma had been assaulted by that terrible man. I dreamt that he had attacked me also. I awoke—"

"Wait, Aunty. Did you say that Amma was attacked by Mr. Pickles?"

She looked at him innocently and asked, "Chandu, did you not know?"

He shook his head no slowly, trying desperately to control the anger he felt welling up inside him.

"I'm sorry," she said, lowering her head. "I thought you knew."

The barrister waited anxiously for him to interpret, but his emotions kept him from saying anything. He connected Amma's illness to Mr. Pickles and shuddered thinking of the sheer humiliation and agony his mother had to endure.

"Who else knew of this, Aunty?"

Her head was still lowered, and she replied, "Uncle and I, but we never talked about it."

"Amma told you?"

She nodded, "And I told Uncle."

"And he knows that you killed Mr. Pickles?"

Again, she nodded. "He wanted me to keep my mouth shut. But I do have a conscience. When we heard Siva garu was in jail for this murder, I knew I couldn't keep quiet."

Chandu interpreted their conversation to the barrister, and his eyes gradually widened as he revealed the tie between Mr. Pickles and his mother's untimely death. The barrister shook his head and said, "That bloody rogue deserved to die." Then he said, "Can she tell us how she killed him?"

He turned to Prema and said, "Tell us what happened?"

She blew her nose into the handkerchief. "After your Amma told me that she had been attacked, I had a dream that I was being attacked. I awoke from that dream petrified thinking that it was a premonition and knew I had to do something. So I waited till everybody was asleep and went to the galley where I found a knife. I then went to find Mr. Pickles. I got lucky finding him in the first room that I looked. His room smelled of alcohol, and he lay there sleeping loudly. I thought of your Amma, Chandu, when I pushed that knife as hard as I could into his belly. I pulled it out and stabbed him again and then again. This is all I remember." She started, weeping again. "It was like I was a different person."

"He got what he deserved, Aunty!" he said and in that moment he found himself wishing that it was him that had taken his miserable life.

"Am I in trouble?" she asked.

Again, Chandu relayed her story for the barrister, and he pinched his lips together. "Let's wait a day or two and see what happens."

*****

Siva was gaunt and tired looking when the barrister appeared in front of his cell holding some documents. He sat in the corner unmoved by the presence of his employer turned attorney.

"I have good news for you, my dear friend," he announced above the noise of a couple natives who were arguing with each other several cells away. "You're going to be released today."

Siva's head moved slowly in the direction of Mr. Mahendhi, his eyes barely making contact. "Today?" he mumbled barely audible.

"That's right, today."

"Thank you, Govindas," he said, slowly pressing his hands together high over his head, "thank you."

"It was nothing. Their case fell apart when their witnesses failed to appear. The magistrate dismissed the case."

Siva let out an exhaustive sigh and said, "So why aren't they letting me out of this hole?"

"You know how these Whites are. They've lost face so they're going to take their time making their way down here to release you. But be patient, my friend. Oh, and I didn't tell you. I started a newspaper and you're going to be one of my editors."

*****

Chandu made a grand entrance onto the grounds of Villa Pravina on horseback amid the clanging of symbols and banging of drums. His father couldn't have smiled wider or looked smarter as he led the way wearing a new cream-colored *Kurtha*. All the pain and heartaches that had left an imprint on his heart faded the day.

By Chandu's side was Sivasambarao. The law clerk turned newspaper editor had been given a new lease on life and reveled in the occasion of his young friend's wedding.

But missing from his other side was Pradip and, as such, a piece of Chandu's heart. Nevertheless, he was determined to stay in the moment and not let past heartaches ruin the festivities.

Where the procession ended in the back of the Villa Pravina, they were greeted by Manisha's family. Prema applied a *Tilak* to Chandu's forehead then placed a garland of marigolds around his neck. Then she handed him a lighted lamp and said, "I'm proud to have you as my son-in-law."

She, too, was able to sleep well again after the barrister, and Chandu assured her that her secret would always remain that—a secret. Not even Siva was told of her deed.

When he was finally able to set his eyes on Manisha, his breath was taken away. She had been transformed into a goddess. Her crimson sari with gold brocade and tinsel was wrapped around her with delicate perfection. She sparkled with gold adornments. Ornate *Mehndi* tattoos decorated her hands and arms, as well as her feet. Hidden within the intricate and skillfully tattooed artwork were their names. It would be Chandu's job to find their names before the wedding night would commence.

Nowhere on earth would have been found a more beautiful young woman then Manisha. Her breathtaking beauty melted away every care and worry, and he counted himself as the luckiest man alive.

They offered puja to Lord Ganesha so that all would go well. It was understood in both the Telugu and Gujarati cultures that the elephant god was a remover of all obstacles and a symbol of peace and happiness.

The priest pointed to the four pillars holding up the canopy under which they stood. He reminded them that they were representative of their parents and that they were to continue their role as mentors in their lives. He glanced over at the pillar behind the priest and tried to imagine his mother holding up the one corner of the canopy. She had always been strong. Her sturdy arms would have easily held up that corner of the canopy. But Chandu always believed her character was her real strength. And she would have loved Manisha as a daughter-in-law.

As the two of them exchanged garlands, he could tell by the warmth of her smile that she had finally accepted him. Her dark eyes were misty from emotion, and the flames from the sacred fire reflected off the moisture in her eyes. He, too, gave into his emotions when his father came over and tied a sacred knot between their clothing, which would symbolize their life long union. Fate, he thought to himself, was an amazing thing.

CHAPTER 27

Chandu gazed at the beauty of his sleeping bride and realized how lucky he was. He was destined to be with her, yet he would have never imagined it several years ago. He once dreamed about a life with Annabelle, but now it was unimaginable. Fate had its way, and he was thankful. His only regret, rather heartbreak, was that it was at the expense of his brother. How he desperately hoped that he would come home.

For now, a single roomed cottage behind Villa Pravina was home for the young couple. Chandu knew that once his family started to grow, they would have to find a bigger place. But they liked having the Mahendhis close by. It was like having another set of parents. And the Mahendhis especially enjoyed having the young couple.

As the barrister had taken on a role of mentoring Chandu, so too did Pravina with the new bride. She was quick to recognize a strong spirit within Manisha. That was something that could serve her well, but she would have to learn to tame her will and let Chandu be the leader, even if he wasn't always right. Chandu would learn from his mistakes, she told her. But Manisha wasn't too unlike her father in that regard.

As for the *Indian Observer*, it was quickly taking on a life of its own as the Indian community waited eagerly each Wednesday for the weekly edition to reach newsstands. The mission was to educate and inform the Indian brethren of the political and social dynamics that were shaping their lives. And while Siva was a reluctant editor, he proved invaluable as one who knew how to speak Telugu, Tamil and a fair amount of Hindi.

The barrister, of course, had his own column where he penned his opinions, and it was there that he often lambasted the Europeans for their authoritarian ways. But over time, he began to realize that one of the biggest obstacles facing Indians in the colony was the Indians. The Europeans that ruled the colony long argued that laborers from India were uncultured and lived in unsanitary conditions. Having resided in London for a number of years, he understood the clash. There was a deep chasm that lied between the European way of life and that found among the laborers who were usually recruited from the lowest echelons of Indian society.

The activist found himself on the horns of a dilemma. How would Indians ever integrate into the fabric of a European colony unless they rid themselves of the practices that Whites found so abhorrent. While he felt obligated, even driven to defend his kinsmen against the harsh criticisms being leveled against them, he knew there was some truth to their rhetoric.

He picked up his quill and began to write.

When the copy of the editorial came across Siva's desk for translation he was taken aback.

"How do you think this is going to be received by our readers, Govindas?"

"What do you mean by that, my friend?"

"Well, you're accusing them of being dirty, lying cheats that have a bad habit of—shall we say using nature as a toilet."

The barrister's hands went onto his hips. "Come, my colleague, I didn't put it like that."

"You did, Govindas. I just summarized it."

"Well, my piece is certainly more diplomatic, but our brothers and sisters need to know the truth. If they ever want to be accepted into this colony, then they have to start adopting European customs."

"I agree, Govindas. I'm just not sure how our readers will take your advice."

He pondered Siva's words and then responded. "Some may not take my admonition the way it's intended, but they need to hear the truth, nonetheless."

*****

Thursday morning was like any other morning. The air was crisp and cool, and the sun would be at their side as the barrister, and Chandu journeyed north from Sydenham to Phoenix. The trip always gave them plenty of time to talk, often planning what they would put into that week's edition. Thursdays were the first day of the week after the Wednesday run, so they would often get a head start on ideas for the next run before reaching the office.

This morning, however, Chandu could tell that the barrister was not himself. He was unusually quiet and introspective.

"Everything all right?" Chandu asked as he snapped the reins.

"I had a bad dream last night, my young friend."

Chandu chuckled slightly. "Must have seemed real by the look of your face."

"If not foretelling." His eyes widened. "I dreamt that a mob of Indians came and circled the office and then attacked us."

"Angry because of what we published yesterday?"

He nodded. "Yes, my friend. That's exactly why."

Chandu tried to put the barrister's mind at ease, "It was just a dream, Mr. Mahendhi. Nothing more."

"I hope so," he replied, but the worry didn't leave his face.

Chandu changed the subject and said, "The Velu's are moving to Asherville."

The barrister's eyebrows rose high into his forehead. "Is that so? We'll practically be neighbors."

He nodded and then added, "Manisha feels strongly about moving in with them once they move over to this side since she is working full time in the factory now."

"So you're leaving Villa Pravina?" There was a hint of disappointment in his voice.

Chandu patted his boss and mentor on the leg. "It won't be tomorrow."

The barrister took a deep breath and pushed his glasses up high on his nose. "Asherville is nice. A lot of up and coming Indians are moving to that area."

*****

As they neared Phoenix, they noticed soot in the still air and could smell the char of freshly burned wood.

"That doesn't smell like rubbish burning," Chandu remarked.

The barrister didn't reply. As they turned onto Stonebridge Street, they could see a small crowd gathered where the small building that once housed Mahendhi and Associates as well as the *Indian Observer*.

Siva met them as they pulled up and looked like he had spent hours putting out the blaze. His eyes conveyed a combination of sorrow and anger as he shook his head side to side.

"This was no accident, Govindas," he exclaimed. "Somebody burned this building down to the ground."

"How do you know?"

"You can still smell the kerosene. This was arson!"

The fire had obviously been set last night shortly after our departure. The barrister had yet to say anything as he walked slowly toward the burnt remains. There was little sound except crackling cinders. All eyes were fixed on him when he started laughing and threw his hands in the air. "It was fate!" He kicked some burnt rubble and said, "It's God's way of telling me something."

Siva snickered. "I know what God is telling me. These White people do not like us and want us to leave the colony."

Seemingly out of nowhere came the remark, "I think you tell the truth, Mahendhi, even if they don't." Everyone turned to find a diminutive older man holding the latest edition of the *Indian Observer* rolled up in his right hand.

The barrister smiled and answered, "I'm glad you think so, my friend, but who is 'they'?"

He motioned with his hands, indicating nowhere specific. "Those who were offended by what you wrote about them," he replied, hitting the newspaper into his open hand. "But I think you were doing us all a favor. We need to hear this from one of our own so we learn to adapt to this place we now call home."

The barrister smiled. "What is your name, my friend?"

He pressed his hands together and answered, "I am simply Muthusamy."

Siva jumped in, "Did you see who did this, Muthusamy?"

He nodded. "No, it could have been anyone. I heard a number of our people grumbling about your newspaper." Then he walked away.

Siva glanced over at the barrister and remarked with amazement, "And you're not even angry."

Again, he shrugged. "You can't fight fate, my friend." He walked over to where his office once stood and kicked away some rubble that exposed a cash box he kept in his desk. It opened effortlessly, and inside was ninety-eight shillings that had remained untouched by the blaze.

The barrister pulled out two shillings and threw one to each of them. Then he asked, "Are we going to just lie down and let this defeat us?" He closed the cash box and walked over to them. "From these ashes, we will rebuild this newspaper. Are you men with me?"

Siva and Chandu exchanged glances, then Chandu answered first. "I'm with you, Mr. Mahendhi."

The barrister smiled and then looked at Siva. "What about you, my friend?"

Siva's brows furrowed toward his nose. "What about Mahendhi and Associates?"

"You mean the law office?"

"That's why I moved my family here from India, Govindas." Siva's tone was petulant.

The barrister stroked his chin as he was often prone to do then said, "I can do well, or I can do good." He walked over and put his hand on Siva's shoulder. "I can be more effective and do more good for our people with this press rather than representing wealthy Muslims."

Siva kicked a piece of burnt rubble. "But how am I supposed to support my family?"

"I'm not asking you to volunteer your time."

"You might as well with what little money the newspaper brings in."

"That's going to change, my friend. We're going to start charging the readers—three pence. And we're going to start selling advertising." Siva put his hands in his pockets, showing little emotion or interest in what the barrister had to say. It was obvious that his dreams of building a life for him and his family had perished in the fire.

But the barrister continued as he kicked a piece of smoldering wood. "And I know just what we should rename the paper."

"Hot off the press?" Chandu joked.

"No," he said, raising the smoking ember toward the sky. "It shall be called *Phoenix Rising.*" He turned toward Siva and asked, "What do you think?"

He shrugged. "Very clever."

"We can do a lot of good with this press, my friend, and I want you to be a part of it."

Siva replied, "We tried that." He motioned with his hand toward the ruins. "Look what it got us."

"That's because we went about it wrong. If we want our brothers to respond positively, then we must be willing to show them not tell them."

"I don't know what you mean, Govindas."

"Well, I guess I'll just have to show you," he said with a broad grin. He walked over and slapped the printing press that was still intact and said, "Right after we rebuild this place."

*****

Prema never imagined that she would one day own such an enormous factory. But the move came rather quickly after the Velus' were contracted to supply men's and boy's clothing for Edmund's Fine Clothes—the largest retailer of fine clothing in the colony. Before long, they had twenty-five seamstresses in their employ and several supervisors.

Across the street from the factory was the Grey Street Mosque, and it was rare to find Europeans moving around in that part of the city. That is, except the Reverend George Stadelmaier.

Some years ago, he had a church several blocks away on Field Street but now spent a disproportionate amount of his time among the Indians. His mission was to convert them to Christianity. The Muslims were largely unmoved by the reverend's efforts but there were some Hindus who did convert. It was usually the poorest of the poor and those who were downtrodden that received what the reverend had to say.

Reverend Stadelmaier never complained. To his naysayers who would tell him he was wasting his time, he would cite the parable in the Gospel of Luke in which a certain man gave a great supper and invited many. Those whom the man invited offered varied excuses as to why they would not attend. The man then extended the invitation to the outcasts of society who were glad to come.

The reverend approached Manisha and Chandu one afternoon outside the clothing factory. He recognized Chandu because he was still in the practice of wearing fine clothing whether he was working or not.

"Hello, young man. Aren't you one of Govindas's colleagues?"

"Yes," he replied confidently, "I'm Chandu Nayadu."

"And this lovely young woman must be your wife."

"Yes, this is Manisha," he replied.

"Reverend George Stadelmaier," he responded, extending his large hand. "Govindas tells me you people are rebuilding the newspaper?"

"Yes, sir," he answered. "We're starting next week."

"And with a most appropriate name, I might add," he said with a broad smile. "Do you happen to know the meaning of phoenix, Mr. Naidu?"

"Uh, it's a bird, from a myth, I believe, that dies and rises again as a new bird?" He chanced upon that story in a book of Russian folklore while living with Siva.

"You're right, young man. I'm quite impressed with your knowledge. The phoenix is a classic symbol of death and resurrection. But it's only a myth, just as you said. There is, however, a story of death and resurrection that isn't a myth. Shall I tell you about it?"

He had a feeling that the reverend was going to tell him whether he was interested or not. He put his hand up to block the hot rays of the midafternoon sun.

"Have you ever heard of Jesus?" he asked.

"Yes, he's the Christian God," he answered. "Reverend, do you want me to become a Christian?"

"It's not what I want, Chandu. It's what God wants."

"I believe in Jesus," he rejoined, but I also believe in all of our other gods."

"Sure you do, young man. But let me ask you a question. Has even one of those gods laid his life down for you so that you can have eternal life? Do any of them desire to have a relationship with you?"

"Are all White people Christians?" he asked with a slight sting in his voice?

"Certainly not," the reverend replied calmly.

"But many of the Europeans in this colony go to church, don't they?"

"Yes, I suppose so."

"Yet these same people who go to church hate us Indians. Is that what it means to be a Christian?" he asked.

The reverend hesitated for a moment. "Young man, that is *not* what it means to be a Christian. Followers of Christ are called to love one another just as—"

"Please forgive me, sir. I don't mean any disrespect, but I'm a Hindu, and I should die that way."

"I'm not trying to be disrespectful either, Mr. Naidu, but I hope you don't—"

"I'm sorry, sir," he said, taking Manisha by the hand. They started to walk toward the carriage and the Reverend yelled in their direction, "I'm always around if you ever want to talk."

*****

As they started their long journey back to Phoenix, he said to Manisha, "Can you believe that White man asking me if any of our gods ever died for us? What kind of question is that?"

She raised her eyebrows and replied, "Well, have they?"

"Of course not!" he snapped back. "What god will go and die for one of us?"

She turned and looked straight ahead, and he was sure that was the end of the conversation. Then she said softly, "Jesus."

He turned slowly toward her, and his brows narrowed toward his nose, "Who have you been talking to?"

She answered coyly, "Nobody."

"Who's been talking to you about Jesus?" His voice was louder this time.

"Devi's been telling us girls at the factory about this Jesus."

"Devi's a Christian?"

She nodded and said, "She prayed with me and asked Jesus to give us a baby."

He scoffed, "And you think that will work?"

"Nothing else has worked. We've been trying for almost two years with no luck."

"I guess we'll see if this Jesus answers prayers," came his haughty reply.

"And if he does?"

He snapped the reins, sending the horse into a faster clip. "We'll see."

*****

In January of 1905, just five weeks after construction had commenced, the first edition of the *Phoenix Rising* was ready to go to press. With a building twice the size as the previous and a brand-new printing press, the barrister was more determined than ever to keep the Indians informed. It was a crucial time in the colony, and the political turmoil was fast coming to a head. It seemed that Indians were going to be pulled in whether they wanted to or not.

But Siva and Chandu convinced the barrister to make the first edition of the *Phoenix* lighthearted. There would be no politics or stories about European dominance and oppression but, rather, stories of human interest, humor with a hint of satire. They wanted to not only bring their readers back but to bring a smile to their face at a time when there was little to smile about.

Take, for instance, the story of a mother of three who had chosen to save her children's school fees in a half empty jar of pickled mango. When it came time to pay the fees, she promptly went down to the school registrar whereupon she handed over the jar and its pickled contents. She was sure that there was enough money in the jar to cover the fees for all three children. She had been faithfully saving all year. As for the pickled mango, well it was a gift for the schoolmaster. It was an old family recipe.

Another story gave a glimpse into the nuances of an evolving Indian society. A diaspora that disrupted the well-established caste system. Imagine the horror of some when constables from the *pariah* caste were suddenly in a position of authority over those of a higher caste. The pariahs were considered untouchable back in India. Being in the shadow of a pariah was enough to "pollute" a higher caste Indian. "What to do?" Chandu wrote in his article, "stay out of trouble, and you'll stay out of the long shadow of the law!"

But they knew that the plan for a soft entry back into the sitting rooms of their readership was about to change when their illustrious managing editor barged through the newly painted front doors of their office.

"Well, they did it!" said the barrister, holding a copy of the *Natal Times* in his left hand.

"Did what?" Chandu asked.

"The newly elected assembly has unanimously passed the Indian Registration Act."

"That didn't take long," said Siva.

"Well, it still has to be approved by Lord Falmouth, but don't expect any hesitancy on his part. He will surely stamp it into law before his morning tea."

"So what to do?" Chandu asked.

He held up his hands. "We will be required to submit imprints of every finger as well as revealing body marks for exact identification. Those who don't register within a month will be sent to jail."

"These Europeans really hate us, don't they," Chandu remarked.

"The final copy hasn't gone to press yet, has it?" the barrister asked.

"Just getting ready to print it," said Siva.

"Hold the press," he said, "I have something to say to our brothers and sisters."

*****

Though Velu was incapable of reading more than three words on his best day, he paid the three pence and carried the folded paper tucked under his arm the entire day. When he went to see Edmund Klein, the clothier asked him, "Is that the *Times*, Mr. Velu?"

"Uh, no, sir, it's my son-in-law's paper, the *Phoenix Rising*."

"Oh," he said with raised eyebrows, "may I?"

Velu handed Mr. Klein his paper, which was now partially unreadable after so many hours under Velu's sweaty arm. Nevertheless, Mr. Klein gingerly unfolded the paper and laid it open on his desk and then pulled his reading glasses out of his top pocket and set them on the end of his nose. He peered over to Velu and said, "I'm interested in reading what this Mr. Mahendhi has to say. He's a fascinating character."

He quietly read through the first few paragraphs then said, "Your leader is saying you Indians must resist this new registration law and be ready to go to jail if needed." He glanced back at Velu and asked, "Are you willing to go to jail to protest this law?"

Velu shrugged. "I don't know anything about this."

Mr. Klein pushed the paper back toward Velu and said, "I can't afford to have you and your workers sitting in jail. Do you understand what I'm saying?"

Velu had never seen Edmund Klein so stern and took a step backward. "I do, sir. I understand."

"Good. Just remember that it's because of me that you now have that big factory down the road and now drive that nice carriage sitting out there in front of my store."

"I know, sir."

Mr. Klein continued, "I don't care how persuasive this Mahendhi chap is, telling you that this is a 'mark of slavery' and 'an affront to your manhood.' He's not paying your bills, you hear?"

"Yes, sir."

"So then there won't be any protesting of this law. Am I right?"

"Yes, sir. You're right," Velu started toward the door and then stopped. He turned around and asked Mr. Klein, "Sir, you're from another country?"

Mr. Klein shot Velu a curious stare. "Yes, I am from Germany."

Velu smiled. "Then you are required to register also?"

"I'm afraid not, Mr. Velu. This government has enacted it solely for the purpose of harassing you Indians. I wish it weren't so, but it is."

*****

When Velu got back to the factory, he took the same paper and threw it on the table in front of his wife. "Mahendhi is telling us Indians that we have to protest against this new registration law that the Whites have passed."

"Why?" she asked as she looked over the quality of some recently stitched garments.

He pointed to the paper. "He says that we won't be men and that we'll be slaves if we don't. He also said that we must be willing to go to jail."

"She looked up from the shirt she was inspecting and with furrowed brows asked, "Did you read that?"

"No, Mr. Klein did."

She resumed what she was doing seemingly unbothered. Velu snatched the paper off the table and put it back under his arm. "Who appointed this man leader over us? Mahendhi obviously has nothing to lose himself. If we all protest this thing and end up in jail, we'll lose our business!"

Prema looked up and said, "But what about all of our workers? What if they decide to protest? Then what good will it do if we register? We will have a business but no workers. They will all be in jail."

His eyes widened. "We can't let them protest. Our factory will come to a halt."

"But how can we stop them?"

"We'll fire them if they decide to protest."

She held her forefinger to her lips, "Shh! We can't do that, Ammandi."

"Why not?"

"Because this thing is much bigger than us."

Velu was quiet for a long moment. Then he leaned over and said in low tone, "All I know is that everyone who works in this factory will have to register for this new law or they lose their job." Then he marched out of the factory.

*****

As the day drew to a close, Siva grew increasingly unsettled. The barrister's not so subtle suggestion that Indians resist the mandated registration even at the cost of their freedom was more than he was willing to personally bear.

"Govindas, I have to speak to you."

"Of course, my faithful colleague, what is it?"

"I don't think you'll find me a faithful colleague after I tell you what I have to say."

The barrister removed his spectacles, "Please, tell me."

Siva's eyes reddened with conviction. "I can never go back to that jail."

He paused momentarily before responding, "I understand, my friend. But keep in mind that freedom comes with a price. And you must remember that there's strength in numbers. None of us will be alone."

"That may be, Govindas, but you didn't go through what I went through. I can't go back to jail, and I can't encourage others to go."

Before the two men finished their conversation, Velu stormed through the front door of the newspaper office. He marched straight over to Chandu's desk and started ranting in Telugu, "How can Mahendhi garu expect us business owners to go to jail? Is he looking for a fight?"

The barrister saw the commotion from the other side of the office. He walked over and asked, "Is there a problem?"

Chandu answered, "My father-in-law is concerned about the article in today's paper."

"Let me guess—he doesn't like the idea of going to jail if necessary."

Chandu nodded.

The barrister turned to Velu and said, "You must understand that this law is meant to humiliate us—to disgrace us. If we give in now—"

Suddenly, Ali Kader and Mohamed Deedad walked in. "Mahendhi, we need to talk you about this story in your paper," said Mr. Kader. "You're demanding that we resist this registration ordinance and be willing to go to jail."

"That's right, gentlemen. I thought that you were also against this ordinance," the barrister asserted while trying to maintain his composure in the face of mounting opposition.

"We are," replied Mr. Kader, "but we are not willing to go to jail."

"If all of us unite together to resist this act, then they can't possibly throw us all in jail. The jail isn't big enough. But look, women in America are doing it right now for the right to vote. If women are brave enough to go to jail, then how much more should we take a stand for our very dignity?"

"You don't understand, Mahendhi!" said Mr. Deedad. "We business owners have a lot to lose. These Europeans may decide to take away all of our licenses leaving us with no way to make a living."

"There is no legal grounds by which they are able to take away your business licenses, gentlemen. As I was saying to Mr. Velu before you walked in, these people want to humiliate us. If we give into this outrageous *act*, then I myself will not be able to walk down the street with my face showing."

"It's fine for you Hindus to do this thing you're proposing. Your people are mostly hawkers and don't have much to lose. We Muslims are merchants and have too much at stake to go against this thing."

"Hold on, Mr. Kader, there's no need to put down our Hindus. We are all Indians, and we all face the same dilemma. Should we not stand united against this treacherous *act* that is meant to bring shame upon our people."

"We may all be Indians," said Mr. Deedad, "but we are two different classes of people with different stakes at risk. And we never asked you to represent us in this matter."

"Please, gentlemen, go home and sleep on this. We have an INC meeting next week, and we can discuss the matter then."

The barrister had skillfully managed to diffuse the situation, but he knew his challenges were only mounting. He took out his handkerchief and wiped the perspiration from his forehead then commented, "These men have underestimated the power of the press."

"What do you mean?" Chandu asked.

"What I mean is that if these men want to break the solidarity of this passive resistance, then I will publish every name of every dissenter along with their father's name, caste, and the village they're from."

"Please don't do that to my father-in-law, Mr. Mahendhi. He will never forgive me as long as I work for this newspaper."

"I wouldn't do that to you, my young cohort. But you must talk some sense into that man."

*****

Chandu understood Velu's dilemma. On the one hand was the barrister's firm conviction that Indians needed to be of one mind in taking a stand against their European oppressors. On the other hand were people like Velu—someone who was getting ahead in life by hard work and determination. Going against the powers-that-be meant possible jail time and the chance of losing everything. And somewhere in the middle were people like himself. He had a loyalty to both sides and wondered how he would manage to walk the fine line that separated the two.

*****

When he told his father-in-law that Mr. Mahendhi was intending to publish the names of those who would go against the planned protest as a way of bringing shame on their families he replied, "How can you work for a man like this?"

"You have to see Mr. Mahendhi's side, Uncle. He's doing what he thinks is best for the whole Indian community."

"It's not best for me and my family or all the employees I have working for me. How is this good for the Indian community?" In a fit of rage, he took his plate of food and threw it against the wall. "It's good for him because it gets him more attention. This man lives for attention."

Nobody dared say a word as he walked over and picked up his plate. He turned to his son-in-law and said, "If it were not for my daughter, I would ban you from my home. But I cannot have you move into our new home as long as you are working for that man. You must continue to live with him."

CHAPTER 28

The INC meeting that preceded the opening of the first temporary registration office was well attended but almost entirely by Indians who were intending to protest the mandated registration. Those who were not intending to protest didn't come. That included a large number of the Muslim community, as well as Velu. Also absent was Siva. He explained to all his colleagues at the newspaper office that his unwillingness to go back to jail would only compromise the movement, so he turned in his resignation. They were all deeply saddened to see him go.

Nevertheless, a plan was devised to demonstrate peacefully outside the registration office which was set up in a vacant building on Grey Street just one block south of the mosque. The barrister, along with Chandu and a couple of dozen other dutiful picketers, led the way on the first morning of registrations. They walked to and fro and back and forth in the blistering hot sun, yet nobody arrived to register. Nobody even seemed interested except a slightly built White fellow who identified himself as reporter for the *Natal Times*.

The next morning, they returned with their signs and the barrister with a copy of the *Times*. On the front page was a small story that denounced the demonstration as intimidation to those who would choose to register. Still, they carried on with the protest for several days and saw only three families cross their path to register. They were careful not to so much as utter a word to those who registered as several constables stood nearby and were looking for a reason to jail them. The barrister simply noted their names and promised to publish them in the next edition of the *Phoenix Rising*.

But on the fourth day, Mohamed Deedad and a group of Muslim businessmen arrived to register early in the morning. As they walked past, Mr. Deedad spat on the ground and very close to the feet of one young picketer named Barun. The young activist was incensed by Mr. Deedad's gesture. As far as he was concerned, the elderly businessman had thrown down the gauntlet. He took his sign and swung it like a cricket bat, hitting Mr. Deedad square in the under section of his torso.

Another businessman who was slight in stature but extremely angered by Barun's actions reached out and thwacked Barun with his open hand, knocking him to the ground. The young man jumped up and lunged toward the businessman, prompting an all-encompassing melee.

It was all the police needed to cart the protesters off to jail. But jail was not where Chandu wanted to be, at least not then. With a deep gash over his eye and a bruised rib, all he wanted was to be home with Manisha.

The small cramped cell only seemed to fuel the barrister's passion for the resistance movement. Even the limp he was left with did little to slow his frenetic pacing from one side of the cell to the other.

"Deedad and his ilk are poison," he ranted. "They're going to do everything in their power to foil this movement." And as their leader labeled the men as traitors and vowed to make public their betrayal, Chandu moved his face close to the only window in the cell for some fresh air. Walking by was Reverend George Stadelmaier. With a Bible in his right hand, he quickly strode by, and Chandu could only guess that he was on his way to rescue some heathens from themselves. While he would ordinarily find humor in his gangly stride and the straw boater hat that was forever blowing off his head, he wasn't laughing now.

"But we mustn't be fearful!" said the barrister. He quickly turned his attention back to the conversation as he continued, "because there can be no remission of sin without the shedding of blood."

"What did you say?" Chandu asked.

"Something wrong, my friend?"

"What did you say about the shedding of blood?"

"I said that we mustn't be fearful because we are on a mission to win without the shedding of blood."

"That's not what you said. You said, '*there can be no remission of sin* without the shedding of blood.'"

Several chuckled.

"You're hearing things, my young colleague."

Was I hearing things? he thought to himself. He peered out the window, but the reverend was out of sight.

Several hours passed when the jailer appeared with keys in hand. They were being released. Standing outside the jail as they filed out was the Reverend Stadelmaier.

"I thought you men might want to spend the night at home."

"Did you get us out of jail, Reverend?" the barrister asked.

"Lord Falmouth is an old friend, and he owed me a favor."

"Well, you're a real friend to the Indians, Reverend."

"I believe God created us all in his image, and we all deserve to be treated the same."

Chandu knew that his boss and the reverend differed on their philosophical positions, but he was impressed how their relationship was able to transcend those differences. After the band of activists made their way toward their respective homes he stayed behind to talk to the reverend.

His face contorted in an anguished sort of way at the sight of Chandu's wound. "You need to get some attention for that injury, young man."

"As soon as I get home, Reverend."

"Did you wish to speak with me?"

"I would like to ask you something"

"Of course, anything."

"What is your opinion of the Indians trying to resist this Registration Act?"

The reverend smiled and said, "Let me first say that your mentor is a good man, and I believe his intentions are honorable, but I don't believe he's on the right path."

"But Mr. Mahendhi claims that he is following the example of Jesus by peacefully resisting the Indian Registration Act."

The reverend chuckled. "The word is *rebellion*, young man. Jesus never resisted or rebelled against authority. He only denounced those who were clearly violating God's law. You must remember that laws and government are instituted to bring order without which, there would be utter chaos. We are instructed to submit to authority as long as those laws being enforced do not clearly violate God's eternal law."

"Do you think that this registration law is fair to us Indians?"

"Well, it might seem unfair, but its intention is to maintain order in a society that gets more complicated every day," said the reverend. "Look," he said with a softer tone, "I don't agree with some of these new laws, but the law is the law, and we have to submit to them regardless. This is why I can't condone Mr. Mahendhi's actions. Unfortunately, he's a victim of one of man's most common afflictions—pride. If he truly wants to follow the example of Jesus, then he would, in all humility, submit to the law." Then he asked, "What do you think?"

"I don't know what to think, Reverend."

*****

Chandu wouldn't be able to hide the deep gash over his eye from Manisha, but he wasn't going to tell her that he spent time in jail. He wasn't even going to tell her about his bruised rib. He knew how she felt about his involvement with the resistance movement, and he already knew how she was going to react.

She'd say, "Chandu, you should quit this movement. You may end up getting yourself killed."

He would respond, "I can't quit, Manisha. Mr. Mahendhi is counting on me."

She would start crying and say, "But look where it's got us. We're considered troublemakers, and we're no longer welcomed by my parents."

He knew her well enough, and he knew that she would be waiting for him at the door before walking over to the Mahendhi's for supper. As per usual, she was waiting for him, and before he could shut the door behind him, she embraced him like he had never experienced. She was sobbing, yet he hadn't even told her what happened.

"It's not that bad, Manisha."

She lifted her head from his chest, and Chandu noticed that she was smiling. "Why are you crying?" he asked with a tone of bewilderment.

She wiped away her tears and said, "I'm pregnant."

"Pregnant!"

She smiled slightly from the side of her mouth. "Devi's prayer worked."

"Oh, you mean…"

She nodded. "Don't you remember?"

"Are you sure you're pregnant?"

"She nodded as more tears rolled down the softness of her cheeks. He took her hand and kissed it. Then he said, "You're pregnant."

A smile swept across her face. "Yes, my love, I'm pregnant."

"I'm going to be a father!"

She gasped suddenly. "Chandu! What happened to your eye?"

Before he could answer she said, "Don't tell me. I don't want to hear it. If you're going to be a father, then you need to quit this resistance movement?"

"That means quitting my job, Manisha."

"Can't you talk to him—please."

"Okay, I'll talk with him tomorrow. Let's not say anything over supper."

*****

By the time Chandu arrived at the office the following morning, he already planned what he would say to his boss. He would tell him that he could no longer participate in a movement that was causing division in his family not to mention within the community and that he would just have to see his point of view. Then he would tell him that he was going to be a father. He thought about it for a second and decided he would tell him about being a father first. Perhaps it would soften him a bit.

So he waited and waited, and with each passing minute, he grew more nervous. Would he really tell the man who had made his schooling possible and had taken him under his wing that he was jumping ship?

Then he suddenly realized why nobody was at the office that morning. They made a plan to meet at dawn's break in front of the registration office. *How could I have been so absent minded*, he thought to himself. He jumped in the carriage and raced into town and to the temporary registration office. But none of the protesters were to be found.

He removed his hat and stepped warily into the registration office. Sitting behind a small desk was a slight middle-aged man with his sleeves rolled up and his collar loosened. He had a pinched face that Chandu suspected was permanent. When he saw him walk in it was apparent that he recognized him from the day before. With a sly smile, he said, "Have you changed your mind and decided to register?"

"Excuse me, sir, but where are the men that were here yesterday?"

"You mean your little band of revolutionaries?"

"Were they here this morning?"

"They were. That is until the police carted them all away."

"On what charges?"

"For being a bloody nuisance, I suppose. We don't need your kind here disturbing the peace."

"Our demonstration *is* peaceful, sir."

"You call what happened here yesterday peaceful?"

Chandu didn't have an answer.

"You can find them all down at the jail, boy, just where they belong."

He hopped into his carriage and headed toward the jail but knew there would be little he would be able to affect upon his arrival. Then he worried they might lock him up as well just for being associated with the protesters. The barrister warned him that they might be jailed for their actions, and everyone agreed that they were ready for such a consequence. But now that he had a taste of the inhospitable and foul-smelling stench of a jail cell, he had change of heart.

He slowed the carriage down to a crawl and contemplated whether he should just go back to the Phoenix office. Then he spotted the Reverend Stadelmaier walking on the footpath, and he brought the carriage to a halt.

"Greetings, Mr. Naidu!" the minister yelled from the footpath. He walked over as Chandu was stepping down from the carriage. "And I see you've managed to escape incarceration this morning."

"You mean the registration?"

"No, I mean you've kept yourself out of jail. How did you manage such?"

"Oh, I was late this morning. By the time I arrived, they were already gone."

He shook his head side to side with his lips pursed. "Remember what I told you yesterday?"

"I do, Reverend, but is there anything you can do to get them out of jail?"

"I suppose I could but what about tomorrow? Are you going to come looking for me again if you yourself aren't in jail? Let them stay there for a day and think about whether it's worth sitting in that cell. They'll be released at the end of the day." He paused for a moment, waiting for Chandu's response, but he had none. Then he said, "You do see my point, don't you, Mr. Naidu?"

"I suppose so,"

"Very well, then is there anything else I can do for you?"

Chandu was prepared to go on his way, but without forethought, he blurted out, "My wife thinks Jesus got her pregnant."

The reverend looked at him strangely. "What I mean is that one of her Christian friends prayed to Jesus for her to get pregnant, and now she is."

He put his large hand on Chandu's shoulder and smiled. "Well, surely, young man, you must have had a role in this."

"Well…"

"Congratulations. I'm very happy for you and your wife. God is good, isn't he?"

"Does this mean that I have to become a Christian?"

He chuckled. "Well, I think God would like nothing more, but he gives us a choice. You can choose to follow him or not."

"But, Reverend, can't I put a Jesus statue alongside our other Hindu gods?"

"Absolutely, Chandu. But let me ask you something." He leaned forward so that he was practically face to face. "What have your other god statues done for you?" He stood up straight and paused, waiting for Chandu to respond, but he was unable.

"I'm not trying to shame you, young man, just an honest question. You see, Jesus has clearly answered your wife's prayer when it was seemingly impossible for you to start a family. Therefore, I believe Jesus is the only God you should acknowledge."

The reverend could clearly see that Chandu was uncertain, even anxious about his situation. "You have a lot to consider, don't you, young man?"

He nodded. "I don't know how Mr. Mahendhi is going to take me leaving the resistance movement. And I know Jesus answered Manisha's prayer. I believe it. But it's going to be hard telling my Nana that I'm a Christian."

The reverend smiled and pulled out his well-worn Bible. He turned to a passage in St. Matthew and read,

> Come unto me, all ye that labour and are heavy laden, and I will give you rest. Take my yoke upon you, and learn of me; for I am meek and lowly in heart: and ye shall find rest unto your souls.

Chandu shrugged, "I don't know what that means, Reverend."

"Of course, I'm sorry, young man. It simply means that Jesus will take all your worries upon himself and, in turn, give you his peace."

His eyes lit up. "I want that, Reverend."

"Very well, then let's pray."

And as the reverend prayed for Chandu, a peace that he had never experienced came over him. His countenance changed, and the reverend was quick to notice. "I believe you were touched by God, son."

He smiled. "I think you're right, Reverend. Does this mean I've become a Christian?"

"Do you believe that Jesus died for your sins?"

"I…" He looked at the reverend with a puzzled look. "Jesus died for *my* sins?"

The reverend put his hands on Chandu's shoulders and smiled broadly. "Indeed, he did, young man. That's how much He loves you."

Tears welled up in Chandu's eyes.

*****

The next morning, Chandu was sitting at his desk with a stack of memos along with some story lines that needed his follow up. Sitting on top was a list with the names of the families that had registered the previous day. He recognized several of the names and knew them to be hardworking business owners and reckoned them to be no different than the Velus. His stomach felt queasy, and he put the list back down on his desk.

His mind drifted back to the encounter he had with the reverend the previous day. He knew in his heart that it wasn't merely words that were uttered as he acknowledged Jesus, but something truly transformational had taken place in his heart.

He leaned back in his chair and started to nod off when the door opened. It was Siva.

"Hello, Chandu."

He startled. "Siva!"

"Uh—is Govindas here?"

"No, he—he's out right now."

He took a step in and asked, "Do you mind if I wait?"

"Not at all. You're always welcome here, Siva."

"I'm not sure if Govindas would say the same. So where is he?"

"Well," he replied hesitantly, "he's in jail right now. He and whoever else were protesting down at the registration office this morning."

Siva shook his head side to side. "This crusade he's on is going to bring our people to ruin."

"How so?"

"We can't win this battle with these Europeans. They have the backing of the biggest empire in the world. If we continue to defy these people, they're likely to crush us like they crushed the Zulus." Then he caught a glimpse of the list of names sitting in front of Chandu and asked, "What are those names?"

"These? Oh, these are uh…" He couldn't think of anything fast enough to avoid fueling Siva's rant. "…the names of the families that registered."

"So you can publish them?"

He nodded shamefully. "But—"

"Publishing names of people who choose to register as if they were criminals. Is he looking to have this building burned down again? It's not right, Chandu. He's only bringing division between our people. If people want to register, they're only doing what is lawful. Govindas has appointed himself as not only our leader but our conscience as well. He has to be stopped."

He got up and started toward the door, and Chandu asked, "Do you want me to give Mr. Mahendhi a message?"

"I was going to talk to him about coming back to work, but I've changed my mind."

*****

Later that evening the barrister paid Chandu a visit at his cottage. He was concerned that he had neither joined the protest nor made an effort to visit the band of protesters in their confinement.

Chandu asked the barrister pointedly, "Mr. Mahendhi, do you really believe that this movement is going to get the registration law revoked?"

His head cocked back several inches. "Are you having doubts, my young colleague?"

"I've been thinking about it, Mr. Mahendhi. It seems that we stand little chance of winning a battle of wills with these Whites. They have the support of the British Empire and—"

"It sounds like somebody has been lecturing you. So let me tell you this: The British Empire does not support this Indian Registration Act. Secondly, if you should want to admit defeat before the first battle is over, then we will surely lose. Now are you telling me you are ready to give up?"

Chandu suddenly felt deflated. The barrister had an uncanny ability to win people over to his side of the argument.

"No, but things are not so great around here, Mr. Mahendhi."

His face grew concerned. "Tell me, my young colleague. I want to help."

"My father-in-law has barred us from moving into their new home."

"Why is that?"

"Because I work for you."

"Oh, I see." He thought for a moment then said, "Is that it?"

"Manisha is insisting that I quit this resistance movement. She thinks it's causing us many problems."

He nodded. "Anything else?"

"I'm going to be a father."

His eyes widened. "A father!" He sat down and said, "That's wonderful news. I'm very happy for you and your bride, but I'm not willing to just release you if that's what you're thinking. There is a compromise waiting to be discovered if only we should seek it."

"I'm happy to seek a compromise."

"Very well. Then let me suggest that you continue on as my editor but at the expense of being involved with any passive resistance movement. Though I would have greatly valued your involvement, I know firsthand the importance of keeping our wives happy.

He smiled, and Chandu chuckled.

"As for your father-in-law, hmm," he said, biting his lower lip. "Perhaps I need to go and speak with him."

"He's pretty stubborn."

"I know, but I can be pretty stubborn also."

"That's true," he said with a chuckle.

"Very well, then you must wish me luck."

CHAPTER 29

Though Velu had a long history of dissidence things were different now. He had a prosperous business and a mandate from his sole client, Edmund Klein, to refrain from any notion of resisting the registration. It was a side of the soft-spoken clothier he had never seen before, and he was inclined to take him very seriously.

So when the barrister challenged Velu that Indians needed to stand strong in peaceful defiance of White tyranny, he held his ground.

"Look," said Velu extending his hand out toward the team of women who were busy stitching the garments that would soon grace the racks of Edmund's Fine Clothes. "I have all this at stake."

"That may be," the barrister said calmly, "but you're allowing a White man to control your destiny."

He knew he hit a nerve. It was a calculated barrister tactic that zeroed in on Velu's Achilles' heel. He heard all the stories that made Velu somewhat of a legend. Certainly, he was back in Korlakota. His fearless defiance of the Zamindar, not to mention his rebellion on the plantation, would be talked about for generations. But over time, Velu had softened. The barrister was trusting that that spirit hadn't been completely quenched.

Velu was silent for a moment, and the barrister watched Velu's eyebrows narrow down toward his nose. He didn't know what was going on inside his head, but he had a hunch that he said enough on that subject. He bid Velu a gracious farewell, and as he was departing, he suggested that his son-in-law was not the enemy, but it was rather those who would rather see Indians move back to India.

*****

Nayadu gave little thought to the politics surrounding the Indians and cared very little about the Indian Registration Act. Mr. Cozen would surely insist that his employees register, and Nayadu would surely comply. He didn't read the paper because he couldn't read. But even if could, he had no interest in the world outside of his family or his little realm on the Sykes Estate.

He had found his little vocation in life and was happy. The only thing Chandu reckoned would make him happier was if he came to know that he was going to be a grandfather. So he anxiously waited for Sunday, his day off from work, to tell him the news.

*****

When Chandu and Manisha arrived late that morning, they found him relaxing on his daybed. Ordinarily, Nayadu would have sprung from his reclining position at the arrival of any guests but not now. He simply smiled and motioned them in with a wave of his hand.

Being married agreed with Nayadu, and his rounded stomach showed that Sonali and Seeli were taking good care of him. But working out in the fields was aging him. His arms and legs were thin and sinewy, and his skin was dark, almost black, from the constant exposure to the sun.

Manisha gave him a kiss on his cheek, and Chandu asked him, "Do you notice anything different about your daughter?"

He cocked his head back and looked her over from head to toe. "No, she's just as beautiful as ever," he said with a smile. Strictly speaking, there was nothing different about Manisha's appearance other than the glow she was wearing since learning she was pregnant.

"I'm with child!" she gushed.

He sprung from his reclining position, and his eyes grew round like chestnuts. "Really? You're expecting?"

Chandu replied, "Yes, Nana, she really is."

He stood and hugged Manisha. A tear streamed down his cheek, and his voice cracked, "I never thought I would have grandchildren."

"You can thank Jesus, Nana," she blurted out.

Nayadu's face hardened into a frown. "Jesus? Why should I thank Jesus?"

Chandu cleared his throat. "Uh, Nana, Manisha's friend Devi prayed that Manisha would fall pregnant."

He nodded and added, "So?"

"Well, Devi's a Christian, Nana. She prays to Jesus."

His face scrunched up while he contemplated what he just heard, and then his eyebrows rose into his forehead. "So this Jesus made you pregnant?"

"Well, not quite like that, Nana."

"No, I know what you mean. This god must have some power."

"We've been trying to get pregnant for two years now."

"I know, I know," he acknowledged with a vigorous nod.

"I'm not praying to any other god but Jesus," Manisha gushed in an almost childlike manner.

Nayadu's face turned serious again, and he turned slowly toward Manisha. "No other gods but Jesus?" His words were slow and deliberate. "Have you become a Christian, my daughter?"

"I have," she replied innocently, unaware of her father-in-law's animus toward her newfound faith.

He looked over to Chandu, "And you?"

He took a deep breath and felt a sudden surge of peace wash over him. He knew how his father felt. He considered him the god of the White man. But barring the notion that Manisha's pregnancy was by sheer chance, Jesus had truly answered a desperate prayer, and it was time to respond.

"I have too, Nana," he replied boldly.

Manisha smiled and put her arm around him while Nayadu sat back down on his daybed. The look on his face was blank.

"So you're leaving the tradition of your father and your father's father and his…"

"Nana, this Jesus has been trying to get my attention for a long time now."

He then went on to tell him of his unexplainable experiences. He told him of the strange vision he had while lying in the army cot in Ladysmith where an older man dressed in white appeared out of nowhere to bring comfort to that dying soldier. Yet nobody else saw him. He was sure that he was an angel and that God had let him witness the peace that awaits those who believe.

And there was no doubt in his mind that the reverend was one of his agents. Though he found his ways and words offensive at first, there was truly no hate or unpleasantness in him, and he grew to admire him greatly. That admiration caused him to strongly consider what he had to say.

Nayadu sat with his legs crossed and often looked away while he was speaking, causing Chandu to wonder whether he was listening. But in reality, it was hard for him to listen as everything his son said was an affront to the traditions of his forbears.

When Chandu finished speaking, he shrugged dismissively. "You're a grown man now, Chandu. I can no longer tell you what to do. But please don't expect me to become a Christian like you."

He looked over at Manisha. She looked innocent as a doe unaware that her seemingly harmless comment would trigger such controversy. He looked back over at his father and said, "As you wish, Nana."

Underneath, he breathed a sigh of relief. He imagined that his father's reaction would have been more severe, not unlike the way he reacted to Ammamma and Thathiyya. But he was older now, and he, like Velu, had mellowed with age.

Manisha changed the subject and asked, "Where are Sonali and Seeli?"

He went back to his reclining position and pointed to the room. "Lying down. Neither is feeling too good this morning."

"Is it anything serious?" she asked.

"No, just some vomiting. They've both been this way for over a week."

"A week!" Chandu exclaimed. "And you don't think it's serious?"

"No," he said calmly, "she feels bad in the morning but is fine after three or four hours."

Manisha looked at Chandu with a curious look and then said to her father-in-law, "That's the way I've been feeling also, Nana."

"Nana!" Chandu blurted.

"What?" He was startled by outburst.

"Sonali's pregnant?"

With a coy grin, he shrugged. "I didn't want to have any children, but Sonali was desperate. What to do but make her happy."

Manisha elbowed Chandu in his side and said, "Seeli also."

Chandu was aghast. "Nana!"

He nodded calmly and said, "She's pregnant too."

"But, Nana, she isn't your wife."

"She, too, wanted children, son."

"How does Sonali feel about this?"

"She is the one who suggested it," said Nana, shrugging his shoulders. "These women will not die happy unless they have children."

"But why can't Seeli go and find a husband before she has children?" he asked.

Nayadu frowned and put his finger across his lips. "You trying to upset them?"

"Sorry."

"You know they're attached in a way we don't understand." He shrugged. "I don't understand it, but I don't mind it either."

Chandu spoke softer this time, "But, Nana, you're too old to be starting another family."

"Hey!" he said indignantly. "I'm still strong as an ox." He scratched his chin and pondered briefly. "I'll be a father and a grandfather at the same time." Then he stood up and moved toward the room. "I have to tell the sisters about this."

*****

On Monday, the barrister showed up early at the registration office with his faithful band of protesters, and before they could pull their signs out, they were escorted to jail. Lord Falmouth had issued an order to remove any public nuisances from the area of which he and the activists had been deemed.

The barrister started to reconsider his strategy. Sitting in jail from dawn to dusk would accomplish nothing and would do nothing to discourage those who would otherwise register. He paced the dingy floor of the jail frustrated that Lord Falmouth had rendered him impotent. Then he was struck with an idea.

*****

When Chandu arrived at the office, he found one of the young protestors sitting on the front step. His clothes were dirty, and Chandu assumed that they were the same clothes worn during the infamous scuffle that landed the protestors in jail. He likely wore them as a badge of honor. He stood and, without a word, shoved the note toward Chandu.

Chandu read it aloud, "Notify the *London Times* and *Hindustan Times* that Govindas Mahendhi refuses to take food until the Europeans repeal the Registration Act."

He folded the note and asked the young man, "Who gave you this?"

"Mr. Mahendhi," he replied.

"He's not eating?"

He shook his head. "No, and he wanted me to tell you to make sure that you tell the world."

The young man handed him another note.

"What's this?"

He shrugged. "It was under this rock here next to your door."

Chandu shook his head in disbelief. "I knew that Mr. Mahendhi was passionate about this cause, but I never thought he would take it this far. These Whites will let him starve."

The young man was few with words but one who was clearly a willing warrior for the cause. He shrugged again. "Can I help you?"

Chandu paused for a moment. "Just let Mr. Mahendhi know that I'm going to make sure that the *London Times* and the *Hindustan Times* are aware of what's going on here."

He sat down at his desk and opened the note that had been placed by the door under a rock. It was handwritten and barely legible, but he was able to decipher its contents. It said, "A great story awaits the newsman who pays a visit to this small, struggling Christian schoolhouse in Stanger."

That was it, no details or even a name to look for. But the cryptic message was enough to hook him. He'd never been to Stanger, but he knew it was a small village about a half day's ride away. He knew the barrister was surely expecting him to visit, but he didn't want to go near the jail—at least right now. He had to follow this mysterious lead.

*****

"Welcome!" said the bright-eyed woman, customarily pressing her hands together. "Who are you?"

Chandu stepped down from his carriage and immediately recognized her as Telugu. He replied to her in their native language, "I'm Chandu Nayadu."

"Ah," she replied, smiling, "you're Telugu." She assumed that he was there to see her husband and said, "I am Pastor Thomas's wife."

He glanced at her longer than what was comfortable, trying to recall where he might have seen her before. She broke the awkward silence by asking, "Did you come to see my husband?"

"Uh—you have a schoolhouse here?"

"Yes, we do. Is that why you're here?"

"Oh," he said, fumbling to pull the note out of his vest pocket, "I was given this note."

She smiled and handed it back to him. "Do you mind reading it?"

"Sorry, yes, of course. It says, 'A great story awaits the newsman who pays a visit to this small, struggling Christian schoolhouse in Stanger.'"

A confused look came over her. "Who gave you this?"

370

"Someone left it under a rock in front of my office in Phoenix."

She smiled and said, "I'm not sure about the great story, but we have a small Christian schoolhouse. Would you like to see it?"

She started walking in the direction of a modest wooden structure that Chandu assumed was the schoolhouse. As they approached, he said, "This is nice."

She smiled out the side of her mouth. "This is our church."

They continued walking past the church and across a small field that was mostly dirt and weeds. She turned and said, "I would love for you to meet the children. They are so precious."

"I would like that."

"But they've gone home for the day."

They came upon the small building and walked inside. There was no door and a window on each side. Tiny streams of sunlight made their way through the holes in the roof.

There were no chairs or desks, only a dozen or so mats neatly stacked in the corner. Grime formed a ring around the wall at knee level where the children were in the habit sitting back against the wall. In the other corner were nooks each containing a stack of papers the children had compiled over the week.

"We pray that God will hold off the rain each morning till the school day ends. Sometimes he says *yes*. Sometimes he says *no*," she said with a smile.

"You need a new schoolhouse."

"We would be happy with a new roof. What's more is the owner is raising the payment we make every month to stay on this property."

"How do you manage to pay the owner now?"

"With the tithes and offerings that come from our church, but our members are very poor."

He was taking notes as she spoke and wanted to ask what tithes were, but his pride stopped him. He simply wrote down what she said and would find out from the Reverend Stadelmaier when he got back.

"Come to our home and rest until Pastor arrives."

The small home in which they resided was on the far corner of the property nestled in the sparse shade of a large jacaranda tree.

Fallen lilac and plum-colored leaves covered the ground, and from a distance framed the modest house in a purplish haze.

Just then the pastor came running across the field and met them as they approached the front door. "Hello and welcome," he said eagerly.

"Shh, you'll wake your son," his wife said in a hushed tone.

"I apologize. I had to visit with a member of our church who's been ill. So who do we have here visiting our humble home?"

Chandu extended his hand. "I'm Chandu Nayadu, and I decided to come after I received this note." He handed the note to the pastor.

The pastor read it and said, "Who gave you this?"

"As I told your wife, I found it by the door of my office."

"So you're here to write a story about our humble little school?"

Chandu was starting to wonder where the great story was, but he kept that to himself. "That's right. Tell me about your school."

The pastor cleared his throat. "Well, the school is quite modest, as you surely must've seen. We have over thirty children wanting to come but can only handle fifteen. They are between the ages of five and twelve. If you had arrived earlier, you could have seen the children, Mr. Nayadu."

"Chandu."

"Mr. Chandu."

"Just Chandu."

"I am Pastor Thomas. Forgive me for not introducing myself. Obviously, you've met my wife, Arti."

"Arti?" he said. Though it wasn't an uncommon name for Indian girls, he had only known of one girl with such a name. She came back into the room with a tray of tea and snacks. He looked at her more closely now, and he was sure it was the same Arti.

*****

Arti had striking light-brown eyes and fair skin, features that were rare among the vast majority of the Indian laborers. Besides that, she was very attractive. Chandu remembered his father and Velu commenting how she was the most beautiful girl they had ever seen when she first boarded the *Chadwick*. Chandu was too young to care about such things at the time. He was more prone to exploring the nether regions of the ship with his friend Imran. But now that he was older, he could clearly see that his father and Velu were right.

"My mother-in-law will be pleased to know that you are doing so well," he said to her as she offered sugar for the tea.

She looked at him with a curious gaze. "Your mother-in-law?"

"Yes," he replied. "Prema. She was the Aunty who looked after you on the boat after you became ill with cholera. She feared—well, we all feared that you didn't make it."

Arti's mouth gaped open. She slowly set the tea condiments on the table and sat on the ground. Pulling her hand to her mouth, she said, "Oh my loving savior, so often I wondered what became of her. I hardly remember that time. I was so sick, you see. I only remember waking up in the hospital. As soon as I was strong enough to walk, I was taken to the North Coast Tea Plantation."

"Wait a minute!" said Pastor Thomas, sitting up on the end of his chair "When did you come to the colony?"

Chandu remembered well the date as he had been keeping track of the days aboard the ship. "It was twenty-sixth, October 1888."

"Of course," he said, slapping his hands together in a triumphant clap. "That's where I saw you! I spent weeks down at the harbor that year praying for sick and dying immigrants." He moved his face close to his wife's and looked her straight in the eye, "That's where I saw you. I prayed for you as you lay near death in the arms of this Aunty."

Arti nodded in disbelief, and her eyes started to swell with tears.

"I don't know which will make the more interesting story," Chandu said.

Pastor Thomas smiled, and he too had tears running down his cheeks. "This is the story that your note spoke of. What I do know is that you're coming here was of the divine."

*****

After some time of reminiscing and recounting their journeys, Arti asked, "Will you join us for supper, Chandu. We're having mutton curry."

"Thank you, but I really must be getting back. Manisha will worry."

Pastor Thomas nodded. "You'll never make it back before dark, and there's no moon out tonight. Are you sure you won't stay and join us?"

"No, I really must get back, Pastor. I hope you and your wife understand."

"Of course, I understand. Why don't you stay and break bread with us, and I'll travel back to town with you. It will be better if you have someone with you if you're going to be travelling in the dark."

He hadn't eaten since early morning, so it wasn't difficult to accept the pastor's offer.

"It's settled then," said Arti. "You do eat mutton, don't you?"

"Uh, no, nothing like that. I'm a Hin—" He caught himself and then corrected, "I don't eat meat."

"But you told me you're a Christian."

Suddenly he felt cornered. He hadn't considered that becoming a Christian would mean eating things that once breathed and walked the earth.

The pastor asked, "How long have you been a Christian, Chandu?"

He shrugged. "Not long."

The pastor smiled and said, "Then that's fine. Arti will make you something."

"Of course," she said from the kitchen. "I already have some tamarind rice, and I'll just make some parathas."

Chandu's mouth started watering. He hadn't experienced the tangy flavor of tamarind rice since he was a small boy visiting with his Ammamma. "This is one of my favorites," he told her.

"I make it all the time for Pastor. It's one of his favorites also."

"Yes, yes," he agreed. "I'm a very blessed man to have such a wonderful cook for a wife."

"You don't happen to make ka-meetha?" Chandu asked.

She poked her head out of the kitchen. "I don't make it often, but on occasion. I'm sorry I don't have cashews, or I would bake one."

"No, that's fine. I would only ask for the recipe so my wife, Manisha, will be able to make it."

"Of course," she said. "But how do you know of ka-meetha?"

"My Ammamma used to make it for me and my brother when we were small boys. We used to visit her and Thathiyya after school without Nana knowing because he had forbidden us to see them anymore."

Arti came out from the kitchen intrigued. "Why were you forbidden to see them?" she asked.

"Because they had become Christians, and we were Hindus. Nana didn't really know what Christianity was. It just made him angry when Ammamma took all their god statues and threw them in the Godavari River. It made him even angrier when they told him he should do the same. That's when he told them that they were not welcome anymore. And that's when we had to start sneaking over there after school without him knowing."

"You boys were quite naughty, weren't you?" she said, smiling.

The pastor listened to his story pensively and said, "I'm sure it was very hard for your grandparents to be Christians in that little village where you grew up."

Chandu shrugged. "I suppose so."

The pastor moved to the edge of seat again. His eyes were alert, and he spoke with assurance. "It's not easy being a Christian, Chandu." He had his attention. "You will have many trials that will test your faith to its very limit. But always remember this—God is forever with you."

Chandu was deeply moved by the pastor's encouraging words. Deep down, he knew there was going to be challenges living as a Christian among the vast population of Hindus. He knew some to be hostile to Christians who were but a small minority of the Indian population. Pastor Thomas's assuring words were just what he needed.

"How much do you think will help put a new roof on that school building?" Chandu asked the Pastor.

He nodded thoughtfully. "I don't know, Chandu. I never considered the cost?"

Chandu chuckled. "Of course, you are busy doing God's work." He stood up and said, "I'm going to write a nice story about your school in my newspaper, and we'll see how much we can raise. Those kids deserve a roof over them."

Pastor Thomas smiled, and a tear streamed down his cheek. "May I see that note you brought?"

He read it aloud and handed it back to Chandu. Then he said, "This is the handwriting of an angel."

Chandu took the note and studied it. Then he glanced up at the pastor and, with a childlike inquisitiveness, replied, "An angel?"

The pastor pointed his finger toward heaven and replied, "Our God knew our need, and he brought you here to us. That's what I know."

CHAPTER 30

Chandu turned down Soldier's Way and parked his carriage in front of the small brick building that he had come to loathe. There was one small, barred window positioned high enough that the person of ordinary height had to stand on his toes to see out.

The putrid stench turned his stomach. It was a smell that he remembered well and had hoped to forget.

Two jailers were on duty, and one recognized Chandu as he entered.

"Here to see your troublemaker of a boss, are you?"

"Yes, please." He was careful to show respect so as not lose favor with them.

"Did you bring him some food? He doesn't like what we give him."

"No, sir. I don't believe that's why he's not eating."

The jailer suddenly turned nasty. "We know why he's not eating. He's trying to bring pity upon himself."

The barrister called out from behind the wall, "Chandu?"

"May I?" Chandu asked the jailer.

"Empty your pockets first."

*****

Chandu poked his head around the corner and was immediately taken by how much weight the barrister had already lost. He found him sitting cross legged with his back against the wall. All the other protesters sat likewise down the row. None of them appeared happy.

"Did you forget about me?" he asked without so much as a flinch. He remained motionless, determined to conserve his strength.

"Never," Chandu replied. "Just busy, that's all."

"You notified the *Times*?" he asked.

"Yes, of course." Immediately he felt guilty about lying to his boss, but he wasn't going to confess now. He would simply notify both the *London* and *Hindustan Times* when he returned to the office, and nobody would be the wiser.

*****

"I have some more bad news for you, Mr. Mahendhi. Manisha told me that her father and his workers are going to register tomorrow."

The barrister's chin fell into his chest. "He has no backbone," he mumbled.

"Not true," Chandu replied. "Velu Uncle has more backbone than anyone I know. I think he's scared he will lose his business if he doesn't register. He has a lot to lose."

The barrister looked up at his acolyte with a look of resignation. "And I suppose that you don't want to publish his name."

"Did you think about all the readers that we are going to lose by embarrassing them to our community, Mr. Mahendhi? We can't be the judge of everyone."

*****

Velu was nervous this morning because today would not be business as usual. In fact, he would not even unlock the doors. He paced back and forth by the front door of the factory while waiting for the employees to arrive and felt a sudden urge to chew on some betel nut to calm his nerves. He gave that up years ago, however, and wasn't going to start back now. Prema was working less hours in recent days and was devoting more time to seeing after Manisha now that she was pregnant. She would not be coming today, and Velu was glad.

As the sun started to rise, the women arrived. Most were early or on time, and a few straggled in late, but Velu cared little about tardiness this morning. He told them nothing, and they contemplated curiously among themselves as to what their boss was up to. He waited until his last worker arrived because he didn't want to repeat himself, and when all thirty-six were present and accounted for, he spoke.

"The factory's closed today."

There were groans heard among them as most didn't relish the idea of losing out on a day's wage, but he continued, "But I'm still paying you."

There were "ahs" and sighs of relief. Some applauded in spite of the fact that they knew nothing of what they were in for.

"The Europeans running this place say we have to report to this registration office up the road and have all our fingers and toes printed in ink. Then they will look for other marks on your bodies that will help them identify you. They will look at places on your bodies that you're shy to show your own husbands."

There were gasps and looks of disgust between them. Velu knew that it wouldn't be hard to convince them any further. "These Whites call this the Indian Registration Act." There was more murmuring as some of them repeated what they heard. Then he said, "I refuse to allow these Whites to treat me like this!" he yelled. His rhetoric was not only stirring up his workers but him as well. There was a buzz of indignation among them, and Velu knew he would not be alone today.

*****

Chandu felt strongly, more than ever, that publishing the names of those who chose to follow their conscience would be immoral. He had become convinced that, while some were determined to resist, most Indians were apathetic toward this Registration Act and wanted to live in peace. Many made it clear that they were unwilling to lose their trader licenses for a cause that was going to change very little in their lives.

Nevertheless, he would notify the *London Times* and the *Hindustan Times* of the barrister's hunger strike. Those papers would seize upon such a story in way that would surely lift the barrister turned activist into a living martyr.

As he headed up Soldier's Way on his way back to the office, he found himself blocked by a procession led by his father-in-law, followed by a couple of dozen women. He quickly surmised that they were on their way to register so he pulled over.

Chandu ran over to Velu and said, "Don't worry, I'm not going to put your names in the paper. I think you have a right to do what is best for you."

Velu smiled and gave his son-in-law a pat on the back. "Thank you, son. I am going to do what is best for me and my family and for these women. We are on our way to protest this registration."

Chandu's eyes opened wide. "Wait, you said that you were going to register to save your business. What happened?"

He shrugged. "I have to be true to who I am. This is how I have lived my life. It's brought me trouble at times, but I have never been one who lets people take advantage over me and my family. Call it a fault, if you must."

"And the business?"

Again, he shrugged. "There are still some bridges to cross."

Chandu looked over at the women who ranged from Manisha's age on up to Ammamma's age. Various degrees of determination etched their faces.

"Why don't you be a part of us, son."

Not only was Chandu caught off guard by the Velu's sudden change of heart regarding the Registration Act but his change of heart toward him. Never had he called him son before.

"Uh…I have work back at the office."

Chandu could tell that his father-in-law was disappointed even though he didn't show it. He proceeded to lead his flock of protesters down Soldier's Way toward Commercial Street, where the Registration office was located. He knew that Velu had a lot to lose, and even though he personally lost the conviction needed to persevere, he couldn't help but admire the man.

Then Chandu was suddenly struck with an idea.

"Uncle!" he yelled.

Velu stopped and turned around.

Chandu ran and caught up with him and asked, "Do you know what to do when you get to the registration office?"

Velu's brows furrowed. "What do you mean?"

"Have you ever protested anything?"

He hesitated for a moment. "Won't there be other protesters?"

Chandu shrugged. "Maybe, but can't say for sure. I would like to show you."

"Come," he said with a chuckle as he put his arm around his son-in-law. "I don't want to get this thing wrong."

Chandu gently pulled away and said, "But I also think this would be a great story for the *Phoenix*. Our readers would be inspired by your courage to risk everything you've worked so hard for. I think Mr. Mahendhi would like for me to write about it."

Velu nodded pensively and then smiled. "Okay, you can write a story."

*****

There were but a handful of picketers demonstrating peacefully when Chandu and Velu arrived along with his bevy of dissenters.

"So what do we do?" asked Velu.

"You must march back and forth in front of the registration office."

Velu frowned. "That's it? We don't get to yell and throw sticks?"

Chandu chuckled. "Not today, Uncle. This must be a peaceful demonstration, or they will throw you in jail."

As fate would have it, Velu's biggest client, Edmund Klein, rode slowly by in his buggy and stopped when he recognized Velu. He motioned with a wave of his hand, but Velu pretended not to see him. Chandu, who never met Edmund Klein, took note of the man and, with a puzzled look, asked, "Who's that White man in the buggy?"

Without looking over, Velu replied, "Turn around. That's our big customer, Mr. Klein. He told me not to protest."

"He's walking this way, Uncle."

Velu let out an expletive. He figured he could easily lie to Mr. Klein and tell him that he and his workers were there to register. That way he could buy some time with his client and figure a way to keep his business. But how would that look to his workers and, more importantly, his son-in-law when he just professed that he had to be true to who he was.

As the clothier neared the gathering of workers huddled in front of the registrar's office, he called out, "Is that you, Velu?"

Velu turned and feigned a look of surprise. "Mr. Klein, what are you doing here?"

"I was on my way to my store when I saw you and your workers. Are you here to register?"

Velu knew that this was a moment of truth. The next words to come from his mouth could effectively send his business into ruin. He cleared his throat when suddenly the Reverend Stadelmaier appeared. He tipped his hat and, with his usual smile, said, "Good morning, gentlemen. You have quite the gathering here."

Chandu was never so happy to see the reverend. He quickly realized his father-in-law was in a difficult spot, and the reverend always had a way with directing the conversation. He towered over the diminutive Mr. Klein as he extended his hand and introduced himself. The clothier reciprocated and added that he was the owner of Edmund's Fine Clothes on West Street.

Hearing the man's accent, he noted, "Ah, you're from Germany."

Mr. Klein smiled. "Yes, there is no hiding that, I suppose. And you are Stadelmaier, also German."

"Yes," the reverend replied, "came here as a small boy with my parents and older sister."

The clothier chuckled. "This is why you don't have an accent like myself. You've been here most of your life."

"That's true," he replied, "and I was raised in an orphanage from the time I was eight years old."

"An orphanage?" the clothier retorted. "I don't understand."

"Quite simple," he responded calmly, "my parents and sister were killed by Zulus whom we were trying to evangelize."

Mr. Klein's face pinched. "This is quite remarkable, Reverend. And you? You were able to survive?"

He pointed upward and replied, "By the grace of my Heavenly Father. I should have also died that fateful afternoon. You see"—he pulled his shirt out of his trousers to reveal thick scar just below his left rib cage—"this is where they sent a spear that went all the way through me. We were all left to die, but I survived."

Chandu and Velu were awestruck while Mr. Klein shook his head in disbelief. "Were you not angry with God for letting your family die in such a horrific way?"

"Yes, I was very angry with God. In fact," his words suddenly thickened, and he paused. He wiped the moisture from his eyes and then continued, "I stopped believing in his existence altogether for years. I was an angry young man with a quick temper and a deep hatred for Zulus. Then one day I was walking down the road heading home—that is, the orphanage—and I passed a Zulu boy about my age who bore an uncanny resemblance to one of the warriors that put me and my family to the spear. Well, I decided that this boy was going to pay the price for my family's martyrdom. Without so much as giving him a chance to utter a word, I knocked him to the ground with a swift blow to the side of his head. I still remember the look of surprise on his face." The reverend shook his head with shame. "I remember kicking him hard in his side. He was very thin, and I probably broke a few ribs with my heavy boots. I remember thinking that he was going to be easy. Then I picked up a large rock and lifted it up over my head. At that moment, I heard a voice as clear as I'm talking to you now say to me, *'I spared your life. Now you must spare his life.'* I saw the fear in that boy's eyes and suddenly realized that I made a dreadful mistake. Then that voice spoke to me again and said, *'Take him home with you and feed him, for he hasn't eaten all day.'* At that point, I knew God was alive and well, and he was speaking to me of all people. Someone who had completely forsaken him."

The clothier interjected, "And now you are a man of God."

The reverend smiled somewhat bashfully, "Well, I developed a profound love for God and his Word, and that has carried me through this life."

Mr. Klein extended his hand and said, "Well, it was a pleasure, Reverend. If I weren't Jewish, I would come and visit your church."

The clothier turned and quickly started making his way back to his buggy. The reverend replied, "Our Lord Jesus was a Jew, Mr. Klein. We welcome everyone."

He waved without turning around, and the reverend simply smiled. "I'll add him to my prayer list."

Chandu turned to Velu and smiled. "I believe God's favor is upon you, Uncle."

Velu was still a little tense as Mr. Klein had yet to ride away. Once the clothier's buggy started moving down the road, he replied, "Which god?"

The reverend overheard Velu's uncertainty and replied, "There is only one God, my friend, and indeed, his favor is upon you."

Velu looked puzzled. "How do you mean, sir?"

"What I mean is that God told me that there was going to be some trouble here unless I got myself over here. I had no idea what He meant, but I was obedient and came over here and introduced myself. I reckon that man was your lahnee?"

Velu nodded, but Chandu spoke for him. "That man was Velu Uncle's biggest customer, and he told Uncle that he shouldn't protest the registration."

"I see," said the reverend. "So you and your workers are here to protest but he thought you were here to register."

Velu shrugged while Chandu replied, "I think so, Reverend."

"And my arrival threw him off your trail."

Chandu laughed. "God used you, Reverend."

"Well, it wouldn't be the first time, Chandu, but I think you already know how I feel about these protests."

Chandu's face turned solemn. "Yes, I remember. You called it rebellion."

"Well then," he said with a tip of his hat, "I'll be on my way."

Chandu drew a heavy sigh and glanced over at his father-in-law.

Velu responded somewhat agitated, "What is this 'rebellion' your friend speaks of?"

Chandu thought for a moment, then said, "I think the reverend means that you're going against authority."

Velu nodded with a smile. "Ah, yes." His face turned serious. "But this man doesn't approve."

"The reverend is saying that God doesn't approve."

Velu's face scrunched with confusion. "Which god, and how does this man know what god approves of?"

"Did you not hear him when he said that God told him there was going to be trouble here if he didn't get himself over here? He is a true man of God. Maybe you should listen."

Velu nodded dismissively. "Do you still want to write your story about me?"

Chandu let out a sigh. "Sure, Uncle."

"And when you're done," he continued, "you and my daughter must come home for supper tomorrow night. It's time."

*****

Hibiscus Street was lined with mostly trees and brush. There were only two houses, the newest belonging to the Velus. The double storied wood frame house sat at the end of the dead-end street and was marked by a long brick drive that ran up the side.

Prema was overjoyed to once again have her daughter and son-in-law under her roof. She hugged them and then rubbed Manisha's belly, which was now starting to show signs of her condition.

"*Pumsavana*," she blurted out. "We have to pray that you would be granted a male child?" (Pumsavana is a rite that mothers who have just conceived go through to prevent the birth of daughters).

Manisha hugged her mother and, with a doting smile, said, "Amma, we would love a son, but we'll be happy with whatever God gives us." She took her mother's hands as she continued, "I hope you'll understand that we cannot do these Hindu rituals anymore."

Prema recoiled. "But why can't your father and I offer up puja to our gods for a grandson?"

Velu interrupted the conversation when he arrived home from the factory. Clearly troubled, he asked Chandu to speak with him out back.

He led his son-in-law far enough away from the house so that the women would not hear, and Chandu noticed beads of sweat on his forehead though it wasn't even warm outside. "Did you write your story yet?"

"Yes, of course, Uncle. Why, is something wrong?"

"You must stop it. I can't have that story out there for people to read."

"But why not? What are you afraid of?"

Chandu hit a chord with Velu that rubbed him wrong. "I'm not afraid!" He caught himself and lowered his voice. "I can't have Mr. Klein reading about me and my workers doing this protest. That's all."

Chandu nodded slowly. "It's too late, Uncle. The paper went to press last night and is being delivered as we speak." Chandu walked over to his buggy and grabbed a copy of the paper and handed it to Velu.

*****

When Lord Falmouth learned that word of the barrister's hunger strike had traveled to London, as well as India, he decided that it was time to have a meeting. He arranged to convene with the barrister in secret for fear of the press. He knew it would do untold damage to his credibility if it were known throughout the colony that he was relenting to the stubbornness of this little Indian lawyer. But more important was the need to court world opinion.

"Mr. Mahendhi, you have been a consistent thorn in our backsides. What are we to do with you?" said Lord Falmouth from behind his large, ornately carved maplewood desk.

The thin and bedraggled activist replied, "What would you like to do with me?"

"Proper decorum would prevent me from saying, Mr. Mahendhi. Let's not waste each other's time. We need to come to an agreement that will satisfy both sides. What is it that you would like from us?"

"We would like you to amend this Indian Registration Act. It is unnecessary and makes us Indians out to be criminals."

"Mr. Mahendhi, you fail to understand that the primary purpose of this *act* is to control the flow of migration into this colony. Many of your people have come into this colony illegally. Therefore, we saw the need to legislate this *act*."

"Very well, Your Lordship. But instead of making this compulsory through law, make it voluntary. Our people would gladly agree to register themselves if it were not for the sting of compulsion. What's more, Your Lordship," he cleared his throat, "we would ask that the restriction on trader's licenses be loosened. Our people are being starved to death through this injustice."

Lord Falmouth stroked his chin as he pondered the barrister's proposal. "Your demands are quite excessive, Mr. Mahendhi, but I shall speak with my cabinet, and I will summon you when we have reached a decision. In the meantime, you are free to go home to your family. I will no longer be responsible if you choose not to eat."

The barrister responded, "With all due respect, that responsibility was never yours."

*****

Chandu and Manisha were settling in for the evening when a familiar voice broke the silence. Standing in the doorway of their small cottage was the barrister holding a candle. It was warm, and his face glistened from perspiration. It was unusual to see him wearing a pancha as he was commonly disposed to wearing tailored clothing no matter the occasion. Neither could help noticing his ribs sticking through his chest.

"Hello, my friends."

Chandu quickly jumped up from the bed. "Mr. Mahendhi!"

"I'm sorry to interrupt you two, but I wanted you to know that I was released late this afternoon after a meeting with Lord Falmouth."

"That's good news. So he agreed to halt the Registration Act?"

He walked over to a small table and set the candle down. "Well, not exactly. I had to negotiate a deal with this chap to make this *act* voluntary and to loosen the restrictions on trader's licenses."

Chandu scratched his head, unsure whether this was a good compromise or not. "Did he agree to this?"

"He will speak to his cabinet and let me know."

Chandu responded rather sharply, "And what about your cabinet?"

He recoiled at his protégé's rejoinder, "What cabinet?"

"Who are you consulting as you make decisions for our Indian brothers and sisters?"

The barrister was taken aback by Chandu's bluntness if not his insight. In that moment, he reflected back to his memory of the precocious boy he met ten years ago. Back then, he saw a boy whom he knew had wisdom beyond his years. Now it was haunting him.

His time in jail without food had weakened him, and the spark that usually animated his speech was noticeably absent. Ordinarily, the barrister would have fired back in defense of the charge, but instead, he picked up a copy of the *Phoenix* that was lying on the table next to his candle.

"Good headline," he said, holding the candle in one hand and the paper in his other hand.

"Did you read the story?" Chandu asked. His tone was softer.

"Yes, of course, I read it. And I read your piece on Velu. You made him a martyr for our cause."

Chandu glanced over at Manisha, who appeared oblivious to the barrister's comment. But it was true, and now he wasn't sure that the story was a mistake. Though Velu would be seen as an iconoclast who was taking a stand for the rights and dignity of Indians in every region of the British empire, there was going to be a price to pay.

"Tomorrow is going to see record numbers of protesters, mark my words. I just hope it's peaceful," said the barrister.

*****

As the barrister predicted, the following day saw hundreds of protestors overflowing off Commercial Street onto adjacent streets. Anyone intending to register found it impossible to move past the throngs of dissidents and, therefore, didn't even try. While some were arrested for being unruly, most protested peacefully, as the barrister had always prescribed, which agitated the Europeans all the more. They knew that the eyes of the world were upon them and that undue retaliation against the protesters would be met with largescale derision.

But it wasn't the barrister by whom they were inspired; it was Ramsamy Velu. His daring to defy the registration at the risk of his very lucrative business for the sake of Indians across the globe was not only inspirational but tangible. Overnight, he had become a cause célèbre.

Velu, however, was at odds with his newfound notoriety. At home, Prema unleashed an unprecedented level of wrath on her husband for making such decisions without her consent and banished him to another room. She would continue to cook his meals but stopped speaking to him altogether.

And then the inevitable—Edmund Klein, true to his promise, cut off all ties with the Velus after he read the story. Without the Edmund's Fine Clothes as a customer, the future of the business was uncertain at best.

*****

The barrister would soon reconvene with Lord Falmouth. "Mr. Mahendhi, we all felt that your demands were excessive, but we have agreed to certain terms. If your people agree to register voluntarily, we will see about repealing the law. As for the restriction on trader's licenses," said Lord Falmouth resolutely, "we will just have to see how your people respond to our agreement. In the meantime, I want you to use that newspaper of yours to get these people off our streets."

The barrister was confident that his negotiations with Lord Falmouth would be considered at least a marginal success. The very next week he went to press with the following headline:

Registration Now Optional

But as readers would soon discover, all was not as the headline purported. Registration was optional but necessary if Indians were to be seen as honorable in the eyes of the Europeans. And any loosening of restrictions on trader's licenses would hinge on this. This hardly seemed like a victory as the headline seemed to convey, but even more infuriating to the readers and especially the business owners was that the barrister had acted independently.

*****

Ali Kader showed up at the barrister's office the next morning, and there was an awkward moment of silence before Mr. Kader finally spoke, "Govindas, I feel like you and I are good friends."

The barrister pointed over to a chair and Mr. Kader promptly sat down. Then he continued, "But I have to tell you that you have angered businessmen across this province by not consulting with us before making a deal with this Lord Falmouth. You negotiated alone on behalf of us Muslims and all Indians. And now you're advocating that all Indians should register out of a sense of duty, and hopefully, Lord Falmouth will stop restricting trader's licenses. I'm surprised that you would agree to such folly."

The barrister looked over the top of his bifocals and calmly replied, "My dear friend, did not you and all your prominent merchant friends willfully, if not gleefully, register last week? Why should you be bothered with any of this?"

"I came here as a friend to let you know that the Muslims are breaking away from the INC because they don't feel you represent their best interest."

The barrister leaned back in his chair and tucked his folded hands under his chin. "Very well, my friend, I suppose you and your coreligionists are happy with the way the Europeans treat you."

"Govindas, you must know that the Muslim merchants had no problems doing business here before the Hindus started arriving here. Now, there are so many Indians here in this colony trying to hawk everything under the sun. You must see our point. We cannot be seen as one with Hindu laborers."

"This is what I understand, my dear Ali. These laborers that you look down upon, breathe the same air, eat food from the same soil, and drink water from the same river. They should be afforded the same dignity as those who try to deny them."

Ali Kader stood up and said, "You're missing the point, Govindas, but I have run out of words for you. You are on your own."

CHAPTER 31

It was no secret that the community the barrister once championed was no longer behind him. He had given up a lucrative career as a lawyer to defend the rights of those he considered kinsmen. Now, but for a remnant of devoted followers, they had abandoned him for someone whom they could trust, someone whom they saw as a true kinsman.

His time behind bars had changed him. The physical changes were obvious. He was gaunt, the result of his refusal to take food. His cheekbones protruded sharply below his sunken eyes, and his bony shoulders slumped slightly forward. And save for his fair complexion and spectacles, he appeared no different than the vast population of poor immigrants who adorned themselves with nothing more than a pancha wrapped around their waste.

But he was no less spirited and perhaps even more passionate about his oppressed kinsmen. He knew that he still had a lot to offer to the cause, but he would need to take a different approach.

*****

Velu had unintentionally risen to become the hero or, more fittingly, the antihero of the oppressed. It was not a role that he wore with comfort, however. He didn't like crowds, and he was uncomfortable speaking in front of large groups. His scarred face and scratchy voice certainly didn't draw people to him. But each line on his dark face came with a story, some that ended well but most did not. It was those stories that had made him into the man he was. The edgy, seditious side of him had long retired, but the remnant of what once was made him an apt iconoclast. Indians trusted him as one who knew the hardships of working from sun up to sun down in the sweltering heat of the cane fields. And he was proof that it was possible to rise above what his caste had foreordained.

But Velu gradually warmed to his newfound status as a radical reformer. Each successive INC meeting in which he was thrust to the forefront as spokesman for change saw him gain more confidence. Yet it was clear that while he knew the end goal, he didn't have a clue as to how to get there.

In the meantime, the barrister was attending the INC meetings incognito. His now simple attire already likened him in appearance to the multitudes. But when he wrapped his head in a turban and removed his trademark spectacles, he was unrecognizable.

He relegated himself to quiet observer sitting in the back row while Velu stirred the crowd. He repeated the same rhetoric from one meeting to the next and splicing it with stories of his rebellious past.

But the barrister's heart was gladdened to witness an unbridled enthusiasm in a young woman named Pooja who also sat in the back. He guessed that puberty wasn't far behind her, yet he could see she was keenly interested in the affairs of the colony.

One evening before the meeting started, the barrister smiled at the young woman and asked, "This interests you?"

She returned his smile and replied, "Oh yes! How can what this man has to say not be interesting?"

The barrister nodded. "Mr. Velu, you mean?"

A broad smile swept across her face. "Of course, Mr. Velu. Who else?"

He suddenly realized that he was perilously close to losing his cover by speaking so freely. But he also understood that she likely had no idea who he was irrespective of his disguise. She was young, and this was all new to her.

"And your family?" he rejoined quickly. "Where are they?"

"My father and mother brought me and my brother here about a month ago, but they never wanted to come back." She shrugged. "They wanted to see what this was all about but lost interest."

He smiled. "But not you."

She nodded vigorously. "Uh-uh. Not me. Me and Mr. Velu are kindred spirits. I've already decided that tonight I'm going to speak with him and see how I can help him with this movement."

If there was one thing that Velu clearly needed, it was help. He had honed his rhetoric over the weeks ad nauseam, but a plan of action had yet to come. The barrister had some ideas but wasn't convinced the timing was right. So he waited, he watched, and he listened.

In the weeks following, he was keen to notice that Pooja was now sitting in the front row. The barrister was also quick to note that Velu had lost the focus he clearly had in previous meetings. While his well-rehearsed words were still fiery and inspiring, he was, at times, distracted by the reverence of one particular individual who was sitting just feet from him.

Instead of slipping out early and going home as he was prone to do, he went and stood behind the building watching as the attendees made their way home. Velu was the last to leave, and Pooja was with him. She jumped up into his carriage, and they slowly disappeared into the darkness.

*****

Chandu was never especially fond of animals, but over time, he developed a profound affection for his horse, Hema, whom he named because of the gold flecks in her eyes. He came to believe that it was those gold spots that gave her exceptionally keen eyesight and kept them out of harm's way on a number of occasions. It was Hema that he saw as the one stable force in his life. She was reliable, never complained, and Chandu often found himself pouring out his problems to her when the rest of the world was unmoved.

Every Sunday he would spend several hours grooming her, and then he would take a trip to Smithfield's Feed Store and load up his buggy with forage, grains, and oats. Hema became so fond of the routine that Chandu had to slow her down on the trip over.

It was at Smithfield's one Sunday afternoon that Chandu ran into Reverend Stadelmaier. It wasn't long ago that he considered his early encounters with the reverend as an inconvenience. But not anymore. Things were different now that he had become a Christian. Little by little, he was learning to trust this Jesus. But for him it was a process. That's why he now looked forward to his chance meetings with the reverend. He knew that it was the next best thing to God himself coming down and speaking to him in person.

"Hello, Mr. Naidu! What a pleasant surprise," he said, holding a large bag of what smelled to be fertilizer.

He smiled. "Good afternoon, Reverend. Doing some gardening?"

"Oh, the manure. Yes, I'm doing some gardening at home." He set the bag down and pulled out a small bag of seeds from his pocket. "I take these, some fertile soil, and a little water and watch God do the rest." He held up a single seed with a glint of wonder in his eye. "Imagine that this little kernel contains within it the design that will enable it to become a large tree." He turned toward Chandu with a childlike enthusiasm. "And not just any tree, but a mango tree."

Chandu pursed his lips as he contemplated Reverend Stadelmaier's words. *Interesting*, he thought to himself.

"Reverend Stadelmaier, why have you never invited me to your church?"

He put the mango seed back into the small bag and replied, "Well, I suppose I owe you an apology young man. I think every believer should attend church service. There are two very good Bible believing churches with Indian pastors, both of whom I had the privilege of discipling. I would recommend either for you and your lovely wife."

"But what about your church, Reverend? I should like to attend your church?"

He smiled and put his large hand on Chandu's shoulder. "If only I had a church for you to attend."

Chandu pulled back with a look of bemusement. "How can you not have a church? You're a man of God. You're a reverend."

"Oh, I used to have a church on Field Street. I had a fairly large congregation, in fact. Then God put it in my heart to go out and invite the disenfranchised members of our community, especially Indians like yourself." He smiled. "Unfortunately, that didn't go over very well with my White congregation, and they gradually stopped attending. A few were even quite angry with me for allowing Indians to come to my services."

"And then?"

"And then I got news one afternoon that the church building had burned to the ground. That was over five years ago."

"And you never rebuilt your church?"

He shook his head no. "No, these nearsighted Whites would only burn it down it again. No, instead, I have become an itinerant farmer, so to speak."

"What do you mean, Reverend?"

"What I mean is that I plant the Word of God into whomever the Lord puts in my path."

Chandu thought back to all those early encounters he had with this man whom he had now come to admire. How he tried to plant the Word of God in him but without success. He realized now how hard his heart had been toward Christians. Now, all he could do was thank God for not giving up on him.

With a paternal gaze, he said, "I can tell something else has got you down, Mr. Naidu. Do you want to tell me?"

He drew a heavy sigh and smiled slightly. "Reverend, do ever feel like you want to just run away and hide from the world?"

"Oh, I think everyone has those feelings from time to time. What's causing you to feel this way?"

Chandu drew a deep sigh. "Manisha's practically ready to give birth to my child, and yet she's hardly speaking to me all because of a story I wrote in the *Phoenix*."

The reverend's face scrunched in confusion. "The story about her father?"

Chandu nodded.

"Wait a minute. I read that story. That was a fine piece of work. I would think your kinsmen would see Mr. Velu as a hero of sort. Would they not?"

Chandu snickered. "Maybe, but not Edmund Klein." He pulled out a handkerchief and wiped his face. "The man took his business away from the Velus"

"Oh, I see," he said, stroking his chin. "They had all their eggs in one basket."

Chandu shot him a curious look. "Huh?"

"Mr. Klein was their only customer?"

"That's right, Reverend."

He nodded in contemplation and asked, "Is that it?"

"I just don't know if we Indians will ever be accepted here in this colony. It can be discouraging at times."

He nodded with a fatherly smile that managed to comfort Chandu before he even uttered a response. "These are challenging times for your people, young man. My intuition tells me that it will take time before Indians are able to enjoy an egalitarian society. And when I say time, I mean generations, unfortunately. It will be our children's children or perhaps their children who'll see the barriers that separate our people removed."

Chandu's face saddened. "So there's no hope that we'll see equality?"

"Young man, I would suggest that you put things in perspective. You've been given opportunities that very few Indians have been given. Sure, hope deferred makes the heart sick, but we hold onto hope if not for today then for tomorrow and for our children. And it's our job to pave the way for them as difficult as it is."

*****

Chandu had yet to get used to the barrister's transformation, and when he walked into the office, he instinctively asked the barrister if he was feeling all right.

The barrister looked at him curiously and replied, "I'm fine. Why do you ask?"

Chandu simply nodded. "Oh, no reason."

The barrister sat down across from his associate and leaned over his desk. "Natal Railways."

Chandu leaned back in his chair and shot the barrister a curious gaze. "What about Natal Railways?"

The barrister stood and started pacing as if he were getting ready to deliver an opening argument. "Did you know that Natal Railways has thousands of indentured laborers breaking their backs to build a railway connecting the mines in the Transvaal to the Port of Durban."

Chandu shook his head no. "No, I didn't."

"Well, it's true. And if we can persuade these laborers to take a bold stand for the rights of all Indians and quit work on the railway, then we can bring the colony to its knees."

Chandu cleared his throat. "Mr. Mahendhi, have you forgotten that you have lost your standing with Indians? How will you persuade them to do anything?"

He sat down and leaned over the desk once again. "No, I haven't forgotten, my friend. That's why we have to convince Velu that he has the ability to forever change the course of South African Indians by choking the lifeblood out of this colony."

Chandu pinched his lips as he pondered the barrister's idea. "I don't know, Mr. Mahendhi. It sounds very dangerous. I can't see these Whites allowing our Indians to get away with stopping the railways from running."

"Of course, this is not without risk. Nothing worth attaining comes without some sort of sacrifice. But you must keep in mind that the eyes of the world are on us right now, and I don't think that these people will do anything that will put them in a bad light."

At that moment, Velu walked through the door. He was smiling and his face was radiant. Chandu and the barrister knew that this was not the man they knew. Velu was motivated by agitation. Following behind him was Pooja. She smiled bashfully while the two men looked on with astonishment.

"This is Pooja, my new assistant," said Velu, gesturing with his hands.

When the two men didn't immediately respond, he cleared his throat and said, "I came here to see if we can get you to print another story."

"Uh, what story, Velu?" the barrister asked.

"Hey!" exclaimed Pooja. "Do I know you from somewhere?"

The barrister recoiled at the young woman's assertion. He wasn't in disguise, but his nasal voice was easy to recognize. Rather than having to explain why he had been concealing himself, he lied. "No, I don't believe we have."

She squinted, trying to focus her memory. "Hmm, you remind me of someone."

He snickered and turned his attention back toward Velu. "You have an idea for a story?"

"Uh, yes. I thought a story telling our community what we're doing would be good."

The barrister shrugged his shoulders. "What are you doing?"

Velu's eyebrows rose into his forehead. "You don't know what we're doing?"

With all due respect, my friend, I know what you're saying, and you do a good job of getting our brethren fired up. But I do not know what you are doing to make things change. I'm listening."

"We're protesting," Pooja blurted out.

Velu tried to hide his embarrassment. "Uh, yes, we're protesting."

Chandu interrupted, "Mr. Mahendhi has an idea that could change everything for our people, Uncle. Would you like to hear it?"

His eyes widened. "Of course, I want to hear it."

The barrister's eyes darted back and forth between Velu and Pooja before he said, "Can we discuss this plan in my office—in private?"

Pooja knew she was being excluded from what was likely very sensitive information. Though disappointed, she politely excused herself. No sooner was she on her way when Chandu boldly asked, "How is Aunty doing?"

Chandu was well aware that all was not well with his in-laws. Manisha was devastated that her parents were merely existing under the same roof and that they hadn't spoken to each other in weeks.

"Oh," he squirmed in discomfort. "She's fine. I think."

He sat down and let his head fall into his hands. He wasn't one to give into emotions, but he had been covering up his heart long enough and tears started running down his face.

"She hates me," he uttered in between muted sobs.

Chandu wanted to console him and assure him that his wife didn't hate him, but he wasn't so sure. All he knew for sure was that he had risen to prominence among the Indian community, but it had come with a great price.

"I don't blame her," he continued. "Our factory closed, and all our workers no longer have jobs. I don't know how much longer we can survive with no money coming in." He shook his head side to side. "I should have never let you write that story about me in the Phoenix."

The barrister nodded pensively and then replied, "May I give you some advice, my friend?"

Velu just shrugged.

"First, you must stop pitying yourself. You are where you are because of choices you made for yourself. You knew well the risk of protesting the registration against the will of Mr. Klein. That's one," he said, holding up his index finger.

Velu's head cocked back, blindsided by the barrister's rebuke.

"Next," he said, holding up another finger, "you must rid yourself of that girl, Pooja."

"Wait!" he objected. "She really believes in what we are doing."

The barrister smirked. "Would you take her home and introduce her to your wife?"

Velu lowered his eyes.

"That's what I thought."

Chandu interrupted, "Velu Uncle, everyone is looking up to you right now."

Velu smiled out of the side of his mouth.

"But," he continued, "this relationship could destroy you and this movement."

"You don't understand, son," he replied with forlornness. "I'm a man, and I have needs."

"Maybe I don't understand these things. But I see a good woman in Aunty. She's pretty and smart and a good mother to your children. She is one worth holding on to. You should go to her on your knees, if you must. You don't want to lose her."

He lowered his head again. Chandu and the barrister knew he was wrestling the advice he was just given.

"You're right. I don't want to lose her. She's a good mother." A broad smile swept across his face. "And she'll make a good grandmother. Now!" he exclaimed, slapping his hand on his knee. "What is this plan that's going to change everything?"

Chandu cleared his throat. "Uh, maybe you should go to Aunty and get right with her before—"

"While we're gathered here," the barrister interrupted. Let me just tell you what I was thinking."

The barrister walked around and stood behind Chandu so that he was facing Velu. "We all know that I have a way of agitating but also inspiring people with my newspaper. Would you agree?"

Both nodded.

"And we have seen what kind of influence you have had on our Indians, my friend. It has been quite remarkable."

Velu smiled.

He continued, "I have identified a weakness in this colony's economy that will collapse without Indian labor, and it's not sugarcane."

"What is it, then?" Velu asked.

"The Natal Railway. They use it to connect the mines in the Transvaal to the Natal Harbor. Right now there is a race between Natal and Capetown to see who can build a rail to the mines first."

"Therefore, I would like to craft a story that will provoke the conscience of every oppressed laborer breaking his back on that Natal Railway and convince them to put down their tools." He removed his spectacles and crossed his arms. "It will be your job, my friend, to lead the strike."

Velu needed little convincing. A sudden fire had been lit, giving him a renewed purpose. This was what he knew he had to do. "Yes!" he exclaimed, jumping up from his chair. "We'll make them stop this Registration Act and give our people back their trader's licenses." He shifted his intense gaze back and forth between the two men. "When do we start?"

"What about your wife?" the barrister asked.

"If I go to her now, then we can forget the strike. My life of leading protests will come to an end."

"Hmm," the barrister responded, "I really do need you to lead this protest."

Velu nodded. "Yes, you do. I will go to her as soon as we get back."

Chandu shook his lowered head side to side.

*****

With the help of the barrister's incendiary editorial, Velu was able to organize over three hundred Tamil railway workers, and on a hot November morning in 1913, work came to a grinding halt. The barrister and Velu, along with hundreds of railway workers, sat in protest of not only the abhorrent working conditions but with demands for the fair treatment of Indians living in the colony.

When news reached Lord Falmouth, he incited the police to be especially unforgiving. Baton-wielding police, along with the railway bosses, physically and verbally harassed the protesters. Some were seriously hurt. The barrister, however, admonished them to suffer gallantly and that the violent reaction of the Europeans was a sign of their weakness.

But Velu had little tolerance for the senseless beatings that were being inflicted upon the peaceful demonstrators who wanted nothing more than to be treated as human beings. Finally, after watching a policeman shoot a protestor that refused to stand, something triggered inside him.

Velu had just spoken with the man earlier that morning. And although he didn't recall his name, he remembered his humility and that fact that he had four children, one of whom was mentally handicapped. And he recalled his eagerness to sit in protest.

He felt his heart thumping rapidly and a sudden rush of adrenaline that he hadn't felt since the time the Zamindar and his henchmen kidnapped Manisha and Pradip.

"Nooooo!" he bellowed as he leapt up from where he was seating just yards from where the father of four now lay dead. He jumped onto the back of burly policeman, knocking him to the ground, and wrapped his arm around his neck. With every ounce of strength that Velu could muster, he tried to pinch off any air that the man might try to breathe.

A large crowd quickly gathered and then *Bang!*

The crowd dispersed as quickly as it had assembled, and when the smoke settled, the policeman was on his back, trying desperately to regain his breath. Lying next to him was Velu. He had been shot in the back and was clinging desperately to life as blood started to fill his lungs.

The barrister ran over to his dying friend and pleaded for him to stay alive. But Velu was unable to speak. When he heard the gurgling of blood, he knew there was little hope. He held Velu's hand tightly as his life slowly drained from his body. Overcome with emotion, the barrister removed his spectacles from his face and silently wept.

*****

Chandu sat staring at the dull, windowless wall of his office. It was a reflection of what he felt deep within his soul, empty and uncertain. He had in mind that he would fulfill his obligation to put out the weekly edition, but nobody was around, and he was numb.

He knew that it would be his job to make sure that his father-in-law would be honored and remembered for his contributions to the effort, but he couldn't even force himself to lift a pen. And the barrister, for his role in the strike, was behind bars again.

He slipped out the back door and locked it. Hema rustled eagerly in anticipation of journeying away from the dry, hot dust that layered the streets of Phoenix.

"Anywhere, girl," he said as he snapped the reins. Hema instinctively started pulling toward the sea. They trundled up the dirt road past endless rows of sugarcane, and then Hema began to labor as they moved up the steep green ridge that separated the coastlands from the interior. As she reached the apex, the vast Indian Ocean came into view. The coolness of the brisk sea breeze took Chandu's breath away while Hema seemed to nod in approval.

He took his hat off and secured it by his side. "Hey, Hema!" he yelled out. "Why do you suppose these Europeans didn't name this ocean after themselves?" He chuckled.

As he gazed out at the roughness of the sea, he flashed back to the perilous journey that brought his family from a tiny village in India, across vast and turbulent black waters to the verdant hills of Natal.

He knew it wasn't fate that brought him to where he was but, rather, a choice that his father and mother made after weighing all the advice they had been given. But he firmly believed that it was the hand of God that had ever so gently directed their steps, even before he knew about him.

As they rolled slowly down the dirt trail, they passed a young boy heading in the opposite direction leading an oxen cart loaded with sugarcane and supposed that he still had long journey ahead to the Tongaat Mill. His heart ached for the young boy. He was sure that he too would have a story to tell, one that would likely be full of heartaches if Indian status didn't change.

Chandu considered that he should have been counted among the thousands that dotted the green hills of Natal. He was no different than the dark-skinned young boy he just passed. He was from the agrarian Kapu caste, and Kapus were farmers. They were born to till the soil, to work the land.

Chandu knew he had a story worth telling, or worth finishing. The story he started writing as a wide-eyed student bound for London recorded the remarkable events leading up to that voyage. He was sure that the chronicle he kept was packed away somewhere. He needed to finish it, if for no other reason than to apprise his children and his children's children. They would have a much different life, a presumably easier life, but they would need to know where they came from and what their forebears endured along the way.

As they neared the bottom of the hill and a T-junction that would force them either north or south toward the port, Hema's ears flicked back, waiting for Chandu's command. He pulled the right rein until Hema had managed to turn the buggy around facing up the hill that they had just descended. He snapped both reins and said, "Take me home, Hema."

EPILOGUE

Korlakota 1939

The train whistle awakened the stranger from his brief slumber. He sat up and asked, "Is this our stop?" He was still a bit groggy from his nap.

The whistle blew again, and the train started to slow down. "Must be," he answered. The man picked up his worn bag, set it on his lap and smiled. "Sorry, did you say you had friends here in Korlakota?"

"Uh, no." In fact, he was sure that everyone he ever knew in this small village was dead or long forgotten. He wasn't sure why he was in Korlakota, only that God had put it in his heart to return.

"You've been here before?"

Chandu smiled. "Oh yes, but it's been many years."

His face lit up. "We like visitors, especially foreign ones."

He grinned. That this villager saw him as a foreigner was amusing. He was Telugu, after all. He could have told him that he was born just a short distance from where they were standing, but for now, he was enjoying his role as the stranger.

"What do you think?" he asked, gesturing toward the train station. "The British had it built several years back. I don't know why," he said, shrugging his shoulders. "The village has grown little since I was a small boy."

Chandu gazed around trying to remember the once-familiar surroundings. "So what was here before the station was built?" he asked.

The man pursed his lips in a way that he was trying to recall. "Nothing. Nothing was here for a long time. But," he said, his eyes growing bigger, "years ago, when I was quite young, there was this wicked man who had his office right there." He pointed to the platform extending out from the small wooden ticket office. "The Zamindar," he said, shaking his head slowly side to side. "Mmm, he got his punishment."

The Zamindar. Chandu hadn't heard the name since he was a young man. He reckoned that were it not for the evil ways of the Zamindar, the Nayadus would have never left Korlakota.

"It was probably right here, right where we're standing." The stranger paused for a second and then said, "I wasn't there, you see, and glad I wasn't. I've seen enough in my lifetime."

"What did you *not* see?" Chandu asked as the man had managed to pique his curiosity.

"The death of the Zamindar and his agent—right here," he said, brushing his foot across the dusty ground. "Those two men did a lot of bad things, but they went too far killing Sunil Bukkaya."

"Sunil Bukkaya," he said abruptly. Chandu remembered his father telling stories of the Bukkaya clan.

"You know him?" asked the stranger.

"Uh, no," Chandu replied.

"People say he would do anything for anybody. That's the kind of man he was. There's a story that he was visited by a stranger who was passing through our village. It happened that the Zamindar paid him a visit at the same time. Word is that Zamindar threatened the stranger's life and that Sunil grabbed his grandfather's rifle and chased the Zamindar and his agent off the property. The next day that Zamindar came back while that family was sleeping. The wife and children were terrified to see the Zamindar and his agent drag that poor man down to the Godavari and drown him."

"Is that true?" he asked, shocked.

He nodded. "When word got around the village of what that Zamindar had done, they pulled together and came here. His office was right there." He again pointed to the platform extending out from the ticket office. "They said it was impossible to tell the Zamindar from his agent when they got done with them. Probably right where we are standing. The two bodies were thrown onto a cart and rolled down to the Godavari, never to be seen again."

"I suppose they got what they deserved," Chandu said, shaking my head in disbelief.

The stranger picked up his bag and said, "Come, my friend, I don't live far from here."

The first familiar site was the temple. Inside Chandu saw several worshipers offering *puja* to *Shiva*. The large deity stared straight ahead with a fixed hint of a smile, seemingly unaware of the adoration.

"So where do you live?" Chandu asked his travel companion.

"We're almost there," he replied.

They stopped in front of a small house that was typical of villagers who lived along the Godavari. "Is this where you live?" he asked.

"Yes," he answered with a smile. "Right here."

"Right here?" he asked incredulously.

The stranger looked over at the humble little home with its thatched roof and rejoined, "Yes, right here."

"You may not believe me, but my Ammamma and Thathiyya used to live in this same house."

The man dropped his bag and turned, his one eye gazing intently into Chandu's. His face turned serious, and words were slow and deliberate. "My Ammamma and Thathiyya also lived in this house."

"I don't believe I ever got your good name, sir."

"Pradip," he replied, "Pradip Nayadu."

Chandu's eyes welled up, and his voice cracked as he replied, "Pradip!" He couldn't believe that the stranger that he been sitting next to for the last hour was his long-lost brother.

"It's me, Chandu!"

Pradip was unable to say anything. He grabbed onto his brother and held him tight. Through tears of joy, he said, "Forgive me, brother, for not knowing you." He looked him over from head to toe and chuckled. "We've gone old, haven't we."

From behind his thick glasses, Chandu replied, "We have, my brother. We have."

"Surely you must be wondering what became of me from the time we last saw each other," said Pradip as they positioned themselves on the mats covering the hard clay floor. His daughter brought them *masala tea*. She bore an uncanny resemblance to their mother, especially when she smiled.

"We named our daughter Archana, after Amma," said Pradip as if he knew what his brother was thinking. Her son cozied up next to Pradip. "Can you say 'hello' to Uncle?" The boy buried his head in his grandfather's *pancha*. "We call him Puvendrun—after our father. Sadly, his father died right after he was born." The two women joined them. "And this is my wife, Anya," said Pradip. She simply smiled as she found a spot for herself to sit.

"Yes, Pradip, our hearts were torn wondering what became of you," he said.

The last we heard you had gone off to fight with the Indian Army."

"There was no Indian Army," he said. "The Indians that arrived from India were nothing more than stretcher bearers for the British Army."

"Stretcher bearers?"

"Yes, we were there to carry the—"

"I know. I know. So how were you—"

"Wounded?"

"Yes."

"We were ambushed one moonless night while we lay sleeping in our tents. Those sneaky Boers came and set fire to our tents. It was horrible. Many Indians and British soldiers burned to death that night. I managed to escape but not without getting badly burned on my face, as you can see. All I knew to do was to try and pull men from the burning tents. But in the end, we lost hundreds of good men.

"We retreated to Colenso, where the British had a base camp and hospital. Many more men died from their wounds. I wanted to return to the frontlines. It was there where at least I had a purpose. But they wouldn't allow me, and yet I didn't have the courage to return to the plantation. I couldn't let anyone see me." He lowered his head in shame while Anya gently stroked his scarred face.

"So," he said, lifting his head, "I came here. Ammamma was living here alone. She was not doing well, and I knew she didn't have long. I moved in and cared for her till she died almost a year later." He shrugged. "I started farming the land here by myself for almost ten years."

Anya took their empty cups away. Chandu realized as he studied his brother that he would have never made him out. His once-handsome face was unrecognizable. His skin, like so many of the older villagers, had blackened from years of working under the hot Indian sun. Nevertheless, he looked strong, and in him seemed to be contentment with what he had.

Pradip continued, "Then one day Anya's mother and father came to me and asked if I would accept their proposal to marry their daughter. I didn't think anyone would want their daughter to be with someone who looked like me." He laughed. "Good thing there wasn't many single men of marrying age at that time. But enough about me, I want to hear about you."

"What can I say?" he said, smiling. "There is so much to tell."

"Tell me about Manisha."

Chandu let out a mournful sigh, "Manisha died several years ago."

Pradip lowered his head, "I'm sorry."

His countenance quickly changed. "But she gave me five beautiful children—all of them married. I named my oldest Pradip. At that time, I believed that we would again be reunited. But with each passing year, I began to lose hope that we would ever see you again."

A tear rolled down from Pradip's eye.

"And I have ten grandchildren."

"All living in Natal?" he asked.

"Yes, of course," he answered. "We're a very close family."

"And tell me about Nana?"

Chandu paused for a second. "Nana passed away about fifteen years ago."

Pradip covered his face, his sobs muffled by the sleeve of his shirt. A tear rolled down Chandu's cheek as he waited several minutes to let his brother grieve. He wiped his face. "My heart ached every day for you and Nana. Many times I thought about going back to Natal, but I never had the courage."

"I have something to tell you about Nana," he said

"What?"

"Nana married again after you left us."

Pradip's eyes grew large with curiosity. "Who did he marry?"

"You remember Sirdar Sunil Reddy?"

"Yes, of course," he replied. "I didn't like him much."

"Yes, he wasn't kind to us. But he died after you left. Nana moved into his bungalow and married his widow, Sonali. Then he had two children with her—a boy and a girl."

Pradip laughed. "You mean we have a brother and sister?"

"That's not all," he continued. "Nana had two more children with her sister, Seeli—a boy and a girl."

"I don't believe you," said Pradip, shaking his head in disbelief.

"True. You have two more brothers and two sisters back in Natal."

"This is too much for me," he said, waving his hand for him to stop. "How can I possibly bear so much news at one time?" Again, Pradip covered his face as he wept silently. Chandu also wept as he gazed upon his long-lost brother.

Pradip abruptly stood up and wiped his face. "Come, brother, let us walk together. I don't like my family to see me in such a way."

They walked out to the narrow road that the two had traversed so many times as young boys, and Chandu asked, "Do you think we could walk by the old house?"

"Of course," said Pradip as they made their way down the dirt road.

"It's been a long time since you and I walked down this road together," Chandu said.

"Yeah, do you remember how we used to come and fill up on Ammamma's *parathas*?"

"Like it was yesterday," he replied.

"So tell me more," he said, "what became of Velu Uncle and Aunty?"

"Ahh, Velu Uncle—he died a martyr protesting for Indian rights. Things were never the same after he died."

Pradip furrowed his brows and asked, "What do you mean?"

"Well, Mr. Mahendhi, you remember him?"

"Yes, of course."

"He took Velu Uncle's death very hard because he was there, you see. And he felt responsible for his death since he convinced him to lead the protest. He left Natal soon afterward and returned to his home here in India."

Pradip nodded. "He was a good man."

"Mr. Mahendhi was a very good man. I believe he was a light that burned so bright that the whole world took notice of what was happening to us Indians down in Natal. It took me many years to appreciate what he did for us Indians. But there was another man, a very wise man who said to me once that it would take generations before Indians would be on equal footing with the Europeans. After living in Natal for almost fifty years, I've come to believe that he was right. I believe it will be another fifty or sixty years before our Indians are afforded the same privileges as the Whites."

"But I hear that Mr. Mahendhi is doing good things here in India for the outcastes," Chandu said then stopped and faced his brother. "Can you imagine an India without a caste system?"

Pradip nodded. "Doesn't seem possible. The high castes have all the power."

Chandu agreed, "They do, indeed. I suppose India society is no less guilty than the Europeans in Natal."

Chandu knew they were getting close as the road rose higher from the bank of the Godavari. Their former home sat on some of the steepest yet skillfully terraced land in the region. The Nayadus had acquired it generations ago for next to nothing because nobody else wanted it.

But gone were the terraces of rice paddies, and gone was their childhood home. Nature had reclaimed the forsaken piece of land. All that remained was a memorial.

"You remember Sangam Bukkaya?" asked Pradip.

"Hey, we were very young, but I remember Nana speaking of him. He was the village elder who worked for the Zamindar."

"That's right, the traitor. His grandson, Sunil, was given our home when we moved away. I told you about him at the train station, remember?"

Chandu nodded. "Yes, I remember the story."

"It was here on our property that he was killed by the Zamindar," Pradip exclaimed, pointing down bank of the Godavari River.

Chandu stood in amazement, contemplating the history of the land upon which they were gazing. He was unsure how many generations of Nayadus had farmed the once-cultivated terraces between the banks of the Godavari and the dirt road connecting the neighboring villages. What was clear, though, was that any trace of their ancestry had been wiped away.

"The house is gone," he said, somewhat disappointed.

"Yes, the Bukkayas tore it down after Sunil's death. Except for the shrine the property has been abandoned."

Chandu pointed out a tamarind tree that stood very close to where the house once stood. "Do you remember that tree?" he asked.

"Of course," he replied.

"Come," Chandu said, "the tree is full of tamarinds."

Concern swept across Pradip's face as he glanced down at the steep trail.

"Hold on, brother," said Chandu. He took notice of a broken tree branch on the side of road and broke off two of the smaller branches, quickly fashioning them into walking sticks. He handed one to Pradip. "There," he said with a chuckle. "We didn't need these the last time we climbed this hill."

"Where did the time go?" asked Pradip.

Chandu glanced around curiously as he kicked the fallen tamarind pods away from the base of the tree.

"What are you looking for, brother?"

"Do you remember our last act before leaving this place?"

"Yes! We buried the arm from Ganesha along with some tamarind seeds."

Pradip sat down in the shade of the tree and pushed some betel nut into his mouth while Chandu took his stick and started scratching at the crusted dirt, hoping to unearth the one last vestige that would validate their memories.

"Don't trouble yourself, brother," said Pradip. "That piece of relic is where it belongs."

Chandu stopped digging and smiled out of the corner of his mouth. "Yeah, you're right." He went and sat down next to his little brother.

The two sat in silence, just gazing out at the Godavari. The monsoons were still a month away, and the river was low. Memories of Amma washing clothes on the large rocks along the riverbank replayed before Chandu's eyes. He turned toward the barren hillside and recalled how Nana would prod the buffalo up the steep drive as she carried large buckets of water to the highest terraces. Every day was spent flooding the top terrace to overflow onto the lower terraces. That was until the Godavari dried up.

Pradip interrupted the silence, "I was angry."

Chandu nodded. "I know you were, little brother. And I'm sorry for what happened."

Pradip shrugged. "I'm not. I made a lot of mistakes when I was young, but as I look back," he said, looking his brother straight in the eye, "I see a purpose in everything that has happened. I would have never met my beautiful wife or had my precious daughter and grandson. I spent a year with Ammamma before she went home to be with the Lord. All these things were of the divine."

A tear rolled down Chandu's cheek.

"When we were on the train, you said you weren't sure what brought you to this little village."

Chandu wiped away the tear and smiled.

Pradip continued, "You made a promise to me before I planted the tamarind seeds that have become this very tree we are sitting under."

"Yes, I remember," he replied, his voice cracking with emotion.

Pradip inched over and put his weathered hand on Chandu's leg and said, "When we were boys, you promised me that nothing would stop us from coming back to our home."

Chandu nodded as a tear rolled down his cheek.

As tears filled Pradip's eyes, he continued, "You kept your promise, brother."

The End

ABOUT THE AUTHOR

J. R. Harrison is a world traveler who has lived in countries such as India and South Africa and Fiji. He has been married to his wife, Jessica, who happens to be South African of Indian descent, for over two decades. They currently reside in Los Angeles.

Lightning Source UK Ltd.
Milton Keynes UK
UKHW011821250522
403525UK00002B/27